Knitting series

"PERFECT holiday reading material. Absolutely perfect."

—My Fiction Nook

Behind the Curtain

"Amy can rock the socks off a blank piece of paper. The rhythm of the words, the flow of the story, her style is just brilliant. I fell as hard for the author as I fell for the characters."

—Sinfully Sexy Book Reviews

"This book is so well written, that even though I have never been involved in theater or dance, I could visualize what they were doing and empathize with what the characters were going through."

—Live Your Life, Buy the Book

"*Behind the Curtain* is an extraordinary story of love and friendship. I highly recommend this book, it is one I will be reading again, and again."

—Top2Bottom Reviews

Ethan in Gold

"I thoroughly enjoyed the emotional journey I experienced and I recommend these books to all who enjoy extreme heart-pulling with your sexy stories. *Ethan in Gold* and all of the Johnnies books certainly delivers!"

—Mrs. Condit Reads Books

"I totally loved this one and continue to think this is a fabulous series. The characters are so well drawn, so fully developed and richly layered."

—Joyfully Jay

Readers Love Amy Lane

Going Up!

"Highly recommended, especially to you Amy Lane fans out there. Don't miss this one."

—The Novel Approach

"As always, the writing style is smooth as silk and a real pleasure to read."

—Hearts on Fire

Shiny!

"To say it is amazing that after so many books I've read from her, Amy Lane still delivers so soundly for me, would be an understatement. Again she wrote a story with characters that are so easy to love and cheer for, it's bittersweet to let them go."

—The Tipsy Bibliophile

"The end of this book was Shiny in true terms, I thought… the kind that never wears off and I sighed pleasantly. It was truly satisfying."

—The Blog of Sid Love

Left on St. Truth-be-Well

"This was a delightful read. The intelligence and emotional quotient that we have come to expect from Amy Lane while being a lighter, easier, and less angsty story."

—GayListBook Review

"If you like stories written with humor, mystery and intrigue, sweet sexy romance and a couple twists that may shock you and a very good short read for a hot summer night this is a must!"

—MM Good Book Reviews

By AMY LANE

NOVELS
Behind the Curtain
Blackbird Knitting in a Bunny's Lair
Bolt Hole
Clear Water
Gambling Men: The Novel
The Locker Room
Mourning Heaven
Racing for the Sun
Shiny!
Sidecar
A Solid Core of Alpha
Under the Rushes

THE KEEPING PROMISE ROCK SERIES
Keeping Promise Rock • Making Promises • Living Promises • Forever Promised

THE JOHNNIES SERIES
Chase in Shadow • Dex in Blue • Ethan in Gold

ANTHOLOGIES
The Granby Knitting Menagerie
The Talker Collection
Three Fates

Published by DREAMSPINNER PRESS
http://www.dreamspinnerpress.com

By AMY LANE

Published by DREAMSPINNER PRESS
http://www.dreamspinnerpress.com

The Granby Knitting Menagerie

Amy Lane

Dreamspinner Press

Published by
Dreamspinner Press
5032 Capital Circle SW
Suite 2, PMB# 279
Tallahassee, FL 32305-7886
USA
http://www.dreamspinnerpress.com/

The Granby Knitting Menagerie
© 2014 Amy Lane.

Cover Art
© 2014 Catt Ford.
Cover content is for illustrative purposes only and
any person depicted on the cover is a model.

ISBN: 978-1-62798-973-2

Printed in the United States of America
First Edition
May 2014

For my knitters and the people I knit for—so, really, for my entire Dreamspinner family and the people I live with as well. You know who you are.

And for T.A. Chase and Devon Rhodes, who spent an entire night reading these stories over again to help me find Aiden's last name and then gave me a perfectly acceptable one when it turned out I'd made a little teeny omission!

The
Winter
Courtship
Rituals *of*
Fur-Bearing
Critters

This one's for John and his husband, Andrew.
Andrew spins, John knits, and together,
they warm the hearts of everyone who knows them.

Chapter 1

Bald

CRAWFORD WATCHED with interest as the new resident of #15 Llama Lane moved in. It was early September in Granby, Colorado, and the snows were not that far off.

Granby, Colorado, part of Grand County, sat in a bowl of a valley which was, itself, set shallow in the midst of the peaks of the Rocky Mountains. According to the computer, it was a mere thirty-four miles away from the more populous Fort Collins, but that thirty-four miles was over a road so treacherous and so winding that they had made it a state park. From June to August, people from all over the world traveled over Trail Ridge Road (otherwise known as Highway 34) in awe. For one thing, it made it to over 12,000 feet in elevation, making it the highest road in the country. For another, it still had six feet of snow on the sides even in July, and it spanned the continental divide. It also had (the nonlocals were wont to complain) a distressing lack of guardrails, but that didn't bother Crawford none. He had a large, comfy barn, a roomy garage next to the mill, and a giant meat freezer. He laid in hay and grain for the alpacas as well as firewood for himself all summer. He made one last big trip to Boulder on the other highway in December and just hunkered down with the alpacas until March. A few trips to the store in the 4x4 would do him then, unless he had to call the vets, but he could handle most of the animal husbandry problems himself.

Crawford was just fine.

But as he watched the young man move computers and electronics equipment into the modest two-story farmhouse in the middle of September, he could not say the same for his new neighbor.

Crawford was out checking the fences, something that was not as difficult with alpacas as it was with other critters. Alpacas didn't mind being closed up none and didn't stress a fence or test it in odd places— not like sheep. Crawford had sheep on the other pasture, sure, and a thick wooden fence over there, too, but here, bordering his new neighbor's scant acre of land, it was not much more than pig fencing, and the alpacas didn't give a hoot. They just hung out and ate the grass, like they did, and ignored the fence. The other side of the fence might as well have been the other side of the world to their amiable little hearts, and since old Mrs. Humphreys had passed away, it had been to Crawford too.

But this new guy wasn't old Mrs. Humphreys.

He was young, for one thing. Midtwenties to Crawford's late-thirties, and bright and shiny as a spit-polished shoe. His hair was cut fashionably long, and he had just enough scruff on his lip and chin to make Crawford think that maybe he kept that scruff full time. He wondered how long it would take for that scruff to grow to beard length, and thought that would be a crying shame, because the boy had a narrow face with a squarish little block of a chin and tip-tilted sea green eyes. His mouth was wide and smiling, with full lips, and all in all, it would be a real waste to hide that pretty face behind what would probably be sandy-brown hair.

He was also quick to talk, quick to smile, and gregarious. He chatted with the movers and took notes of the good places to eat (there were really only two places where the locals ate, and Crawford listened shamelessly enough to know that the movers knew those places too) as well as where he could find a movie or help if he needed it.

"And if you need help," one of the young men said (Robbie, Clarence and Angie's boy, who used to be a hell-raiser in high school but who had settled down now with a wife and two kids), "Crawford here might help you. He's queer, but don't let that bother you none, he's harmless."

Crawford refused to flush under the boy's sniping and stared at him until he blushed instead, mumbling something about checking the overhead and disappearing into the truck. The new kid moving in grinned brightly.

"Well since I am, too, that won't be a problem," he said with such sunshiny goodwill that Crawford found himself smiling back from his side of the fence.

The two movers took in this information with widened eyes and flushes, and the new kid just rolled his eyes and continued to chat, putting them both back at ease quicker than Crawford had ever been able to. In a few minutes, just that much, they drove off in a choking cloud of diesel exhaust, leaving the kid with his little city car and a thoughtful look on his face as he surveyed his house.

God, Crawford thought uncomfortably. There had been so much those two yahoos had *not* told him.

"You're going to need more firewood!" he hollered shortly, and the kid looked at him in surprise.

"Really? There's a gas heater and a whole stack against the side of the house—"

"The gas guy doesn't always get out regular, and what's against the house will only do you a week."

Crawford was twisting lengths of wire over a hole, and he carefully wrapped that last end so it didn't snag on the alpaca's valuable fur, and then stood and pulled off his work glove.

"Rance Crawford," he said shortly, shaking hands with the boy.

That thin face lit up, and Crawford's work-roughened, lanolin-softened hand was suddenly grasped tightly in bony fingers as the boy pumped his hand with some enthusiasm.

"Hi! My Aunt Gretchen talked about you! I'm Ben, Ben McCutcheon. Gertie sort of left me her place."

Rance nodded. "I'd wondered how that went. She had a whole passel of relatives out here right after she died. You weren't one."

Ben grimaced. "Yeah—she was really my great-aunt, and my mom was sort of the black sheep of the family. It was mostly just her and me, you know? We used to come out here once a year or so when I was little, and I sent her Christmas cards after Mom passed. I didn't know it, but I was apparently the only member of her family who didn't think she was batshit crazy or just want her little acre in Colorado."

Crawford had to smile, because Gertie Humphries had been a tough old bitch who'd once threatened to shoot his best stud because she claimed he scared her best laying hen. Rance had cured her of that in a hot second—he'd knitted up some of Burlingame's top-notch fleece into a hooded shawl that the old girl had worn even on her deathbed.

Yup, Gertie had liked him in the end, which was why he'd been sorry to see that swarm of kin around her house, likely counting chickens for their celebration dinner. He hadn't seen what had broken them up and sent them scattering, but now that he'd met the boy, he heartily approved of Ben.

Although that could have been just because he was pretty enough to make Crawford do the pee-pee hard-on dance.

"So," Crawford said, eyeing the weathered little cottage dubiously, "you're going to settle in here during the fall?"

Ben grimaced. "It's a little colder here in the fall than it was in Sacramento," he admitted.

Crawford stood and straightened, picking up his lightweight denim jacket and putting it on again now that he wasn't sweating in the thinning sun. "How cold was it in Sacramento when you left?" he asked judgingly, and Ben looked sheepish.

"Ninety-five degrees."

Crawford knew his eyes had widened. It was laughable. Here in Grand County, near the end of September, at ten o'clock in the morning, it was around fifty degrees. "It may make sixty-five by the afternoon."

Ben shrugged. "It's been sort of a shitty long summer."

Crawford just looked at him. "What's winter like?"

Again, that shrug. Like living through snows was going to be no big deal. "Mild. Lots of rain—if we're lucky."

Crawford nodded and sighed. "You're going to need a list," he said on a grunt. "You going to keep the chickens?"

Ben nodded. "Aunt Gertie liked 'em."

"The rabbits?"

"Why not?"

"She's got an old sheep named Millicent and a yapping piece of coyote kibble—"

"Yeah, I'm keeping Millie, but my mom's least favorite uncle took Biddy-Bye for his grandkids to play with."

Crawford shook his head. Stupid fucker. "The little shit's gonna eat herself some fingers."

Ben chuckled and sighed happily. "Yeah. I hope they're his."

Crawford turned to him with nothing more than a raised eyebrow, and Ben blushed. "They weren't nice to my mom," he mumbled, looking at the small house in the middle of the overgrown grasses. A shrill autumn wind sang through the valley, and the grasses rippled, but even through the ever-present shushing, Crawford heard him when he added, "They weren't nice to me."

Crawford nodded then and gathered his tools, rolling them in the leather holster and putting it in the saddlebag. He had a tractor and a motorcycle, but those things made the beasties skittish. A horse was still a good idea with fifty acres to tend.

"I'll make you a list, then," he said decisively. "Things you'll need, shit to prepare for. Winter's not a joke here. You'd best take it seriously."

Ben looked at him and smiled, and it was a child's smile, open and clear and trusting. His green eyes lit up, and he nodded, even as he shoved his hands deeper into his pockets. "I'd like that," he said happily. "That would be really kind of you. I've got money—I just don't know what to do with it to prepare."

Crawford looked at him bouncing on his toes in his tennis shoes, shivering a little in his long-sleeved T-shirt. "Money's a start. When's it run out?"

"It doesn't!" Ben smiled again, this time proudly. "I work from home. Independent game companies send me their code, and I clean it up for them. They call me the Bug Man—it's sort of cool."

Crawford thought his eyes might bug out of his head. He knew about the Internet, and they got it fine in Granby, but a hotbed of media development they were not. "And you thought you'd relocate here?" He had to ask it. He absolutely had to ask it.

Ben couldn't look at him anymore. The ever-present wind had blown the clouds over the sun, and the temperature had dropped again. He tilted his head up to the sky anyway; it was vast and open, horizoned by the Rockies on all sides.

"Do you have any idea how high your heart can soar in a place like this?" he asked. His nostrils flared a little, like he was scenting the wind and the animals and even the snow that would probably visit in November.

Crawford's pee-pee hard-on dance stilled for a moment, and he found himself looking hungrily at that young, pretty face. "You forget," he said softly, not thinking about the sky at all. He'd gotten lost in the sky years ago—he was well aware he'd never find his way back.

Ben pulled his attention earthward, still shivering, but now looking peaceful and not lost in the sky. "It's beautiful," he said simply. "And I was really loved here. I sure would appreciate that list. Should I come over for it?"

Crawford's brain shorted out. He didn't want Ben coming over to his place. He was not ashamed of it—the mill, the connected store, the house next to that—he was proud of all of them. It was just that suddenly, these places were... *personal*. They were personal, and he only wanted Ben to see them if *he* was going to be *personal* too.

"I'll bring it in the morning," he said. "On my way to town. I'll take you. There's firewood for sale. You're going to need it. I've got a truck."

Maybe, with a little bit of revising, he might have made the whole speech a little more rock-bottom terse, but it was the best he could do on improv.

Ben didn't seem to care, though. He nodded seriously, like a child taking orders. "What time?"

"Eight thirty." Because he was up at six, the lumberyard with its supply of firewood opened at nine, and he had to be back at ten thirty to open the shop. He could do it, he was pretty sure. "I'll have the list," he added before swinging himself up on top of his patient horse. Everclear had sat docilely, eating grass and giving Sourmash, Edna, and Hankity the evil eye so they'd stay away from him, but as soon as he felt Crawford's weight, damned if that gelding didn't give a disgusted little snort and jerk his head toward Miss Gertie's place instead of away from it. Crawford gave the reins a little jerk back and eyed the horse with suspicion. It didn't pay to give the horses their head too much—they tended to think worse of you.

"I really appreciate the help," Ben said, his gratitude as open and as transparent as the sky.

Of course he appreciated the help. He was like to freeze to death without it. Crawford grunted something, probably something socially inept and grim, and swung Everclear away and down toward the mill. God, he had shit to do.

Chapter 2

Scarf

CRAWFORD WASN'T sure exactly how it happened. He finished tending the fences, tended to the animals, and went into the shop. His two journeymen were there, running the mill itself, and Ariadne, his frighteningly appropriately named apprentice, was in the shop, talking to a nice middle-aged woman about qiviut.

"Yeah," Ariadne was saying. "We're lucky. We've got a co-op agreement with a First Nations reservation up in Canada. They collect the fiber after the musk ox molt. It's expensive because it's sort of painstaking, you know? That's why we usually only spin it lace-weight. A skein big enough for a shawl will cost you about $150 to $200, but we have smaller skeins if you want to ply it with another fiber so it goes a little farther."

Ariadne looked up at Crawford and grimaced as he settled his jacket and ball cap on the peg inside the door that led to the mill. He shut the mill door, because the twins (Jeremy and Aiden, unrelated in any way except being white with sort of brownish hair) were about to start the drum carder, and the thing was a *bear*—it was sixty years old if it was a day, and even though it was a small model, it was still the size of a kitchen table, if a kitchen table was a half-ton of prickle-studded metal. The damned thing groaned like hell's bitch when you started it up, which was why they saved all their carding for once a week and then carded all the goddamned day.

"Do you have any yarns that are plied with qiviut?" the woman asked. She was petting one of the lace-weight skeins that Ariadne had placed on the shelf right next to the register to both discourage theft and encourage questions. (As of yet, Crawford had not met a kleptomaniac knitter, but Ariadne insisted you just didn't want to put temptation in anyone's path.)

"I think Crawford has been hand-plying some skeins to determine manufacture," Ariadne said. "That barrel over there, labeled 'experimental,' has all sorts of prototypes at a reduced rate."

The woman, plump, graying, with a surprisingly unlined face and a stellar smile, walked over to the barrel and pulled out a skein of rose-gray/sea-foam green alpaca/merino blend. She read the label and stroked the yarn itself and absolutely glowed up at Ariadne. "This is gorgeous," she murmured. "It's sock weight, isn't it?"

Ariadne looked at Crawford, who nodded. "There's some nylon in there for strength," he confirmed. "And more than enough for a pair."

"Ooooh…." Then she giggled. "Oh, I'm awful, aren't I? I really wanted some qiviut, and here I am, groping your sock yarn!" Fascinated, she went back to looking at the various experimental combinations, some of which Crawford and Ariadne (who specialized in fiber) had decided to put into production or to continue to experiment with and some of which were simply passing tickles that didn't look as good in reality as they had when Crawford or Aiden (who was Crawford's second in colorwork) had dreamt them up.

"If you like those," Ariadne encouraged with no compunction in the least, "we have some Sweeps over in the other corner of the store."

"Sweeps?" Oh, Ariadne had the woman now. The woman was a tourist—and probably one of the last of the season, before the snows. After the tourists went, it was all about working to build the stock and selling to the town regulars until the skiers arrived, and when the snow got too deep to travel, it was all about Internet sales, designing new stock, locals gathering for gossip, and dreaming of spring until the tourists returned around May.

The thing about tourists who bought yarn was that they tended to buy a *lot* of it. Crawford's mill—Craw-Daddy 'Paca—sold to small yarn stores (known in the trade as the LYS—or Local Yarn Store) around the country, but a yarn connoisseur wouldn't always be able to get hold of his stock, even on the Internet. And the Sweeps and Experimentals were always one-of-a-kind items. The Sweeps were mystery fiber, usually the actual sweepings from the mill floor after a number of dyed fleeces had been carded and spun. The results were bizarre, odd, and sometimes oddly beautiful. The Experimentals were whatever Crawford and Ariadne felt like coming up with when they were hand-spinning. Of course marketing was always a consideration, but sometimes, they simply put together the rovings that moved them to see what they got.

"Yeah," Ariadne said, standing up from behind the counter in a swirl of multi-colored skirts and a hand-knit wool/alpaca cardigan, all done in purple, gold, and brown. "Here, let me show you."

Crawford rolled his eyes at her, because she was such a ham, and she wiggled black eyebrows over warm brown eyes and a slightly Roman nose. Ariadne wasn't a beauty—had never pretended to be one—but she was one of the happiest women Crawford had ever known. Her husband, Rory, was an artist who sold in one of the tourist traps in Grand Lakes, a town just down the road, but Ariadne had always preferred fiber arts herself. She said she could understand going to all that trouble for something if it was practical, but she didn't have the patience for something going on the wall. Crawford had always felt that way as well. He'd learned to knit at his grandmother's knee and had inherited the sheep property from his father. He hadn't had the stomach for eating the critters but had loved the idea of the process, from first to last. The mill had been his dream since business school in college, and he'd made it come true one small investment at a time.

He'd lucked into Ariadne about ten years ago. She'd been young, just out of college, and unemployed. She and Rory had moved to Colorado from Seattle right after they'd gotten married, and no one wanted to take a risk on a kid with (at the time) cropped green hair and an eyebrow ring. She'd taken his sign for help wanted at its word, and he hadn't said one thing about her being a little small for the work. She'd toughed out the grueling physical labor with the mill, listened when he'd explained plant-dyeing techniques, and learned how to spin and knit right alongside him. In the meantime she'd gone from a defensive kid with a butch haircut, ripped jeans, and an eyebrow ring, to a woman comfortable in her own skirts—and an eyebrow ring.

And still desperately in love with her husband.

It was the one thing Crawford really envied about her, but he could forgive that because she was really his dearest friend.

The customer left with nearly three hundred dollars' worth of Crawford's most fanciful colored wool, and Ariadne sighed and collapsed into the padded office chair next to Crawford's spinning wheel and stool. While she'd been schmoozing, Crawford had, aided by the moaning *kerchunk kerchunk kerchunk* of the giant drum carder, established a treadle rhythm and begun spinning a big fluffy rust-brown batt of alpaca/merino into a thin ply of yarn. He thought this sort of robust color might call for a thicker yarn, so he made plans to ply the singles a couple of times until it was heavy worsted weight. He had an idea for it, but he didn't want to put a voice to it.

"So, boss—do I get my bonus?" Ariadne teased, pushing her slender arms over her head and arching into a stretch. She was three months pregnant and so thin that you could already see the fullness at her waist. She claimed that her back kept tightening up with the strain, and Crawford had taken her out of the mill for the duration of the pregnancy. She'd put up a gratifying fight on that one, but then she'd thrown her back out just doing laundry and had to concede. Something about the weight distribution was just wonky, and Crawford was coddling her like a blind kitten.

This baby was as close as he was ever going to get to fatherhood. It was going to be loved.

"Yup. I'll add one more item to the layette," he said mildly, and Ariadne's eyes lit up.

"Yeah? Because this mysterious layette is killing me! You won't tell me colors or... or styles or...." Her eyes got big. "You're designing it, aren't you? The whole thing, from the fiber to the colors to the designs, right?"

Suddenly she popped out of the chair and squealed, throwing her arms around his neck and making girl noises. "You are you are you are! Oh, Crawford, I can't wait to see it!"

Crawford's eyes widened with a little bit of alarm. "You'd better wait! It's going to take me forever to knit!" It was, too. He'd started spinning and dyeing the yarn in small batches and taking it to his little house, which sat about fifty feet from the back of the shop, toward the livestock acreage but not *too* close to the alpaca pens. In the evening, before he fell asleep, he watched television or read and knitted quietly on the tiny socks or the matching hat he'd already started. He figured when December hit and he needed to see bright oranges and yellows, greens and blues, that it would be the time to work on the blanket, so it could sit in his lap as he worked with the fingering-weight yarn. But that project was going to have to wait for a night, he thought helplessly as he watched the singles spin out between his wide, blunt fingers. This thing, this soft, sturdy, natural thing, it was calling him, loud and clear.

Ariadne was smiling at him, oblivious to the uncomfortable thing growing on his heart like singles on a bobbin. "I can wait for ya, Craw—I always could." She looked at what he was spinning curiously. "That's sort of neat—rustic, natural colored. Very nice."

Crawford still blushed when she complimented him, and she did it often for just that reason. "It's fleece," he muttered. "I met the new neighbor."

Ari smiled prettily at him when he looked up, and he blushed more.

"He's gay," she said almost gleefully.

Oh crap. "I am aware," he muttered. "How did you know?"

"Because Gertie told me when we nursed her through the flu that last time."

They both sighed. They missed Gertie.

"Why'd she tell you that?" Seemed like an odd thing to bring up.

"Because she suspected you were and she wanted me to know it was okay."

Crawford let out a sigh. "Well, that would be a load off my mind if she wasn't dead and all," he snapped. God. Why did it have to be about the gay? He could live most of his life a sexless eunuch (except for the little thing he had going in Boulder with a man he suspected of having a lot of other little things going on and who mostly gave Crawford a one-off once a month out of pity) if people would just pretend he didn't exist. He was happier that way.

"Crawford!" Ariadne clapped her hand over her mouth and looked at him in horror, and Crawford did his best to tuck his misanthropy back under his belt.

"I'm sorry," he muttered. "That was a shitty thing to say."

"It totally was!" Her eyes were still big and horrified, and he winced. She was the only person on the planet who talked to him at all, and seriously, why would he want to go and freak her out like that?

"I just...." He sighed and glared at the singles in his hand. God, he loved spinning. Usually, the even keel of it, the sweetly repetitive motion of treadle, wheel, and yarn, kept his bastard in check, but apparently he wasn't doing enough of it. "He was pretty," he said at last, startled into saying the truth because he couldn't afford to lose Ari, and he *really* wanted to be that baby's Uncle Craw.

Ari sighed and reached out and ruffled his unruly, past-his-ears coarse and curly auburn hair. "Oh, Craw," she mumbled. "What am I going to do with you?"

"Call me an asshole, because I am one," he sighed, but he had to admit her touch did soothe something as edgy as an angry wind that threatened to rear up inside him.

"You're a good man, mostly," she said softly. "You just need another good man to make you happy, or you're going to get all bitter and alone out here."

Crawford grunted. "Maybe I'm just bitter and alone anyway."

"Maybe so," she conceded, but he could tell she was humoring him. "You sure have been trying to win a grumpy bastard contest since I've met you."

He felt his lips move in a pattern only vaguely familiar to either of them. "*Trying* to win? I *won* that contest, hands down!" But he smiled when he said it.

Ari laughed, and her hand moved to his stubbled cheek. Unlike Ben McCutcheon, Craw's stubble was neither intentional nor artfully arranged. It just happened because he forgot to shave, and his beard grew in, dark auburn, sort of like his hair, but with more gray.

"Sure you did. Maybe you could enter another contest now, you think?"

"You need two players for that game, Ari, and in a town this size, you know that's not going to happen."

"You just said he was pretty."

"Yeah, but just because he's pretty doesn't mean he wants to play."

"All you said was you needed another player, Craw—you've got one. Now make him see you're not just the only game in town, you're the best one too."

Crawford glared at her and was going to say something else— anything else—to get her off this subject when he was just starting to find some comfort in it himself, when the bell rang and a customer walked in. Ari stood up to greet them, and Crawford went back to his grumpy bastard therapy, which some people confused with spinning.

THE NEXT day he was at Gertie's house (Ben's house!) early. He got out of the truck, leaving it to idle in the driveway, and stomped to the door, a bit of knitting clenched in his hand.

Ben came out, wearing a thin denim jacket like Crawford's, except Ben was shivering in it. His hands and head were bare, and his teeth were chattering in the fortyish cold of the pre-sun Rockies in the fall. "I saw a coffee shop when we drove in," he said by way of greeting. "I don't suppose we could stop there, wherever we're going."

"Sure," Crawford grunted as Ben shut and locked the door. Locked it. Like someone was going to break into it. Right. "Here. Put this on."

Ben took the thing from him and looked at it, open-mouthed. "It's gorgeous," he said, surprised. "Are you sure—"

"Did I give it to you?"

"Yeah."

"Put it on. Your ears are red."

The hat was that dark, rusty brown at the rolled brim and in the center of the crown, but the rest of it was a sweet sea-foam green in seed stitch, for interest. (The seed stitch had been a bitch to decrease evenly, but Craw doubted this kid would even look to see. It didn't matter. The kid's notice of the details or lack thereof did not take away from Crawford's pride in his work.) The rusty brown kept the green from being too effeminate, and Crawford was pretty sure it looked fashionable and not gay. His eye for that sort of thing had been good since he'd taken a few design classes in college to go with his business degree, and Ben didn't seem to have any reservations about jamming the soft blend of alpaca and wool on his head and shuddering blissfully.

"My God, it's softer than a baby bunny's ass!" Ben raised his hands to pet the fabric, and Crawford grinned.

"You coming? If we want your coffee, we'd better get to it."

"Did you make this? Thank you!"

But Crawford was uncomfortable with praise or thanks. "Get your ass in the truck," he snapped, and Ben looked at him with bemusement—at the same time he obediently hopped in. Thank God,

Crawford thought. He'd stayed up late the night before knitting that thing, reasoning through the pattern, going into his stash for just the right color of green, creating a hat that looked casual at the same time it actually was sort of a wonder of engineering and creativity. Thank God that kid was going to be reasonable about this, since it was absolutely clear that Crawford had fair to partly lost his mind.

Chapter 3

Loose Ends

"DID YOU feed all your critters?" Crawford asked as the truck heaved its way down the road. It was an old Chevy half-ton with a primer-spot paint job and an engine that could haul a herd of cattle, if the trailer hitch didn't fall off first. It purred like a kitten, but it also rattled your brain around in your skull because the suspension sucked wind. Crawford was going to have to do something about that.

"Ye-eah." Ben's voice rose and fell as they hit a pothole, and he clenched the help-me-Jesus bar above the window. "Thanks for the instructions, by the way—I take it you were the one who fed them all after Gertie passed?"

Crawford grunted. Not that Gertie's relatives had noticed.

"Well," Ben said, taking the grunt for what it was, "that was really nice of you. That sheep is scary—she thinks she's the kitten, but she's the size of a horse!"

Crawford grunted again, because that was about the size of it. "We'll shear her in the spring, if you want. We did for Gertie, gave her cash for the fleece."

"Oh sure—was that why Gertie kept her?"

Craw shook his head. "She was supposed to be lamb chops. Gertie couldn't do it." Poor old gal had been broken up about it, too— she had a fixed income, and she really couldn't afford one more critter after the dogs. The sheep had been a stray off a nearby ranch, and it had seemed like a windfall until the slaughter-man had arrived. Craw had stepped in, and Gertie had loved the damned animal almost as much as her dog ever since.

Ben was looking at him like he knew there was more to it than that. "She nibbles" was what Ben said. He held up a sleeve that was a little sodden and had bits of grass on it. "Do the other things, the llamas—"

"Alpacas."

"Yeah, do they nibble like sheep?"

Craw frowned. "No. The girls will spit if they don't want to be mated, but then, wouldn't blame them."

Ben blinked and then opened his eyes *really* wide. "I don't... God. Don't tell me what that looks like."

Craw thought about it, his eyes moving restlessly on the road as he tried to figure out if there was any other way for the long-necked, long-legged critters to go. "It looks like two alpacas fucking, mostly," he said apologetically. "Of course, sometimes, the boy can't get his boy parts past the girl's furry ass, and he needs a little help, so then it looks like two alpacas fucking while their handler's giving the one on top a hand job."

He looked sideways as Ben's giggles took over the car. "Well, I didn't say it was a picnic for the *handlers*."

And that was it. Ben, the pretty man he'd been trying to impress, was leaning back in the seat of his truck, poinging like popcorn in an old metal pan and laughing so hard there were tears tracking down the beginning creases at the corners of his eyes.

Apparently the alpacas weren't the only ones who had made a fucking impression.

GIVEN THAT, Craw was surprised when Ben offered to buy him coffee. Crawford took him up on it, and Ben asked him if he liked anything special. Trying not to blush like a weenie, Craw asked for one of the lattes with pumpkin spice, and Ben's grin was comforting and infectious.

"I love the dessert-tasting ones. I'll get one, too, extra whipped cream!"

Ben ran into the coffee shop while Crawford sat in the truck and watched him. He smiled at the people in line, chatted with the girl at the counter, and sallied some sort of farewell as he backed out of the glass doors, coffee in hand. Oh Jebus—there was the counter girl, running up to him with a pastry bag and smiling prettily into his face. Craw knew her, too—her mom had come into his shop for her yarn since he'd started the mill—and she waved at him as he sat in the truck.

Craw waved back, dumbstruck, and stared at Ben as he fumbled the door open and clambered in, two cups of coffee, pastry bag, and all.

"What?" Ben said, handing him a large-sized something that smelled sweet, syrupy, and like dessert.

Craw backed the truck out of the parking lot and then took the coffee, shaking his head. "People *like* you," he said, and then could have kicked himself when he sounded wistful.

Ben didn't seem to hear it, though. He grinned, sipped his coffee appreciatively, and sighed in bliss. "I'd talk to the devil if he was the only one in the room," Ben agreed.

"Why's that?"

Ben smiled, shrugged, took another sip.

Crawford took one while he was waiting for an answer and almost closed his eyes too. Something about Ben's infectious smile seemed to make the coffee better. Maybe the girl had made it better *for* Ben, Crawford thought, and then took another sip. Nope—couldn't figure it out.

"My mom and I moved around a lot when I was little," Ben said into Craw's coffee meditation.

He startled and spilled a little on his lips. Well shit, here was the hardware store—this conversation was about to be history, right when it was about to get good! But Ben didn't stop talking, and Craw was grateful.

"I was left with different babysitters while she was trying to find jobs. I guess I just got good at making friends and fitting in."

Craw sighed. "Me too," he muttered, then grimaced. "The single mother part. That other shit I just couldn't do at all."

Ben made a hissing sound, and Craw looked at him in concern. "You okay?"

Ben's eyes were suspiciously bright and shiny when he looked back. "Peachy," he answered, something tight about his face letting Craw know that he was trying to restrain himself. The boy had a face a baby could read, but he apparently decided not to share with the playpen. "Should we go in?"

Craw didn't bother to answer but got out of the truck instead, and he heard the answering slam as Ben closed his door too. As they were walking, Ben jerked his head around to look at the truck and then shook it like he was laughing at something.

"What?"

"I'm just not used to not hearing an alarm being set, that's all." Ben made the time-honored clicking-an-electronic-device motion with his thumb and finger and then made a "poit-poit!" kind of whistle.

Craw cracked a smile. "You saw the inside of it. Would *you* steal it?"

It was true—the half-ton was old enough to have bench seats, and the upholstery was so bad it was covered by a sheet so the springs and worn padding didn't poke through or stick to your clothes. Behind the seat was about everything a man needed—a car-repair tool set, a fence-repair tool set, around 250 feet of rope, first aid kit, solar blanket, blah, blah, blah, blah—but most people didn't look past the crusty interior design to see that other shit, and Craw was glad. He didn't have to guard the damned thing with electronics that made "poit-poit" sounds.

Ben pulled up one side of his mouth and shook his head. "Guess not."

Craw had scoped out Gertie's little house already. He took the list of things Ben would need if he was going to survive the winter with any comfort whatsoever out of his pocket and gave it to a disbelieving Ben.

"Insulation in the ceiling? Are you sure?" Ben looked at the list dubiously. "Wouldn't she have had that?"

"Not an inch of it," Craw growled. "It was cold enough to freeze off an alpaca's balls—and they're covered in alpaca's *fur*, and that's about the warmest shit you can find on the planet. I have no idea how she lived so long in there."

Ben's eyes got big, and he nodded obediently, putting in the order with the guy behind the counter in the insulation department. The guy was somewhere near Crawford's age—Craw had seen him in one of the town's three bars, where Craw hung out on the odd evening he couldn't stand his own company anymore. (He still had to stand it—there wasn't a gay bar between Granby and Boulder, but at least in a regular bar, he could hear male voices arguing over game scores.) He had a forehead that sloped to his nose and a nose that sloped to his chin, he helped to coach the high school baseball team, and he seemed to think he was God's gift to the world of athletics and home repair.

"So I hear you're staying in Gertie's place?" he asked, writing the specs for the insulation as well as the day Ben had set aside to come get it. "And that you're queer like Craw here." The clerk looked up at the two of them and smirked. "Lucky you two, a chance to get you some right down the street."

Craw *wanted* to grab the guy by the shirtfront and slam his head down on the counter, but he restrained himself. "Just 'cause you put a mating pair in a pen doesn't mean one of 'em's gonna go ass-up," he snapped. "We're just guys getting some fucking insulation, you mind?"

The guy turned red and mumbled something apologetic, and Ben grimaced at Crawford and rolled his eyes like a mother reprimanding a teenage daughter.

"Don't mind Crawford," he said, smiling that charming smile at the guy. "He just likes to take the happy out of gay, that's all."

The clerk brightened, and they eventually got out of *that* department and started moving down to the lumberyard before they looked for emergency supplies.

"Jesus, Crawford." Ben said with a smirk as they walked away. "Way to embarrass the guy—he was just trying to be friendly."

"He was being an asshole," Crawford muttered.

"Well, it was nice of you to compare us to mating animals," Ben said, and Crawford's eyes went big, because that hadn't been his intention at all. "Because, you know, that doesn't set back the GLBT public image fifty years at *all*."

Well, shit. That hadn't been his intention. How had that come across all wrong? "I was just saying...." Crawford hunched his shoulders and shoved his hands in the pockets of his fleece-lined denim jacket and tried to come up with words. "I just meant that I can get ass if I need it. If I come poking at ya, it's not because we're in the same pen."

Ben stopped, and Crawford didn't notice until he'd gone forward about half an aisle. He turned around and realized that Ben had the same look of shocked horror on his face that Ariadne had shown the night before. Oh crap, he'd done it again. Still. "What?"

Ben stopped and laughed, like there was no other way for him to respond. "Nothing, Crawford. I just don't know how anybody could get a mixed signal with you, one way or another."

That cheered Crawford up, actually. Good. Because Ben was still pretty, and Crawford was starting to think about giving him a nudge to see if he'd maybe not spit if they were put in the same pen. "Call me Rance," he said cheerfully, and the expression on Ben's face was as though something had dawned on him that maybe he'd not thought about before.

"Okay… uhm… Rance."

"It was my grandfather's name," Crawford told him. "C'mon, firewood next."

They got firewood, and then they got window insulation, because if there was a blizzard, then the double paning wouldn't be enough. Ben had also made a list of the things he'd need to improve the outlet situation in the little house. The electric lines and Internet access to the area had been recently updated. Ben just needed the equipment to make sure his computers could work in the house itself.

"You can install all that?" Crawford asked, impressed. He was handy with a hammer and could work magic on the equipment in the mill, but he'd had to hire someone to run out the industrial-level generator and fuse box that he needed to run the mill itself.

"Yeah," Ben said, his customary smile in place. "You sort of have to know how to do that shit. I mean, maybe not *have* to. I know lots of software engineers in the computer business who haven't even cracked open the top of their own hard drive towers, but I like looking at the way things are put together, knowing the thing behind the thing, you know?"

Crawford raised his eyebrows. "Like the critter behind the fleece behind the yarn behind the hat?"

Ben's smile widened, and his hand went up to the sea-foam green understated masterpiece on the top of his head. "Like exactly," he said with a nod. "The Discovery Channel—one of my favorite places to be."

Craw thought about it. "Yeah—I'm not too crazy about Shark Week, though."

Ben shuddered. "Me neither. It's why I stayed away from Southern Cali." They both nodded in complete agreement and then moved on to their next department.

After an hour they had spent a lot of money, but Ben seemed to think that was par for the course, so Crawford didn't worry about it for him. They had also held a conversation that had not gone awkward, and

Ben had listened to every bit of Craw's advice about living through the cold.

Ben had also offered some of his own resources in terms of movies, Internet, and basic entertainment, because on those days when getting out to tend to the livestock was as far as you or anyone else was going to get because of the snow, boredom got to be a real factor in Granby.

As they were loading supplies into the back of the truck, Crawford started to wonder about maybe giving the boy more than a hat and maybe offering to give him a little poke in the pen, and then Ben smiled that guileless child's smile and Crawford thought maybe not. Maybe all that sweetness was too gentle for the likes of Rance Crawford, and he'd be better off with knitwear.

Maybe.

But still, after dropping Ben off and tending to the alpacas and sheep, he walked into the mill to see if the twins needed help setting up the spinners. It was an intricate job, and they always welcomed the help, but they weren't just welcoming Craw for the help.

They wanted to know about his date.

"Wasn't a date," he snapped, and Aiden grinned, the expression pleasing in his all-American-boy face. Aiden probably should have gone away to school after his graduation three years before, but he was that rare fish, the kid who grew up in a small town and loved it and had no dreams of escaping, ever. (Sort of like Craw had been, after school.) Aiden loved working in the mill and really loved the nitty-gritty end of fiber production and working for a small company. He got to create his own colorways and help plan some of the new fibers they would spin. He'd been school valedictorian, but working for Craw still seemed to be a dream job, and Craw paid him the best he could.

Jeremy was a few years older, an ex-con who had served two years for check fraud. He still had the pretty, slicked-back looks of a good con man, but Craw had given him a job because Aiden had needed help and Jeremy had been panhandling in Boulder. After buying the guy lunch and enjoying the hell out of Jeremy's schtick (but only believing about a quarter of what he said), Craw had asked him if he'd ever done an honest day's work in his life.

Jeremy, in a surprising burst of sincerity, had said no, because he'd never had an honest boss in his life.

"You think I'm honest?" Craw had asked curiously, and Jeremy's shoulders had shaken.

"I think if you weren't such an ass sometimes, a decent con man would have screwed you six ways to Sunday," Jeremy had replied, enjoying his third breakfast on Craw's dime.

"Then come work for me. I've got a full-time employee and a kid coming by after school, but it's getting too big for us."

Craw had driven Jeremy from Boulder to the mill that very day and set him up in the little apartment in the back of the barn. Once Jeremy got the hang of working with his muscles instead of his quick wits and liar's tongue, he did a pretty good job. Aiden had spent a day with him in the mill and then one with him on a supply run and came back saying that it was a good thing they had to wear earplugs most of the time, or Jeremy would drive him to murder. But they *did* have to wear earplugs most of the time, so Jeremy was safe and Aiden could retain his own sunny personality. Jeremy had moved into his own apartment since, and the boys had become inseparable—Aiden didn't even need earplugs anymore except when they were doing loud jobs.

But setting up the spinners was not a loud job, and on this day, neither of the boys was leaving Craw the holy fuck alone.

"Hey, Jer!" Aiden called, and Jeremy looked up from where he was running a hand-spun end through the machine to the spool. "Craw says it wasn't a date!"

Jeremy rolled his eyes. "Did you bring him a gift?" he asked, and Craw blinked. That hat had looked awfully pretty perched on Ben's head, but it hadn't really been a… well, it wasn't flowers. Did gay men do flowers? More importantly, would *Craw* do flowers if he had the chance? The thought made him itch. Christ, no.

Jeremy's customary laughter crinkled his eyes, making him look younger than early thirtysomething. "So there was a gift. How about food?"

"Coffee," Craw grunted, aligning his own spinner so it was in the same spot as the last one and ready to begin.

Jeremy laughed. "Well, there was food, a gift, and you spent your time shopping. I'd say it was a date!"

Aiden squinted at Jeremy. "That's all we did last Saturday!" he said, a little bit of surprise in his voice. "I thought you weren't gay!"

Jeremy widened his eyes big enough to look shocked. "Well, I didn't know you were!"

"God, what a dumbass!" Aiden shook his head. "Jesus, how can you give advice on two guys dating if you don't even know what two guys do if they're *not* on a date."

Craw looked at the two of them helplessly. The spinner was ready, the day's millwork was about to begin, and suddenly Ariadne seemed like better company.

"I want four hundred hanks, 420 yards," he said. "Make sure the roving stays consistent. It's for socks."

"We going to dye today?" Aiden asked, and Craw figured they could.

"You've got a plan?" he asked, and Aiden brought up a color scale sampler that he'd put together with pastels on a piece of nice artist's parchment. Craw looked at it, surprised. Peach, pink, fuchsia, with an overdye of red.

"This is real pretty," Craw said, and looked at it critically. "But it's sort of girly—you want to throw together another sampler with some blue or some brown in it, so we can do two batches?"

"Womanly?" Aiden asked with raised eyebrows and a leer.

Crawford grimaced. "Yeah, whatever. Show me what you got, and we'll do some roving like this. I've got some yarn stores who've got hand-spinners and are asking me if I've got any product. I like this—would like it better with some blues or neutrals, but I like it. It's as good a place as any to start."

Aiden nodded. "And maybe we can try spinning up the dyed roving and then overdying, you think?"

Oooh.... Visions of the color, saturated, shifting, like a river of visual emotion, moved behind Craw's eyes like running water over a streambed. "Yeah," Craw said dreamily. "Do that. I want to see."

He snapped out of it, which was hard, because Aiden's color visions were usually *so* seductive, and his best sellers, and then pulled out his own chromatic scale. "Here, for the people with testicles," he said.

Aiden looked at it approvingly. "Oooh, boss, I like—and not just 'cause you're the boss, either!"

Rust and teal—but not a teal that sat by itself. It started so dark it was almost green-black and then slid up and down the tint and hue scale until it reached sea-foam green. It had been the last thing Crawford had done after he'd finished Ben's hat—the hat had inspired him, sort of, and he liked where it had led.

"Maybe not quite so extreme on the dark end of it," Aiden murmured to himself. "It's sort of retro… if we keep it a little lighter here…." He wandered off murmuring to himself, and Crawford knew that whatever he came up with, it would be good.

"I'll be back to put what's on the bobbins on the hanks and help with the dying," Crawford said to no one in particular. "I'm going to go check on Ariadne."

As he walked away, he heard Jeremy saying, "Oh God, what kinds of rainbow wooly madness are the two of you going to put me through today? C'mon… lemme see the magic paper… c'mon, Aiden, you know you wanna let me see it!" and he had to laugh. God, Jeremy was a pain in the ass sometimes—but Aiden seemed to like him.

As he walked in to talk to Ariadne, he was thinking about that color scale, thinking about the leftover yarn he had, and, for no reason at all, thinking about Ben's statement about not having to worry, ever, about where Craw stood. Craw had to fight not to go find more of the yarn he'd used on Ben's hat and start him another project.

THE NEXT day, he was still fighting that urge when he drove into Boulder, the better to deliver shipments personally to the three local yarn stores there.

He had hired a rep who worked with a couple of different companies for much of his business, but Boulder was special because he had to go there anyway and because local business was good business.

Besides, he had a steady lay in Boulder, and usually that would be a cause for some special treatment right there, wouldn't it?

But as Craw went about shaving that morning, he looked at himself in the mirror, saw the square jaw under the stubble, the rectangular face, the brown eyes and the bold nose, he couldn't help hearing Ben's words too.

I just don't know how anybody could get a mixed signal with you, one way or another.

He'd made the hat. They'd gone out for coffee. They'd spent time shopping. He'd been thinking about maybe nosing about the boy and showing his interest.

Maybe going to get his pole polished out of habit was not such a good thing to do at the moment.

"Hel*lo*, handsome!" Stanley said as Craw balanced a couple of really big boxes and came through the door. He raised his plucked eyebrows theatrically and held his hand to his chest. His hair plugs were working, and his straw-blond hair was coming in thicker over his pink scalp. Craw was glad for his sake. Stanley was vain, and he'd been worried about that the last time Craw had come by.

Stanley was also unapologetically gay, as opposed to Craw, who was mind-your-own-fucking-business gay. "Hiya, Stan," he said gruffly. "Hang on a minute. I've got another load."

Stanley managed one of the larger yarn boutiques in Boulder, and the owner specialized in local yarns. Craw had been, uhm, making deliveries at Ewe'll Love This! for about five years, and to Stanley for about that time too. Stanley possessed no scruples about seduction, or about monogamy, and the first time Craw had brought a delivery by, he'd followed Craw into the bathroom and bent over the sink with a wrapped condom sticking out of his plumber's crack. Craw had been pretty fucking horny right then and had taken him up on that. He'd continued to take him up on that for the last five years, and he'd been planning on doing it today, too, it was just that....

Well, maybe a guy like Ben would think that was giving out mixed signals.

Craw sighed. Stanley was not the type to take this well.

"Here, baby," Stanley chattered, "let me show you where we're putting those today." He led Craw to the back room, talking the entire time about supply, demand, and the irritating ability of little old ladies to come in and ask for cheap acrylic yarn. Craw usually listened politely, because, well, Stanley was planning to bend over for him in the bathroom, and it only seemed fair. But today, he was wondering how to break it to Stanley that he wasn't planning on going to the bathroom, not even to pee. He'd actually stopped before this particular delivery, because usually his morning coffee hit him as soon as he rounded the corner for the store.

So he grunted in response to shit he probably should have spoken in response to, and Stanley didn't notice until Craw had all the boxes stacked and was pulling out the literature for the new colorways and fiber lines that he'd started since his last delivery, nearly three months earlier.

Stanley waved those away. "I can read that *later*, Craw. Now it's been forever—I don't expect you to dish, big guy, but, you know... the least we could do is... dish?" He darted his eyes to the front door, where the open sign had been turned closed side out, and raised his eyebrows.

Crawford flushed. "Uhm," he said, shifting his weight from foot to foot. Receding hairline or not, Stanley had *the* sweetest little bubble-ass, and it was usually tight and very often lubed and stretched soft around the rim if he knew Craw was stopping by. Even though Craw wanted an actual partner, like pretty much any other man in the world, a little bit of mindless bouncing off that bubble-butt had given him a whole lot of joy—and Stanley, too, he hoped.

Stanley raised his eyebrows. "Uhm?"

Craw looked away and flushed. "I've got a new neighbor," he said unhappily, knowing he was going to fuck this up like a stud critter's crushed testicle. "He's... he's nice."

Stanley rolled his eyes. "Well, bring him by and I'll blow him! But first, c'mon—I've got about fifteen minutes before the aqua class gets out across the street, and I'm swamped!"

Craw grimaced and tried to imagine Ben just bending over the bathroom sink while looking over his shoulder and hissing, "Hurry, dammit, I'm on a schedule!" Somehow, he thought sex with Ben would involve a lot more kissing. His lips were the softest pink under the fuzz of that trendy beard. Craw sure would like to kiss them.

"He's not that kind of nice," Craw said, his voice firming, and he tried to do right by this man who certainly had been happy to do *him*. "But you have been. I'll... uhm. You know. I'll miss doing that. But maybe next time, I should just bring you coffee, okay?"

Stanley let out an irritating little passive-aggressive whine-sigh. "Oh, *fine*. But if you want a piece of ass the next time you come by, you'd better bring the fucking lube, Craw. Honestly—I've been looking forward to this all day, and you're going to blow me off for some guy who's 'not that kind of nice'?"

Crawford did something a little out of character then and leaned forward and kissed Stanley's cheek.

Stanley stopped his tirade and looked back, bewilderment clearly written on his fashionable little oval of a face. It was, after five years of fucking in the bathroom a few times a year, probably the only time they'd ever kissed.

"I'm ready for someone that kind of nice," Craw said gently. "I think he's that kind of nice."

Some of the bitchiness pranced out of the room. "Well, Craw, I never knew that's what you were looking for."

Oh. Well, Craw hadn't known Stanley would have offered him that. "Neither did I," Craw said. "Until I saw him."

Stanley sighed and rolled his eyes. "Jesus. Could you at least get me a fucking coffee *today*, and then come back and mind the register while I go pull out the butt plug? Those things aren't made for long wear, you know?"

Crawford's eyebrows about hit his hairline. "So *that's* how you're always ready." Well hell—that was good to know.

"Well yeah, Craw—you're hung like a fucking bear. A boy's got to have some prep, right?"

Crawford nodded, although he was a little bit flattered by the belated compliment, and walked toward the front door to get that coffee. "Pumpkin latte?" he asked. There was a Starbucks two doors down in the strip mall.

"As if!" Stanley sniffed. "There's not enough sit-ups in the *world*. Venti, black, two Splendas, no cream. And hurry. Those women don't fuck around after aqua class."

Craw did hurry, not wanting to think about what Stanley was going to be doing in the bathroom during his absence. But even as he walked over and placed the order, he was thinking about something completely different. He was thinking about that colorway he'd just had Aiden dye, and how there was some worsted weight that rust color to complement it, and how good the sea foam green blended with the teal would look with Ben's green eyes.

And he was thinking about maybe Ben being that kind of nice.

Chapter 4

Carding

SO THERE were a fuckton of things to do to alpaca and sheep fur before you sat down in your soft lounging chair to knit.

There was the shearing first, but that usually happened in the spring, and then there was washing and carding and carding some more to combine the fibers, and then pulling it through the carder to make roving, and then spinning it from the roving into yarn, and then dying it after designing the colorway, and then picking out a pattern that would complement the fiber and the color and the thickness, and then....

Then, there was making something lovely.

If pressed, Crawford would refer to the next few weeks as carding.

It started the day after the visit to Boulder and the unexpectedly painful moment with Stanley. That felt like a cutting of the old to make way for the new. A shearing, of sorts.

So Craw had his fleece, his original fiber materials—him and Ben. They would be the alpaca and the merino wool, spun together. He bathed regularly, and he assumed Ben did, too, so he figured they could skip that step in their analogy and move on to carding.

Carding got rid of the brambles, the stickers, and the random bits of flotsam in the wool, and aligned all the fibers so they were in the same direction. It also got the two different fibers used to each other so they could be spun together equally.

Crawford started out by marking when Ben was outside, tending to his small acre and his unassuming animals. It usually happened in the morning, which was good, because that was when Crawford was tending his own stock, and Craw got into the pattern of being down on that end of his property, feeding the alpacas and the sheep and making sure their pens were secure.

The first day he did this on purpose, Ben looked at him a little oddly. Craw rode the horse directly for the corner of the yard where

Ben was standing, then dismounted and began feeding the animals, who looked a little surprised.

Craw could have smacked himself, but then, subtlety had never been his strength.

He looked up at Ben, who stood scratching his one sheep on the head, and did his best to make small talk. He was lucky Ben was feeling cooperative.

"You need help getting that insulation installed?" he asked, and Ben shook his head.

"No, thanks. I'm actually okay with the do-it-yourself stuff. All that time as an electrician."

Oh. Well, shit. Craw didn't have a lot to offer. Home improvement for the tenderfoot had been his ace in the hole. "You got your computers and shit set up?" Good. Get him to talk about work. Craw seemed to remember something about getting people to talk about themselves from college.

"No, but I will. I've got a nice consulting check coming in this week. It'll hold me until spring, so I've got time."

Well, there went that conversational gambit, but still, Ben had stopped scratching the sheep's head and was now leaning against the fence post, a look on his narrow, pretty face that said he was willing to continue to engage in this conversation if Craw was game. His beard scruff was especially nicely trimmed this morning, but Craw could hardly say *that*, could he?

"How about the critters?" he asked a little desperately. Jesus, talk about broadening a guy's skill set!

But as it turned out, he got lucky on this one, because Ben could *not* shut up about the rabbits. "They're really wonderful!" he said after about five minutes of describing personality traits and bunny quirks and the whole "bathing them in the bathtub" thing that sort of made Craw's eyes bulge out. "I was afraid they'd bite at first, because, you know, the only part of Bugs Bunny that sticks out is his teeth. And they do nibble if you're not careful, but mostly, you have to worry about their back legs. If they get unhappy, they can scratch." With that, Ben pulled back the sleeves of his Henley shirt, and Craw was appalled to see some ugly red slashes up on his forearms. He actually *twitched*, wanting to go doctor those up, even though he likely had some bruises and some scratches of his own from dealing with critters. This wasn't him. This was *Ben*, with the light-up-the-world smile. *Ben* didn't get hurt.

"Lucky they didn't get made into stew!" Craw grunted, and Ben looked at him with that familiar outrage on his face.

"Jesus, Craw! They're just little bunnies!"

Crawford turned red. "That just looks like it hurts," he mumbled. "I take it you got them all penned and everything."

Ben apparently forgave him for being a bastard, because he nodded and his face got all eager again. "Yeah. I made them a pen for the front yard. I saw it in the lumber store, actually and went back and got it. You want to see?"

Rabbits? Really?

"Yeah," Craw heard himself saying. "Yeah. Sure. Here." This side of the field sported an overhanging oak tree with low branches stretched over Craw's head, leading to a sturdy trunk. Instead of trotting the quarter mile up to the gate for the fence or climbing over a fence that was mostly pig-wire, Craw reached up, grabbed the branch, and swung himself awkwardly over the top of the pig-wire, leaving Ben to look at him with that uncomfortably familiar shocked expression.

"Oooooo-kay," he said, inviting Craw to laugh with him.

Craw didn't see anything shocking or funny about it, though. It was just practical. "Where's the rabbits?"

Much of Gertie's land was pretty lawn, different from the long grasses of Crawford's land. It was scarcely an acre—the little white house was right in the center of it, with the back end facing Craw's property, complete with lean-tos and pens for the sheep and the rabbits and a roost for the chickens. The rabbits were in the front yard, huddled together in the wind, nibbling on the grass in a little wire contraption that was, apparently, designed to let smallish critters enjoy the great outdoors without becoming somebody's food.

They were, Craw understood, big for their kind. Lop-eared bunnies did have a certain charm, and their fur was long and silky. There were two black and white spotted rabbits and two brown ones, and as they sat in their pen, they seemed placid enough. Okay, well, two of them seemed placid enough. The other two were—

"Oh for Christ sake!" Ben exclaimed. "Are they doing what I think they're doing?"

"Fucking?" Craw asked, to make sure he wasn't surprised at something else. "Yup. I'm pretty sure that's what they're doing."

"Well, shit. Gertie told me she'd had them spayed."

Craw had to laugh. "I think she got the two brown ones spayed and neutered—the black and white ones she got from the fair this last year. They're sort of a breeding pair."

Ben looked at him and rolled his eyes. "Well, that *would* explain the separate cages." The female let out a squeal at his feet, and Ben eyed her sourly. "Yeah, you have your fun *now*, sweetheart—you're going to be up to your eyeballs in baby bunnies in about three months." He looked at Craw unhappily. "It'll be so cold! Will they be okay?"

Craw shrugged. "That's what the fur is for. Besides, that lean-to and the rabbit hutch are nice and snug. I helped Gertie do that when she got her first pair, long time back. Did you brush them?"

Ben nodded. "Lots of fur came off. I kept it." He blushed and looked away. "I wasn't sure…. I mean, you've got the shop and the mill…. I thought you'd be interested."

Crawford couldn't help the smile that creased his blunt features. "Of course I am! Gertie used to save me the brushings too. I might not do anything with them immediately, but I usually find a place to work them in." And then, belatedly, because it was thoughtful, "That's really nice of you. Thank you."

Ben smiled back, looking for all the world like a child who had pleased a big brother or a parent. "Well, you've gone out of your way to be nice to me," he said. "Returning the favor."

Crawford blushed. Oh geez. Quid pro quo. He didn't *want* quid pro quo. He wanted… well….

The male rabbit gave a little *squee* of completed copulation at his feet, and the two bunnies separated, panting. The male gave the female a little bit of a nuzzling, and the female gave an irritated chuckle and a hearty hindquarter kick to the male's face as if to say, "Fuck off, asshole! You've done enough damage!"

Okay. Crawford didn't want *that*. But that part where the one rabbit had been riding the other? Yeah. That had been promising. He wanted *that* with some foreplay and a lot of afterglow, and maybe some, "Gee, Crawford, you *are* a nice guy, and I'd really like to do this frequently, if you don't mind me saying so."

Except with more grunting, moaning, and hot male kisses and stubble burn and maybe a blowjob or two. And breakfast in the morning and dinner together and sharing each other's day and....

Well. Maybe he was moving a little too fast. After all, look where that got the boy bunny.

"That's a real nice offer," he said, knowing the pause had gone on too long while he'd been watching hot rabbit sex. "Thank you."

He looked up and caught Ben's eyes on his face, like Ben had been looking at him and trying to read him like a book. "Here," he said after a moment. "I'll go get the bag. I'm curious as to what you'll do with it, I won't lie!"

And Crawford had his first real inspiration of this entire courting business, because suddenly, his shop and his mill and even his house didn't seem too personal at all. "Would you like to come by tomorrow and see the business?" he offered.

Ben turned around from the door of the little cottage. "I'd love to!"

CRAWFORD WONDERED if he should have... primped more for Ben's visit, but then he figured that if Ben couldn't take the business—and Crawford—as they were, well, things probably wouldn't work out anyway. For a moment he thought that maybe he'd go back to banging Stanley when he made deliveries, but the thought of Ben not liking the business just made his heart too sore to think of Stanley at all. That night Crawford took a look at his orderly, colorful little shop with its white walls and brilliant rainbow of yarn colors and his clean, no-nonsense mill next door, and decided that this was his home, and maybe a little bit of optimism wouldn't be out of order.

Apparently *something* was, because as he settled down to his afternoon spinning (he was spinning up the variegated teal roving that Aiden had dyed the day before), he actually *broke his thread*, which was unheard of almost since he'd first taken his foot to the treadle nearly twenty years before.

"What in the fuck?" Ariadne said. She'd watched him do it as she'd chattered on about her husband trying to paint an ultrasound in rainbow colors and failing because he kept getting the details too fine, and suddenly she couldn't stop staring at Crawford's bewildered expression or talking about what a dumbfuck he was.

"Jesus, Crawford! You... what the hell were you doing? I mean, you *never* break your yarn. That's such a rookie move! And you're working with what? Merino and alpaca? That doesn't break! Well, what are you waiting for! Splice it back together and reaffirm my faith in the universe! What were you thinking about when you did that?"

Crawford smiled, and the look he gave her must have been mighty helpless in texture, because suddenly her face got all soft.

"Really?" she asked quietly. "You were really thinking about him?"

"How do you know who he is?" Crawford asked, looking at the frayed ends of the yarn-to-be between his fingertips.

"Because you said ten whole sentences about taking him shopping for weatherproofing, Craw. That's something of a record. You took a week-long trip to Denver last year that didn't get talked about that much."

"He's coming to visit tomorrow," Crawford said apologetically. "No. It's not a date. He's just being neighborly." His hands started moving independently, and he licked his palm to make the spit-splice work better.

"Are you sure about that?" Ari asked gently, and Craw gave the wheel a couple of pumps to get the spinning past the break. That done, he stopped spinning, because it was clear he needed to have this out, or he'd never get his spinning even.

"He likes baby bunnies," he tried, wondering if even Ariadne spoke enough Crawford to put that connection together. "He likes baby bunnies. He thinks they're cute. He scratches the sheep on the head like a kitten. Ariadne, do I *look* like the kind of person who would do that?"

Suddenly his big, battered, lanolin-soft hands—the hands that could spin and knit and repair a fence and pick a horse's hoof and rope a critter down to shear—were covered by Ariadne's small, delicate little hands with electric blue nail polish at the tips.

"You don't *look* like the kind of person who could do that, Crawford. But I've seen you do it just the same. Hey—he's talking to you. I mean, *Jesus*, that's an improvement over every other gay man you don't know, right?"

Crawford managed a half smile, half scowl. "He's only talking to me because I made him a hat."

"Yeah? What're you going to make him next?"

Oh crap. The sad truth was he was already started on the project.

BEN LIKED the shop. He must have—he spent over an hour just wandering around, petting each kind of yarn while Crawford and Ariadne waited on customers. He didn't say anything, although he did look wistfully over his shoulder when Crawford took a break and took him on a tour of the mill.

"You want some?" Craw asked, and Ben startled and looked at him almost guiltily, blushing.

"Yes, and some yarn too!" he quipped, and Crawford blushed, not sure if that meant what he thought it meant, so he was relieved when Ben just kept on talking. "I don't know how to knit, though."

"Ariadne could teach you," Crawford offered, and Ben looked up at him sideways.

"Not you?"

Crawford blushed even harder. "Ari's a real good teacher. I'm sort of horrible. I managed to teach her, but only because she kicked me in the shins and called me a grumpy asshole so I remembered to lighten the holy fuck up."

Ben laughed, the sound echoing off the ceiling and the concrete floor of the big room that housed the mill proper. "Well, then, maybe I'll ask Ariadne when it starts to get a little colder. Something about knitting during a cold winter's night has some real comfort appeal, you know?"

Craw nodded. "Now see, here's the fleece room. After the critters are sheared, we wash the fleece to get the dirt out, and we've got to do this a couple of times with the sheep, and the water can't be too hot, or the fleece will crimp and we'll lose all the lanolin, and here's the big sinks that we do that in...."

Crawford loved the mill. He loved the big machinery and the tiny thread that seemed to come from it, and he loved the big vats of dye and the unexpectedly beautiful hanks of yarn that came from *that*. He took Ben through it piece by piece, often giving the history of each piece.

"Yeah, we had to make do with a whole different piece of equipment until two years ago, when a small mill in upstate New York went belly-up, and I took a trip up to convince the owner to let us buy his industrial-sized one."

"He brought me to flirt with the owner's daughter," Jeremy said sourly.

Crawford caught the look Ben gave him. It was appreciative—as it should have been, because Jeremy had a pretty face and appealing smile—but it was also a little repulsed.

"God, if we hadn't needed that damned piece of machinery so damned bad…. It was *almost* not worth it!"

"Didn't you tell me you slept with her?" Aiden asked, and Jeremy rolled his eyes.

"Only to make you jealous!"

"Yeah, *that'll* work."

The two wandered off, bickering, and Ben looked at Crawford in true confusion. "Are they…?"

Crawford shrugged. "Nobody knows. They spend more time together than any married couple I know, but as far as I know, neither of them's gay."

Ben's look was pitying. "Aiden definitely is," he said, considering it carefully, "but I'm not sure about Jeremy."

Crawford blinked and steered Ben outside so he could meet the alpacas. "How would you know that about Aiden?"

"Because he's obviously getting over a long-term crush on *you*, genius! Do they bite?"

"I told you, no," Crawford shot back, trying to disguise the fact that he had almost tripped on a nothing, he'd been so surprised. "And I think you're full of shit!"

Ben shrugged. "Yeah, you go ahead and think that. What's this one's name?"

"Burlingame. He's one of three studs, and his coat is rated extremely superfine. See how light it is?"

"Yeah?"

"Yeah, alpacas come in nearly thirty natural colors—that one there is really rare. It's a tough decision whether to dye it or to spin it raw. Seriously, you think he had a crush on me?"

Ben smiled that sudden, sun-in-an-open-sky smile. "Yeah, why— would you return it?"

Crawford grunted and shook his head. "Nope. He's way too young for me. And too nice. Gotta be careful with that kid—I'll squash him flat."

"What about me?" Ben asked.

Crawford wanted so badly for that implication to be there in his eyes that he told himself it wasn't so he didn't dash his own hopes. "You're tough," Crawford said gruffly, thinking about Ben's startled laughter when Craw had been mean to the sales clerk. "You'd fight back. That's good."

Ben's smile was so bright it made Crawford's eyes sting.

BEN STARTED stopping by on a regular basis after that, often with some coffee or a muffin, sometimes with something healthy for Ariadne, who immediately recruited Ben to help her do a virus scan on the computer she'd set up for inventory. September blew slowly into a crisp and bright October, and Ben visited the shop in the afternoons while Craw made a point of seeing him in the mornings. Ben could charm Crawford out of his most surly, obnoxious funks, and Crawford….

Well, one early October morning as Ben was out mowing his lawn, Craw saw that his thin denim jacket was hung up from a branch of the tree Craw had used (often now) to get into Ben's yard. Ben was sweating a little with the exertion, but Crawford knew as soon as the lawn was mowed (all one acre of it, give or take a few fruit trees and some random granite boulders that just sort of hung around the sloped planes of their stretch of the Granby bowl), Ben would be shivering his thin, under-fatted ass off.

Good. Craw had a plan for that.

Ben's back was turned, and he was at an angle not to see Crawford as he scrabbled over the fence, threw his newest gift on the branch with the jacket, and scrambled back. He was back on the horse and trotting quickly back before Ben even turned the damned mower around and figured out that he'd been there at all.

That was okay. Crawford had made his presence known.

Ben was wearing the scarf and the hat when he came to visit. It was warmer in the afternoon, so he was a little red-faced and sweating some, but Crawford appreciated the gesture.

"Wow, Ben," Ariadne said, looking at him with appreciation. "That's some mighty fine work. I hope *whoever* made that for you also has time for *other things* he's supposed to be working on!"

"He does," Crawford said mildly, and Ari smiled. Then she raised her eyebrows and made a less than graceful exit, and Ben came up to lean over the counter, watching as Crawford spun happily.

"This yarn is different than the hat," Ben said tentatively, and Crawford smiled up at him, his hands working on automatic.

"More complex," Crawford agreed.

"Why?" Ben smiled a little and looked up as he asked, like he wanted to know the answer but also like he was asking it just to exchange words with Crawford.

"Because I know you better," Crawford said primly. "More complex you, more complex yarn."

Ben grinned then, and Crawford wondered that the sun did not just hide behind the clouds in shame, the smile was so bright. "I wonder what you'll have for me next," Ben said confidently, and Crawford was suddenly struck with some fear.

"I only do so many things right," he said sharply, and the hurt on Ben's face was so acute that Crawford cursed himself and stood up, disregarding his yarn tangling around the bobbin. "I just...." He grimaced and then just finished. "My knitting is simple," he said desperately, hoping Ben would read between the stitches with this one. "My knitting is simple," he said again. "I can make anything you want with it, but it will always be simple."

Ben's hurt went away, and his smile this time wasn't that charm-the-birds-from-the-trees brand of sunshine. This smile was much gentler—much more Crawford's dye lot, actually. "Simple is good," he said. "I've lived through complicated. Complicated hurts. Simple sustains you. Complicated makes you hungry for simple."

Crawford wanted to know about complicated. He wanted to know what kinds of simple Ben hungered for. He wanted to figure out the things Ben needed that Craw could make for him.

Oh, how Crawford hungered to knit for this man.

Chapter 5
Tangled

ARIADNE SAID the moment was promising, but Crawford, well, he was cautious. Ben was not his first rodeo, and Stanley hadn't been either. He'd ridden a few times like the alpaca johnnies, and after a few randy pokes, he'd been spit at and had that horrible, disdainful sniff of rejection. Not a lot of men could put up with Crawford's raw way with words or his obsession with fiber. His business meant everything to him, or almost everything. He really, really wanted to find someone to share it with.

He'd rather give away half his stock as winter wear than give up his heart to someone who wasn't going to keep it warm and cozy in baby-bunny fur gloves.

Which was exactly what he made for Ben the third go-round.

He didn't know what that yarn he and Aiden had developed was going to be. A subtle midnight teal with a rust overdye, it was, as Aiden said when he saw it, very much Ben's colors, and Aiden had helped Craw put up a cone of it special, spun with the bunny fur. (Ben had kept bringing them bags, just like Gertie had done, and they had some very lovely batches of Sweeps because of it.) Aiden hadn't said anything as he was helping Craw with the task, but he had once brushed the yarn with his index finger, a sort of wistful look on his face as he did so.

"Craw, if you were going to make a yarn for me, what colors would it be?"

Craw thought about it. "Sky blue," he said, matter-of-fact. "Sky blue, with little dots of rust and gold, like a field of spring flowers under the Easter sky."

Aiden nodded his head then, as though that made sense. "Not as dark as this?"

Craw shook his head.

"You don't think I'm dark, do you? You think you have to be older, more complex."

And Craw had known then, known that what Ben had seen in a moment was true. "Yeah, Aiden. You need to find someone who likes that spring sky color, you think?" There. How was that for subtle?

Aiden blushed, so apparently not very. "I don't know if he's... uhm. You know. Like us. Like us and Ben."

Crawford didn't spend any time wondering how he could have been so blind. That was what happened when you surrounded yourself with your gruff, growly grizzly bear shell. All of the deer, rabbits, and even the occasional fox ran around behind your back, hoping not to piss you off. Aiden was too young for him. Even if Aiden had been Ben's age, Aiden would have been too young for him, and Ben was not.

Crawford couldn't help him with the other thing, though. His way of courting might not work for another soul on the planet. "If he is, he is. If he's not, he's still your friend. And if he's not that, I'll fire him. Fucker." But Craw doubted it. Jeremy might be able to talk a rabbit out of its tail, but Craw was positive he had some honest affection for the boy.

Aiden looked at him dryly. "Life's very simple for you, ain't it, Crawford?"

Crawford shrugged. "Yup." And then he went down to the south pasture to check in on Ben. The time had long passed when he could claim he was checking on the fences, the critters, or even just to see what crossed the road down there. Nobody was fooled. Ariadne had started chiding him about bringing sunflowers. Aiden had started asking him if he could rent Gertie's cottage when Ben moved in with Craw.

Craw told them both that nothing was certain and that all he was doing was being neighborly.

But he was starting to be neighborly with a hard-on an awful lot.

Ben was pretty—he'd seen it himself a thousand times. But he also cared for the critters and spoke nice to Craw's staff. He was honestly interested in the knitting and had been taking slow, patient lessons from Ari. And he got Crawford's sense of humor like nobody since Ari and maybe Aiden and Jeremy.

He liked to smile in a way that tugged Crawford's heart right up to the stratosphere like a kite.

And the man sure did appreciate knitwear.

October swept on to November, and Crawford rode the horse down to the end of the pasture to watch Ben raking leaves. He hadn't had to mow the lawn since the last time Craw had seen him, and he'd gradually started wearing oversized hooded sweatshirts underneath his denim jacket, along with his hat and his scarf, because November was a little bit brisk. The snows hadn't come enough to stick yet, but Crawford kept waiting for the day Ben would cave and go buy a parka or something warmer than a denim jacket and a hooded sweatshirt, and the day hadn't come yet. Besides that, there was the purely physical desire to see more of Ben when he walked into the store, which couldn't happen unless he took off the hooded sweatshirt. This was a shame, because his waist was narrow and tapered, and his chest was a little broader than his waist, and his muscles were small and defined— all things Crawford had noticed under the T-shirts and such he'd seen in the early fall but which he could not appreciate now that Ben was freezing to death.

Today, his hands were red and swollen from raking leaves in the cold, and Crawford sighed. Ben was pretty good at the weatherproofing. He had shown Crawford that the little house with its doily-covered couches and elaborately carved furniture was now much warmer and a good deal more hospitable than it had been. So Ben had been right—he was good at home improvement in general. It was just *Ben* that needed to be weatherproofed with some skill.

Crawford reached into his pocket and stroked the coarser wool of the project that had been riding him the night before, reflecting on this very dilemma. Well, he thought, he was a fast knitter but not in such a hot hurry as a suitor. Maybe it was time he stepped things up a bit before Ben's balls dropped off from exposure.

He pulled his hands out of his pocket and put on his own leather-covered gloves so that when he swung himself over the fence, his hands wouldn't sting like a sonovabitch from the cold.

He dropped lightly to his feet to see that Ben had leaned the rake against an aging pear tree and was walking forward, a welcoming expression on his face. Two months they'd been doing this, and Craw had come to treasure that expression more every day.

"I'm going to have to put in a gate," Ben said, grinning. "You keep doing that, eventually that tree's going to just drop the limb out of sheer irritation."

Craw flushed not because he thought he was fat or irritating the tree any, but because Ben had sounded like him. He rolled his eyes and pulled the half-mittens out of his pockets. They were made with the dark teal yarn with the veil-dyed rust overtones that Aiden had helped to mix, much like the scarf that Ben had wrapped warmly around his neck.

"Here," he muttered gruffly. "Give me your hands."

Ben had that look on his face—that bemused look that he often wore when talking to Crawford—but he put his hands out obediently and let Craw slide the half-mitts on. He didn't move his hands when Crawford was done and instead clasped his fingers lightly over Craw's, holding Craw's hands in his as he examined the mittens.

"They're not soft," Crawford said into the sudden heart-thumping silence. "They're not soft, but I've got some alpaca spun with that rabbit you gave me. It's real fine. I was going to make you some inner gloves for these to go over, but they take time, and...." He trailed off and swallowed and found that even though he had gloves on, he was stroking Ben's cold, red, work-roughened fingers as they peeked out from the opening of the half-mitts. "You just looked so cold."

He couldn't look at Ben then. He couldn't bear the thought of pity, or amusement, or anything else in his eyes. He'd make those gloves, the ones with the fine wool, and bring them, and then Ben's hands would be warm too.

Ben's fingers tightened over Craw's. "You don't need to coddle me, Crawford," he said softly. "I can take care of myself."

Crawford concentrated on the backs of Ben's hands and the new half-mitts. He'd put a cable on them because the cable was a little more complicated than the simple seed stitch on the scarf or the hat, and he wanted Ben to know he wasn't stupid. "You need a winter coat," he said softly, still not looking up. "We could go into Boulder tomorrow, if you want. I've got some deliveries to make, we could make a day of it. Stop for lunch and...." He swallowed. He must not make too much of this. He mustn't. He was a big scary man in a big-skied windswept place, and he must not frighten the new, amazing creature who had wandered into his paddock before he had time to sniff around a bit and decide Crawford was really all warm fur instead of just grim, spitting attitude. "It would be… it would be fun," he finished lamely. "We could have a good time."

"Yeah," Ben said, that sweet thread of humor stringing through his voice. "We could have a *great* time. Pick me up at eight thirty?"

The change in his voice gave Crawford permission to look up, and when he did, instead of Ben's usual bemusement, he saw something dark and yearning in his eyes.

"You have really amazing eyes, Rance," Ben said quietly. "You don't need to look away from me."

Crawford wanted to say something nice back, something about how ever since he'd seen Ben's eyes he'd been obsessed with capturing it in yarn, but that wasn't what came out of his mouth. "I'm not complicated," he said. "There's nothing deep or interesting going on in my eyes." Not like what he saw in Ben's eyes: Ben, who could charm half the town with a smile and a quick comment or who could look up at the Colorado sky with such yearning and such joy.

"I had complicated, you know." Ben's eyes darkened now to almost the same teal color of the half-mitts on those hands that were still holding Craw's.

"I assumed," Crawford said cautiously. He hadn't wanted to pry.

"We had separate apartments, and *he* at least, had separate other lovers, and I was just… just me. I just wanted one lover, and one place, and someone to keep me warm and listen to my bullshit and tell me a little about his day. But… it was…." And his voice grew bitter and black like burnt coffee, and Crawford felt bad and helped him finish the sentence. "Complicated," they said together, and Ben's bitterness faded, and his smile came out again.

"I told you, I like simple."

Crawford nodded. "I… I'm doing Thanksgiving this year." Thanksgiving was in a couple of days. "It's just me and Ari, her husband, the twins. Aiden has his own family, but he likes it at my place or Ari's. Jeremy just has all of us." As he spoke, Ben took a few steps in until they were eye-to-eye and so close he could feel the heat of Ben's breath. "Would you like to come?"

"I'd be honored," Ben said, and Crawford shook him off.

"Don't be honored. Just be there."

Ben pulled away his hands away and turned around, muttering something about killing a fucking moment, and Crawford sighed. Oh God. He really had. Ben had been there—he might even have thought about kissing, a thing that Crawford hadn't done in a *very* long time, but Crawford and his irritable pride.

"Tomorrow, then?" Crawford said, as humbly as he could.

Ben turned around and smiled then, and if his smile was troubled, his words weren't. "I'd love to."

THE DAY went well. They started with coffee, and Crawford let Ben get the coffee, because whatever Ben said to the girl inside sure did give her a loose hand with the cream. The whole town knew he was gay; she must know he wasn't flirting for real. He just had that effect on people—they wanted to give him things. Crawford could testify.

The trip itself was good, although the roads were icy and negotiating the twelve-something hairpin turns up the mountains and out of the valley was tough. Crawford was lucky his upper-body strength was considerable from wrangling sheep and alpacas, doing the shearing, and wrestling with the mill. Hell, his entire life made him a good candidate for steering his monster-beater of a truck.

Ben kept up a steady stream of conversation, so he must not have been worried. "I had to take a trip to Boulder last week," he said like Crawford hadn't noticed his absence keenly, "and I can't get over the... the *sky* in this state. In Granby, it's amazing... it's like you're the smallest Cheerio in the bowl full of sky!"

Crawford didn't even hardly have to respond. "It makes you feel big and small at the same time."

"It does, and that's why it's funny how sometimes the animals just make everything standard-sized again. I feel important and the world feels big and the sky doesn't make—" Ben stopped himself, and even though Crawford was driving, he caught the quick, darting look his way.

Crawford was wrestling the wheel at the moment, so even *he* was surprised when he heard himself say, "Make what?"

"Make it feel like what you want doesn't matter."

They had 200 yards of straightaway then, and Crawford managed a look square into Ben's eyes. "What you want matters," he said soberly, and then he was on another fifteen-mile-an-hour hairpin turn, and he only hoped what Ben said was "What you want matters too."

Lunch was good. They ate at one of those steakhouses with the girls in the tight T-shirts, mostly because the steak was good. Crawford dug into his twenty-two ounce T-bone and watched with amusement as Ben damned near charmed the tits off their blonde waitress. She left, giggling, after leaving Craw an extra baked potato and some bacon to go with it, all on the house, and Crawford swallowed a mouthful of steak and said, "Are you sure you're gay?"

Ben laughed, his eyes crinkling warmly in the corners, and primly wiped the scruff around his chin. "Yeah, Rance. I'm absofuckinglutely sure." Something about the way he was looking at Craw made him think sincerely about kissing the man before the end of the day, and for a little bit of time, he let that thought, that wildly optimistic plan, warm him from his stomach to his chest to his balls. He even let it make him sweat.

Then they stopped to make a delivery to Stanley, and it all went to hell.

Ben insisted on coming in, and that was embarrassing. Crawford stammered and turned redder, and then, because he was socially damaged, apparently, blurted, "I used to bang this guy in the bathroom. I don't know how nice he'll be."

Ben grew very, very still. "Uhm, used to? When did you stop?"

"About three months before you got here," Crawford said, because he delivered about once every two months.

Ben wasn't fooled, though. He raised his eyebrows. "So how often do you deliver?" he asked pleasantly.

Crawford sighed. "Every three months."

Ben's eyes narrowed, and he got out of the truck without another word.

He beat Crawford in, because Crawford was carrying two boxes of yarn, and he didn't offer to help with the other two cases of roving that were tucked into the back of the truck under the bungee cords, either. Crawford lumbered in, and Stanley pointed disinterestedly to the back room. He wore a thin little smile, and he and Ben were busy showing shark teeth to each other and discussing... well, Crawford wasn't sure what they were discussing, but he thought it might have been him.

"So you've known Rance long?" Ben asked after offering Stanley the large coffee Craw had insisted on bringing.

"'Bout five years," Stanley said, as though that meant something. "But I call him Crawford."

"That's funny," Ben said using that tone of voice that said it was pretty much the opposite of funny, ever and always. "I've known him for two months, and I call him Rance."

"Oh, honey," Stanley said, his voice dripping with something that would gag a bee, "you can't ever know Crawford. It doesn't matter how deep he gets under your skin, baby, he'll always be just one mysterious bundle of grizzly fur, wontcha, Craw?"

Craw was on his way out to get the second load of boxes, and his sudden involvement in the conversation came as quite a surprise. "Huh?"

"I'm just saying that you don't let anyone get too close, do you?"

Stanley seemed to be challenging him in some way, and Ben was looking at him like he needed Crawford to defend him somehow.

"Of course I do," Crawford said, feeling puzzled. "I live right next to my store. People have to get close or I wouldn't sell any stock."

He looked at Ben to see whether or not he'd said the right thing, and Ben's eyebrows were squished in together over wide, shiny eyes, as though he couldn't decide either, but he was looking at Crawford like he still held some value, so Crawford smiled back into his pretty sea green eyes.

"You're right," Ben murmured. "You do let a select few get close."

"You have a store next to your house?" Stanley asked, and Craw shrugged and went back out into the shortening day to get the rest of the stock.

He came back in, and Ben was looking less like he wanted to cry and more like he wanted to think, so Crawford had to hope that was a good thing. "That oughta do you through Christmas, Stan. Have Alice give me a call if you need more stock, okay?"

"Okay, fine, Crawford. You can take your pretty little skank here and motor any time." Stanley was looking at a stock clipboard

Ben took a deep breath and then put on his most charming expression. "So nice to meet you, Stanley!" he said, his voice so jovial it could cut through frost on a pane of glass. "I can't wait until Craw's next delivery. I'm sure I'll be coming with him then, too."

Stanly pulled up his lip and looked bored. "Good to know one of you will be coming *sometime*, then," he said, and then jerked the fingers of his hand in a little wave. "Buh-*bye*."

Craw grimaced. He and Ben climbed into the truck in the fading light, and he was conscious that the wind had picked up and there were snowflakes swirling lightly from the clouds overhead. But true to Colorado's fickle little heart, there was sun shooting under the cloud cover, turning the sky in the west the same orange and pink that Aiden had tried to capture with his last color chart.

"I'm sorry about that," he said as he started the truck. "The outfitters is right around the corner from here. We can get you a jacket you can move in that'll keep you warm, okay?"

Ben nodded but didn't say anything. In fact, he kept his eyes fixed on that strange, sun-snowy horizon.

He was preoccupied through shopping, too, and in the end, Craw just picked the waterproof/windproof lined coat with the faux-denim exterior, and Ben put it on his credit card without protest or even much interest.

The drive home was melancholy and quiet, and Crawford was too invested with not killing the two of them on the icy road to protest much. When they pulled up in front of Ben's house (Craw no longer thought of it as Ms. Gertie's), he got out of the truck and swung around, the better to help Ben down.

"I'm not a girl, Rance," Ben said, his sadness too strong for his words to sting. "I can get out of the truck myself."

Crawford sighed and stood, his bare hands buried in his pockets, shifting from one foot to the next. "Yeah, but… I want…." He stopped, feeling stupid. "I want to take care of you."

Ben grunted, the sound so much like Crawford's own that Craw's head snapped back in surprise. "In what way, Crawford? Seriously. In what way? Like Burlingame, the alpaca? Ariadne, the mommy? Aiden, the kid who's got a crush on you? Maybe like Jeremy, who was just lost until you showed up? You take care of everybody, Crawford—how do you want to take care of me?"

Crawford looked at him and floundered for words. "I... God. Your smile is so pretty," he said by way of introduction. "You just smiled that day, with the movers, and I... I went home and designed that yarn just for you."

Ben's eyes crossed. "So you take care of me with yarn?"

"You got a better idea?" Craw asked, truly at a loss.

"Jesus, Crawford—you go home and knit your goddamned fingers to the bone, but have you ever once thought it would be easier to kiss me? A guy could freeze his dick off before you'd offer him a hand job, couldn't he? You'll go and bang the counter guy at the yarn store before you even fucking—mmmmmmmffff...."

Crawford was devouring him. His hands were on Ben's slender shoulders and his rough, hard mouth was plastered against Ben's sweet, soft, pillowy one, and Ben was opening the barn door for Crawford and letting him pillage the stock.

Oh God, the guy tasted good. He tasted like the chocolate they'd eaten in the car on the way back and like the gum he'd chewed after that, but it was more than just what he'd eaten. His lips were soft and his tongue was inviting... hell, it was fierce, and Crawford opened the same way.

Ben made an *mm-mmm-nummy* sound and thrust his tongue in and tasted Crawford the same way Craw had just tasted him. Craw wasn't good with kissing, but he'd made sure the lead-in to this one was nearly two months long, so he was okay with it. Ben invaded, and Crawford wrapped his arms around Ben's shoulders and crushed their bodies together between their parkas in the swirling snow, and Ben just cuddled up next to his chest and ground up against his groin and made Crawford feel warm all over.

He wasn't sure who pulled away first, but his cock was stiff against the placket of his jeans, and his breath was being forced out in pants. Ben was literally whimpering, and he had one leg wrapped around the back of Crawford's thighs as he tried to grind up against the front of Craw's leg and get off. They had just come to the part of the kiss where it was either back off or go down on each other in the snow, and thank God someone had the good sense not to go that far.

Craw wasn't completely sure it was him who had it, either.

"God," Ben panted. "God. There's only one thing I want right now, but I've got to go put the heater on in the lean-to, and you've got to tend stock, and it's late and…."

Craw nodded. He had an hour, maybe two, of chores to do—they both knew it. He swallowed and placed a brief, promising kiss at the corner of Ben's mouth. "I'll see you tomorrow," he gasped, and then, over Ben's whimper of protest, he said, "I'm going to have a question with me. You decide how you answer, okay?"

"God," Ben panted, "you got a question that'll go with *that?*"

Crawford didn't have enough left to laugh. "Well," he said with the kind of snuggle that made Ben's ribs creak and the muscle between his own shoulders stretch out, "I didn't say it would be in words."

They didn't let go after that, but they didn't talk much either, and Crawford managed to brush Ben's cheek with the side of his nose and to notice, even in the darkness, that Ben had a few freckles on his cheeks that the scruff didn't cover.

"Why don't you shave?" he mumbled, his lips rasped by that little bit of stubble.

"Why don't you talk?" Ben answered, making a *hmm* sound as Crawford explored him, and those were the last words they had.

Crawford kissed him one more time—oh God, so sweet—before he found himself back in the truck and on the small dirt road to tend to his critters.

He did his chores by rote, making sure the animals were warm and happy in the barn before he retreated to his house and started the fire in the modified Franklin stove in the middle of his kitchen. His bedroom was right above the kitchen itself, and with the gas heat on and a little bit of wood, he could have a floor that didn't make his feet ache with cold when he woke up the next morning.

As he took off his outerwear and tramped the snow out of his boots and put everything to rights in his small little home, he realized that sleep was going to be a damned long time coming.

He might as well work on Ben's question now.

He pulled out alpaca yarn, some in rust and some in teal, and worked quickly, whipping the thing up in no time. He liked it—it made him laugh—and it sure did answer one of the questions Ben had hurled at him when he'd had his fur ruffled, didn't it?

He liked it so much he made another one, in different colors, just to give Ben a choice. He looked at his handiwork—knitting as joke and knitting as a proposition of sorts—and smiled. No, Crawford didn't talk a lot. But sometimes he got his point across just fine.

Chapter 6

The Curious Behavior of a Mated Pair of Furry Mammals

BEN WAS wearing the fingerless mitts as Crawford approached, with a pair of thin black factory-made gloves underneath them. Crawford's eyes narrowed at that violation, and then he remembered that he'd had other things to do with his time and that Ben had still been cold.

Crawford had walked this time, leaving Everclear in the stable, mostly because after the trip the day before, he felt like it, and Ben's little pasture fence was really not that far away. Ben was out in front of his house, salting the walk to keep it from getting icy. It was a little early for that—most folks tried to show more fortitude that way—but Crawford applauded the effort. His sweet little California bunny might actually keep hopping until spring.

Ben looked up as Crawford swung over the fence, and he set down the bag of salt and rolled the top shut. "Morning, Rance," he said mildly, but there was some hope in his eyes.

Crawford's smile was pure and whole. No one in the whole world had called him "Rance" since his mother had passed about six years ago, and damned if he didn't love the way Ben said his name.

Ben's own smile grew slack, and his mouth opened a little, and as they stood, just looking at each other, those pretty eyes grew round and excited.

Something is going to happen.

Crawford blushed. Well, it was sort of up to him now, wasn't it? He pulled his gifts out of his pocket and put them into Ben's hand. Ben opened his hand and held both choices from thumb and forefinger, regarding them with sort of a shocked awe.

"You said you had a question?" Ben asked, his voice squeaking.

Craw looked at his handiwork, still pleased. "You said your dick was going to freeze off," he said matter-of-factly. "These will make sure it doesn't."

Ben's eyes practically crossed. "They look a little, uhm, narrow to fit."

Crawford's smile widened. "I'm pleased to hear that. They'll stretch."

Ben's entire body was shaking with silent laughter as he looked at the unmistakably phallic tubes of wool, each of them complete with a contrasting color on the mushroom head and the scrot sac for the twins. One was teal and rust and one was purple and gray, but it didn't make a difference. What mattered was where they would be worn and who would know they were there.

"Uhm...." Ben closed his eyes and opened them again, but no, they hadn't magically changed into a sweater or anything while his eyes were closed. "Rance." His voice squeaked. "You, uhm, said you had a question for me?"

Crawford nodded. His voice sobered, and his grin faded as he said, "Wear my work."

Ben's entire body stilled. "Wh—" he started out, but there must have been something in his throat, because he coughed to clear it and then tried again. "Which one? When?"

"Whichever one you want. Tonight. As many nights as you can stand me after that. We're getting ready for Thanksgiving tomorrow. Stay the night. Help me and Ari cook. Stay that night. Be with me when my friends arrive. Just...." Crawford looked past him for a minute, to his little house, to his animals, and even beyond, down the swept hill into the little valley of Granby and up across the mountains and into that infinite sky. "Just know that if you want to sleep in your own bed, for a night, for permanent, that when I want you, I want *you*. Not just the guy down the road."

Ben's eyes grew gentle. He put the cock cozies in the pocket of his parka and took a few steps in. "Is that what you've been worried about me thinking?" he asked seriously, and Crawford shrugged, digging his own hands even deeper into the pockets of his jeans.

"We're two gay men in a very small town," he said by way of explanation. "You didn't know that... that my whole world stopped when I first saw you smile." He was seriously sweating now, and it wasn't warm. He could actually see steam rising from under his collar. How completely embarrassing.

Suddenly Ben's face was in his vision, his green eyes kind. "What was it you said? Something about 'just because you put a mating pair in a pen doesn't mean one of them's going ass-up for the other one'?"

Crawford knew his eyes went big. "You remember that?" he squeaked. God. Who knew his voice could break that hard?

Ben nodded, some of his smile coming back. He took a step, and another, until they were close, intimately close. "I don't go ass-up for just anyone, Rance," he said softly. "It's got to be someone who's kind, and thoughtful, and simple enough that only an idiot doesn't know where he stands." His mouth turned down, like maybe he was thinking *he* was the idiot, and then he kissed Crawford so gently it damn near hurt. Crawford started to lean into the kiss, make it a serious thing, when Ben pulled back.

"I'll see you tonight, after chores," he said, and he didn't smile, and neither did Crawford.

"I'll be waiting."

THAT NIGHT, after settling everyone down to bed, Crawford did a quick cleanup of his room. He threw all the clothes in the hamper, changed the sheets, and then hit the shower and hit it hard, paying special attention to all his intimate puckers and below-the-belt creases. He shaved close, used deodorant, brushed his teeth, combed his hair (which was sometimes a hit-or-miss proposition), and then put on a clean pair of sweats and a sweatshirt that didn't have any holes in it and his leather moccasins, and he settled down to knit some on Ari's layette. He was working on the blanket now, in its fantastical rainbow colors and its fingering-weight precious yarn, and he figured the project really would keep him occupied for much of the winter, with some time out to knit Ben a sweater for Christmas.

That last idea startled and pleased him, and he was well on his way to planning it out while his hands moved independently, so enchanted by the prospect that the knock on the door startled him.

And set his heart thundering in his ears.

He dropped the blanket in the basket and tried not to run to the door. When he opened it, there was Ben, a little backpack over his shoulder, his new jacket on against the November cold, his hat firmly over his head, his scarf nestled in against his neck, and his fingerless mitts on over those hateful factory-made gloves that Crawford would replace as soon as possible.

But still, Ben smiled up at him, and Crawford smiled back and let him in. He came, stomping the snow off of his boots and setting his backpack by the door before starting to take off his gloves and his jacket.

They still hadn't said anything, and Crawford could only look at him hungrily, wondering if they'd be able to talk easy when it was done or if they would be there, together, moving, thrusting, screaming, all night long. He figured either one would be fine.

Then Ben got rid of his outerwear and stopped to unlace his boots, but he did an awkward little shimmy as he bent. His grin up at Crawford was wicked. "You know," he said conversationally, "this thing sort of itches. You, uhm, wouldn't want to help me take it off, would you?"

Spots danced in front of Crawford's eyes. "I, uhm… oh Christ." All his blood just went south. "Hell yes. Yes. Yes, I want to help you take it off."

Ben stood up then in his bare feet and grabbed Crawford's hand, tugging gently. "Then let's go do that," he said, rising excitement in his voice, and Crawford followed him up the stairs.

They didn't talk much after that.

The hallway was dark, and by the time they got to the bedroom, Crawford didn't care much about turning on the lights. One minute they were padding across the carpet, and the next minute their mouths were fused together, and Ben's hands, only a little chilled, were running over his stomach, up his ribs, palming his chest as he scraped his thumbs delicately across Crawford's nipples. That last one made Crawford keen, because suddenly his cock was so full, so achy, that it actually hurt to be teased like that, even from his nipples. Ben must have known it, too—he made a chuckle in the back of his throat, and Crawford pressed deeper into the kiss and grabbed Ben's slender hips and hauled him closer, grinding up against him and letting him know that this was business this time.

Crawford bent down and kissed Ben's belly button, a dark divot in the pale flesh of his soft stomach, and then stood up, stripping off Ben's shirt as he stood, planting kisses, nibbles, laves with his tongue as he went. He got to Ben's nipples and stayed bent, suckling until Ben went, "Waauuuhh…. God… Crawford… killing me. This thing doesn't stretch *that* much!" with his hands clenched in Crawford's hair until it stung.

Crawford sank to his knees then and pulled the tab of the button fly open, *really* wanting to see if Ben was wearing his silly little gift.

Well, it wasn't so little now.

For belonging to a smaller, slender man, Ben's cock was exceptional, and Crawford was always appreciative of functional art. At the moment it was jammed into the cock cozy, and Crawford was all about setting it free. He slid the cozy off slowly, because he knew it would tease, and Ben's gasp as Craw inched the wool over his cock was tortured.

The end was already slick and shiny with smeared precome, and Crawford grinned up at him. "Bet that itched," he said, and Ben tilted his head back and groaned. Crawford set about making that better. He liked this part—he liked making his tongue flat and licking the head and sliding his lips over his teeth and making his mouth nice and wet. He *really* liked the taste, and the fullness, and the sounds Ben made when he pushed his head forward as far as it would go. And he *loved* it when Ben thrust hard into the back of his throat like he couldn't help himself.

He stayed there, kneeling, kneading the backs of Ben's thighs with his hands, then moving up to his backside and kneading harder. The side of his hand slid into the crease, and he got another surprise. He pulled back and looked up, skating his fingers in the freshly applied lubricant and giving the handle of the little rubber plug a flick. It was all he could do not to bury his head against Ben's flank, yank that plug out, and then convulse and come in his sweats.

"You got wants you want to voice?" he asked gruffly, sticking his tongue out to a point and playing with the edge of Ben's crown. Ben was circumcised, which was fitting, because his cockhead was naked and unprotected. It needed a cock cozy, or Crawford's mouth, just to keep it warm.

"I've got a powerful need...." Ben gasped as Crawford opened his mouth again and pulled his cockhead in. His hands tightened and he stopped Crawford, who held still, Ben's cock half in and half out, and just watched the play of pleasure and intention ripple across Ben's face. "God, Crawford, I'd really love to go ass-up if you'd just poke me, okay?"

"Geeeeraaawww...." Crawford really *did* bury his head in Ben's slender, muscled flank this time. He held on there for a moment, arms wrapped around Ben's waist, until the need to come was beaten back a little, and then he stood and pushed Ben back against the bed.

"Ass up!" he commanded, thinking they would probably not get a chance to watch television tonight because he was going to want to do this face to face and spoon-style and maybe even sixty-nine before morning came, but right now, ass-up was absolutely imperative.

And there Ben was, his ass stretched and ready, wiggling in the air. Crawford had about a breath to rub his hands over the whiteness of it before a hard shudder took him, and he conceded they didn't have much time. First he stripped naked and then grabbed a condom off the bed stand, watching Ben just stay there obediently, waiting to be mounted and fucked. Even the brushes of his own hands or clothing on his skin was like fire, and everything, from his hands to his breath to the sounds he was making without meaning to, shook. He pulled the plug out without much ceremony, and Ben's long howl into the comforter was pretty satisfying.

But not as satisfying as shoving his hard, hurting cock into the place where the plug had been.

This time, Ben's howl cracked up an octave or two, and Crawford reached around his waist and hauled him up so they were flush together, so close they *had* to be fucking or there wouldn't have been any room for Crawford's erection. He plastered his big hand up on Ben's throat and nuzzled his ear. "All good?" he asked, and Ben shook his head and whimpered.

"So good. So good. God, don't stop now, Rance, please?"

Crawford put his hands on Ben's shoulders and pushed him forward, and then... oh God, and then thrust into him for all he was worth.

Ben made noises during sex, lots of them, grunting, pleading, begging words, and every noise ramped Crawford up that much higher, especially when Ben gave a huge, howling cry and convulsed, his hand moving on his cock clumsily and his broken half sobs muffled by the blankets.

"You come?" he asked, and Ben's "Auuhh-huh!" was mostly yes, so he finally, *finally* let the tingling, smashing thing that had built up at the base of his spine, behind his balls, in the pit of his groin, explode, spilling so hot and so hard into the rubber that it scalded.

He fell over Ben's back then, his arms spasming around Ben's chest, and listened to Ben laugh breathlessly as their combined weight slowly squashed them flat into the bed. They stayed there for a while, and Crawford placed a smattering of tiny kisses along Ben's slender shoulders, and Ben made a luxuriating sound in spite of Craw's solid body on his.

"Rance?"

"Hmm?"

"How early do we have to wake up?"

"'Bout eight, if we're going to feed our critters."

"Mmm…." Ben pushed his shoulders up, and Crawford rolled over to let him, sliding out of his body as he did so. Ben turned to face him and scooted until they were cuddled together in the faint chill of a room at night in late autumn in Granby. "What time is it now?" he asked, kissing Crawford's chest the way Craw had kissed his shoulders.

"'Bout nine, why?"

Ben pulled back and looked at him, those green eyes that spoke of the sea, both salt water and grass glinting wickedly in the dark. "Because we can do all sorts of things before we go to bed," he said happily, and Crawford nodded his head yes and then started round two with a kiss.

THE NEXT day was a fog of exhaustion and tending the stock and then cooking and preparing for the celebration of thankfulness that both of them would give their whole hearts to. But that was the day.

The morning was waking up with Ben plastered against his back, both of them tired and smelling strongly of sweat and sex and in sore need of a shower.

And very, very happy.

"Rance?"

"Yeah?" Craw rolled over and stretched out his arm, the better for Ben to lay his head on Crawford's shoulder.

"How hard would it be to put my bunnies in your barn and my sheep in with yours?"

"Not hard at all. Chickens too?"

"Yeah."

"Today?"

Ben's artfully tousled hair was now tousled for real, and it was no less charming for that. He looked at Crawford from his position on his shoulder and rubbed restless patterns on his chest until Crawford caught his hand and tangled their fingers. "Not today. When it's handy."

"It'll be handy next week," Crawford said, feeling warm and full, and almost like it was Thanksgiving but better, just waking up next to Ben. "You sure?"

"You sure you want me?"

Crawford chuckled dryly and kissed Ben's forehead. "Wanted you since before I knew you," he said softly. "You think I knit for just anyone?"

"You don't?" Naked vulnerability there, and Crawford put that to rest right there.

"Only folks I love," he said, trading naked heart for naked heart.

"How'd you know so soon?"

And Crawford didn't have an answer for that. He couldn't put into words the expression on Ben's face when he'd first stood on his land and held his face to the wind, or the winsomeness of his smile, or the absolute joy Crawford found in watching him charm the world at large. He couldn't express how happy he would be to have a man at his side for Thanksgiving, at his table, with his friends, one who made him proud to be himself.

"You looked like my kind of critter," he said, and then buried his nose in Ben's shoulder until he giggled like a child. "Smelled like him too. I just don't know why you'd want to get poked by a grumpy fucker like me."

Ben reached out a hand then and rested it on his cheek. "It could have been your eyes," he said lightly. "I'm a sucker for deep brown eyes and the red hair to match—mm. Just fucking mm. It could have been the fact that you went out of your way to be nice to me. Or that you can make me laugh. Or that you seemed to get me without even trying and that you liked to hear me talk. Hell, it could have been that any idiot can see you're hung like a walrus."

"I am?"

"Hey," Ben laughed, "Stanley's words, not mine!"

"Oh God!"

"But that wasn't what pushed me over the edge."

"No?"

"No," Ben said firmly, pushing himself up so he was perched on Crawford's chest, smiling down with happy-evil eyes. "It was the knitting."

Crawford laughed. "The knitting?"

"Yup. You courted me with alpaca-fur woolens. How could I resist?"

Crawford rolled his eyes. "It was all I had," he confessed, feeling foolish.

"It was perfect," Ben said, suddenly very, very sincere. He kissed Crawford on the mouth then, morning breath and all, and Crawford's arms tightened around his shoulders. Later there would be friends and food and cooking and joy, but right now, he was just very thankful.

Thankful indeed.

Rance Crawford's Pattern for an Above-Average Cock Cozy

(also fits neatly over a tube-shaped bottle of lubricant)

Yarn: Worsted weight, colors of choice.
Needles: Size 6 DPN
Gauge: 5 stitches per inch
Shaft:
C-O 24 stitches; distribute stitches along three needles.

Work in stockinet stitch for, uhm, six inches is average. (Eight or ten if you're lucky, I guess. But if it's eight or ten, you may want to C-O another four stitches. Just saying.)

When you get to the head, increase four stitches.

Work 1 round even.

K5 stitches k2 tog

Work 1 round even

K4 st. k2 tog

Work one round even

K3 st. k2 tog.

Work one round even

K2 tog. Around

K2 tog. Around.

Break yarn, thread through remaining stitches twice, and pull tight, tie bigass knot at the base of the yarn, and trim the little trickle hanging off, for good humor.

Scrot sac (these directions are for the big-balled. For the average-balled, feel free to lighten up on the increasing):

At the base of the shaft, pick up and knit 12 st.

Working back and forth (for the moment) purl one row.

Increase to 24 st. in the next knit row.

Work back and forth for eight rows; end with a purl row.

At end of row, pick up six stitches FROM THE PURL SIDE TO THE KNIT down the side of the flap, pick up 20 st. on the bottom, and pick up ten stitches up the other side. (Yes, this will gather a bit. So does the equipment it's meant to cover.)

Work back and forth on the 32 stitches for about 2-3 inches. Bind off, leaving a 12-inch tail. Fold the side stitches (the ones picked up after the flap was knit) together and sew together with tail. Finish off. Take another 12-inch length of yarn and do the same thing for the other side stitches. Finish off.

How to Raise an Honest Rabbit

Chapter 1

Dishonest Work

JEREMY DIDN'T really know his last name. His father was a con man and his mother was history, and he went through so many different identities as a kid helping his dad on the grift, that all he knew of himself, really, was that he was a bad person. He had to be. His one skill set was relieving people of their money.

He was okay at it. When he was a kid, he simply sat by his father's side and looked hungry (not hard to do) when his father was selling encyclopedias, bibles, or "free" ammo, depending on the area they were canvassing. As a blooming adolescent, he hit colleges and sold magazines, just like the legit kids doing the same thing. His specialty was selling to the chubby, lonely girls who looked like they had money but no attention. He paid attention to them, talked to them as they sat under the dappled leaves of a picturesque tree looking intellectual and dreamy, and walked away with checks ranging anywhere from ten to a hundred and ten dollars, without having to even give them a kiss. He stayed young looking well into his twenties, so that was pretty much his job, right up until he went to prison.

He and his father supplemented their income with the usual grifts—Three-Card-Monte, The Fiddle Game, The Good Samaritan, and The Embarrassing Check—and Jeremy was a decent student. When the other kids were graduating from high school, Jeremy and the old man were having "clear the apartment" drills—they could completely relocate their lives in less than five minutes. Once, when the cops were banging on the door and they were sneaking out the window of a walk-up in Chicago, they'd done it in two. Jeremy figured he and the old man could probably have continued to con the world as an unbeatable team pretty much forever, but two things happened.

The first was that the old man got shot when he conned the wrong guy. One minute, Jeremy was waiting in the shadows of an old Vegas casino while Oscar signed over a phony deed to some property in Utah, and the next, the guy pulled out a .45 and blew him away. Jeremy stood there, holding his breath, sinking into the curtains of the theater, and making sure nobody saw him. He stood there while Mario Carelli shot his father again in the head to stop him from twitching; he stood there while Mario had his goons haul away the body and wash the floor; he stood there while Mario started asking if anyone would actually miss some con man with shitty shoes and a cheap suit.

He stood there when Mario's favorite goon, Gianni—who had gone down on Jeremy the night before, while Oscar and Mario had been hammering out the final deal—had shrugged and said, "I dunno, boss. He had muscle with him, but the guy was hired and not that bright. For all I know, he took a powder when he heard the shot."

Gianni had known exactly where Jeremy was standing, and he knew that Oscar was Jeremy's father, and he knew that Jeremy was almost twenty-six years old and thinking about maybe going to college for real. Oscar had spent a long time building the pig-in-the-poke con, and Jeremy had a long time to spend with Gianni, telling him as much of the truth as he could, because you don't tell a guy your old man is scamming his mob boss, even if you're starting to feel a little bit bad about it. Jeremy had "sweetened the pot" with a lot of marks, both male and female, and Gianni's mouth on his cock hadn't been unexpected. The unexpected part was the sweetness of Gianni's shy smile at the end, and the way he'd carefully done up Jeremy's slacks and then kissed him passionately on the mouth. Jeremy had returned the kiss, a little bit frightened by how real it was, because until that exact moment, he'd thought sex was the biggest scam of all.

So Gianni took a big risk for Jeremy, and Jeremy repaid him by staying right in that exact spot—surrounded by stage curtains, trying really hard not to piss his pants—until his father's brains were cleaned up off the floor and Mario Carelli stalked off with his goons, chuckling about the look on the old man's face. Even after they were gone, Jeremy stood there, swimming in his own sweat, feeling it drip from his calves to his ankles to the nylon socks inside his dress shoes.

He was thinking that his daddy had told him to hang back the night before because he had a grifter's sense the con had gone bad. Oscar hadn't been a Hallmark father, and Jeremy would eventually figure out that he'd been sort of screwed in the parenting department as a whole, but in this case, Oscar had done his son a solid and worried Jeremy might get hurt.

He was thinking that Gianni would be dead right now if Jeremy had breathed or whimpered or pissed his pants after that whopping lie Gianni told, but Gianni still told it, all because of a blowjob and a kiss, two things Jeremy hadn't thought much of at all.

He was thinking that for his whole life, he'd thought love might be the biggest con of all, and all of a sudden, it was the only real thing, and he was swimming in it, suffocated by it, just like he was suffocated by the wool curtains and swimming in his own sweat.

HE MADE it out of there eventually, but by the time he got to their shitty hotel room, it had been raided by Mario's men, stripped of his and Oscar's backup money, the mattress upended, and even his small cache of possessions trashed and stolen. He'd been out of hope when he went rooting in the dresser for their last-hope-stash tucked into a defiled bible, but he was suddenly rewarded.

There in the little cavern carved into the glued pages was not only the cash, but also his father's wallet and ring—two things he knew had been in Oscar's possession when Oscar had been shot.

He looked at them and swallowed. *Gianni.* Gianni had taken a hell of a risk for him, and there it was: his chance to walk away.

And he did, but walking away was harder than it sounded. Two months later, he was in Denver, trying to get a nice woman at a gas station to give him cash for a bad check. She'd been smiling at him tentatively, coyly, starting to blossom under his insistent charm, when he noticed the fading bruises around her mouth, and his heart sank. Yeah, the rich girls under the dreaming trees in the colleges used to look at him the same way; he'd known they were neglected, worried out of the confidence that would have kept them safe from a predator such as him. This woman hadn't had her confidence neglected—she'd had it beaten out of her, and that didn't really sit right with him. How was getting swindled out of fifty bucks going to make that situation any better? Then the child had walked in, a little boy, five at the most, saying, "Mommy, do we have to wait in the car?"

Jeremy's brain did some sort of horrible rise and dip then, like a roller coaster, only uglier, with more vertigo. His stomach heaved with a combination of hunger and self-revulsion. He shoved the cash back in her hand and hissed, "What's the matter with you? Don't ever give your cash to strangers." Her eyes widened, and her mouth pinched narrowly, and he saw in that moment the ugliness that ugliness had made of her. Yeah, she'd known what he'd been selling, and she'd wanted it, desperately, needed to buy it, even for a moment, and he'd just ripped it out of her hands.

He turned around and walked out of the gas station and into the November cold, well aware that she was probably raising a ruckus behind him but not caring. His vision was dark and spotty, not just from the hunger, which was acute, but from the realization of what he was. He was a bad guy. A swindler, a con man, a thief, and a crook. The woman's name had been Linda—how many Lindas had he taken money from over the years? How many Lindas had put their faith in his fast-talking pretty face and been betrayed and injured, yelled at or beaten, or simply just cheated, because he thought his right to eat was of more priority than theirs?

He was a bad guy. He was one step away from the guy who'd put a bullet in his father's head and hosed his father's brains off the floor.

When the cops caught up to him, he was squatting in the dirty snow, dry heaving because he hadn't eaten in three days.

His public defense attorney sucked. He should have gotten thirty days for fraud, maybe—but suddenly they were bringing in all the shit he'd done with his old man, even the stuff they couldn't prove he'd done, and the woman (sporting fresh bruises from her husband) came in and said that Jeremy gave her a split lip to boot.

He ended up spending two years at Fort Lyon, a lovely place that let him out in the yard once a day and gave him many opportunities to take a dump in public.

It had been surprisingly peaceful, stuffed in that cell with his monosyllabic cellmate and his rapidly burgeoning conscience. Nothing to do but read, write, and think. He was maybe one of the very few people in that place to actually take the child's advice to sit in a corner and think about what he'd done.

He wasn't thrilled by the experience, really. It was hard. He would have been wrong to say he relived every con and every score, because he was a petty con man, and he'd made his life off small potatoes. One small potato looks very much like another one, and after they'd been boiled and peeled, the only thing left to do was mash them—and that's just what Jeremy did. He boiled his experiences in his head, peeled them and mashed them, and decided that what was left in his head was not what he wanted to be living with for the rest of his life.

He got his GED at Fort Lyon, and started taking college courses. He managed to work too, in the laundry, and when he was discharged after two years, he thought he was well on his way to becoming an honest citizen.

He was so wrong.

Nobody would hire an ex-con. Nobody. He was discharged, not paroled—he had no resources, and even if there had been any, he wouldn't have asked. There had been no bonding for him in prison. No brotherhood. His first cellmate had been in there for manslaughter after a DWI—a lifetime con man and a detoxing banker? Their best quality as a couple was that they were good at leaving each other the fuck alone.

Jeremy was released in December. For a month, he managed to live on soup kitchens, washing dishes, and the Christmas kindness of strangers. Later, he would wonder why he hadn't taken to giving blowjobs for food money, and it took him some time to realize that it was because he'd never considered himself a victim. He'd always been looking for a way, an avenue, an alternative—that kind of optimism gave you confidence. It kept you from being meat. It made your shoulders swing in such a way that nobody would dream of asking you if your ass was for sale, because if they did, you might have a comeback that would shrivel a dick forever, and who wanted that from a cheap piece of ass?

But in spite of his continued optimism, his trolling of the Goodwill for clothes that made him look like he could hold down a job, his haunting of the YMCA to keep clean and groomed, and his insistence of hauling around his own sheets so he didn't get lice at the shelters, by January, he was more than a little bit desperate.

He started haunting one particular street corner in Boulder, where little old ladies frequented a family style gym and a yarn store. If he stood there between the time they got out of the gym and swarmed the yarn store, he could almost always win some food for breakfast or lunch from them, and while panhandling lacked dignity, it was at least honest. Life didn't get much more honest than "Please give me money because I'm hungry," or at least it hadn't for Jeremy at that point.

Then, after about a week, he saw a big guy, not too burly, with curly red hair on his head and growing out in what was probably an unintentional beard, fighting his way through the flood of little old ladies like a bear swimming against a salmon tide.

One nice woman, a regular with short white hair, kindly eyes, and a velveteen pantsuit, who always liked to talk to him about his day, had just finished pressing five dollars in his hand. "Okay, dear—now, don't get this wrong, but I hope not to see you next week. You say you're looking for work; I'd like to see you find it!"

Jeremy had nodded and smiled, but inside, he was dying a little for lack of hope. He'd used the library computer to fill out applications for everywhere—dry cleaners, pet stores, lumber mills, coffee shops, everywhere. There were jobs to be had, but you had to know someone first. The only person Jeremy had ever really known was probably rotting in a shallow grave.

Suddenly, the big guy with the red hair was right there, glaring at both Jeremy and the little old lady.

"Helen," he said—and his voice rumbled too—"is this guy bothering you?"

The woman smiled up at him and patted his arm like he was some sort of tame giant-frickin' afghan dog. "No, Craw—he's a good boy. Did you bring in new stock today? You know I love your stuff."

The guy grunted. "Ariadne's dyed up some Sweeps. You'd better hurry—there's a swarm."

The little woman looked up in honest alarm, and, without another word to Jeremy or the big-furry-bear man, darted into the store to go at it in some serious elbow-to-midriff competition for what appeared to be a big bucket of brightly colored yarn that didn't seem to follow a rhyme or a reason in terms of color or size or anything.

Jeremy watched her do battle through the big plate glass window and then sighed. "Helen" had given him lunch money, and now he got to go search the want ads fruitlessly over some food at Denny's. Well, some days it had just been over coffee, and some days, it had been a full-out meal. Some days he'd even been able to find work too—stacking pallets, loading shit onto a truck—but the fact was, although he wasn't weak, he didn't have a powerhouse physique. There were guys with more powerful bodies and harder hands who could do a better, faster job of it, and he was often passed over at the train yard when people were looking for spare hands.

And nobody gardened in January in Colorado.

So when he noticed the big guy was just watching him through narrowed eyes, Jeremy had a moment to think that he'd been getting off easy. He'd made it through two years of prison by trading cigarettes and helping to smuggle in luxuries, and thus had not had his pretty little body violated in any way he didn't want it to be. (He hadn't wanted it to be. Once you started having sex in prison, that sort of thing got around, and pretty soon, you were the prettiest girl at the prom. He'd kept his sexuality to himself, and people had left him alone.) For just a second, he thought he might have to actually whore himself out to do honest work.

Then the guy had wrinkled his nose and said, "Five bucks? You're gonna get lunch for five bucks?"

Jeremy smiled greenly. "Denny's—they serve cheap breakfast all day, unless you're gonna hand me a ten!"

The guy laughed shortly. "It's gonna take more than a ten to fix those shoes."

Jeremy looked mournfully at his feet. They were the same shoes he'd worn into prison, and they'd started out pretty good quality, but now the leather was cracked and the sole was worn thin enough to let in the dirty, melted snow. "Yeah, there's nothing like a good pair of shoes, you know? First thing I'm going to buy when I get back on my feet is a new pair of shoes."

"Got any plans to get back on your feet?"

Now that Jeremy felt his person wasn't in imminent danger, he could patter like the pro he had been. "I'm gonna get me a sales job, right? 'Cause I'm good with people. But first I'm gonna work under the table for a bar, right? 'Cause I'm good with people, and then I'm gonna get me some new threads. But before I find that bartender job, I need me some breakfast—and the bigger the breakfast, the better. So, can you spare a ten?"

The guy laughed and stuck out his hand. "I'm Crawford, and I'll buy you some lunch, how's that?"

Wow—lunch and a five in his pocket, and he didn't even have to put out. (The guy was over six feet tall, and Jeremy didn't even want to speculate on the hole Crawford would rip if he decided that wasn't the case. Jeremy was just as happy not to have to break his record for not bending over to eat, thank you very much!)

It was lunchtime, but Jeremy ordered breakfast, because he loved eggs and toast, and he was ebullient over the first meal. He bolted it down in an all-fired hurry, because his stomach was doing all the talking in his body, and it needed some frickin' chow. Of course, he could talk and eat, so he started spinning all sorts of pie in the sky, about being a salesman and owning his own store and then going to college and getting a law degree. "Because the way I see it, being a salesman is just a legit way of being a con man, right? So I've already got the groundwork, and I know how to talk, and I'm pretty sure I could sell water to a duck, right?" (That's one of the key things the old man had taught him—people would do almost anything to avoid being rude.) "So I figured you'd—"

"You'd sell people shit they don't need, and your only claim to honesty would be not ending up in prison?" Crawford asked, and Jeremy blushed and mopped up the eggs on his plate with toast, and then started using his finger for the last of the egg. A heavy silence might have fallen then, but Crawford signaled the waitress with two fingers and a point to Jeremy's plate. Jeremy opened his mouth and then closed it, and Crawford took a swallow of coffee and then looked at him like he expected an answer.

"Well, how am I going to pay for the law degree?" he asked, but he was watching with wide eyes, realizing that all that beautiful food was going to be for him as the waitress walked back to the kitchen and called a double of his exact order. For no reason he could think of, his voice cracked as he said it, showing the cold winter sunshine peeking through his thin fictions, like the snow saw through the holes in his shoes.

He swallowed, and Crawford took another swallow of coffee. "You'd make a great lawyer," he said meditatively. "Those fuckers'll suck the life outta you with words too."

Jeremy didn't have a comeback for that. He was too filled with visions of food, real food, not just enough to keep him on his feet, but enough to gorge on, to make himself sick. He swallowed, his mouth suddenly watering like it hadn't when they'd walked into the diner, and he felt like he had to work for his money. He *had* to talk, *had to*, because that was all he had to pay Crawford back for the second and third helpings of food coming his way.

"Yeah," he said, swallowing again. "Yeah, they'll suck the life outta you, but you know, you get a good one, and good things'll come your way, right? So, you wanna be that person, the person who can make the rain come. My daddy, he talked all the time about the rain comin' down, and how that's all a man can want is to make the rain come, and I figure a lawyer, he'll be all about makin' it happen, but only a good one, right? I wouldn't want to be a bad one, because the bad ones, they get you put away for...." He swallowed again, and the waitress brought him the two servings of toast that went with Crawford's order and he just looked at them, suddenly just touched beyond words. The first meal, that could have been a fluke, but this was... God, this was the rain coming down, wasn't it?

"How long?" Craw asked, his voice gruff, and Jeremy didn't even think to lie or evade.

"Two years," he said, watching numbly as Craw picked up the little jar of jam he'd seen Jeremy use and started preparing the toast. Craw handed him the plate and Jeremy ate automatically.

"How old are you, son?" Craw asked softly, and Jeremy swallowed toast down so he could answer.

"I'll be twenty-eight next month," he said, and Craw nodded, like Jeremy had looked that old, which he hadn't used to, and Jeremy's pride flared. "Yeah, I know I look young, but I coulda picked your pocket a dozen times if I'd tried, and if I hadn't been going straight, you'd be signing me your first born by now, so don't worry about me being young. I can take care of myself, but thank you much for the breakfast just the same."

"Kid, have you done an honest day's work in your life?"

The waitress took that moment to drop off his first second breakfast, and Jeremy looked at it longingly. It was like suddenly he realized he'd been caught in a long con, and if he took a bite of those eggs, he wasn't going to be able to wriggle his way out.

He really wanted those eggs.

"No," he said simply, picking up his fork and shoveling them on a second piece of toast. "I don't even know how. You're the first honest man I've ever known in my life."

"You think I'm honest?" Craw asked curiously, and Jeremy's shoulders shook.

"I think if you weren't such an ass sometimes, a decent con man would have screwed you six ways to Sunday," Jeremy replied frankly, because Craw *had* been an ass—he'd broken every law of conversation Oscar had ever taught him. If Jeremy had been on the grift, he would have walked away from this one—guys like Craw would call you on your bullshit because they just didn't give a fuck.

Craw nodded, a faint smile on his mouth under the unintentional beard. "Good. Then come work for me. I've got a full-time employee and a kid coming by after school, but it's getting too big for us. I'll teach you honesty."

Jeremy blinked and ate another bit on automatic. "You'll teach me honesty?" he said numbly. *Oh God.* Suddenly that sounded harder to learn than lawyer shit. "How's that going to feed me?"

Craw shrugged. "I can put you up in a tack room until you get enough to rent an apartment," he said, obviously having thought this out. "I can feed you until then too." Craw's eyes swept the bustling streets of Boulder, full of human sheep and pigeons, all ready to be fleeced and plucked, if only Jeremy hadn't sworn off fresh game. "The only catch is you'll have to leave this shit behind. I live in Granby."

Jeremy shivered, just hearing the name. It was the last stop before the Rocky Mountains—Jesus, he didn't even know the road to Granby was open this time of year!

"This is the only jacket and shoes I got," he said, his heart sinking.

"Will you work for me?" Craw asked.

"Yeah," Jeremy said, not even bargaining for clothes and shoes. It was a job. It was a job, and a place to stay, and food. Jeremy hadn't realized how desperate he was until he was offered all three of the things he wanted most, when he'd just gotten used to a full stomach in the warm diner.

"Then I'll get you what you need," Crawford told him, and Jeremy looked at him with gleaming eyes.

"Why?" he asked, wanting to hear something, anything, that would make sense.

All he got was a shrug. "Aiden needs your help."

Jeremy took one more bite of the second plate of eggs and then started mopping up the yolk again. "Who in the hell is Aiden?"

And Crawford just laughed.

Chapter 2
Honest and Lonely

AIDEN RHODES turned out to be a kid, a little taller than Jeremy, with muscles just starting to define and hands and feet that were just starting not to be outrageously proportioned. He had curly dark blondish hair a little lighter than Jeremy's, light brown eyes that were a little closer to green, and a sturdy sort of grace that transfixed Jeremy the moment Craw introduced the two of them.

Craw had driven him from the diner to a Walmart for some better clothes, then back over the hill with its hairpin turns and into the Granby valley. It was a pretty drive—if you didn't mind the imminent threat of boulders crashing down on the battered, uncomfortable half-ton truck—because there were snow-covered trees. Of course, the best thing about places like Colorado and Montana was that gorgeous, amazing sky.

Crawford explained his setup on the way—there would be horses, sheep, rabbits, and alpacas (an animal Jeremy could not quite picture in his head), and a mill that spun fur and fleece into yarn. Jeremy would be expected to help with everything from feeding and grooming the animals to working the complex mill machinery and manning the dye vats. The millwork sounded okay—a lot like the laundry at Fort Lyon—and Jeremy found himself reassured. He would be doing something specific and useful, and he wouldn't have to sit down and be still and stay in the same place. Of course there wouldn't be people to talk to, and he wasn't sure what Oscar would say about that, earning a living that didn't involve selling anything or talking anybody out of their money, but Crawford had promised him a small room with a shower cubicle and a toilet, and he already had new clothes.

If the promised food and some spending cash arrived as agreed upon, Jeremy thought maybe he was well on his way to honest living.

And then he saw Aiden—really saw him. Aiden had a smallish, thin face with a square, if short, jaw, and eyes the color of green-shadowed earth. Yeah, yeah—if you looked at them from a distance, they were brown, but when you got close enough to shake hands, you could tell the difference. The kid was bundled, because it was January and cold, and wearing a brown store-bought hat and brown hand-knit gloves with little white specks all over them. But Crawford introduced Jeremy as his new full-time employee, and Aiden took off his gloves to shake Jeremy's hand with a wide, welcome smile, revealing long, artistic fingers, battered and a little scarred from hard work.

And for a moment, Jeremy thought he was at the far end of a dark tunnel, and Aiden was the light at the end of it. Jeremy reached out his hand automatically to shake the young man's hand, and when those fingers wrapped around his palm, he felt something jerk awake inside him, unhappily. That wide smile, with white, even, teeth—this boy had been cared for.

"Good to meet you!" Aiden said with quiet enthusiasm. "Awesome, actually. I don't graduate from high school until the summer, and even then, Craw said he's going to make me take college classes twice a week, just to make sure college isn't going to take, so he's really going to need the help around here."

High school. High school? *High school?*

"Well, I'm hoping I work out, sir," Jeremy said, feeling bright and brittle, like all his words were cracked lacquer over a dirty table, and everybody could see the table was rotten and covered in filth, but they sat at it politely, because the words covered the worst spots, and the table was trying, right? Trying to be something serviceable and worthy, and you couldn't hold all the scars on the top from all the dirty deals against it, right? Because it hadn't even known it was a table, and it had better things to do, until all those scars and that dirt was laid, and so some shellac was all it had, until it got sanded and repainted, right? And words did that, they covered the dirty, and so….

"I'm hoping I work out real good. I like animals, you know that? I don't know much about 'em, but I love 'em, I sure would like to go see 'em, okay? Can we go see the horses—no, don't start with the horses; fuckers are big. Let's start with the rabbits. The rabbits are small, and I think I'll be real good with 'em, because I ain't a threat to no one, and rabbits'll see that, you think? I think so. So, high school, right? You get good grades? You must, if you're going to college you're probably real smart and getting good grades. That's a good boy.

You gotta do that, you want any future. So, what're you going to do with all them good grades? Probably like, a teacher or a lawyer or an engineer—"

"A designer," Aiden slipped in, sounding a little desperate. Jeremy had scoped out the small barn they were standing in while he'd been talking.

"A designer?" He saw the small pens, up off the ground, with a scattering of droppings below, on clean straw. He walked straight over to the pens and just stooped and looked, and although he didn't touch, he just stared at the black, brown, and white creatures inside. They all had long, carefully groomed fur, floppy ears, and were surprisingly big—maybe fifteen pounds a bunny. "I'll bet you're good at it," he said, unaware that his voice had dropped to a low hum. "I'll bet you can design a use for these guys, right? Something for their fur? 'Cause it's lovely. They're real sweet critters, but all this fur, it's gotta be a burden in the summer, a sure burden, I'm tellin' you. These guys, they need to have all this extra fur go somewhere, right? Is that what you design? 'Cause this is a yarn mill, and I can't think of anything finer than something made of this fur right here."

His voice was low, soft, and he put a tentative finger in the cage to rub the rump of the critter with its back against the side. The rabbit startled and then relaxed into the request, and Jeremy stared inside, entranced. The fur was so soft, his battered finger, brown and cracked from the time on the street, almost couldn't feel it. He hummed a little, settled into that rub, and the rabbit was apparently tame enough to be petted like that. He turned back around and saw that Craw and Aiden had moved a little closer to him, exchanging glances like they were talking together like old friends.

And he remembered that he had to keep talking, to cover up that he was a battered table, covered in filth, bad money deals, a few drugs, cheating, lying, conning—it was all on his top and needed to be hidden.

"Will I get to tend the rabbits, Craw? 'Cause that would be a sure pleasure, oh yes it would. They seem peaceable critters, and with any luck the sheep will be the same."

"Tending the stock is sort of everybody's job," Aiden said, looking at Craw and then back to Jeremy like maybe there was something wrong with Jeremy that Craw didn't clue him in on. "You can do it as often as you want. But maybe you want to see the mill?"

Jeremy nodded and then turned around and saw the sheep, huddled in the barn, and then the two horses, back in the corner and then—

"Whoo-ee, wow! Are those them 'paca critters you were goin' on about? Those are amazing! Lookie them, all tall-necked and smug-like—and all that fur. Is that fur soft—can I touch them like I can touch the bunnies? Because that would be a surefire treat."

Aiden sputtered for a moment. "But, we gotta tend to the—"

And Craw cut him off, which surprised Jeremy, because even while he was just taken with the urge to go pet the critters, as strong as any kid's urge in a petting zoo, he could hear himself nattering on and on and on, and was disgusted. If this were a con, he would have sure as hell lost the mark.

"Yeah," Craw said shortly. "You go pet the alpacas. Aiden, show him how to touch 'em so they don't spook, and where the food is kept and how we water. Make sure you do it slow, show the steps. He doesn't know a fucking thing about livestock, and we can sure as shit show him."

Aiden cast Craw a resentful glare then, and Jeremy thought miserably that all that lacquer hadn't done its job. Instead of covering the dirty spots on the table, it had just been loud and cheap, an unconvincing veneer.

"Yeah, I'll show him. Sure would be great if he could stop talking long enough for me to get an instruction in edgewise, but I can sure show him."

He took Jeremy to the pen, and Jeremy just *looked* at the alpacas, thinking they looked alien and helpless and smug and he loved everything about them. He reached his hand out with a jerk, and the big brown one he was closest to startled back, and Aiden made one of those "hanging on to my temper" sounds that parents make all the time.

"They're like the rabbits," he said, his voice clipped. The hand he held out, though—that looked easy. "You hold still, and you gentle them, and then you get firm so they know they're safe. And after they know that, you can just keep petting them when you want."

Aiden followed through with his words. He held his hand out until the big brown sheepish-looking alpaca nudged his hand, and then Aiden stroked his long neck firmly while the critter arched under the stroking. Aiden wasn't skittish and he didn't take shit—that thing started butting his head against Aiden's chest, probably looking for treats, and Aiden shoved him away, even though he was bigger, and, well, a critter. "I said no," Aiden said mildly, and then the alpaca, who was about Aiden's height, just stood, looking eye to eye with this beautiful kid, and allowed himself to be loved.

Jeremy swallowed hard. This kid... *this* kid knew what the world was all about, and he hadn't hardly left Granby. How was it this kid walked this earth like he was a part of it, and Jeremy had only ever felt like a flea on its back? There had to be a flaw, Jeremy thought. He was begging for one, because the things this boy was making him think were not appropriate for a grown man, oh no they were not, eighteen years old or no.

And oh, that kid was as smart as Jeremy had thought—he knew *everything*. He took Jeremy through his paces for the rest of that day and the second half of the next. (Aiden and his family went to church, while Jeremy slept late in his snug little cot in the tack room. Yeah, sure it smelled like horse and alpaca poop, but there wasn't anyone trying to steal the little cache of stuff he'd managed to smuggle in the sport coat he'd been wearing when Craw picked him up, and no one groping him while he slept. And he could open the door and wander out to the snow if he so desired. As far as he was concerned, the furry critters were the best roommates *ever*.) But when Jeremy wasn't in his little room, reveling in his freedom, he was in Aiden's presence for those first two days, reveling in the quiet civility of a genuine good boy.

Jeremy may have tried to talk the boy's ear off, but he was also studying him like a bug.

Good boys didn't lose their temper, even when their companions could not seem to stop talking psychotically for hours upon hours. Good boys didn't swear—much—and good boys double checked all of their work to make sure it was done right. Every time Jeremy was tempted to cut a corner—leave half a feeding for later, not give enough water, leave some horse/sheep/rabbit/alpaca crap where it was—Aiden was there, telling him that the critters would suffer if he didn't get his shit together. Every time Jeremy was tempted to shirk his duty on the mill, Aiden was there, explaining to him all the terrible mangling things that could happen to the both of them if the machinery was not kept like God's watch, and Jeremy learned, task by task, not to shine anyone on or shirk his basic duties. Jeremy would talk and talk and talk, and Aiden?

"Are you listening, Jeremy? Yes? Okay. This thing doesn't stop once we engage it. You need to do all of this while the machine is running. No, don't ask me questions right now, I'm working it. So, the automatic cutoff button is down here, and the rack is right here, and the carding hooks will eat you alive if you don't freakin' watch it, okay?"

And Jeremy would nod, and listen, and wonder how this smart kid with the good home could stand even to look at Jeremy, and every time he thought this, Jeremy would start talking again. It was cheap shellac on his tarnished soul, but it was like his daddy used to say about his teeth and hair. Keep 'em brushed and shiny, and folks might not notice you ain't soled your shoes in quite some time.

So Jeremy talked—and he might just have talked himself out of a job and a life, he realized later, if it hadn't been for two things.

The first was that Aiden bought himself a pair of earplugs.

Yup, Jeremy had to hand it to the little shit. They had to make a delivery run together in Craw's big beat-to-hell half-ton with the zero-suspension, and Jeremy nattered on and on and on, and then, about the time they got to Ft. Collins (and they went the long way too, because Highway 34 was closed most of the year) Jeremy noticed the tiny red plug sticking out of Aiden's ear.

His relief was tremendous. If the kid didn't hear him talk, he didn't have to talk, and the second half of the trip he spent quietly, happy in his own head, thinking about whether or not Craw would let him take a rabbit out of the cage and hold it. Yeah, it was true, their back legs could rip a man to ribbons, and Jeremy sported some lovely red scratches from trying to get too close, but man, just to hold something that big, and that soft, gentle it against your chest, feel its breath—Jeremy wanted nothing more in this world than to hold one of those bunnies. There was a big bruiser too, a smudged gray bunny, that Aiden had started to call Harvey for no reason Jeremy could fathom. He had the same gentle, dumb animal look as the other rabbits in the hutch, but he was a little bigger, and he seemed to be something of a slut. He would rub himself on all the other bunnies, until they'd get sick of him and bite his ears or kick him, and Jeremy thought maybe, maybe if he held that bunny and petted him special, maybe he could charm that bunny into not being the big, slutty pain in the ass he was making of himself to the other bunnies.

Couldn't hurt, right?

So Jeremy lapsed into his own head with a sigh of relief, dreaming of holding that fluttering soft-as-a-dream creature of muscle in his arms, and pretended he didn't hear Aiden talking about how great earplugs were to Crawford. Craw, for his part, just grunted and said he reckoned they got everything he needed, and told them to go inside the shop because Ariadne had hot chocolate for them.

Jeremy had ignored him and gone back to gaze at the rabbits instead. He was a little leery of both Ariadne and the shop. The woman wore lots of black-rainbow clothes and had brightly colored red-black hair, but underneath that, she was plain. The plain part was fine, because it was usually easier to charm a plain woman than it was a pretty one, but she didn't seem to *need* anything from him. She could talk almost as much as he could, charmed customers into buying the yarn that Craw's mill produced without any help from Jeremy at all, and was decent enough with the numbers for the store. Jeremy couldn't *do* anything for her, and his daddy always said if you didn't have a service to sell, you didn't have much. At least with Craw and Aiden, he was selling his work on the mill and his time with the animals, his time doing deliveries, his service as a worker. With Ariadne he didn't have anything at all. She had a husband—a strapping artist, with blond hair, a gentle beard, and a shy smile—and really? He didn't know what to say to her.

So he was more than confused when she came out to see him with a mug of hot chocolate.

"It's warmer inside," she said, and he couldn't argue with her. The barn was a haven in a sea of snow, and Jeremy had been made to understand that snow was a possibility until April, if not May.

"Thank you, ma'am," he said politely, taking the mug from her and wrapping his bare hands around it. Craw had bought him work gloves, which he appreciated, but he'd noticed that everyone else seemed to have hand-knitted gloves, and he figured he would have to make him some of those. He'd come to love the look of them—the hand stitching slightly irregular, the yarn lush and perfect. The colors he was easy with—he didn't have no particular preference that way— but the texture, that was the thing.

"You don't like coming in the shop," she observed, and he darted a glance at her, unsure of how to respond.

"I… mm, that chocolate is really wonderful, thank you kindly," he said, smiling to put her off a little, and she just raised dark eyebrows in what was really sort of a thin, sharp-nosed face.

"Why don't you like coming into the shop?" she rephrased deliberately, and he looked at the bunny again.

"It just seems silly to try to sell the yarn," he said, wanting to bury his cold hands in Harvey's fur. "It's so beautiful, and you can pet it, and hell, I don't even know how to knit the stuff, but you can just… just touch it, and why do you need to even try to sell it? It seems like people would just be coming from everywhere to love it, just shell out a twenty to take some home to hold." He turned to her then, and saw that her green eyes were very wide. "No ma'am. I can sell shit that ain't there, but how'm I going to sell something that's real? It's like… like gilding the lily, like my daddy used to say. Just having me in the store, telling people why they have to have something, that's just poor salesmanship there. And I would. I'd just…. It'd be like Harvey, there, but it couldn't scratch ya. It's one thing when you're working on it, taking it from the carder and putting it on the spinnerets, because then there's hard, metal things and you're all busy keeping it safe from them, but once it's prettied up, it's… it's irresistible, and I wouldn't want to walk in there and walk out with my pockets full of yarn. I like this job, and I don't even know how to knit."

She was as slender as a spider, and only a few inches shorter than he was, but when she wrapped her arms around his shoulders and squeezed, he was amazed by her strength.

"You come and ask, Jeremy, and I'll teach you how to knit, okay?" She was such a little pip, but most of the time, she scared the shit out of him.

Jeremy turned toward her, feeling a little hunted. "It's an honest craft, ma'am, and I don't know who I'd knit for."

She smiled a little. "Knit for yourself, or me, or Craw, or Aiden. We'd be honored, right?"

He felt unaccountably shy. "I wouldn't make anything beautiful right off."

"Well, no one does. Everyone's first efforts are mangled and sad. They get better. It's part of why we do it, because it's proof we can become better at something if we try."

Jeremy's heart gave a hard pound. "There's proof of that?" he asked, almost terrified that it should be so. If there was proof, then... oh God. What if he tried to knit and he never made it better?

"As long as you keep trying, even if you never get it to work the way you want, isn't that proof?"

Jeremy nodded then, and clutched his mug of hot chocolate to his chest. "Yes'm, I reckon so."

Ariadne smiled. "Well, how 'bout you let me teach you inside? It's horribly slow today. I've got nothing better to do."

So that was the other thing that happened that helped him feel easier in his skin while he was being honest. Ariadne taught him to knit.

She started off teaching him how to knit what she called a "swatch," but when he found out that a swatch didn't do nothing but just be a square of knitting, he called that a cheat, and she sighed. She started talking about measuring and multiplying and he didn't want to admit to her that he'd never been one of those savant grifters who could tell you the vig on what some guy made on the track two months ago after subtracting the bookie's percentage and tipping the runner. He and his daddy had only worked in big, round, whole numbers, because that's all Oscar could keep in his head too.

"Okay," she said at last, her patience imposed upon, but not really stretching, "how about this. You know how to cast on, right? You know how to count? Well, cast on eighty stitches on these needles."

Jeremy blinked at her. "But, you said yourself you don't know how big I'm going to make the stitches when I do this," and Ariadne nodded.

"That's right. This is a new yarn, we don't have a gauge for it— this is a guess."

"What if it's not enough?" Jeremy asked, a little horrified. "What if it's too small?" and she patted his knee. They were sitting behind the register in the store, which was a tidy and yet overstuffed clutter of yarn in the most amazing range of colors Jeremy had ever seen, and Jeremy was starting to feel like Harvey the rabbit did when Jeremy had petted him for a good long time. It was like his skin was so full, he was growing complacent and catatonic with satiation. Crawford had come in once to see where Jeremy was, because he and Aiden were fixing to feed the stock and Jeremy liked that part of his day. Jeremy had gone to stand up to go help, but Ariadne grabbed his hand and pulled him back down.

"He can say hi to the guys later, Rance. Right now he's learning to knit."

And Jeremy expected a fight (after he got used to the idea that Crawford had a first name, and that it wasn't a usual one) but what he got was that thing Craw did that wasn't a scowl and wasn't a squint and didn't register disapproval, but basically meant the man was trying to figure stuff out but didn't want to chat.

"'Kay," he said in assent, and then turned away, and Jeremy was left in the February quiet. He was too intent on the knitting to talk, and he found that Ariadne's questions to him could be answered like Crawford answered questions—with a minimum of well-placed words.

Cast on, okay, one stitch at a time, and he did it, muttering the rhyme Ariadne had given him to help him remember how. "Under-the-bush-around-the-tree-through-the-door-and-home," he said, then, "One."

"So, Jeremy, Craw says he found you looking for work in Boulder. What kind of work were you looking for?"

"Under-the-bush-around-the-tree-through-the-door-and-home," he said. "Honest work. Two."

"So, what kind of work were you doing before?" She was knitting quickly and efficiently on something lovely and green.

"Under-the-bush-around-the-tree-through-the-door-and-home. The kind that gets you in prison. Three."

"Oh," she said, nodding quietly, not even dropping a stitch. "What kind is that?"

"Under-the-bush-around-the-tree-through-the-door-and-home. Four. Under-the-bush-around-the-tree-through-the-door-and-home. Five. The fake check scam. You get someone to give you money and write them a check for it. Under-the-bush-around-the-tree-through-the-door-and-home. Six, seven, and eight."

She let him cast on for a few moments in silence, and he had all eighty stitches on the needles before she spoke again.

"It looks a little big, hon."

Jeremy looked at it in alarm. "How many should I take off?"

"Eight," she said immediately, and he did without question. "Okay, now snap the shorter end until it's only about three inches, okay?" And he did, just using his hands. "Good. Now, remember the knit stitch? Let's do that, all the way across."

"Under the little man's legs, pull out the loop, push the old one off the building, listen to him scream... aaaaaahhhh...." He giggled as he made up his own little chant for knitting and he heard a wonderful sound.

Ariadne was giggling too. "That's really fucking morbid," she said, but she kept laughing, so that was okay. He grinned at her and went back to his knitting, repeating the chant about the little man with every stitch while his hands got used to the motion, a little surer every time.

"So," Ariadne said when he was absorbed back into the quiet whirr of the heater. Someone—probably Craw and Aiden—had started the spinner in the attached building that held the mill. It made a soothing "kachunk-a-chunk-a-chunk-a" as they worked, and Jeremy was once again lulled into it. "How was prison?"

"Under the legs, pull out the loop... yadda yadda, off the building... aaaaauuughhhh.... It was okay. I was good at the black market thing. They left my ass alone."

That made Ariadne drop a stitch, and Jeremy looked up at her, still tranquilized by the quiet. "Well, isn't that what everyone wants to know? I mean, I look like easy meat for a prison, but no one wanted to touch me. It was okay. I got my GED. That was good."

Ariadne had stopped knitting by now, but Jeremy didn't want to. "But yeah, Jeremy—but what about... I don't know, freedom? Not taking a leak in front of the whole world? What about that?"

Jeremy worked his next three stitches before he answered her. "All that stuff sucked," he said frankly, although he didn't let any word pictures in his head because the idea made him shudder and feel a little queasy. "But I wanted to be honest, and it was easy in prison. You keep your nose clean, trade with people, make 'em happy. No temptation to grift, to steal. You steal in prison, you get your ass ripped and your guts shivved. So it was easy to be honest." He looked at the knitting in his hands. He was done with the first row of knitting and didn't know what his next step was. "Now that I'm out, I don't know what to do next."

He looked up when she put her hands on his and reversed the knitting, putting the full needle on the left and the empty needle on the right. "Next, we learn how to purl," she said quietly.

He smiled, and realized that it was not a good smile. Usually when he smiled, he made sure to pull his mouth back far enough to pop his dimples and to make people see the grooves in his mouth and the lines at the corners of his brown eyes. His daddy had told him that the dimples and the eyes were his moneymakers right there, but he wasn't trying to make money—or at least not this moment. He was just trying to knit a fucking hat.

"I meant in general," he said, feeling a little ashamed at having to confess to having a really deep thought.

"So did I," she said gently. "One stitch at a time. It works for both."

Suddenly his grin went all the way, because he liked that. "Okay, so what next?"

"Okay, now take the right needle, and put it from back to front in the stitch…."

JEREMY TOOK his knitting to his little room that night, after he wandered around and said good night to the critters. He liked the way the big ones slept, standing up, simply continuing on in peace. They made stamping noises and continued to breathe in great puffs. He also liked the way the bunnies huddled in their little box filled with fluff, under the small oil heater Craw had plugged in for them. They all seemed so peaceful, there with their compatriots.

Jeremy loved that he could sit in his room and feel like one of them, but not have to worry about whether or not someone would be testing him to see if the fresh meat could fight back (he'd had to once or twice) or trying to steal his black market stuff.

In the past month, he'd gotten happy and used to saying good night to them, and now, as he sat in his tiny room and listened to them breathing while he knit, they kept him at peace. He liked the knitting, liked the rhythm of it, the way it seemed to fill the empty spaces without any words on his part. Craw had given him a small television, but this night he didn't turn it on. Instead he took a stitch at a time and thought of Aiden.

Aiden had put those earplugs in and had sat serenely, looking out at the world with eager eyes. Jeremy had discovered this last month that, although still in high school, Aiden was eighteen, and he'd designed a lot of the yarn colors in the shop. Craw talked to him like he was fully adult and listened to what he had to say in return. For his part, Aiden walked up to Craw like a member of a team, his shoulders back, his small, intense face usually set in adult lines, and everything about him screamed business. He corrected Jeremy's fuckups patiently—and Jeremy felt like he made a lot of them. The only time Aiden really snapped at him was when the talking thing got out of hand, and Jeremy didn't know what to tell him about that. Sometimes, when they were working on the equipment together or dyeing the yarn or washing the fleece or any of the hundred small chores that kept the mill in business, Jeremy would look at him and think he was beautiful, and then remember that Aiden was a high school student and Jeremy was twenty-eight years old.

Jeremy kept knitting and thought that maybe, he'd make the hat for Aiden.

He stopped himself from thinking about anything that would come of it. Aiden should go to college, and even if he didn't go to college, which he should because he was so damned smart, he should not, not ever, look at Jeremy. He should, in fact, keep looking at Craw with that spark of eagerness in his eyes. Yes, Craw was in his thirties, but Craw had the ranch and the mill and the shop, and those were things that Aiden loved. For a moment, Jeremy thought about making the hat for Craw instead, but he didn't think Craw would appreciate it. For one thing, Craw and Ariadne seemed to knit for each other, and Jeremy got that. Ariadne was married and perfectly happy, but Craw was the person she knit for. Craw really only had Ariadne in the world, so she got that lovely lace shawl/scarf she'd had bundled around her neck and shoulders that afternoon, in autumn brown and a deep rose pink.

Jeremy didn't really have anyone to knit for, he thought, and for the first time, the thought made him feel forlorn in his peaceful, quiet little hole in the barn. Then he decided that, whether the boy liked him or not, Jeremy would knit for him. It would make this rush of quiet not roar so loudly in his ears.

THREE DAYS later, he pulled the hat out of his pocket and sort of threw it at Aiden, half ashamed. He'd asked Ariadne to help with the decreasing and then he'd cast off and stitched the crown shut and down the side, but....

Well, it was not perfect. The stitches were lumpy in places and thin and tight in others and it was... well, a little big.

Aiden looked at it and smiled. "Hey! You're learning to knit!"

Jeremy smiled back, a little desperately. "Uhm, it's for you if you want it, because, I guess because people do this for other people, and I didn't know who to knit for, but I figure I see you every day, and you have homemade hats but you keep wearing one that's store-bought and I figured that's no good for a guy who works at a knitting place, but it's a little big, and I don't know how to make it fit—oh fuck." Because Aiden had put it on while he'd been rambling, and it was *very* wide and too big at the bottom, and it looked more like a potholder on his head than a hat. "Oh fuck. I'm sorry. Give it back."

Aiden laughed and shook his head and put it in his pocket. "Hell no! Here, I'll take it home and felt it and then block it, and I'll bet you it'll be just about perfect."

Felt it? Block it? Oh shit—he'd just learned how to *knit* it. "I'm sorry, Aiden," he said, feeling as lost and stupid as he probably ever had in his life. "I don't know what either of those things mean."

Aiden smiled, and unlike some of the grudging smiles he'd given in the past, because he was obligated to teach Jeremy something or stuck doing something with him, this smile was warm and confident and full of sunshine.

"Here—let me teach you some more about fiber, okay?"

And Aiden got out a pad of paper and a pencil and made some sorts of awesome drawing showing how a sheep's hair was made with lots of little hooks, and when you got them warm, they opened and when you got them cold, they closed, and when you got them hot they got so open they twisted and grew even more convoluted and so shrank even more, and he showed Jeremy a piece of felted knitting and a piece of felted roving.

Jeremy listened, not talking, and when Aiden was done, he said, "Okay, so untreated wool—you wash it in warm and then cold and then warm and then cold and the fibers hook on themselves and the piece shrinks. You block it—get it wet and then stretch it to a form to dry—and it will stay in that shape."

Aiden nodded and said, "Yeah. You don't have to felt stuff to do that—sweaters will stay in that shape when you do that too."

Jeremy wasn't paying attention to his smile this time; he just knew it lit his face. "That's... that's very cool," he said, blinking at Aiden. "Same stuff, just mess with it until it's the right shape." Like before, when Ariadne said the key to life was purling the next row, it just *sounded* bigger, sounded more important than wool. "I like that." He smiled again at Aiden, and at that moment, Craw came thundering in wanting to know why the dryer and the second carder hadn't been started up yet, and the two of them got their asses up and back to work.

And work was good.

It was loud and it was dirty, and it could be dangerous if you weren't paying attention to what you were doing in the mill. The critters were the same. Jeremy came to appreciate his boots after being bullied and stepped on and generally herded by the critters he was supposed to be herding. But he liked them too. You couldn't con a sheep, and alpacas couldn't write bad checks. Rabbits didn't care if your smile was pretty, and although they liked to hump everything in the cage, he didn't have to worry about one violating him in his sleep. (After the DWI guy, his second cellmate had tried to get frisky. Jeremy had spent his whole life on the road; he did know how to fight.)

The machines did exactly as you told them, and when they got ornery, you had the right to smack them on the sides (not too hard or you'd hurt your hand) and fiddle with them until they worked. Just like in prison or on the grift, though, if you didn't pay attention, you were going to get hurt. Two days after Jeremy gave Aiden the hat, Jeremy got his hand caught in the smaller drum carder and Craw had needed to take him to the hospital for stitches. He was pretty sure he'd never forget *that* lesson again.

Aiden came to the hospital with them, and Jeremy sat between them on the bench seat of the truck, a cloth wrapped around his hand and his head spinning from the ibuprofen and Vicodin that Ariadne had fished out of her purse as Craw was wrapping his hand. (What was it with women and carrying around a pharmacy, anyway? Jeremy hadn't met one woman who didn't have some sort of first aid in her shoulder bag. Considering he'd managed to shove his whole life in his pockets and make do not just once but many times, the thought boggled him.) He was trying to explain to Crawford why he couldn't go to the doctor.

"I can't," he slurred. "Hand doesn't hurt, just wrap it up and I'll be fine."

Aiden's snort of irritation actually helped to focus Jeremy's wandering attention. "If I have to look at it, Jeremy, it's going to make me sick. How 'bout if we let the doctors take care of it, okay?"

Jeremy shook his head mournfully. "You don't understand. They're going to need to know who I am!"

Craw's grunt was no less irritated than Aiden's snort. "Ex-cons get medical treatment same as everybody else, Jeremy. You've got workman's comp insurance through me—it'll be fine."

Jeremy whimpered. "Yeah, but that wasn't my real name either!"

Aiden looked at him, eyebrows drawn, and Jeremy avoided his gaze.

"Never mind," he said, trying to keep his head. It shouldn't matter. "If it was good enough for the prison system, it's good enough for the hospital. I'm sorry. I... we... I'm just good at avoiding hospitals, okay?"

"Well, yeah," Craw said, and Jeremy must have been out of it, because Craw sounded a little disconcerted. "But you've gone straight now, right? You don't have to worry about hospitals."

Jeremy gave in and leaned on Aiden. Aiden surprised him, for a kid, and wrapped his arm around Jeremy's shoulders. "Everyone thinks I'm Jeremy... crap, what's my last name?"

"Stillson," Aiden said, and Jeremy heard the humor in his voice.

"Yeah," Jeremy mumbled. "That was a good one. Jeremy Duane Stillson. I could keep that one. It's got some prison on it, but not too much hard use." He inhaled, thinking Aiden smelled fresh, like kid, and then suddenly he smelled salty, like sweat. When the kid spoke again, there wasn't any humor in his voice.

"Jeremy, if Stillson's not your name, what is?"

Jeremy giggled. "Who knows? Only Oscar knew, and I think we lost those papers in Abilene… or was it Albuquerque? I forget. I'm not real fond of the southwest. Vegas sucks ass."

"Who was Oscar?" Aiden asked, and Craw made a shushing noise, but Jeremy would rather listen to Aiden. When he was talking, and his face got all relaxed, and he forgot he was irritated with Jeremy, his voice and his smile were like sunshine.

"That was my daddy," Jeremy said, and for a moment, with the drugs and the blood loss, and the general well-being from having that stringy young arm around his shoulders, Jeremy could remember that daddy had the plans and made sure they ate and was the one who told him where to go and what con to run. It had been comforting, knowing someone else knew the con.

"Mm…," Aiden murmured, rubbing his arm. Jeremy let himself relax on Aiden's chest, with his eyes closed. God, when was the last time Jeremy had touched another human being like this? Unbidden, his woozy brain summoned the picture of Gianni it held for only special occasions. Gianni had looked at him, his mouth still shiny, and he'd smiled, and Jeremy had wanted a hug so damned bad. But Aiden's insistent voice interrupted that memory and the regret that went with it. "Jeremy, what happened to Oscar?"

Jeremy's brain was all gray and fuzzy, like the old blanket Oscar had kept in back of the big Ford Taurus they'd driven for a couple of years.

"I think I'd rather pass out than answer that," he said truthfully, and so he did.

HE'D BEEN surprised at the hospital. Craw and Aiden had stayed, since the hospital was in Boulder, and turning around and going back over the mountains to Granby hadn't seemed like a great idea that night. So Craw had gone out and gotten food, and the nurse had let one of them sleep on the couch and the other on a cot, and generally, they'd had themselves a little party when he came back. Jeremy ate from the hot plate in his little tack room and bought packages of ramen noodles, bagel chips, and big jars of peanut butter. These he hoarded in various places in his room—under the cot, under the kitchen sink, in the cupboard across from the bed, of course, and even in the shower when he wasn't using it. Given that, he was almost ebullient, in spite of the doctor's admonition that he needed to rest.

He had *guests*, and that was something that, sure as water was wet and snow was cold, he'd never had in his life if he wasn't trying to con them.

At first, he'd been a little afraid that Aiden was going to keep asking him questions about Oscar, but apparently he and Craw had come to an understanding about that. Instead, they focused on Aiden's coming graduation, and his registration in the junior college outreach in Granby, and Jeremy listened ravenously for details of Aiden's life—his teachers, his parents, his sisters, any girls he might have dated. He heard plenty about the first ones, but nothing about the last, and he didn't pry about that, figuring he could have all the fantasies he wanted as long as Aiden didn't know otherwise. And fantasies were good. Jeremy was still older, and still tarnished, and still not in Aiden's league, so Jeremy kept his fantasies chaste and to himself. It was enough that the boy was eating takeout in his hospital room. All he ever wanted, in fact, so he'd stop there.

"Graduation sounds like a real good idea," he said when Aiden fell silent. "But I don't know if I could go to college. If I'm not gonna be a salesman and then a lawyer, I'm plum out of ideas. I'll have to read some—"

"Granby's got a library," Aiden said. The boy was working on his second giant hamburger, and Jeremy wanted to smile. He'd have been eating another one too, but with the drugs and the pain and everything, that wasn't sitting well in his stomach. "You could always check out a book and return it."

Jeremy blushed. Of course you could.

"That's a real good idea," he said pleasantly, thinking that he still wasn't comfortable checking things out when he was never sure how long he was going to be somewhere.

"I mean, you're not going anywhere, are you?" Aiden asked, and Jeremy scowled for a moment. It was like the kid had read his mind.

Jeremy looked at his hand, which the doctor said had damned near been chopped off. "Not unless I get fired," he said mournfully, thinking he probably couldn't work three-card-monte if he did, and he was done kiting checks.

"Not gonna happen," Craw said gruffly. "As long as you want to work for me, Jeremy, you're going to have to leave us first."

Jeremy looked at the remains of his sandwich and wrapped it carefully. He set it down in the bag next to him, which was also wrapped carefully with the rest of his steak-cut fries. "I got nowhere to go," he said, not looking at anything but the food.

"I know that," Craw said, and Aiden stood up and grabbed the bag to clean up.

"Save it!" Jeremy cried, suddenly afraid. "Boy, you don't ever throw away food, don't you know that? You save it for later—you don't never know when you're going to have to go without!"

Aiden looked at the bags in his hands and looked on the verge of snapping something obvious, but Craw cleared his throat behind the boy, while scratching that stubble of red beard. "Go ahead and put it down, Aiden. Don't worry, Jeremy. You'll have enough."

Jeremy smiled gratefully. "Thank you, sir. That sets my mind at rest." He was tired then. The combination of drugs and trauma meant that as soon as he was done eating, he was close to shutting his eyes. He excused himself abruptly, crossed his arms in front of him, and fell asleep.

He woke a little when there was a rustling at his side, and then he heard that now-familiar rumble of Craw clearing his throat. "Leave it, Aiden. He wasn't fucking around. He'll look for it."

Aiden made a sound of frustration, and Jeremy imagined him, throwing that muscular body back on the tacky blue couch in his room. His hair was growing long, and since it was as unruly as a tangled skein, it was right in his eyes. Jeremy liked that, although he worried that the boy might get himself hurt in the mill like Jeremy had, just because he couldn't see.

"Craw, it's not like he's gonna wake up and eat it!"

"Yeah," Craw said, and Jeremy relaxed a little more into his sleep, because Craw was answering questions so Jeremy didn't have to. "It is. Aiden, I know you grew up with a nice family and food on the table every day, but not everyone had that—"

"I know it!" Aiden snapped, and there was more than peevishness in his voice. "I don't want him to have to, that's all. I want him to trust that there's going to be food tomorrow and trust that he's got a place to stay. He's a pain in the ass, but it would be really great if I didn't think he had one foot out the door."

Craw's sigh was eloquent. If Jeremy was on the grift still, he'd copy that sound, so he could use it to his advantage. "Well, you're not helping with all those questions," Craw grumbled. "What're you trying to do, gut him?"

"I don't want to *gut* him," Aiden protested, "I want to *get* him. I don't understand the things he does, Craw. He's got jars of peanut butter all over his little room, you know that, right? He's *always* eating. *Always.* But he never finishes what he's eating, he just tucks some of it away for later. It will *spoil* before he touches it after he does that. And I don't get the talking thing—he talks all the time, but I swear I don't think it makes him happy."

Craw grunted. "Yeah, I think you're right there. I think the quiet makes him happiest. You gotta think, though. He made his life as a con man. He just turned twenty-eight, he spent two years in prison—he's been doing this all his life. There's shit that con men do—eating on the run, not letting a mark get a word in—he may not have graduated high school, but he's a grand master at bullshit or die."

Aiden made a hurt sound. "He made me a hat," he said softly.

"Yeah?"

"Yeah. I took it home and felted it a little and blocked it. It's not half bad."

"Well then."

"Well then what?"

"Well then, make him something back. Once he thinks he owes you, he won't leave until he's paid you back."

Aiden started to chuckle, and it was a little bit of an evil sound. "Okay, Jeremy the grifter," he said softly. "We're gonna make it so you *need* to stay."

I already need to stay, Aiden. I need to see you grow and be a man.

But Jeremy couldn't say that either.

Chapter 3

One Foot Over the Line

WHEN JEREMY got his first weekly paycheck in February, Craw asked him if he wanted help setting up a bank account. Jeremy said no, thank you, as long as there was a check-cashing place in the little town of Granby then Jeremy could get along just fine. He still had his little bible with the gouge out of the middle, and that would do him just like it had his daddy. In fact, that bible had been what let him get away after his daddy was killed, because if Gianni hadn't left him that cash in there, Jeremy wouldn't have been able to afford the bus ticket that let him blow town.

Not that the bible was the only place he stored his little packets of cash. There were the usual spots—in the mattress, in the pocket of the one sport coat he owned, in a plastic bag behind the toilet—all sorts of good places a con man would know to put money, and it was a good thing, too, because Jeremy wouldn't have known what to do with Aiden's gift otherwise.

About a week after Jeremy mangled his hand, he was still on nonmill duty. He worked mostly with the critters and the dye vats and the drying room since the gauze over his healing hand was likely to get caught in the machine works, even if he could move pretty close to normal. He had just finished brushing the rabbits and cleaning the hair (lots of it since it was spring and they were shedding) off the brushes and into bags to be spun into some specialty lots, and when he turned around from the cage, Aiden was standing behind him, smiling fiercely.

Jeremy took an inadvertent step back flush with the rabbit cage, his ass pressing up against the wood. Usually when someone looked at him like that, he was about to be conned, or the cops were on his tail, or someone was looking to get him in the lunch line and he needed to come up with some swag, stat. It was the smile of someone who knew something Jeremy didn't, and Jeremy felt a stab of betrayal. *Aiden?*

And then Aiden pulled his hands from behind his back and produced two brightly knitted brown-green-and-blue mittens, the kind with the ribbing around all the fingers, but that let the fingers and thumb see air, so that you weren't trying to do stuff with wool over your hands.

Jeremy blinked at them, and Aiden huffed in annoyance. "Go on, take them!"

Blink. "They're for me? Whatever for?"

Aiden's jaw clenched, and Jeremy was suddenly back three months before when every question he asked about the mill made the boy look like he was going to whap him upside the head. "They're a gift, dumbass! Same reason you gave me the hat!"

Aiden was, in fact, wearing the hat—and he'd been right. The felting and the blocking had made the thing smaller, and it hugged Aiden's ears. It was, in fact, a little warm for spring, and the gold-tinted purple and cobalt blue looked more like autumn than spring, but Aiden was wearing it anyway.

Jeremy reached out with one hand, keeping the other behind his back, and stroked one of the half-mittens with a finger. Green, brown, and blue—he'd never really thought of colors before, but he liked these. The yarn Aiden had used was one of their sturdier yarns—100 percent wool, and it had gone through the expensive chemical treatment so it wouldn't felt like Aiden's hat. Jeremy figured it was wise to use that kind of yarn—it would last. But sturdy or not, it was still soft and giving underneath his fingertip, and he found he'd crushed it a little in between his thumb and forefinger before he snatched his hand away and put it behind his back with the other one.

"So," Aiden said, impatience creeping into his voice, "take them!"

Jeremy shook his head. "Those are real nice," he said, darting his eyes up to Aiden's frustrated face. "They're too nice for me. You give those to Crawford or Ariadne. Your dad, maybe." He smiled ingratiatingly, anything to still the panic like one of the rabbits when a human was trapping them in strong arms.

Aiden scowled, grabbed Jeremy's arm from behind his back, and pulled his hand up by the wrist. Jeremy wasn't going to fight him, since his movements weren't cruel, and he allowed Aiden to open his hand

and put the mittens into it. Aiden forcibly closed his fingers over the precious little bits of wool then, and Jeremy clung to them as he stepped back. "If you don't want them, you're going to have to tell me honestly," Aiden said, and Jeremy couldn't tell from his tone whether or not he'd guessed the real reason Jeremy wouldn't want them.

"They're too nice," Jeremy said weakly, because in his fingers they felt warm and soft and so well crafted. He'd dyed this yarn, he realized. He'd washed it and dried it and carded it and sorted it into roving and spun it. Aiden had taken the last step and created something with it, but Jeremy had helped—he'd helped make something real.

It was, perhaps, the only reason Jeremy didn't chase Aiden down and spin a black lie. Jeremy had helped make these, and they were real. To lie to Aiden because Jeremy was afraid of strings made them a con, and Jeremy had worked so hard to avoid cons. He could have conned three times his paycheck, every time he went into the check-cashing place, but he didn't. It was just like prison: you don't shit where you eat. But in prison, he would have gotten a shiv in the gut. The penalty for fucking up here, in Granby and at Craw's, was so much worse.

So Jeremy didn't con anymore, and he had to take those pretty little half-mittens, because Aiden made them.

He put them in his bible, and stashed some of his cash in the pockets of his good pair of pants, the pair he only wore when they were going to Boulder, because Craw would take him and Aiden out to dinner when they did that, to a place where the girls all had big tits and tight T-shirts and seemed disappointed that none of the guys at their table cared to ogle.

The next time they went there, Aiden asked Jeremy why he didn't look, and Jeremy looked at one girl and then back at Aiden and shrugged. "That shit gets bought and sold all the time," he said, quietly enough so he didn't offend the young lady. "I'm getting my shit sorted—I'm in no place to close that deal." It was true enough. He'd always been amenable to sweetening the pot when he and Oscar had been on a con—with either sex—but now? When there was no con? When his johnson was not in the pot to be offered? He was starting to realize that Gianni's shy smile had meant so much more to him than other smiles of the same sort from young women around the country. It was amazing what you figured out when you were selling yarn instead of blown sunshine, right?

"Twenty-two ounce rib eye, med rare, loaded baker with a salad to start. I don't see you looking," Jeremy said that last part to Aiden, so he didn't have to give voice to any of the other truths running through his head.

"Aiden's too young," Craw rumbled.

Aiden rolled his eyes at them and put down his menu. "Sixteen-ounce prime rib, raw, garlic mash, and soup. I'm too young, Jeremy's not ready—what's your excuse, Craw?"

Craw eyeballed them both, looking bad-tempered, which was par for the course. "I'm gay, you morons—whole fucking town knows that!" And before either Jeremy or Aiden could answer, he signaled the waitress, and they placed their order. After that, Jeremy started talking about ways to publicize Crawford's new line of yarn that he, Aiden, and Ariadne had been working on. Part of it was to cover any awkwardness, yeah, but part of it was because it was something he wanted to talk about. He got Craw being gay and not wanting the whole world—or even any of the world—to know or give a crap. There were personal things—the last girl or boy you kissed for real, the first of each, where you thought your daddy might be buried—these things should be kept in your bible. These were things that could haunt you in a con, or be used against you when a con went belly-up. Jeremy had been given a little room to keep his personal things. He wasn't going to just barge into Craw's room because they had some of the same stuff.

And Aiden and Craw just went along with it, following Jeremy's reasoning until Aiden said he'd draw some posters up and maybe they could borrow a big silk screen from the art department and—

"Wait a minute," Craw said, squinting at him. "Aren't you out of school in two weeks? I could swear we have graduation to attend."

Aiden stopped and laughed a little. "Yeah. I keep forgetting. You guys are coming, right?"

Craw shook his head. "Well, yeah, but an invitation would have been appreciated, dumbass!"

Suddenly Aiden looked panicked. "Fuck. I have them—I have them at home, done up and stamped." He looked right at Jeremy. "Yours is addressed to Craw's house, but you're coming, right?"

Jeremy blinked at him, opening and closing his mouth. "I... don't you gotta dress up fancy to those things?" he said after a moment.

Aiden shrugged and the waitress—God, she was pretty, with dark hair and a pouty little mouth and hooters that really weren't too big for her tiny waist—arrived with their food. She looked hopefully at the three of them, trying to make conversation, and Aiden was too busy fuming at Jeremy and Craw was too busy digging into his chow, so it was up to Jeremy. He smiled at her and winked and called her "darlin'" and asked her to bring steak sauce and told her about yarn. She walked away laughing, and Jeremy got to his steak, which was, thank God, still warm, and looked to see that both Aiden and Craw were glaring at him.

"What?" he asked, his mouth full of steak that was as melty as butter.

Aiden looked away, his eyes narrow with what looked like hurt, and Craw rolled his eyes at the both of them. "You're coming to Aiden's graduation, asshole. I'll buy you a fuckin' suit."

A part of Jeremy relaxed then. It had all been taken from his hands. God, sometimes he just needed that, because making decisions in the honest world was not as much fun as they made it out to be in the joint; that was for damned sure.

"Well, fine," he conceded, swallowing. "I just didn't want to shame him, that's all. It's a big fuckin' deal. The boy's got to know we're proud."

Aiden perked up then and grinned. "Yeah?" he said happily. "What was your graduation like, Jeremy?"

Jeremy took another bite of his steak and tried not to mourn that it didn't taste as good as the last one. "The guard walked by my cell at mail call and shoved an envelope in the slot," he said, thinking about it. Wasn't a *bad* memory. "I got a book that day too. *Brave New World*. You know, I didn't understand that book at *all*? I asked if I could sign up for a college class just so I could ask someone who would know what that book meant." That last bite of steak went down fairly easy, so he took a bite of loaded baked potato next, and then smiled up at Aiden, who was looking at him with bemused eyes.

"It's about mankind fucking up his future by making identical humans to do identical jobs."

Jeremy wrinkled his nose. "Now see? As long as people knit by hand, that ain't ever gonna happen."

Aiden and Craw both opened their eyes really big and asked Jeremy what he meant, and that's what they talked about during the rest of the lunch. It was a good lunch, too, and afterward, when they got back to the mill that Jeremy was starting to think of as home, Craw told Aiden he'd buy them some silk screens so they could make posters, as long as Aiden would design them, and he told them both that he had a line on a large drum carder that was still dangerous but that did three times the work as the old trio, so they wouldn't have to leave it on all the time, and that he'd probably ask them both to go to Philadelphia to get it.

They were grand dreams, pie-in-the-sky dreams, and while Aiden got all excited because he seemed to think they would happen, Jeremy got excited because they sounded like con man dreams, and he understood those. They weren't disappointing if they didn't come true—they weren't supposed to come true. They were just the sort of dreams that got you to the next con.

Jeremy didn't tell Aiden that when they got back to the mill, though. They helped Craw unload the dyeing supplies and the machine parts they'd gone to pick up, and Jeremy and Aiden needed to go fetch some machine oil, because they'd forgotten.

As soon as they pulled away from the mill, sitting on its small rural road of green grass dotted with happy alpacas, Aiden said, "So, Craw's gay. What do you think of that?"

Jeremy frowned at him. "I mostly think it's his own business. Why?"

Aiden shook his head. "I think you're mostly right, that's why. Just wanted to check."

"What would you have done if I'd been an asshole about it?"

Aiden rolled down the window for some air, even though it was still chilly in early May, and thought before answering. "I think I would have been pretty disappointed," he said after a few minutes. "You're shaping up to be an okay guy. I'd hate to think less of you."

Jeremy hoped it was too dark for the kid to see his face clearly, because although he was pretty sure he babbled for the rest of the trip to the hardware store, he was damned positive that he smiled.

AIDEN'S GRADUATION was almost Jeremy's undoing. It was. He'd never smoked, because his daddy said it was the kind of habit that put people off and made them not trust you, just from the smell of smoke in your clothes, but he'd heard cons talk about trying to quit, and how something stressful would come up in their lives—getting arrested for one—and they would go right back to their old habits.

After Aiden's graduation, Jeremy felt an almost overwhelming temptation to run out and sleep with the girl from the local coffeehouse and make off with her car, her cat, and her life savings.

It was just that everyone was so *nice*.

Jeremy got into the processional—he loved watching all the students come out in their caps and their gowns, looking all embarrassed and proud. He spotted Aiden right off—the boy had gotten his hair cut into something short that spiked over his brow—but his small, earnest face and pretty smile were like a searchlight, calling Jeremy's attention. Listening to the rest of the ceremony was sort of boring, and when some girl stood up to sing a really sappy song—badly—Jeremy, Ariadne, and Craw met anguished eyes. You didn't want to say anything mean, but God, you didn't want to listen, either!

But after that Aiden actually got up to speak—because as much as Craw called him a dumbass, he was apparently smart enough to be the salutatorian—and Jeremy's world narrowed to just that golden boy on the stage.

He was talking about… about all the stuff Jeremy had talked about. About making something real, and about not living your life to be like everyone else. He talked about how the things you made with your hands were as important as the things you made with your brains, and how dreaming was important but so was doing. Jeremy was entranced. It was like Aiden had taken everything Jeremy had learned between being a con man and an ex-con and a guy who worked at a yarn mill, and made it real, just by using words. And Aiden credited *him*—calling Jeremy a coworker—and Jeremy just blushed with pride. And then Craw grinned at him, and all that pride turned to horror.

Oh Christ. What if he fucked this up? He was having such a hard time just living a normal life—what if he fucked this up and let that golden boy down?

The thought alone was enough to send a wave of sweat washing through his body, suffocating him, turning his stomach to water and his bowels to ice. Although he sat through the end of the speech and tried to enjoy the pride in their boy (and he was the one with tissues in his pocket for Ariadne, who was sniffling against her husband's shoulder) and then the recessional and all of the other business, it was all he could do to stop his own shaking. He thought he just might have calmed down enough to be a real human when they went to greet Aiden on the football field and tell him congratulations.

Aiden's family was there—it felt like there was a million of them—Mom, Dad, brothers, sisters, grandmother, aunties—and in the middle of that crush of people, Aiden's mom, Susan, turned to him and said, "Hiya, Craw! Oh, and you must be Jeremy!"

She was a sweet, perfectly average middle-aged woman, with a happily lined face, faded brown hair, and pretty green eyes with gold lashes, almost like her son's. She walked right up to Jeremy and hugged him and said, "We have heard *so* much about you. It's really time we had you over for dinner. How about next week?"

It was damned near enough to send him screaming to a big city for some three-card-monte.

He pulled his con man's smile out of his jacket pocket, though, and told her that next week would be a fine time to have dinner over at their house, and then accepted his hug from Aiden like he was a decent person and deserved that quick touch of heaven.

"Jesus, Jeremy—you're sopping with sweat!" Aiden laughed as he pulled away. "You just got those clothes!"

Jeremy blushed some more. "Guess I got the one spot of sunshine in Colorado," he said, that tight con man's grin firmly in place. "You did real good, Aiden. Best speech I ever heard!"

Aiden's grin was nothing but euphoria at a job well done. "Well, it was pretty easy, considering you did most of the writing of it at lunch that one day. You heard me give you credit, right?"

Jeremy shook his head and a real blush and a real smile chipped at the con man's façade. "You shouldn't have done that," he mumbled. "The words were all yours." He felt Aiden's hand on his shoulder and he went to look up, but then Aiden's sister wanted a hug and wanted to brag about how she was going to be valedictorian in two years and Aiden could chase her dust, and Jeremy was left blessedly alone.

There was a caravan from the high school football field to Craw's house, because Craw had volunteered (with a lot of prodding from Ariadne) to host the after-graduation party, and Jeremy rehearsed his exit strategy in the car on the way over.

Of course he had an exit strategy. He was going to have to leave all the peanut butter behind, but he just might be able to put all the cash (and five months of working legit while Craw paid his rent and fed him once in a while had given him a surprising amount of that) in a small duffel and walk away. It was May. He could sleep in the small, clean alley behind the bus stop that night and hop on the bus in the morning. He'd done it hundreds of times before he was twenty; it was no big deal.

Jeremy walked into Craw's pleasant, spacious farm house, where he'd been asked many times to sit down to dinner with Craw himself, or to lunch with all of them when Craw felt inclined, and smiled genially. He wandered the crowd, making sure he talked to everybody, hugged a sniffly Ariadne, clapped Craw on the back since the old bastard was too proud to be surly, and shook a lot of matronly hands with the world's nicest family.

His smile was tight and shiny, spiffy enough to pop that dimple in the back of his cheek, and he tried very hard not to let Aiden see it. He was pretty sure Aiden knew what that smile meant.

He'd thought he'd done it too. Everyone thought he was at the party, having the time of his life, until he had his hand on the kitchen door to slip off across the driveway to the barn. He looked up to take one last scan of the room, his eyes prepared to stop extra long and sad on Aiden, when he realized that Aiden was across the room, glaring at him as he left.

Well, shit. Jeremy slid out extra quick, figuring he could be down the driveway and halfway down the road home before Aiden even got out of the room to look for him.

He underestimated Aiden's determination.

He had all of his cash packets on the bed with his bible and was shoving them into the small duffel he'd had with him when Craw had taken him in, when Aiden barged into his room. Jeremy grabbed his bible and clutched it to his chest as he whirled around to confront the boy, and he wasn't sure if it was for moral strength or protection.

"You're *leaving*?" Aiden's voice cracked on the word, and Jeremy tried really hard to find his smile. He didn't think he succeeded, though—he was pretty sure it flitted back and forth across his face like a moth.

"Not leaving, just… just relocating. Finding a different place, someplace nice people won't find me. You understand, right? I'm not the sort of person you have around nice people, and your family, they're nice people. Need some distance, right? Aiden, you've got to admit, you don't want me at your mom's table. I mean, I'm good and all for a work buddy, but you don't want me at your dinner table, not with little girls and nice ladies, and your grandma and such. She's a real nice woman, you know, going to be one of those batshit crazy dames that wears pajamas and a feather boa in a few years—I'd love to hang out at the park with her and play chess and talk about boys she knew, but not at the table. Table's the place for family—what are you doing?"

Aiden had taken the two steps into the tiny room necessary to be face-to-face, and grabbed the bible.

"Put it back, give your apologies to my mother, and get back in that room."

"*What*?" Jeremy cried, honestly confused. "Give my what to your mother?"

"If coming to dinner with us scares you that much—" Aiden yanked on the bible and Jeremy was undone enough to let it slip from his hands while saying, "I've eaten in prison, dumbass! Your family doesn't scare—" Oh shit. "—me."

The bible fell on the ground between them, opening up to reveal the little box inside, and Aiden looked down at it and then looked up at Jeremy, more than bemused.

"I thought those things were only in movies," he said, stooping to pick it up.

"So does everyone else," Jeremy muttered, stooping to get it back from him. "That's why daddy had one made for me when I was a kid." Aiden beat him to the bible, and Jeremy just squatted there in an agony of embarrassment.

"You kept them in your bible?" Aiden asked, looking at the fingerless mittens, neatly folded next to his stack of big bills. "Why didn't you wear them?"

"They're too nice to wear," Jeremy said miserably. "I didn't want to wreck them."

Aiden looked up at him, and his eyes were shiny and his face was tight and sort of scrunched up. "If you stay, Jeremy, I'll make you more."

Jeremy's face felt scrunched up the same way. "There's no need," he said gruffly. He took the bible away from Aiden then and closed it, making sure the mittens were carefully stashed while he took the wad of bills and shoved it in his pocket. They both straightened up, standing close enough to each other for Jeremy to feel Aiden's breath on his face.

"I... I'm not good enough for your mother's table, Aiden. I used to sell bibles to women just like her, and those bibles were never going to show up. I... I don't know how I can sit there and make nice conversation with her. It...." What was he going to say? It froze his bowels and made him want to throw up? No. He had some claim to being a man, after all. "It wouldn't sit right," he said lamely, and Aiden nodded and looked away.

"If I promise you don't have to come to my house, would you put your shit away and come back inside?" he asked quietly, and Jeremy looked around wildly. His stuff was everywhere, piles of peanut butter and ramen noodles—there were mice that liked to live in the grain bins, and some of the ramen had fallen victim to them. There were open packages and little crumbs all over. And he couldn't even *remember* where he'd been keeping all his cash.

"I... I need to clean up," he said apologetically. "Maybe you should go back and—"

"I'll go get the dustbin and a broom," Aiden said decisively. "You can hide the cash while I'm gone."

Jeremy looked at him with naked gratitude. "Okay," he said, just so happy to have a plan. "I can do that."

Aiden nodded, and swallowed, some of his earlier passion coming back to shudder in his voice.

"Jesus God, Jeremy. If I hadn't gone to follow you, Christ knows where you'd be right now."

"Waiting for a bus," Jeremy said without thinking. "That's usually where most escape plans end."

Aiden widened his eyes. "I'll have to remember that. Uhm, Jeremy?"

"Yeah?"

"Have you thought maybe about getting an apartment? Maybe if you made it a little harder to walk away, you'd find it a little easier to talk to us first."

Jeremy blinked and looked around the room. It was tiny, yes, maybe twelve by twelve—but that still made it bigger than the cell he'd shared with the DWI guy, and a lot more inviting than the swelter of curtains he'd hid in the night his daddy died.

"But, if I did that, I wouldn't have near so much cash," he said, smiling his con man's smile. Aiden was apparently not buying tonight. Who said high school didn't teach you anything?

"The cash is to buy stuff with, idiot. What good's the cash if you don't have a home—" Aiden shook his head. "I'll be back with that broom. Let's hurry, or they'll start to think we're out here making out."

Jeremy shook his head. "You got pretty girls in there—they'll be more suspect. They'll probably think I bound and gagged you and took your cash."

Aiden stomped off then, swearing under his breath. It sounded like "Oh *fuck* no, I'm not having this conversation right now," but Jeremy couldn't be sure. He was busy looking around the tiny room, wondering if he could eat half a jar of peanut butter in one sitting so he could shove his cash in one of those.

Chapter 4
Scary Noises and Pie-in-the-Sky

JEREMY KEPT trying to knit better. Ariadne still helped him. He tried another hat for Aiden; even though it was technically summer, Colorado still had brisk falls, crisp springs, and cold-as-fucking-hell winters. They were a stone's throw from the Rocky Mountains and Highway 34, where there was snow all year round, and a hat was certainly practical enough. Ariadne hinted that maybe he might want to try a scarf for his third project, since those couldn't really *be* too big or too small, and he reckoned she was right. He just might make *her* one when he was done.

He never intended to make an entire scarf in two days. That happened just after the sheep had to be put down, because somehow, the knitting made even *that* better.

Sheep were nice critters, and Jeremy loved to pet them between the slitted eyes until their heads began to loll, but they weren't always big on personality. It was no matter. Craw had enough property that, if they seeded it with alfalfa, the sheep could be moved from corner to corner, and the alpacas too, cleaning fields and feeding themselves in sort of a perfect example of synergy right there. As long as Craw bought them the vitamin-rich saltlicks, they were happy critters.

Too happy, apparently, because the morning Jeremy woke up early to the sound of wild dogs showed him one of the worst bloodbaths he'd ever seen.

He was still wearing moccasins and his boxer shorts, and was running for the field with the broomstick in his hand after shouting for Craw, when he came across the three savaged sheep. The dogs—four of them—were still buried up to their muzzles in sheep gut, and Jeremy started shouting at them, swinging left and right with the broom, trying to get them away.

It wasn't until the largest one, who looked like a cross between a Rottweiler and a bear, looked up and started growling at him that

Jeremy realized he may have been just the tiniest bit reckless. He held the broom defensively, ready to do battle with the monster, when there was the sudden crack of a rifle, and the lead dog fell down dead. The others scattered after that, although Craw picked two of them off as they were running, and Jeremy was left alone with the three slaughtered sheep.

Well, two slaughtered sheep. One was left alive.

Jeremy ignored the others, lying in puddles of blood and innards, and rushed to the sheep who was on her side, bleating a little with every breath. The sheep didn't have names, and Jeremy didn't know this one from any other critter in the flock, but he did like the critters, and it pained him to see them hurt.

"Craw?" he called, but Craw was still galloping down the field, trying to get the other dog. You didn't want to leave a wild dog out there—the one wild one would form a pack that others wanted to join. "Craw?"

"How's she doing?" Aiden asked, coming up breathlessly, and Jeremy squinted at him.

"What are you doing here so early?" he asked, feeling stupid. "And on a Sunday."

"Was going to cook you guys breakfast," Aiden said, grimacing. "My mom's idea. She said since you weren't up to the family dinner, I should cook for you. Heard the shots and came running—how's she doing?"

Jeremy looked at poor Ma Sheep mournfully. "I don't know. Reckon the vet can fix her up?"

Aiden gasped when he saw the mess of her lying about the grass. "I don't know how she's still alive now!" he muttered. Then, "Craw! Craw! Get your ass over here! The dog's gone! We can call the sheriff to come look for it, but the sheep needs you now!"

Jeremy felt like ice had just frozen over a big blank spot in his head. "Why does the sheep need him?" he asked. "If the vet can't help her, what's Craw going to do?"

Aiden's sigh was ragged. "He's going to put her down, Jeremy. We can't just leave her like this."

And Jeremy's brain slid on that icy blank spot—and Jeremy just checked right out of his own head. He stood up abruptly, backing away from the sheep. "No, no, of course not. But I can't be here for this. I can't. I mean, I know it has to be done, but you're gonna need goons to hose the brains off the floor, and we're the goons, and I can't be the guy who does that, I just can't. I gotta go hide, safe and warm, and not see this. I can't see this. I can't. No no no no no no...."

He turned around and ran, aware that Aiden and Craw were having a hurried conversation and that Aiden was suddenly right at his side, sprinting like a champion to keep up.

"Where we going?" Aiden asked, out of breath, and Jeremy looked at the copse of trees up over the rise.

"Gotta hide," he mumbled, and made for that copse of trees, wearing his boxer shorts, his moccasins, and not a damned thing more. They made it to the small cluster of shade, Aiden right at his elbow, and Jeremy wrapped one arm around a small oak tree and hung on, trying to keep his knees from buckling. "Oh God," he whispered, not even sure who he was talking to. "Has he done it yet?"

As if in answer, there was a rifle report across their little slice of Granby, and Jeremy's grip on the tree loosened. He slid away, leaving raw scrapes on his chest and arms, and fell to his knees in the spiky litter of oak leaves, trying hard not to retch. His vision faded to black and he shivered too hard to catch his breath, and his stomach twisted over itself in an effort to void something he hadn't even eaten yet.

And Aiden was right down there with him, that arm wrapped around his shoulders, whispering into his hair, telling him that it would be all right.

Eventually, it was just the two of them breathing, and Jeremy relaxed into Aiden's arm a little.

When he spoke, it was in a small voice. "I reckon we can go back now," he said, and Aiden grunted. The boy was wearing jeans and a T-shirt, and he smelled like boys' sweat and boys' shower stuff, and Jeremy was, for a moment, entranced.

"Why'd you come after me?" he asked. It was embarrassing, having this boy see that part of himself spilling all over the earth.

"Craw said you were going to need someone. Craw's smart that way." Hero worship. The boy's voice was thick with it—even thicker in the past few months since that trip to Boulder. Jeremy couldn't blame him—weren't many men as full-out strong and smart and doing that thing they loved the most while the world could kiss their collective or singular ass. He was a good model for Aiden. Hell, Jeremy watched him appreciatively sometimes too. He was a good-looking man—strong, assertive, with a strong jaw and fine eyes. It would make more sense for Jeremy to have a crush on Rance too—but that's not where Jeremy's heart was, and he knew it. Wasn't he supposed to know better?

"I'm better now," Jeremy said into the silence. "I'm sorry to trouble you like this." He made an effort then to stand up, but Aiden's arm stayed strong around his shoulders.

"Shh," the boy whispered. "Just stay for a minute, okay?"

Jeremy nodded. He said, "In a minute. In a minute we'll go back," but he stayed there, accepting comfort and body contact for much more than a minute.

"Jeremy?" Aiden said softly into his hair.

"Yeah?"

"Sometimes you make me feel so young."

"You are young, boy. It's nothing to be ashamed of."

"I need to be older," Aiden muttered. "I need to be old enough to deal with this shit. Someone's gotta." He shifted beside Jeremy and stood heavily to his feet, then reached his hand down. "C'mon, man. Craw's got clean up. You and me are gonna go make breakfast."

But breakfast wasn't enough. Jeremy got dressed and joined Aiden in the kitchen, following his directions there just like he did in the mill. Craw came in and they sat down, and they ate in strained silence. Jeremy spent all of a minute to feel bad for Aiden—this was obviously supposed to be sort of a treat for them.

He'd been sitting in his seat, looking at congealed eggs and bacon for a while before Aiden stood and put a nice, brotherly hand on his shoulder. Jeremy shot up, knocking his chair over backward and then backed up, tripped over his feet, and fell on his ass. He glared at Aiden and shouted, "What'd you do that for?"

"'Cause I said your name three times, dumbass! Where the hell were you?"

Jeremy opened his mouth and then shut it again and then opened it and said, "Vegas," sort of weakly, and he didn't miss Aiden and

Craw's shared look, but he couldn't do anything about it either. He stood up then and righted the chair and brushed by a patiently waiting Aiden to get his plate.

"That was right good chow, Aiden," he said genially, and wondered that their ears didn't bleed, because he sounded high and screechy, even to himself. "I'm sorry I'm feeling a bit poorly." He scraped his plate into Craw's compost bucket. "I'll just take this out and maybe feed the rest of the critters today, all right?"

"I moved the sheep inside," Craw said gruffly. "They'll be restless."

Jeremy nodded. "I'll try not to bother 'em none. They had a rough morning." He rinsed off his plate and put it in the dishwasher, and then gave a little nod of dismissal and walked out the door. He made it through his chores and realized that being in the big barn, even with the horses and alpacas out in the other pasture, just sort of soothed the savaged parts inside him. On a whim, he went and got the yarn and the needles for the scarf he'd been planning to start for Ariadne, sat down in a corner of the barn where he could see the sheep, and cast on.

It got hot in the barn—it was June, after all—and his hands stuck to the alpaca blend and the needles. Sweat trickled down his scalp from his hair and then seemed to pool and join a river down his spine, but... but that repeat, it just felt so good. It soothed him so nicely. Craw came out and asked him if he'd like some lunch, and that was his only indication that time had passed. He said no thank you, got up stiffly to use the john and to run some cool water on his neck and drink some. It was Sunday. Besides the critters, he was mostly at loose ends anyway, so he went back out to that corner again and kept knitting. The sun slanted and it grew cool in the barn, and it got hard to see. Craw came in with a plate of dinner, took the yarn from his unresisting hands, and pulled up a chair.

"Aiden's worried about you," he said gruffly, and Jeremy looked at the dinner—eggs and bacon, his favorite, and pretty much what he'd refused to eat that morning. It didn't look all that appetizing now, but he took a piece of toast and made a good go at it. He figured if he shoved the food in his mouth, his con man's sensibilities would take over, and he'd eat, and it worked for a bit.

"He shouldn't be," Jeremy answered with his mouth full of food. "He's got all sorts of better things to worry him. He should be out looking for pretty girls, not worrying about a washed up con man."

"He's worried about his friend, jackass. What was going on in your head this morning?"

Jeremy couldn't have eaten another bite if his life depended on it—and he actually knew what that was like for real. "Nothing of importance. You know me, Craw. A braintrust, I'm not."

"Fuck. Fine, asshole. I've got a line on a big drum carder—it'll cut your work in half, but you have to drive up to Pennsylvania in the flatbed to get it. You and Aiden. I figure we work double-time this week to shore up our stock, and you two take a week or so for the trip. You up for that?"

Jeremy gaped at him. "I thought that was pie-in-the-sky," he whispered, genuinely flabbergasted. "I… I mean, who does that?"

Craw squinted. "Well, I had enough profits to put them back into my shop, Jeremy. It's how I had the means to hire you."

Jeremy shook his head. He didn't have the words. How did he explain to someone that his whole life, he'd been waiting for the day when the rain fell, with plans to dance in the rain then? How do you explain the bone-deep knowledge that this thing you con for, lie for, cheat for, ain't *never gonna happen*? That the biggest con of all is telling yourself that it will? How could he tell Craw that saying you were going to do something and then making it happen was, for Jeremy, as unlikely as Craw settling down with a nice girl and breeding like bunnies?

"Does that mean you don't want to go?" Craw asked, still oblivious to Jeremy's epiphany, and Jeremy shook his head again.

"No, no, I'll go. You're not gonna send that kid off to Philly by himself, right? Someone needs to make sure he stays outta trouble."

Craw grunted. It was getting a little cooler, which was nice, but Jeremy had been stewing in sweat, and he was a little bit chilly now. "Quite honestly, Jeremy, after that thing you did today, I'm pretty sure it's Aiden going with you to keep you outta trouble."

Jeremy looked miserably down at Ariadne's scarf, his face screwed tight with shame. "Can't argue there. Well, good. Kid can keep an eye on me. That's fair."

Craw grunted. "Stand up, Jeremy, and grab your knitting. You're coming inside tonight, and you're sleeping on the couch. I've got a television. Haven't used it in months. God knows, maybe something intelligent finally started. It would be an improvement."

Jeremy was bemused. He was also, he understood, in no condition to make his own choice in the matter. Craw told him to, and so he would.

He stood up and grabbed his knitting and spent a quiet evening on Craw's couch, comforted by Craw's breathing and the steady clacking of his needles along with Jeremy's. He stayed up long after Craw got up, bitched about the stupid television show (Jeremy hadn't been paying attention), and went to bed. In the morning, Craw woke him up and told him to go shower and get dressed, and then said he'd block the simple garter stitch scarf Jeremy had finished in the wee hours of the morning.

Jeremy spent a minute staring at it—it was bright fuchsia with black highlights in the yarn, like Ariadne's hair. He hoped she'd like it. For some reason, imagining her reaction when he gave it to her was the one thing that got him off the couch at all.

"IS THAT all you're bringing?" Aiden asked, looking at the tiny duffel over Jeremy's shoulder. Jeremy looked at it too. It had a spare change of clothes, three pairs of underwear, three pairs of socks, his bible, and enough yarn for three hats, which was a plum luxury. It also had a small wad of cash in one of the zippered pockets, one in the bible, and he had one in his pocket.

"I lived for two months on less than this," he said, thinking about escaping from that wrecked hotel room with the bible tucked close to his chest. Aiden raised his eyebrows and Jeremy shifted, suddenly embarrassed. "They weren't *comfortable* months," he confessed. "I figure if we're staying in hotels on the way up, we'll find a washer/dryer. It'll be fine."

Aiden shook his head and picked up his considerably bigger bag. "You got any books in there?" he asked critically, and Jeremy shook his head.

"Nope," he said, although he had a lot of books stashed under his bed in the barn. They were all paperbacks, gleaned from library sales and garage sales and anytime a book was on sale sales. He was aware that if he ever had to bugger off, the books wouldn't be coming with him, so he didn't want to spend full price on them, but he didn't want to risk leaving them behind, either.

Aiden shook his head. "Your room open?" he asked bluntly, and Jeremy shrugged. It didn't have a lock. So far, the only person who had entered without his permission was Aiden, that one time. Aiden shoved his way in there, Jeremy on his heels, and to Jeremy's surprise, he dropped to his stomach and started rummaging around under Jeremy's cot. He came back with *1984*, *Yarn Harlot: Free Range Knitter* by Stephanie Pearl-McPhee, and *Ravished* by Amanda Quick.

"Not *1984*," Jeremy said quickly. "I started that one. It depressed the hell out of me. Get me another Amanda Quick—she's fun."

Aiden did a double take at that and said, "How about some Jennifer Crusie too?" he asked, and his voice was saccharinely ironic, but Jeremy didn't care. He was gonna go with no books at all because he needed to travel light, but if Aiden insisted, he wanted something fun.

"Yeah, sure. I like her too. Why's my reading so damned important anyway?"

Aiden narrowed his eyes. "Because you don't talk when you read, dumbass, and I love you like a brother and would rather not kill you."

Jeremy swallowed. Loved him like a brother? That was sweet. Not what he'd been sort of yearning for, without putting words or pictures to it, but an improvement over "God, I can't fucking stand you," which is where Jeremy was pretty sure Aiden started out in the matter.

"Yeah, get two books by her. I've seen enough violence in my life."

Aiden came out from under the bed and looked at him quizzically. "I was being metaphorical, you know that, right?"

Jeremy flushed. "Yeah, I knew that. You're a nice boy, Aiden. You wouldn't even deck me if I got outta line."

Aiden came out with four books and looked at Jeremy's little duffel, which was stuffed full. "I'll put 'em in my bag," he offered, and Jeremy took him up on it.

He didn't even think to ask why Aiden didn't give him shit about having romances in his collection, even when Aiden's books turned out to be all spy thrillers and stuff. It didn't matter. Aiden loved him, even if it was like a brother.

THE TRIP turned out to be all right, for the most part. Aiden drove first, because he confessed to getting a mite carsick on the curvy parts if he didn't, and he knew the road out of Granby well enough. Jeremy sat next to him and knit, which he could do well enough now to keep his eyes on the road. The knitting took just enough of Jeremy's attention that he didn't spend too much time talking, but not so much that he couldn't answer at all.

They had just cleared the mountain range and were on their way to Boulder—in fact, they were passing the prison, the maximum security one, not Fort Lyon—and Aiden, right after a discussion of colorways and the color wheel that left Jeremy's head whirling in a blinding mix of rainbows and words, knocked Jeremy's happiness with the trip right out of the truck.

"So, Jeremy—what happened in Vegas?"

Jeremy looked desperately to the road and realized they were going about sixty-five miles an hour in the flat bed, and if he jumped out now he'd kill himself.

"Why you gotta ask me that now!" he mourned. He'd been so happy!

"Because we're going too fast for you to jump out of the truck, and you're not driving so you can't wreck it."

Jeremy glared at him. "You're so matter-of-fact!" he accused. "This is my stuff. I don't go into your room and steal your peanut butter—"

"I give you my peanut butter for free," Aiden said practically, and Jeremy shook his head.

"All I know about you is—"

"That I want to design, that I have a nice family, that I've lived my whole life in Granby, and even though I've seen other parts of the world on school trips and such, I really want to live in my hometown. You know I think Craw walks on water, I'm a complete bastard when I'm training someone—"

"You weren't that bad!"

"I was horrible to you, Jeremy. You were so out of your element, and I acted like a pissy little kid. Anyway, you know all that and you still want to hang out with me. But you got something just fucking awful in your head, and it's hurting you. So, maybe, can you maybe 'fess up?"

Jeremy didn't say anything. For fifty miles. After a while, he realized that Aiden had been waiting for his response, and he hadn't had any words for it, and had just sat there, with his knitting in his hands. So he picked up his knitting and worked, very carefully, stitch after stitch, trying to put the bang and the blood he didn't see and his father's twitching body out of his head.

They got out at a rest stop to stretch and piss and get gas and to switch sides. Jeremy didn't say much then, either. Aiden went into McDonald's, and even though Jeremy usually really loved their chocolate chip cookies, he went to Carl's Jr. instead. They met back at the truck, and Aiden held out a little bag in his hand. Three chocolate chip cookies, in the little paper wrapper.

"Thank you," Jeremy said, moved.

"I'm sorry I blindsided you," Aiden said softly. He turned and leaned against the quarter panel of the flatbed, and Jeremy followed suit. "Craw says he's a bastard because he hurts people's feelings whether he means to or not. He figures it's just as well if everyone expects it, and then when he apologizes, they know he means it."

"You're nicer'n Craw," Jeremy said with some contemplation. He pulled out a cookie and nibbled, then settled into the enjoyment. He loved these cookies—the softness, the chocolate chips, the brown-sugar sweetness. He closed his eyes with the last swallow, and offered Aiden the second one from the bag.

Aiden took it. "You wouldn't know it by what I just did to you," he said softly. "I just want to know what hurt you."

"So we could share the hurt?" Jeremy pulled the last cookie out of the bag and broke it in half. "That's not friendly." He offered the other half to Aiden, and Aiden smiled a little and took it.

"Neither is letting someone suffer by themselves. Think about it, okay, Jeremy?"

They each took a bite out of his half of the cookie. "What good will it do?" Jeremy asked musingly. "I'm okay."

Aiden swallowed. "Well, if I have your secret, and you're still my friend, maybe you'll feel secure enough to get yourself an apartment, maybe."

Jeremy looked at the last bite of cookie while Aiden threw his last bite in his mouth. "Why would I want to do that?" he asked the cookie. He almost never ate all three. He almost always left that third one in the bag and folded the bag up and put it in his pocket.

"So I could come over and watch movies, for one!" Aiden said laughingly. "My brothers and sisters all watch Discovery channel, Ariadne and Rory get too gross and romantic, and Craw hates television with all of his black heart. You get a TV, and I'll be able to come over and watch romantic comedies on DVR."

Jeremy smiled a little and popped the cookie in his mouth without thinking. "Action movies too?"

"My favorite kind," Aiden said, smiling. He turned and started walking away from the truck. "Come on!"

"Where are we going? Don't we have to get on the road?"

"We're getting a six-pack of cookies. Three more to share and three more so you can sleep tonight, okay?"

Jeremy trotted after him, feeling strangely happy for having been so miserable during that fifty-mile stretch. This road trip might be okay after all.

And in the end, it was. They drove all day for three days, and at night, Aiden went swimming (and, after talking Jeremy into spending some of his cash on a suit, so did Jeremy) and they worked out the kinks from the road. Then they spent the evenings watching television and knitting, or lying, each on his bed, reading books. It was funny that for all of Jeremy's quiet yearning, those moments lying on adjacent hotel beds, reading, were some of the happiest of his life.

Philadelphia, though—that almost put a kibosh on Jeremy and Aiden's friendship forever, and it was something Jeremy didn't even realize he was doing until it was almost too late.

The problem was, the man selling the mill was retiring, and he hadn't consulted his family. More specifically, he hadn't consulted his *daughter*, and she didn't want to break the mill up into parts.

"I was raised in there!" she complained to her father while Aiden and Jeremy stood by uncomfortably. They had needed to rent a good-size crane to pick the damned thing up off the ground and get it on the flatbed, and apparently, they'd needed two forklifts and a giant wheeled pallet to get it off the floor of the mill in the first place. So when they arrived at the mill—which looked gutted and sad on the lush farm outskirts of Philadelphia—the thing had been outside on the pavement, and the crane had been next to it, set up and ready to heft the giant piece of machinery onto the flatbed so it could be tied off about a thousand times with those sturdy, nylon-covered steel cables. The owner—a giant of a man, both tall and wide, with a fuzz of gray hair on his liver-spotted head—was riding one of those electric cart things, because, Jeremy reckoned, that much weight would be rough on a body. And his daughter—a narrow-waisted, narrow-nosed rake of a woman, stood arms akimbo, and tried to bully her father into keeping a thing from a place, by her father's account, she had never visited.

"You were raised in our home, by the nannies!" her father returned. "And I'm sorry about that, but your mother passed away, may she rest in peace. Now I don't know what got into you right now—"

"You didn't even ask me!" she snapped, and he sighed.

"Katherine, you weren't even around. You live in Manhattan, for sweet Christ's sake. What do you think you're going to do? Come here and run a company you don't want to have nothing to do with? Now can't you see these two boys are waiting on us?"

Both of them turned around and grimaced at Jeremy and Aiden, who were leaning back against the flatbed, watching the show. Aiden saw the scrutiny and glared, but Jeremy? He'd seen this scenario before. He knew what his role was—he'd played it many a time.

"Now don't worry 'bout us none," he said with his con man's smile, the one that made the dimples pop. He flashed that dimple particularly at Miss Katherine, who, bless her, did what she was supposed to do too, and turned red. "We're just going to scare us up a hotel room, while you two hammer this out. Don't make no sense, getting 'tween family, and don't we know it!"

He turned to Aiden, who was looking incredulously from the two mill owners back to Jeremy. "Hotel room? We were supposed to—"

Jeremy kept his smile and winked. "Now don't you fret none, boy." He turned to the mill owners again. "My young protégé here is worried, because we hadn't planned on a hotel room in these parts. He lowered his head and looked at Miss Katherine from under long, dark lashes. "Now you wouldn't happen to know of a nice motel, Miss Katherine? One not too tight on the pockets of two hired hands? If it's some place you know about, well then, maybe we could do business later tonight, after you hash this out with your daddy here—"

"I'm in the Courtyard Marriott, right down the road," she said quickly, her face so red she was flushed and dewy. "If you two get a room down there while we get this settled, I'll pay for it, I promise."

Jeremy allowed himself to look sheepish. "Why, Miss Katherine, that would sure settle us some. Our boss is a good man—but he's a hard one, and tight with a dime. Just knowing you could put us up, that might go a long way to ease his anger if this trip should prove to be fruitless. I'll tell you what. Me and the boy here will go check ourselves in, and you can come looking for us later on. I would surely love to chat with you about what this mill meant to you, Miss Katherine. That way you would know your cherished memories are in good hands."

Her smile did indeed light up her face, and when her lips weren't compressed they were plump in a wide mouth. Her whole face gained a softness when she looked at Jeremy, and Jeremy sighed. *Yup.* Could be, he was going to have to take one for the team. Well, wouldn't be the first time. And this way, he'd be helping Craw, and therefore helping Aiden and Ariadne, and that would sit a whole lot better than just getting an extra wad of cash for himself.

"What the hell was all of that?" Aiden asked angrily as they got back in the truck. Even though Aiden had driven them there, Jeremy had taken the keys, to keep the illusion that he was the older, more experienced man, and Aiden was the boy in his charge.

"I was giving her a way to settle with her daddy," Jeremy explained.

"By letting her know you were for sale?"

"Well, wouldn't that piss her daddy off?" he asked, although he was pretty sure just getting that harpy of a woman off the man's back would make John S. Katan's life a lot easier. "But this won't make him mad. He'll see it as me getting her around a little. She'll get to spend an evening feeling special, and Craw'll get his goddamned gi-fuckin-normous drum carder. It's win-win, Aiden—don't tell me you don't see it!"

"Well, *yeah*! Except you've got to whore yourself out like... like...."

"Like a whoring con man on the grift?" Jeremy asked, stung. Well, mostly because it was true, but he was stung anyway.

"And what do *you* get out of this?" Aiden asked, but he sounded defensive now, and Jeremy could tell he felt bad.

"I get to help Craw," Jeremy told him truthfully, and Aiden sighed. God. Wasn't much either of 'em wouldn't do to help Craw, now was there?

Sure enough, they got back to the hotel, walked out to get themselves something to eat, and had just finished their swim, when Miss Katherine walked into the pool area. She was still dressed in a nice linen summer dress, with shoes that cost what Jeremy made in a week, and she knelt by the pool with every confidence that the skirt wouldn't quite cover her knees and that Jeremy would sneak a peek just for fun.

He pretended to, but seriously, white cotton panties were not going to do it for him at this stage in his life.

"So," she purred, "since you're all settled here, you wouldn't want to come over to my room so we could talk, would you?"

Jeremy smiled. "Why, ma'am, I'm hardly dressed."

"Well, I won't be uncomfortable if you won't," she murmured, and Jeremy amped up that smile.

"I'll just go tell young Aiden where I'll be."

Aiden was doing laps in the deep end, and Jeremy splashed some water to get his attention. The boy straightened up, and Jeremy saw what he'd been seeing for the last four days—the strong, tanned, well-defined lines of a hairless chest, with little shell pink nipples peeking out as Aiden stood up in the five-foot area. Jeremy himself was barely five foot eight, but Aiden had grown three inches in the past six months. He was past six feet now. He was so beautiful—Jeremy had always thought that, from the first time the boy had shaken his hand—but now, it hurt even more. After this, he'd be completely out of Jeremy's reach.

Aiden looked at him and shook his head. "Please don't do this," he said softly, and Jeremy swallowed. It wasn't like the boy had ever been in his reach in the first place.

"I'll let you know how it goes," he said softly, and winked. "Just think, boy. This could be the only thing I could give Craw that he couldn't do with his own two hands." He giggled. "Literally!"

And then he turned and hoisted himself out of the pool, very carefully not looking Aiden in the eyes.

He grabbed a complimentary towel on his way out and held the gate for Miss Katherine, then followed her to her room.

She was up on the second floor, with a king-size bed, and Jeremy looked around appreciatively. It was a nice hotel—better than the Motel Sixes they'd been staying at, and the king-size bed brought to mind all sorts of things that Jeremy had never done. Of course, he hadn't had Miss Katherine in mind at the time, but, well….

It wasn't like Aiden would do those things with him anyway. It was good to remind himself that Aiden was probably not gay. A girl would appear in his life. She had to, so Jeremy could stop dreaming and feeling old and perverted and hopeless.

"So, Jeremy," Miss Katherine said into the sudden silence, "what is it you can say that you think will change my mind?" Her voice was shaking, and for the first time, Jeremy realized that she was nervous. In that moment, he felt bad for her, and in that moment, he realized that this wasn't honest. *That's* what Aiden had been trying to tell him. Oh hells. What to do now?

Well, he had more than one treasure in the grifter's pot, didn't he?

"Well, ma'am," Jeremy said gently, "don't get nervous now." She looked up at him and he winked, and proceeded to make a show of still toweling off his lean little body. "I'm still sort of wet—I don't even want to walk on the rug like this, so I'm not likely to do anything you're not nice and comfy with, okay?"

"Okay," she said, sounding surprised.

Katherine's nerves seemed to crank down a notch, and Jeremy smiled at her, this time a smaller smile. "You miss your daddy, don't you?" he asked, and was gratified by her startlement. "I mean, you moved away 'cause you thought you hated this place, but your daddy, he wasn't a bad sort?"

She shook her head and moved over toward the bed—not with innuendo, he was pretty sure, but because it was an easy place to sit.

"He was good to us," she said softly. "He was right, the nannies raised us, but he came home at night and tucked us in. He made sure he was off holidays, was there for every birthday. I... I mean, I call him once a week, but...."

"But since you moved away, it don't feel the same, does it?"

She smiled a little and shook her head. "No."

Jeremy nodded. "So, he's getting rid of this piece of his life that you remember, and you feel like he's getting farther and farther away, right?"

She had blonde hair, coarse and graying, pulled back into a braid, and she tucked a strand of it behind her ear. "It's like you can read my diary," she said softly.

Jeremy shook his head. "Naw, ma'am. Just my own. Now see, the thing is, you keep thinking that cutting ties with this place is going to make him float away. What you don't see is that having it gone is going to make the two of you free!"

"Free?" Now that she wasn't simpering or blushing or bitching, she was, indeed, a pretty woman.

"Yes'm. He's going to be free to spend the time he didn't used to have, and you're going to be free to visit him without remembering the place you hated for taking him away."

"But...." She stood up in aggravation. "But you've seen him! He's practically housebound! He can't come to Manhattan!"

Jeremy nodded. "Well, ma'am, I didn't say you weren't going to have to give some things up. But he gave things up for you, didn't he?"

She nodded. "You're very wise."

Jeremy shook his head. "Not so's you'd notice."

They spent another hour there, him standing on the three-by-three tile foyer, her sitting on the bed, and when they were done, he had an agreement to go pick up the carder in the morning, and she'd pick up the hotel tab for making them spend the extra day. She got off the bed then and came close to him, close enough for him to smell her perfume, for her to put her hands on his shoulders. It didn't do nothing for him, but it was nice to have the human contact.

She leaned forward and kissed his cheek. "You're really a dear man, do you know that?" she said softly, and he backed up against the door, opening it behind him.

"You have a nice evening, ma'am," he said. He took a couple of steps down the walkway before he scrubbed at the lipstick mark she left on his cheek with the towel.

AIDEN LET him in when he knocked, and seemed surprised to see him.

"Jesus, Jeremy—you were only gone an hour. You must be damned good in the sack!" Aiden threw himself on the bed in a sour huff, but Jeremy knew his moods by now, and Jeremy realized it was something that the boy would forgive.

Which was good, because he didn't want to talk about that. He didn't. He leaned back against the door, thinking that this here was a good kid, and he'd opened the door for Jeremy when Jeremy really didn't deserve it.

"My daddy," he said, without knowing he was going to say it, "was shot in the head in a deserted casino when a con went wrong."

Aiden sat up in bed, horrified, his tanned face going shock-white even as Jeremy said the words.

"I saw just that part, and then I hid in the curtains, right as the body was hitting the ground. Carelli didn't see me, he didn't hear me. One of his boys knew I was there, but"—he wasn't going to talk about that either, not now—"but for some reason, he didn't say anything. And I sat there, like a fucking coward, for something like four hours, while they hosed my daddy's brains off the floor and dragged him off the stage and buried him Christ knows where. I got away, grabbed my bible, and grew a fucking conscience. You know the rest, Aiden. It's not pretty. So now you know me. A whoring, cowardly, thieving—"

"Shut up," Aiden said, looking Jeremy in the face and wiping his eyes with the back of his hand. "You're my friend, dumbass. Stop talking shit about yourself. Just stop it. I don't want to listen."

Jeremy nodded and wished like hell he could go over there and comfort the boy, but he wanted him so badly, it was like to be crawling out of his skin.

"Well, fine. What do you want to do instead?"

Aiden stood up and walked over to him, wrapped one arm around his shoulder, and steered him toward the bed.

"Is she really paying for the room?" he asked, and Jeremy smiled a little. Aiden had showered, and he smelled clean, and like a young man and not a sweaty kid.

"Yessir."

"Think she'd mind if we ordered room service?"

Probably not, Jeremy thought. She'd been pretty happy when he left.

"What'd you have in mind?"

Aiden grinned. "I've been looking at the menu while you were gone. Do you know they have a chocolate-chip-cookie vanilla-ice-cream sundae?"

Jeremy's vision went sort of deliriously swimmy. It could have been the thought of heaven on a plate, but it was probably Aiden's bare skin on his shoulder. It didn't matter. Two minutes ago was on his list for the bottom twenty or so in his life, but he was filing this moment right here away in his top ten ever for awesome.

"Yeah?" Chocolate chip cookies and vanilla ice cream. God yes.

"Yeah."

"I say we get in on that action, you think?"

Aiden sighed and collapsed against him, a little bit boneless and very, very comfortable. Jeremy might have closed his eyes then, just at the sweetness of it, and when Aiden spoke again, his breath tickled Jeremy's shoulder.

"I thought you'd never ask!"

Chapter 5
A Square View to a Clean Sweep of Sky

IT WAS like he'd told a lonely woman in a hotel room. Giving up big burdens can sometimes set us free.

Jeremy got back to his tiny room in the barn, and the mice had gotten into his ramen stores again. He ended up throwing it all away. Aiden had bought him books at every town on the way back from Pennsylvania, and Jeremy looked around and realized he'd be up to his eyeballs in bags of books if he didn't either give them away or find a bigger place. That night, instead of sleeping off a very long trip, he sat up late and counted his little packets of cash and realized that he could afford a couch, maybe, if it wasn't expensive, and a nice television if it wasn't huge, and maybe some plates and dishes and things. Hell, he could even afford a toaster.

Craw shut down the mill the next day so he could have workmen install the giant carder, and Jeremy woke up early enough to ask to use the phone. It was the first time he'd made that request, ever.

Craw looked at him through his customary irritability. "What in the fuck are you planning?"

Jeremy blushed. "Was gonna look for an apartment nearby," he confessed. "We're only a few miles out from the town. If I get a used bike, I could ride it to work."

"I got a used bike in my garage. You can have it. Got an old bed frame in there too."

Jeremy knew his mouth opened a little, his face going slack with surprise and gratitude. "I'd been planning to buy a couch," he said in wonder.

"To sleep on? Sounds like a quick way to a bad back. Get a couch. Get a mattress. Me and Ariadne, we got enough shit between us, you shouldn't have to get much more'n that."

Jeremy nodded. "Aiden's number—"

"In the address book by the phone. I'm *sure* that's how he wants to spend his day off."

Jeremy couldn't help but cringe from Craw's customary sarcasm, but he felt like he owed the boy, since he'd been the one who'd been pushing for it.

Aiden showed up forty-five minutes later in his mom's minivan, with two extra large caramel lattes, because although Granby didn't have a Starbucks, they did have a local coffee place that *wanted* to be a Starbucks and proved it by putting extra dessert in their big latte drinks to show their sincerity. Jeremy approved.

The apartment hunting was actually a pretty short process—there were only a few complexes in all of Granby. One of them—the largest—was for the people who came during the winter to work at the ski lodges or during the summer to work the dude ranches, and they only signed three-month leases. Aiden heard that and grabbed Jeremy literally by the neck and pulled him out of the manager's office without so much as a how-de-do.

"What?" Jeremy asked, confused. "I didn't even get a chance to see the apartments!"

"Three months? I make you bare your soul for three months? After what we've done to put up with each other, it should be two years at the least."

Jeremy grinned, unable to keep his glee inside. "Think you can put up with me that long?"

Aiden rolled his eyes. "Count on it!"

The second one had two buildings that were built in the eighties, one of those square stucco affairs in which every apartment was a square cut into smaller squares. The buildings faced each other, and one of them backed up against the grocery store and the other one backed up against the lumber store. Aiden took one look at Jeremy's face and said, "Fuck it—even I can tell this looks like prison," and turned the car around. "Don't worry, Jeremy. This last place is perfect. You'll like it. It's on the outskirts of town, but I can give you a ride in, 'cause it's closer to my parents' place. It'll be good. Trust me."

Granby was in the flat part of a bowl valley. If you followed the highway a little, you came to Grand, and both were mostly tourist towns. The residents made their living providing either for the people who lived there or for the tourists who visited there. There were a couple of ski lodges that filled in right quick (and could be accessed when the roads closed in the winter by a small airport outside of town), a largish pond/smallish lake outside of Grand, and between the two towns, maybe four restaurants total, a pub, a bar and grill, and a diner that you might be able to eat at without going broke.

The place Aiden took Jeremy was on the way out of town, toward Grand, where the houses were set on large, rolling tracts of land, before the little cluster of tourists' chateaus on the lake began. Jeremy looked at the rolling hills dotted with houses and finally thought to ask an obvious question.

"Do you live in one of those houses?"

Aiden rolled his eyes. "Yes, you oblivious bastard, I live in one of those houses. We can see it from the apartments. I'll show you there."

The apartments were, in fact, a line of small cottages, each one about two feet from the other, and they were tiny, tidy spaces. Each one had a small kitchenette with cupboards, a stove, and a small dining area that walked right into the living room. There was a doorway that led to the bedroom, and an adjoining bathroom. The whole thing formed a nice little square, but the window from the kitchen overlooked those rolling hills with the great farms on them. The window in the bedroom looked up into the mountains.

Jeremy turned a slow circle in the living room, looking to the valley and then behind him to the mountains.

He ran up to the kitchen sink for a moment and said, "Show me!"

Aiden laughed and didn't even ask him what he was supposed to show. He put his head close to Jeremy's and pointed out the farthest house, the one that was smallest from their vantage point. It was white, and even from this distance Jeremy could tell it had a wraparound porch.

"That's a real nice house," he said softly, and Aiden was so close, Jeremy had to close his eyes when he nodded and their cheeks brushed together.

"Yeah. And I wouldn't mind living about this close to it. Close enough to see my family, but far enough away that I didn't have to share the fucking bathroom."

Jeremy laughed. "I hear ya," he said, but he was thinking that he and his daddy had always shared hotel rooms. It had been too close in those last years. Some nights his daddy would go out and find a woman, and there were always nights when Jeremy was expected to sweeten the pot, but in the end? They had slept in adjacent beds and talked about the con like it was going to get them something, and they hadn't ever, ever said anything important.

Aiden pulled away and looked at him. "It's got a two-year lease," he said softly. "Do you think you could be happy here?"

Jeremy looked around and smiled shyly. "I think it's better than a motel room," he conceded.

Aiden grinned. "Is it better than the spare room in the barn?"

Jeremy considered that one seriously. "I'll miss the critters at night," he said honestly. "I don't know that I've often slept in a room on my own."

Aiden's eyes had gotten big at that. "That's twisted. I had to beat my little brother at arm wrestling to get my room to myself." He shook his head. "That's horrible."

Jeremy looked around then and thought about being alone here. "Being in the same room as someone and not being alone are two different things," he said. "I think I'll buy some curtains and things," he added. "Sheets and some posters and I need to find a bed and...."

He turned to Aiden and wondered at the full, gentle smile on his own face. "You want to help?"

It took a week for the couch to arrive, but they had the bed there—a nice queen-size with a spanking new mattress and box spring on Craw's old wood frame—the next day. With the couch came the television, but with the bed came the bags of books and the clothes, and in the interim there were dishes (an old set from Ariadne) and curtains (new) and sheets (also new). There were posters (Jeremy realized he liked movie posters—he couldn't say why) and a framed picture of him, Aiden, Craw, and Ariadne that the three of them gave him as a housewarming gift.

Aiden even brought plants.

And just that quickly, he had a real life.

It was much like his life had been for the past six months. He woke up in the morning and Aiden was there to take him to work. On days Aiden didn't work, he biked himself, and when it got too icy to do that, he took a whole lot of his little packets of cash out and bought a used car, a Toyota, with four doors and a red-primered quarter panel on a gold body. He learned how to pay bills, and it wasn't nearly as bad as his Daddy had always told him it would be, and he already loved going to work, so that wasn't bad either.

And then, there was the miracle thing, the thing he didn't question for the next two years, even though he probably should have. It was a small, simple thing, something so natural and easy that most people would have missed it, but he didn't.

Jeremy treasured it, but he didn't question it.

There he was, sitting in his apartment in that first week, appreciating the hell out of the brand new couch. He was drinking a beer and watching Friday night TV on his new TV/DVR/VCR setup—he had a thing for *Grimm*. Suddenly there was a knock at the door, and when he got there, Aiden was there with a quart of chocolate milk (which Jeremy already had) and a homemade pie from his mother.

And a movie.

Jeremy opened the door, bemused, and let him in.

"You mind?" Aiden asked. "I've got *Safe House* on DVD and no one in my family wants to watch it."

So they did.

It was the beginning of a tradition of sorts.

Sometimes they watched television, sometimes a movie, and sometimes sports, but Friday nights (and sometimes Saturday and sometimes Monday or Wednesday nights) came to mean Aiden at his place, with snacks. Sometimes Ariadne and her husband joined them, and a couple of times, when Rory was out of town, she slept on his couch anyway, so she didn't have to be alone. Craw would come, when it was sports, and generally? Jeremy came to understand that although he might live alone, he was not really alone. He had friends. He had family. For two Thanksgivings, he sat at Craw's table with everybody, and they said a sort of mangled, uncomfortable grace. For two Christmases, he knitted his fingers to the bone, testing his creativity, stretching his abilities. He learned how to read a pattern, and how to make cables, and how to make lace. He knitted some samples for the shop on occasion, but mostly? He knitted the way he'd seen all the rest of them knit—for each other. He took a page from Craw's book then, and poured his heart into his knitting. Aiden didn't get a hat that first Christmas, he got a specialty-made cable sweater. Ariadne got a shawl from a colorway that Aiden helped Jeremy design, just for her. Craw got a big felted messenger bag for all the errands he had to run in the truck.

He realized that these were the only gifts he'd ever given that were honest. He kept working to make them better. And in return? He got everything. As far as gifts went, Ariadne usually knitted him a sweater, and Craw was good for a warm, fluffy blanket. And Aiden? Aiden's gift was always the same. His birthday, Christmas, Valentine's Day, Flag Day, Aiden gave him a pair of gloves or mittens, with fingers or without, in every color from brown to neon pink to something in between. He tested new yarn or got fancy with old, until Jeremy couldn't keep them in his bible anymore.

He bought a floor safe instead.

Yes, the floor safe was a good idea, he thought critically. It was heavy enough to be unwieldy but could still be picked up, it fit under his bed, and it held the packets of cash he used to convert to cashier's checks in order to pay his rent and his bills. And it fit every pair of gloves that Aiden had ever given him.

He'd stopped buying ramen because he hated it, but he still always had extra jars of peanut butter on hand. There were some parts of being a con man that he could choose to leave behind. Having the ability to pick up the important stuff and run with it was not one of them.

And he might have stayed exactly that way, celibate, happy, conning nobody but himself, except two things happened.

The second thing was that Craw decided to hire a delivery service to come get the yarn and take it places. The first thing was the reason why he had to hire the guy, and that was the arrival of Ben.

CRAW HAD put off repairing the fence because he didn't like to leave Ariadne in the store, now that she was pregnant. She was only a few months along, but her spider-thin body wasn't helping her any, so she wasn't even allowed to walk into the barn. The men forbade it, and she humored them.

So Aiden and Jeremy were deep into their morning routine the September day that Craw came up from repairing a fence and told them that a new neighbor had moved into old Mrs. Humphries' place. Aiden and Jeremy had been part of the neighborly brigade that had brought Mrs. Humphries food and helped her tend her animals before she passed away, and they'd been sorry she'd passed. They'd also been more than curious at the tales of a great-nephew who had been given the place over the objections of her rather awful relatives.

When Craw came in, his eyes were a little wider than usual, and his face was a little bit blotchier. His mouth had been pushed out full and a little bit soft, and Jeremy had taken one look at him and then one look at Aiden.

Was Aiden going to be crushed?

Aiden had simply asked Craw if he seemed like a nice enough guy, and Craw had nodded his head. "He seems a mite tender for the area," Craw had confessed, and Jeremy had to admit that if Craw and Ariadne hadn't been watching out for him with alpaca sweaters and blankets and socks, he might have gone sprinting back to the southwest just because it was warmer come winter.

"You going to make him something?" Aiden asked curiously, and then Craw had done something truly frightening.

He'd smiled, and he'd blushed.

He'd stammered his way out of the mill then, saying something about taking the guy to the hardware store and wouldn't *that* be romantic, and Jeremy had looked very carefully at Aiden. Aiden didn't *look* like a guy who'd had his heart crushed, so maybe his hero worship was intact.

"What do you think?" Jeremy asked him, dying of curiosity.

"I think they're going to be our main source of entertainment here all winter," Aiden said thoughtfully.

"I guess we'll know when Craw asks you to do his colorway," Jeremy said matter-of-factly. It was the game they all played—finding a person's colors and having either Aiden or Craw design their yarn. Craw was better with texture, it was true, but Aiden? Aiden was a true genius with color. His yarns were spectacular and original, and Jeremy had been knitting long enough now—and ordered from other people's stock, just to see—to be able to say that without bias. Between Aiden and Craw, they were well on the way to being a name—a brand people went to, every time they visited their local yarn store. Craw was even thinking of hiring a yarn rep, instead of just selling through catalogues. The business was growing, and Jeremy was proud to have been a part of that, even if it was only as muscle.

Aiden nodded. "Yeah," he said softly, and then cast Jeremy an inscrutable look. "But then, I'm still trying to find your colors."

Jeremy, who had gotten used to Aiden sitting on the end of his couch and fighting feet with him as they got comfy, and who had learned to sit next to him in the truck or in his living room without marking every breath he took or growing hard and aching *every* time he caught a nuance of young man, sweaty or clean, was suddenly very, very squirmy.

"You ought to be concentrating on someone who matters," he said automatically, and Aiden shook his head.

"Jesus, Jeremy. I spend more time at your place than I do at my folks'. Who is going to matter more than you?"

Jeremy almost said, "Craw?" right then, to get that out in the open, but the drum carder let out a sound like a wounded goat, and they suddenly had bigger fish to fry.

But the next morning, that whole thing sort of busted itself open, and Jeremy was left in a quandary.

Craw came in, muddled and embarrassed and tongue-tied and dear, trying to pretend like taking Ben the tenderfoot out to get his hardware supplies hadn't been a big banner moment in the life of someone who, Jeremy had often thought, could possibly be the world's most solitary man.

It sounded promising.

"Hey, Jer!" Aiden called, and Jeremy looked up from where he was running a hand-spun end through the machine to the spool. "Craw says it wasn't a date!"

Jeremy rolled his eyes. "Did you bring him a gift?" he asked, and Craw blinked. He looked distinctly guilty, so Jeremy laughed for him and crinkled his eyes at the corners. "Oh, so there *was* a gift. How about food?"

"Coffee," Craw grunted and fiddled with his machinery. The machinery was not really Craw's strongest asset in the millwork. Jeremy and Aiden did most of the work there, so when he came in to help, well, he was competent, but Jeremy could tell he was working really hard to be that way. And that didn't stop him from laughing at Craw's obvious evasion.

"Well, there was food, a gift, and you spent your time shopping. I'd say it was a date!" He grinned then, because it would have been great to know that Craw was out getting some—and hell, it might soften the guy's temper up a little too. Then he caught Aiden's suspicious squint and blushed.

"That's all we did last Saturday!" Aiden said, a little bit of surprise in his voice. "I thought *you* weren't gay!"

Jeremy widened his eyes because he'd heard the emphasis, subtle as it was. *You* weren't gay, as opposed to *Aiden*. Who apparently was. "Well, I didn't know you were!"

"God, what a dumbass!" Aiden shook his head, and his casual pose didn't stop Jeremy's heart from thundering in his ears. "Jesus, how can you give advice on two guys dating if you don't even know what two guys do if they're *not* on a date?"

He would have just stood there, looking helplessly at Aiden while the earth reformed beneath his feet, but Craw spoke up, apparently unaware that everything had changed.

"I want four hundred hanks, four hundred twenty yards," he said. "Make sure the roving stays consistent. It's for socks."

"We going to dye today?" Aiden asked, and Craw shrugged.

"Why not? You've got a plan?" he asked, and Aiden brought up a color scale sampler that he'd put together with pastels on a piece of nice artist's parchment.

They talked colors for a minute, and Jeremy tried to convince himself it hadn't happened. It had been easy—so easy—for the last two years, to pretend that perfection hadn't been sitting on his couch three nights a week, waiting for him to make a move. He'd wanted it—oh God, sometimes the urge to rest his hand on Aiden's calf or his knee or the back of his neck had just been overwhelming, but he hadn't. He hadn't. Because Aiden, there and happy, having shown up with pie and a movie, had been about the best thing to ever happen in Jeremy's life, ever. The thought of more than that... it was painful, because Jeremy would have to turn it down. "Maybe not quite so extreme on the dark end of it," Aiden murmured to himself. "It's sort of retro... if we keep it a little lighter here...."

But Aiden wasn't talking to Jeremy now, and he wasn't making eye contact. He was immersed in his dye work, in the designing that he did so well, and Jeremy took that for a good sign. Aiden wandered to his position at the spinner, staring at his color chart and murmuring to himself, and Jeremy gave him his space for a minute.

Craw issued some more orders about the stock they'd be making, and for a moment, he and Jeremy exchanged glances and then looked at Aiden. Whatever the boy (man—twenty now, he was a young man) came up with, it was going to be good.

Craw left and Jeremy decided that they could tease now, because it had been his imagination, right? He came over to Aiden's shoulder and started to wheedle. "Oh God, what kinds of rainbow wooly madness are the two of you going to put me through today? C'mon… lemme see the magic paper… c'mon, Aiden, you know you wanna let me see it!"

Aiden cast a sorrowful glance at him then, as Craw left the barn, and Jeremy subsided under the weight of that look.

"You didn't know about me?" he asked quietly.

"It was Craw," Jeremy said, and he realized that he must have gotten the habit of being honest, because that had come out exactly as he'd thought it. "I didn't know if it was hero worship or… or a crush. I never could figure it out. I figured once I did, it would be okay. I'd know."

Aiden blinked at him, and then, for the first time since Jeremy had met the boy, standing as confident as you please in the middle of all this dangerous machinery and complicated honest work, he backed away from something.

"Well, now you know. Come *on*, let's get this shit done! I've got class tomorrow, but I promised myself a movie at your place the day after that!"

Jeremy was happy then, like he could already taste the pies Aiden's mother sent. Aiden was gay, but it wasn't going to change them, and Jeremy could sit in quiet contentment, on the other side of the couch, for as long as Aiden wanted to come over for movies.

The next day, when Aiden was gone, Ben came in. Jeremy looked up from his work—he was manning dye vats since Aiden wasn't there to help with the machinery—and saw a sweet-looking man with hipster's stubble, curly brown hair, and sea green eyes. On top of his head was an even sweeter little hat with a rust-colored brim and a teal-colored crown, and if Jeremy had to guess he would have pegged it as Craw's work, because it was sturdy and rugged and practical. The man had his hands in his pockets and was looking around the barn with interest.

"Is Craw about?" he asked, and Jeremy shrugged.

"I think he's in the shop. You must be Ben."

Ben smiled. "I have no idea who you are. Craw's not great at conversation."

Jeremy laughed, tickled. "That he ain't. I'm Jeremy—don't mind me. I'm a hired hand, nothing more."

Ben nodded and wandered over to look at the hanks of wool drying on the racks. "How long have you worked here, 'hired hand'?"

"Oh, two and a half years or so," Jeremy said, not thinking about it because he was hefting a hank of wool out of the vat on a pole. He stopped suddenly, and it was a good thing the wool was dripping over the dye vats, because otherwise he would have made a right mess. "Wow. That's a good long time."

"Yeah," Ben agreed. "That sounds like it's got some permanence. So you'd know then."

"Know what?" Drip, drip, drip and *swing* and there went the hank on the drying rack. The first three times he'd done this, he'd dropped the hank on the ground and almost cried. Turned out, they got rinsed off in a few minutes anyway, so he shouldn't have worried.

"If Craw's seeing anybody," Ben asked, the corners of his mouth quirking like that should have been obvious.

Jeremy rolled his eyes. "He's seeing you, right?"

Ben's chuckle was dry. "He gave me a hat."

"Yeah, well, for Craw, that's like a declaration of intention. You want someone who skywrites, go to another town." Drip, drip, drip *swing*.

"So, how long do I have to wait for his next move?"

Jeremy all but giggled. "Well, I hope you're around for the spring thaw. In two and a half years, the closest thing I've heard to Craw talking about his personal life is when he told us he was gay."

"Yeah?" Jeremy looked up and saw that Ben was extraordinarily pretty, and his eyes were lit up with laughter. "How'd that go?"

Jeremy shook his head, remembering Aiden's small, pretty face—rounder then, because it was more than two years ago—as he'd fastened his brown-green eyes hungrily on Craw's face.

"Well, Aiden asked Craw why he wasn't ogling the waitresses in the steakhouse, and Craw replied, ''Cause I'm fuckin' gay, ya moron!', and there you go. Personal enlightenment, Rance Crawford style."

Ben giggled then, and Jeremy liked the sound. He could see how Craw had been so smitten, but, well, the guy wasn't Aiden.

"How'd you guys take that?" he asked, and Jeremy shrugged and went back to fishing the last hank out of the vat.

"I think Aiden was pleased, really. He had a bit of a crush on Craw back then." He laughed a little. "For about five minutes it gave the kid hope, but he might have gotten over it by now."

"How about you?" Ben asked, and Jeremy looked up and met his eyes. He knew why the fifth degree. Ben was interested—*very* interested, apparently—and he wanted to make sure he wasn't stepping on anybody's toes.

"Craw's a good man," Jeremy said, liking this honesty thing more now than maybe he ever had. "But he's not my type."

"So, Aiden?"

Jeremy looked up sharply. "Two and a half years," he said, a little wonder in his voice. "Two and a half years. I've known these people better than people I've known in my entire life. Why would you assume I'm gay?"

Ben shook his head. "Because you light up when you talk about them."

"I light up when I talk about Ariadne too," Jeremy said flatly, not liking this game anymore.

"It's Aiden, isn't it?"

"I'm way too old for him," Jeremy cautioned. He pulled his con man's smile from his toes, when what he really wanted to do was have a thoughtful conference with this stranger and confide in someone, as he hadn't maybe his entire life. "And I'm sure he'd tell you that I irritate the holy hell out of him, so maybe you'd better match elsewhere."

He grinned up at Ben, hoping to get the man to share in the joke, but Ben was looking thoughtfully at him instead. "I think I'll let you do that," he said quietly. "Now tell me what you're doing here. I'm really frickin' curious!"

Jeremy laughed and gave Ben a basic overview, and told him that sometimes they dyed the roving too, which is what they called "dyed in the wool," and how sometimes they sold roving for other people to spin.

"Why would I want to spin it myself?" Ben asked, unconsciously touching some dried hanks of dyed sock yarn. "You guys do such a good job of it!"

Jeremy grinned. "Here, let me show you." They had samples on hand, one spun by Ariadne and one spun by Craw, for when Craw opened the mill up for tours. "See here?" he asked, showing Craw's chain-plied and Ariadne's neat single. "This is the same roving, dyed the same way. How you spin it for use, that makes it a whole different yarn." Ben's eyes got really big, and Jeremy nodded appreciatively. Ariadne's yarn blended the different colors of the dyed roving subtly, gently, in one continuous color change. Craw's spinning made them clash more, put the sky blue with the magenta instead of having it fade into violet and then purple and then red.

Ben's grin was infectious—but then, so was Jeremy's, so they had a real good moment. "That's really cool," Ben said, impressed, and Jeremy nodded.

"I've always thought so myself. Did you want to see more of the mill?"

Ben's regret was honest. "I've got work to do." He sighed. "Besides—maybe Craw himself'll give me a tour. But, uhm, would Craw's people mind if I came back? Made myself at home a little? I do like this place, and I haven't even seen the store!"

Jeremy nodded sincerely. "Welcome to! Speaking as one of Craw's people, I can't see him not wanting you around."

Ben walked away, leaving Jeremy to work, and Jeremy thought that he couldn't wait to share the juicy details of the conversation with Aiden. The boy had been right—the new guy would provide plenty of entertainment over the long winter.

The next day, Aiden was unusually quiet. When Craw brought Ben in for a tour, he kept darting furtive glances from Ben to Craw when they weren't looking, so much so that he didn't notice when Craw got the trip with the drum carder mixed up with the trip Jeremy and Craw had taken the year before to get the small knitting loom that they'd used to capitalize on the "knit-from-the-scarf" thing that had been going on lately.

But Jeremy had never been one to quibble over details. He'd tried to sweeten the pot on that trip as well, although he'd done so to Craw's complete horror. However, it made a good story, and it made Ben laugh when he said it, and making Ben laugh helped Craw.

"Yeah, and I had to flirt with the owner's daughter too!" he cracked, and suddenly Aiden's furtive looking between Craw and Ben stopped, and Jeremy had the boy's complete attention.

"I thought you said you slept with her!" he snapped, and Jeremy knew, in that moment, that they weren't talking about the trip with Craw. They were talking about the trip two years ago, when Jeremy had let Aiden think that because it was easier than explaining about going honest.

Well, that hadn't been particularly honest of him, had it?

"I just said that to make you jealous," he said with a smirk, because he wanted to see Aiden laugh.

Aiden rolled his eyes, which was just as good.

"Yeah, *that'll* work," he said, and then he and Jeremy walked outside to go start rounding up the sheep.

"I did, you know," Jeremy said mildly as they walked, and Aiden shook his head in exasperation.

"God, Jeremy, you know, it would really fucking help things if you, just once, gave a straight answer to something."

"Yeah, fine, shoot!"

"Okay. Have you ever had a girlfriend?"

Oh, *that* was easy. "No. Next answer."

"Have you ever had a boyfriend?"

Also easy. "No. Next answer."

Aiden's eyes were narrowed. "Okay, when was the last time you were with someone?"

Oh *ouch*. Talk about making a guy feel old. "Nearly five years ago. The night before my daddy was killed."

Aiden sucked in a breath, and for a moment, Jeremy thought maybe that reference alone would let him off the hook. But not with Aiden, that was for sure. The boy was tenacious.

"What happened?"

Jeremy pulled out the memory again, of Gianni's shy smile, the hesitant kiss. It was faded now, and after spending two and a half years in the company of good people, decent people, he'd come to realize that there was so much more to love and affection than just the smile and the kiss. But there'd been loyalty there, and risk, and he wasn't just going to throw that away.

"A blowjob," he said nostalgically, "and a kiss. And someone who saved my life just by not telling anyone I was there."

Aiden reached out then and grabbed his hand as they were walking. Jeremy was going to startle, going to protest, but he looked to his side and in spite of the firmness of his hand in Aiden's, Aiden was looking out to the field with the sheep.

It was like their joined hands weren't really happening.

Oh, but they were. And Jeremy's heart was pounding, and his breath was coming quick, and his skin was going hot and cold in the late October afternoon. Suddenly Gianni's face faded from his mind, and all that was left were their fingers, twining together, and the knowledge that even when Aiden let go, he'd still be at Jeremy's place that night with a movie and a snack.

That knowledge alone made the touch of their fingers delirious and golden, like the autumn sunlight on the fields. It was something Jeremy wanted to soak in, wanted to grip to his chest or put in his little vault under his bed. But he couldn't. All he could do was hold Aiden's hand and feel the touch of Aiden's thumb across the back of his knuckles.

They separated when it was time, but Jeremy realized when they started yelling at the sheep to come into the barn that the whole time their hands had been touching, he hadn't felt the need to talk, not once.

Chapter 6
Hello, Stranger

AIDEN SHOWED up on Jeremy's doorstep as promised, with fresh-baked chocolate-chip cookies, a half-gallon of chocolate milk, and caramel lattes. It was like the trifecta of Jeremy's favorite things, and he was putting the milk away so they could have it later with the cookies, saying, "What's the special occasion, boy—I'm feeling spoiled!" when he realized that Aiden had moved in between the two counters that made up his kitchenette. Jeremy was trapped, his back against the refrigerator, a counter on either side, and Aiden's boyish young face, with its short, square, earnest jaw and brown-green eyes, was right there.

"Uhm, we're gonna miss the start of the show—"

"We're watching a movie. I brought it, remember?"

"Oh yeah, well, you know, let's go sit down before the lattes cool down, they sure do smell good from here—"

Aiden kissed him. Jeremy was so stunned he just stood there, with his eyes wide open and his lips stiff as boards, and then he heard Aiden's exasperated sigh and that made him smile a little, made his mouth relax, and Aiden's lips just felt so good, he closed his eyes.

Aiden's mouth on his was warm, and open, and wet, and unashamedly sensual. Jeremy leaned against the refrigerator and just let the boy do what he was doing, because it was soft, and sweet, and oh so beautiful. His tongue swept in and Jeremy had to suck on it a little because it tasted so good, and Aiden's hands came up to frame Jeremy's face, holding him steady, holding him still until Aiden was done with the kiss. He pulled back and gave Jeremy a chance to open his eyes.

"What was that?" Jeremy asked, breathless and wounded.

"That was me telling you I would really rather you not flirt with anyone else, girl or boy, if you don't mean it."

Jeremy found himself nodding dumbly. Okay. Fine. God, his whole face was tingling. His world was exploding. All the reasons he'd been feeding himself for the last two and a half years for why this would never happen were disappearing like hot breath in the cold.

"Is that all?" he asked.

Aiden nodded, thinking carefully. "For now," he said. "I don't want to spook you."

Jeremy was going to argue, like they did, about how he didn't spook easily, but Aiden knew him. *Knew* him. Aiden knew that he was as skittish as one of Craw's bunnies about certain things. "You're too young for me," he said, because honesty had been working for him so far. "And you're still mooning after Craw."

Aiden's smile was all confidence, and since that had been one of the things that had blinded Jeremy about him in the first place, Jeremy couldn't even argue. "Jeremy, as far as I can tell, you're one blowjob up on me in real emotional experience here. Unless you can prove you ever fell in love, I say we're even on the age thing. And as for Craw? He's set his cap for Ben, and I'm not stepping in on that."

Jeremy didn't like being second, he realized, not even to Craw. The little bit of hurt there allowed him to push past Aiden with what even he realized was a pout. "You don't even know if I'm gay," he said, and he didn't miss Aiden's rolled eyes.

"Yeah, Jeremy. *That's* the thing that's in doubt."

Jeremy scowled at him, but when they both took their coffees to the couch, Aiden sat deliberately on Jeremy's end, swung one leg up and set the other leg on the floor. He met Jeremy's eyes and said, "Sit here," patting the cushion between his legs.

Jeremy opened his mouth and closed it and tried to think of the reasons he shouldn't, but he'd exhausted all his ammo in the last round. He sat obediently, and Aiden pulled him against his chest, which had filled out in the last two and a half years. Now, it was plenty wide enough to support Jeremy's slight, wiry body as they sat and watched *You've Got Mail*, perhaps the sappiest movie Jeremy had ever seen, but one of his favorites. It must have been. Aiden had brought it over a zillion times.

It seemed sparklier this time. Aiden's arm was wrapped around his shoulders, and his chest was beneath Jeremy's cheek. Jeremy closed his eyes at one point so he could see if he could hear Aiden's heartbeat against his ear, but Aiden still had a sweater on, and that wasn't going to happen. It was okay, he figured dreamily, as the final kiss happened on the screen. This was as good as he reckoned it got. Aiden didn't seem to want to move as the credits wrapped up, and Jeremy thought it was okay then, that he just lay there, his head on Aiden's chest. It wasn't anything irrevocable, nothing they couldn't take back. It wasn't a promise or a trap, wasn't the police knocking at the door, wasn't the "I love you" that had been itching at Jeremy's skin since pretty much the trip to Pennsylvania. It was just them, Aiden's hand rubbing slow circles between his shoulder blades, that lovely song about rainbows playing in the background.

Then Aiden spoke softly. "Jeremy?"

Jeremy startled and started to clamber up. "I'm sorry, I'll get off you."

"Jeremy." Aiden's arms tightened around his shoulders, keeping him in place.

"You gotta let me go!" Jeremy laughed, trying not to let on that he was a little alarmed.

"Just look at me," Aiden said softly. "That's all."

So Jeremy tilted his face up and looked.

"What do you see?"

Jeremy smiled softly. "The boy who knew everything when I got here," he said, remembering that dazzling confidence, the way Aiden had known and loved the mill with all his heart, and had wanted to add to it, putting his stamp on everything it did.

"I'm not a boy anymore," he said seriously, with that same dazzling confidence.

Jeremy looked carefully. His face was carved into tender lines, but it wasn't a boy's face any longer. He would be twenty-one this winter, and Jeremy tried to remember what he'd been doing at twenty-one. When the answer turned out pretending to be sixteen on Monday and a college student on Tuesday, he thought that maybe Aiden's twenty-one was a mite older than Jeremy's had been. Aiden's twenty-one didn't have any make-believe in it. He simply was.

"No," Jeremy said softly. "No, you're not."

Aiden's hand came up to his cheek, and he bent his head down, but it was clear that if Jeremy wanted in on this kiss, he was going to have to push himself up into it. The thought of another breathless kiss left him aching with arousal, a thing he'd almost forgotten about in the last five years, and he had a vision of kissing Aiden hard, grinding up against him, soothing that ache at his groin.

And just like that, his heart hammered like a startled rabbit's and he rolled off the couch.

Aiden shook his head and laughed shortly. "You're not going to make this easy on me, are you?"

Jeremy looked wildly around, and for a moment was tempted to run into his room and fetch his floor safe and take off. Of all things, it was his curtains that kept him off the road. Ariadne had been experimenting with cotton yarn and lace, and she'd starched him up a couple of lace valances for his kitchen curtains. His eyes settled on those and he found that his breath started to still.

In the meantime, Aiden had gotten up off the couch and grabbed him by the shoulder. "You couldn't run anyway," he murmured quietly. "I happen to know you promised Ariadne you'd be here to help with the baby. Don't worry." He squeezed Jeremy's shoulder when Jeremy startled again. "I'm leaving. I've got class tomorrow; you're safe. But I'll see you at work the next day, and we're not going to pretend this never happened. And I'm coming over in the evening, and television is your choice. I've got to do homework anyway."

"Then why—"

"'Cause you're my reward, Jeremy. I've been a good boy, growing up. I've done all the right things, and I've loved doing them. And maybe not at first—maybe it took a little time, even, practically a whole goddamned week—but you became the person I most looked forward to in the world. And I need you to get used to me here in your space, so just know that, okay?"

Jeremy was looking at him helplessly now, his vision a little swimmy, his heartbeat receding as he tried to come up with something to say, something honest, that would let Aiden know that this was a horribly stupid thing for such a smart boy to want.

But that was the problem with being an uneducated con man. When you wanted those words, and you needed them honest, that was when they were most likely to desert you. It didn't matter. Aiden kissed his cheek sweetly and then let himself out, and Jeremy was left, his cock throbbing and his head swimming, and so lost for words or a con or a plan or a reason to run that it was all he could do to sit trembling on his couch, close his eyes, and remember the way Aiden's mouth had felt on his.

AIDEN WAS good to his word—not that he'd ever *not* been good to his word, that Jeremy remembered. Two days later, they worked together like they had for the last few years, bickering good-naturedly, talking in code when they weren't bickering. They were good at reading each other's minds by now, and their day went by pretty nicely. Ariadne made them come up into Craw's kitchen for lunch, because it was getting a little nippy to be eating outside toward October, and Rance was watching the shop while she sat down and ate. They ate soup and chatted genially, asking about Ariadne's pregnancy, which they were all concerned about, making sure she stayed off her feet, and generally being the family they'd grown into over the years.

Then, as Ariadne was sitting down to her soup, Aiden told the first lie Jeremy had ever heard him utter, and he was both thrilled and appalled. It happened for the strangest thing too. Ariadne wanted to come over to see a movie.

"So, you two," she said with a small smile, "Rory's out of town tonight, and Craw asked me if I wanted to go to the movie playing at the old warehouse." It was a community theater—they charged three dollars admission and you sat on foldout seats and ate really cheap popcorn. Mostly an event to socialize, really; they ran a different movie every week. "If you don't invite me over to your place, Jeremy, I'm going to have to go see *The Expendables*. Again."

Jeremy was about to open his mouth and say that she was welcome like she always was, but Aiden jumped in and said, "I'm sorry, Ariadne. My mom is trying out her cooking on Jeremy tonight. He promised he'd come visit so he could play guinea pig."

Jeremy gaped at him. He just stood at Craw's old stove, holding the teapot because Ariadne did love her tea, and stared at Aiden with an open mouth as that boy done opened his mouth and told the world's most prodigious whopper.

Ariadne sighed in disappointment and concentrated on her soup and home-baked bread. "That's too bad," she said. "Well, keep next movie week open for me, would you, Jeremy? Rory's got another show next week, and God knows what they're going to be showing then!"

Jeremy nodded and managed to put the teakettle down before he scalded himself, then he and Aiden sat down to eat themselves. But as soon as Ariadne went back to the store and they were alone, cleaning up, Jeremy looked at Aiden like he'd just turned around and kicked a baby bunny.

"What in the hell was that?" he asked. "She's our *friend*, and we just told her a—"

"A social lie," Aiden said, setting the dirty dishes down at the sink without flinching. "It's something two people do when they want to be alone but they don't want the world to know they want to be alone."

"But... but *why*?" Jeremy started to run the water. Together, they'd have this taken care of in no time. "Why couldn't we just let her come over?"

Aiden closed his eyes and pinched the bridge of his nose. "Because, Jeremy. Because I need you to not take any excuse to run, and I need you to see that I'm safe, and I need you to see that it's just me. It's not because we're family, and it's not because I don't have other offers, because I do, and it's not because Rance has Ben now, because it wasn't really Craw in the first place. Craw was hero worship. You are my person. You need to know that. So we're going to start with me, in your home, doing my homework while you do something quiet, and you remember that we don't even have to do anything to make each other happy."

Jeremy scowled at him. "God, you talk a lot," he muttered, and Aiden reached an arm around his waist and kissed his cheek.

"Yes, sweetpea, and you love me for it."

"Oh shut up!"

"You first!"

"I'm going to make the alpacas kick you!"

"The alpacas are too lazy to kick anyone!" Aiden laughed then, and Jeremy shot back, "No, they just don't care enough about you to hurt you," but he was laughing too. This was their code, and Aiden was right. It made him comfortable.

That boy was more of a surprise every day.

AIDEN DIDN'T do homework *all* night. He closed up his books around nine thirty and yawned and stretched. Jeremy looked up from the couch—and the book in his hand—and smiled a little. "All done and ready to go home?"

Aiden snorted. "Done, yes, but not ready to go home." He went to the refrigerator and poured a glass of chocolate milk, then cut himself a slice of pie. "You want one?"

Jeremy smiled a little. Chocolate cream pie. Aiden's mama was a wonder. He wasn't sure what Aiden had said to her about him not coming to eat, but the woman sure did like to spoil him with sweets. He enjoyed talking to her when she visited the mill, and Aiden's brothers and sisters too. In fact, a little part of him was starting to whisper that maybe, just maybe, he could sit down at their table and not be embarrassed at all.

"Yes, thank you," he said, starting to stand up.

"No, stay there," Aiden told him, and circled the couch to set the pie on the big wooden coffee table. He came back with the chocolate milk, and Jeremy was already blushing from the tending to. Something occurred to him then, something he dearly wanted to ask but wasn't sure if he could.

He picked up his pie and looked at it thoughtfully before taking a bite.

"What does your mama think about all the time you spend here," he said, wondering.

"Oh, she knows," Aiden said with a smile and a giant mouthful of chocolate and whipped cream. "I told her in high school that I was gay and that I wanted you. She cried a little, told my dad while they thought I was asleep. They said whatever they needed to that let them hug me in the morning, and let me tell anyone else who cared to know. She thought you could use some raising up first, so she started baking you pies since you wouldn't come by. What?"

Jeremy shook his head a couple of times and took a carefully measured bite of pie.

"Your world is awfully pretty to be inviting me into it," he said when he'd finished. His brain had damned near screeched to a halt and the wheels on his ore cart were spinning in shock.

"What do you think your father would have done?" Aiden asked softly, and Jeremy laughed a little, but not in a nice way.

"He didn't care," Jeremy said thoughtfully, remembering Oscar's complete indifference to anything Jeremy had wanted. "He told me that if I could stand to kiss a boy as well as a girl, it made it easier to sweeten the pot. I never told him which one I liked better, and he never asked if maybe I didn't want to kiss people just to get their money." Jeremy took another bite, lost in giving words to a thing he hadn't spoken of in a long time. "He liked my looks," he said speculatively. "I mean, when I was a teenager, he made me take real good care of my skin and my teeth because he said those were my moneymakers right there. Told me to always keep my hair slicked back—said it looked professional." Jeremy took another bite, but savored this one, because the memories had grown less bitter as they'd grown more distant. "I don't know. Maybe I should stop doing that. I don't think it's me anymore."

Aiden scooted a little closer to him and reached his hand up to the back of Jeremy's neck and knotted his fingers in the hair that fell across his collar. It was straight and brown, and Jeremy usually put some product in it to make it stay slick. "Yeah," Aiden said, thoughtfully. "I think it would feel better under my fingers if it wasn't so gooped up. Feel free to leave that part of your childhood behind."

Jeremy laughed bitterly. "Boy, if you only knew how much of it I've left behind already."

Aiden's caress on the back of his neck never stopped. "So tell me," he said quietly, and no one was more surprised than Jeremy when he did.

He started with the small stuff, sleeping in cheap motel rooms his whole life, never knowing when or where the next meal was coming. He moved on to the hard stuff—being cute for woman after woman who thought she was getting a family but was getting fleeced instead. He moved on to the crap things he'd done, seducing the Miss Lonelyhearts, kiting checks, or selling shit that wasn't there. He talked about never feeling close to anyone, and being pretty sure his father thought he was a commodity instead of a son. By the time he was done talking, Aiden had taken his pie plate out of his hands and pulled him back down on top of Aiden's chest, where he was starting to feel more and more comfortable.

"So," Jeremy finished, feeling stupid and talked out and fragile, "there you go. Life of a dyed-in-the-wool con man."

"It's not just how you're dyed," Aiden said above him, dropping a kiss in his hair. "It's the sort of fiber you're made of, and how you spin yourself. And there's always overdyeing and how you're knit."

Jeremy chuckled. "That there is one analogy I can't ever use again," he said, his brain boggling with following it through.

"No." Aiden nuzzled him then, and Jeremy was feeling raw enough to turn his head and tilt it back for a kiss. "You go ahead and use it. You made yourself into something fine and sturdy, Jeremy. It doesn't matter what you were made to be when you didn't have a choice, you're a good man now."

Oh God. No. No no no no…. He tried to scramble up, but Aiden wouldn't let him. That boy wrapped his arms around Jeremy's shoulders and used his leg over Jeremy's thighs to make him sit right there.

"Don't go," he whispered. "It's okay. Whatever you gotta feel, you feel it right here."

And it was too late anyway. His face was wet and his breath was shaking and he thought maybe the last time he'd done this he'd been about seven years old and Oscar had thrown him some gauze and told him to be quiet because he was on the phone. Jeremy had gone into the bathroom and cried, because the kids who had taken him out had been bigger and scarier, and Jeremy had fought good but he'd wanted some reassurance and hadn't gotten any. And he'd learned to do without, right down to the morning after Oscar had been killed and he'd realized that Oscar had loved him just enough to keep him safe.

And now someone beautiful and golden and perfect was holding him and telling him it was going to be all right, and he couldn't do anything but cry.

AIDEN SPENT the night in his bed, both of them in T-shirts and sweats, and the fact that Jeremy had a spare pair of sweats to lend someone was as much a sign that his life had changed as anything else, he guessed.

They didn't say much, but Aiden called his mom and said he was crashing on Jeremy's couch, and Jeremy thought that might have been the second lie he'd ever heard the boy utter.

"I'm a bad influence," he mumbled as they were falling asleep. Aiden had scooted close enough for them to touch, but seemed to know that Jeremy would not have appreciated being the little spoon, not tonight. It was an alien enough sensation to have someone in his bed.

"Yeah?"

"You don't ever lie," he murmured.

"Jeremy?"

"Yeah?"

"Tomorrow night, I'm going to go down on you. I'm going to take your cock in my mouth and I'm going to stroke it and cup your nuts in my hand and—"

"Aiden!" Jeremy sat up in bed and stared at him, truly shocked. His cock was also fully erect, just from the words, and he shivered, suddenly very much aware of what a void he'd existed in these last five years. He hadn't even wanted to dream of Aiden—the boy had been off limits, and thinking about him that way just hurt. He hadn't even wanted to try. And thinking of anyone else that way hadn't been honest, and God, you couldn't be just a little honest, at least Jeremy couldn't. He had to be honest all the way, and running away to Boulder to get laid had not been in that way! Kisses, and hugs, and cuddles on the couch, and suddenly dirty talk, and it had taken a while but his body—his *sexual* body—was finally coming to understand that the boy meant business, and it was going to get a workout soon. If his terrified rabbit heart would give it a chance, that is.

"I'm just being straight with you, Jeremy. I'm damn near twenty-one, and I'd like to relieve both of us of our virginity as soon as you're ready. But you know, as honest as I'm being with you, I'm not so excited about telling my mom that, okay? Can we accept that once you've been honest as a teenager, you get to tell social lies as an adult?"

Jeremy fell back in bed and curled up on his side, all the better to nurse his throbbing penis. "I'm thirty years old," he muttered, and Aiden gave up on the whole "give Jeremy his space" thing and curled up over his back, reaching down with his hand so that it passed under the elastic of Jeremy's boxer briefs.

Jeremy gasped, and Aiden murmured, "Only in years, Jer," before wrapping those long, battered, able fingers around his cock.

"Nungh...." Jeremy didn't even remember the last time *he'd* beaten off. But Aiden's hand, sure, confident, stroking along his shaft, up toward the head... oh God... talk about being aroused at the speed of sound! Jeremy was pulled back some more into Aiden's front, and he felt Aiden's own arousal at his backside. It didn't frighten him like maybe it should have—instead, he ground against it, and then forward into Aiden's hand and then back into Aiden's groin and then forward and... oh God. Aiden was playing with his crown, and his slit, and then grasping back to his base and....

Jeremy whined. "Aiden...."

Aiden gasped and ground up against him again. "Aiden, what?" he growled. "Aiden, faster? Aiden, harder? Aiden, can I grab your—"

"I'm *coming*!" Jeremy interrupted, and his whole body went hot/cold and convulsed, his vision washed white, and he let out a long whine as his cock spattered and wept over Aiden's clenching fist. At the first spurt, Aiden buried his face in Jeremy's neck and ground up some more on Jeremy's backside and then bit down hard on Jeremy's shoulder and groaned. Jeremy felt the spreading wetness then, seeping through Aiden's sweats and then through his own, and the part of him not reeling in shock and embarrassment was exulting with a terrible sort of joy.

And then the practical part of him, the part not overwhelmed, started to laugh weakly, even as Aiden pulled him closer and nuzzled his neck.

"Boy?"

"Jer?"

"You know I've got two pairs of sweats and you're wearing one, right?"

Aiden chuckled weakly. "I'll go get the washcloth; you get us some new boxers and the blanket from the couch. We're not *trying* to stay virgins here, Jeremy. I think we'll be all right."

It was. They cleaned up, both of them blushy and not meeting the other's eyes as they turned around and wiped themselves off, and then they put on Jeremy's last two pairs of clean boxers and climbed into bed. Jeremy set the alarm early so he could do laundry, and they settled in again. This time, Aiden made sure Jeremy was facing into his chest, and this time, he kissed him chastely on the mouth before they fell asleep.

Jeremy thought the sound of Aiden's breathing was like music.

AIDEN DROVE them to work the next day, and it was like it always was. They stopped for dessert coffee, bickered over whether scones or croissants were better, argued over whether it would be a rough winter or an easy one, and discussed whose beat-up car was going to die soonest. (Aiden's beat up car was a Ford; Jeremy's was a Toyota. Jeremy secretly thought Aiden was right—the Ford was just going to refuse to turn over one day, and be solid, still, cold, and dead. He offered to have a service for it when it happened, too, since Aiden had been driving it for nearly five years.)

The only thing that was different was that whenever they stopped, Aiden put his hand on Jeremy's knee and squeezed. He didn't take his eyes off the road, mind you, but he just touched, softly and possessively, and not long enough to make Jeremy uncomfortable.

Jeremy almost jumped out of the car every time he did it—but less and less far.

When they were driving up to Craw's, though, Jeremy looked up at the sky and gasped. Craw's place was in the western part of the valley, tucked into the mountains that made up the sides of the bowl, and as such, it got the sun the latest. The sky above Crawford's place was just barely touched with dazzling sun, and there was a little bit of gold in it, and the solid suggestion of that heartbreak blue color that was always the October sky. There were also wisps of darkness, of dark purple, the suggestion of black and even dark green.

"Now *that*," Jeremy said, "is your color. It's perfect. It's like that hat I first made you—that's why I started knitting it for you. It was *that exact* color."

Aiden looked at the sky and then looked at Jeremy as he pulled the car into the icy shade next to the barn. "That color?" he said, his voice holding hints that there was more in his head than Jeremy might suspect. Well, the boy was smart—always had been smarter than Jeremy—so that was to be expected. "I thought you didn't do the color thing."

It was true. Jeremy had no talent for designing colorways or yarns, but he was pretty good at picking out the right one for the right person. "Yeah," he said, still looking up at the sky. "I don't make the colors, but that one—it's you. It's gorgeous and golden, and just a little bit dark. It's awesome."

He stopped self-consciously, aware that he'd just given away a whole lot of himself, just looking at the sky.

"Sorry about the dark thing," he said, putting his hand on the door, but Aiden stopped him with a hand under his chin.

"No, I like it," Aiden said quietly, still thinking. "I do. Nobody else saw that in me—you did. And you still love me."

Jeremy's eyes got really big, and he lunged out of the car quickly enough to almost skid on the icy gravel under the car. He didn't say anything else about the color of the sky for the rest of the day, and Aiden didn't either.

Chapter 7
Hidden Cache of Dreams

EVERY DAY they watched as Ben and Craw did a delicate courting dance of knitting and visits, where success was counted by the rising joules of heat in their eyes. It got to the point where Ariadne came in to talk to the two of them when Ben and Craw were in the shop because, in her words, "That much sexual tension makes me want to hump a phone pole, and that's just not attractive in a pregnant woman."

Every night, whether they saw each other or not, they grew a little closer. On the nights when Aiden was at Jeremy's—and they were together often enough that he'd started to leave clothes there, including lots of pajama bottoms and a pair of slippers—that closeness was a frenzied, sloppy delight of the physical and emotional that scared Jeremy as much as it exhilarated him.

The night he took Aiden into his mouth for the first time was amazing. Aiden's flesh was hard, and large, and the taste of his skin all at once made Jeremy spurt precome into his own shorts. Aiden's crown was wider than his base, and Jeremy thought that was *wonderful*, wonderful enough to lick him, repeatedly, from the base to the end before taking the whole of him into a careful mouth. Aiden tried to warn him, but Jeremy didn't care. He was dying for Aiden's come in his mouth, he was *dying* to taste him, to have that sensual trust, something he'd never had before, because it was always marks blowing him and never the other way around.

His lips were sloppy with spit and Aiden's clenching hands were tight in his (productless) hair and he was damned near humping the mattress, he wanted everything so bad. He knew his ass was clenching, begging for something he'd never had and never given, and Aiden's groan above him as he spent, salty and thick, into Jeremy's throat made his stomach clench hard enough to cramp as Jeremy saw stars too, and came.

When he was done, Aiden reached down and dragged him up so they could look eye-to-eye. He pushed Jeremy's hair back from his face and kissed his sloppy mouth, wiping the corner of it with his thumb.

Something in his eyes was... was young and dazed, and Jeremy looked down in a fit of shyness. "What?" he asked defensively, and Aiden nuzzled his forehead.

"You got all shy," Aiden said softly. "It was sweet."

Jeremy buried his face into his pillow. "Well, it was my first blowjob on the giving end. I was hoping I did okay."

Aiden pulled him close, wet sweats and all. "You did great, Jer. Sometimes, I just forget I'm your first in so many ways."

Jeremy grunted then, reluctant to say how many ways, but Aiden wasn't having any of that. "What?" he asked, and Jeremy shrugged.

"There's lots I ain't done," he said, and Aiden nodded.

"I'm starting to guess that," he said. "You know that's where we're heading when you're ready, right?"

And suddenly Jeremy was not ready, not ready at all. He rolled out of bed then and ran to the bathroom for a cloth. He came back and spent an assiduous moment wiping Aiden down before pulling up his sweats, and then he changed his own.

He was in the middle of pulling up a new pair of boxers and throwing his sweats in the hamper when suddenly Aiden stood right there, looking at him gently.

"What?"

And Jeremy was still too raw to tell the social lie. "If you really did still love Craw, it would gut me," he said, and Aiden nodded, then swallowed.

"I don't love Craw," he said quietly. "Craw thinks my color is the summer sky—he doesn't think it's all the dark things you see and still love. I knew that, you see, even before I talked to him the other day. Me and Craw, it was only ever hero worship—and it cut both ways. But the fact that you'd say that, right now? That there's your rabbit talking, Jeremy, and you need to calm him down." Aiden shook his head. "If you rabbit on me now, I'm the one who's going to be lying down, bleeding, you understand?"

Jeremy looked at him, stricken. "Oh no," he said, horrified. "You told *Craw*?"

Aiden grunted. "I told him I didn't think you were gay, and the fact that he bought *that* whopper shows that he doesn't know me at all."

But Jeremy was too distraught over the other thing he said, the scary thing, to pay any attention to that. "You never shoulda bet on me, Aiden. I told you, I'm a pig in a poke, I'm a bad bet—I'm a check on an empty bank account and a 'good Samaritan' and...." Jeremy couldn't catch his breath, and Aiden caught him under the arm and helped him sit down while he hyperventilated on Aiden's shoulder for a few minutes. Eventually, his breathing calmed, and Aiden rocked him softly until he was ready to lie down and sleep.

They woke up early, because it was Jeremy's turn to drive the next day, and he needed gas. While Aiden propped himself up on his elbow in the bed, he watched as Jeremy pulled out the floor safe and opened it. Jeremy didn't worry about Aiden knowing the combination or where all his money was, but he did try, very hard, not to let Aiden see what else was in that safe.

Unfortunately, there were so many pairs of them (as well as the occasional hat) that Aiden couldn't help but see them when three or four popped out.

"Omigod," Aiden spat out, rolling out of bed like the little kid Jeremy was starting to doubt he had ever been. "Jeremy, you keep them in your *safe?*"

Jeremy grunted and pulled out a little packet of cash and then shoved the escaping mittens back into the safe and shut the door. "Where else do you expect me to keep them?" he asked, wishing he'd waited until Aiden was in the bathroom.

"*On your hands!*" Aiden cried, standing up and putting his hands on his hips and then at his sides and then on his hips, like he couldn't decide what to do with them at all. "Jeremy, don't you get that whole 'knit for each other' thing? I wear your stuff *all the time!*"

Jeremy nodded, gratified. "Yeah, you do. That makes me really proud."

"Then why are you putting what I made you in a floor safe?"

"Because it's special," Jeremy said, completely confused. "Where else would I put stuff that's special to me?"

Aiden stopped in the middle of Jeremy's room and ran his hands through his messy, curly hair. "Don't you see?" he said, and he sounded hurt and Jeremy would do anything, anything, to take away the hurt. "You put that stuff in there, and you don't have any faith that there's going to be more."

Jeremy froze, opening his mouth and shutting it and then blinking really hard. No more? Aiden wouldn't be making him another pair at Thanksgiving, and one at Christmas? This would be their third Christmas—last year's pair had been thrummed, which meant there was undyed lamb's wool knitted on the inside of the coarsely knit mittens to keep his hands warm in the bitterest of cold. "Of course there's going to be more," he said softly, and Aiden sighed.

"Okay then, open the safe."

Jeremy gaped.

"You heard me. Open the safe. Open it."

Jeremy had a moment to say "Don't boss me around...," but he trailed off because Aiden was looking at him implacably, and he found himself on his knees, doing the combination again. Aiden grunted, rooting through the safe until he came back with the very first pair he'd ever given Jeremy, the kind without the fingers on the top, so it made it easy to work but kept you warm in the late fall.

"God, Jeremy," Aiden muttered. "I've watched you go without for the last three years and thought you were at least thinking of wearing them. It's like a kick in the 'nads to find them all in here."

Aiden sounded sincere, and Jeremy reached out that same timid finger to pet them. "They were just so nice," he said apologetically. "I didn't want to ruin them."

Aiden shook his head and took the first mitten in one hand and Jeremy's unresisting, work-hardened hand in the other. (Daddy had always told him to moisturize and make sure his hands were businessman's hands, but Jeremy's hands had calluses and blisters after his first month at Craw's. Ladylike con man's hands were the first thing to go.) With rough movements—and shaking fingers—Aiden slid first one mitten and then the other over Jeremy's hands.

"You wear them," Aiden said, his voice gruff. He wouldn't look at Jeremy, he was so upset. "I know you're going to go shower, and I want them on your hands again before we leave the apartment, you hear me?"

Jeremy closed his eyes. One pair. What could one pair hurt? It was like when he spent the money on the car. He'd earned more. He had enough of a cache; he could maybe wear one pair.

"Okay," he said, and was unprepared for Aiden to roughly palm the back of his head and haul him in for a kiss.

Aiden broke off and shook his head again, his eyes bright and shiny. "You will gut me yet, Jeremy no-last-name. For all you're being careful, you will rip out my innards, and you won't even come back to shoot me and make it better."

Jeremy's eyes got big at that. "I don't want to hurt you, ever," he swore, and Aiden grimaced.

"Wear my gifts, asshole. Just wear them." And then he stood up and shooed Jeremy into the shower.

SO THEY reached equilibrium, and they might have stayed that way, Aiden spending three or four nights a week at his place, neither of them talking about the increasingly passionate, very adult relationship that took place behind the closed doors of Jeremy's little apartment. But then there was that other thing. There was Ben and that other thing, and Ben was good, because he made Craw happy, but the other thing was a test, and Jeremy was just lucky he passed.

Thanksgiving arrived, and Jeremy and Aiden arrived at Craw's place with three dishes—one a pie from Aiden's mother, who, apparently, had spoken sternly to Aiden about bringing Jeremy by soon, and Jeremy felt a little pressure around his chest and shoulders for that one, but no imminent anxiety attack, not just yet.

The other two were scalloped potatoes and sweet potato pie, both of them cooked at Jeremy's apartment, and they walked their dishes in carefully over the thin layer of new snow that coated the ground between the driveway and Craw's walkway.

Ben was there—and he had the sleepy, comfy look of a man who'd stayed the night, and Jeremy groaned, because Jeremy had predicted it would take until spring and Aiden had predicted it would happen before Christmas.

"All right, all right," Jeremy groused. "You win. You were right."

"Right about what?" Craw asked, taking the casserole dishes from them and setting them on the counter.

Jeremy rolled his eyes. "Right that you two finally got together before Christmas. I thought for sure it was going to be spring."

Ben laughed. "Yeah, I got tired of waiting. Stubborn bastard."

Craw scowled at him, but Ben just smiled, shining goodwill in the face of that lowered-brow threat, and Jeremy watched as the look on Craw's face went... well, slack and stupid was about the only thing he could think of. He looked at Aiden helplessly, but Aiden?

Aiden met his look with a misery of his own, and Jeremy realized that he was hurting the boy by his lack of commitment, sure he was, just like he'd sworn he'd never do.

So when Ben mentioned over dinner that if things went well (and the way he was looking at Craw like Craw had made the sun rise over the bowl valley, Jeremy really didn't have any doubts) he might be up for selling his grandmother's house—or at least renting it out, maybe even before spring, because he was moving his equipment into Craw's house before Christmas—Jeremy was feeling reckless.

"Excellent! That means I can move out of my tiny apartment!" he said, and he caught Aiden's eyes on him, burning and intense. Jeremy flushed and looked around to see if anyone else saw, but no one else did. They were all digging into the chow, and that was fine.

"You'd have to get a bank account first," Aiden challenged, and Jeremy swallowed.

"Yeah, well, I guess I'll have to decide on a last name before then," he said, and Ben looked at him.

"You don't have a last name?"

Jeremy flushed and realized that the bad part of expanding your family was that they all had to know who you were.

"Long story," Aiden deflected neatly. "I'm more interested in what it would take to get Jeremy in that house."

Ariadne looked up from her plate. She wasn't looking great, and Rory was worried at her side. Jeremy thought that it was a good thing it was winter, because the shop wasn't going to be getting a lot of business, and maybe they could let Ariadne rest at home a little more. God knew, they were all rooting for the baby.

"Probably nothing more than Jeremy's good will," she said with a smile, and Jeremy flushed under the look. "Ben and Craw made the place more than livable, but we'll have to see come spring."

Aiden grumbled, "I don't know if he'll make it to spring," and Jeremy winced. Craw and Ben were busy talking about what it would take to get Ben's computer equipment into the house—he was a computer engineering consultant, and there was a lot of equipment and a lot of power supply concerns—so they didn't hear.

But Ariadne, who was still looking pained, saw Jeremy's face and then looked back to Aiden's and closed her eyes.

None of the men would let her do dishes, so she told them all to leave her alone in the living room—but made sure Jeremy was on hand to tend to her.

"Rory's too nervous," she confessed, white faced. "We didn't want to tell Craw until after dinner, but we're flying out this evening to the hospital in Boulder. It's not going really well, and Rory's worried about me and I'm worried about the baby."

Jeremy gulped, alarmed. "Oh no—do you want me to get Craw?"

"I want you to tell me what's going on between you and Aiden before everybody starts herding around me like the sheep."

Jeremy paled. "We're... you know...." Oh God. How come Aiden, who had always been so honest, could tell such amazing whoppers, but Jeremy the fucking con man couldn't even come up with a little fib? "He's got a really strong will," Jeremy confessed to his hands. He was wearing the half-mitts—it was cold enough for full-on gloves outside, but neither one of them had mentioned the stash in his safe.

"So do you," Ariadne said quietly. "What do you want?"

Jeremy sighed. "To be what he needs."

"Well then, sweetie, you've already succeeded. You just have to accept that he loves you."

Jeremy fought off something really sappy and curled his lip. "It's hard not to accept when he's jamming it on top of your head like a felt hat."

Her spidery hand smacked his cheek lightly. "Well, good. Now that I know my boys are taken care of, I can have Rory take me to the hospital and we can take care of my baby, okay? Could you go get him? We're going to have to leave sooner than I thought."

Craw, Ben, Aiden, and Jeremy all bundled her carefully into the SUV and watched disconsolately as Rory drove her to the airport. Craw had called for a waiting emergency plane, and they already had the doctor on call, but still.

They loved her, and they were worried.

"I don't know if she has enough knitting," Craw said mournfully, and Ben patted his cheek.

"We can drive into Boulder tomorrow and bring her some, okay?"

"Yeah," Aiden said. "We'll take care of the critters."

Craw nodded. "That's kind of you. I think we should do that." He sighed and raked his hand through his curly auburn hair. "And while we're at it, we need to put ourselves on a delivery schedule. If she's out of the store, none of us will be up to making the drives out to drop off stuff at the local stores. Or to the post office, either. That'll be one less thing we have to worry about."

Ben perked up for no reason that Jeremy could fathom. "No more deliveries to Boulder?"

Craw's mouth twisted up at the side. "No, Ben. Not for me."

Ben's quiet smile could not be contained for a moment, and then they all sobered. "Excellent. Well, I don't know about you guys, but I'm in the mood for some pie."

AIDEN'S MAMA sure did know what she was doing when she made pie. That and the thought of the delivery guy to take over that one job were about the only things that could comfort them that night until Aiden and Jeremy were back in Jeremy's bed, their naked shins tangled together, their naked bodies heaving against each other.

They came, just from doing that, and Jeremy sighed into the hollow of Aiden's neck. "We're getting good at this," he remarked, and Aiden chuckled.

"We're awesome at this, Jeremy. What would you think about moving on to the other thing—at least giving it a try?"

Jeremy froze and tried very hard to say, "Yes. Yes, sure. That would be great." He couldn't, though, and Aiden's sigh was longsuffering indeed.

THE MONDAY after Thanksgiving always sucked. Jeremy hadn't known that as a con man, but he sure was feeling it now. He and Aiden had spent much of the weekend planning Christmas gifts for everybody else, and then looking at each other speculatively and trying to figure out what the other would want. They'd ended up in bed a lot, and had eaten a lot of pie, but Aiden had needed to go home Friday and Sunday night, and Jeremy had been forced to remember that it was a small town. Aiden wasn't going to get himself his own place because it wasn't practical. Apartments weren't a dime a dozen in Granby, and that's where Aiden wanted to live, and where Jeremy would prefer he stay.

No, if Aiden was going to stay at Jeremy's house all the time, they would have to make it official, and Jeremy would have to go over to Aiden's house and meet his mama and all those nice people, and they were going to have to tell Craw they'd been seeing each other almost since Ben had arrived on the scene. Craw was going to have to see that Aiden wasn't the boy he'd thought and that Jeremy was just as fragile and as needy as Aiden was.

And just as strong too.

But it was that last part Jeremy wasn't sure about, especially when the new delivery guy showed up to pick up a shipment bound for the east coast.

Aiden was there to greet the guy and sign the paperwork, and Jeremy heard them talking as he walked up with another big, light, unwieldy box. It was such a surprise, because he didn't recognize the voice, and he didn't recognize the back of the guy's head and the dark hair around the ears didn't ring any bells either.

Then Jeremy got up even with him. And dropped the box at his feet.

"Gianni," he said blankly, and Gianni's eyes got really big. He looked at Aiden and then took two steps forward and grabbed Jeremy's arm—not hard, just firm enough to pull Jeremy to the side of the truck like they were going to have a little conversation.

"Hey!" Aiden squawked, and Gianni glared at him.

"Kid, we're just having a fucking moment here, okay?"

"You be nice to him," Jeremy growled, and Gianni's eyes widened some more. Jeremy sighed. "Aiden? Me and…." He scanned Gianni's uniform—he was wearing his shirt over a thermal shirt, and his nametag was in plain sight. "Johnny, here, we're going to go have a little conversation. Don't worry about it." He had a thought and added, "I'm not going nowhere."

And that's what it took to settle Aiden. He stalked up to the porch, his entire posture hostile, and just glared at the two of them as they stood by the truck.

"Jesus, Jeremy," Gianni muttered. "You must be really off your game to just blurt out a guy's name like that."

Jeremy swallowed. "I ain't been in the game for five years," he said, and the number sort of blew him away. It had been more than five years ago that Gianni had saved his life. Gianni obviously recognized the timeline too.

"Really? You quit after that?"

Jeremy shrugged and looked at him. He was older than Jeremy by about five years, and there was some gray at his temples and some fine lines at the corners of his eyes. He was still handsome—damned handsome—but that moment, that breathless shyness between them that one night, that had been crushed under the heel of five very different years.

"My daddy was the only one keeping me in the game," he said truthfully. "So what about you?"

Gianni sighed. "*I* am a long story. Can I meet you somewhere? Jesus, Jeremy—at least you owe me a beer and an explanation for how you got here!"

Jeremy nodded. That was the truth. He did owe the man, and you didn't default on a debt like that. Or at least *Jeremy* didn't. Not now. Not after five years of honest.

"There's a bar in town, not far from my apartment," he said. "It's sort of a redneck place, but they serve good beer and garlic fries. I can be there at nine—the Monday night football crowd should be easing up by then. The Broncos aren't playing anyway—it's not gonna be that big a crowd as it is."

One corner of Gianni's mouth curled up. "I thought of you a lot," he said softly, and Jeremy looked up at the porch, where Aiden stood with his arms crossed and a wounded look on his face.

"Me too," Jeremy said. He stood back then and shook Gianni's hand. "I'll see you later." He pretended not to notice the stroke of a thumb on the inside of his wrist, but Aiden's scowl, even from the porch, told him that he knew something was up. Jeremy needed to find the words to tell him, because the image of Aiden, gutted and bleeding on the floor, was not going away, even if he knew it was just a figure of speech.

Chapter 8

Honest

"WHO WAS he?" Aiden asked, walking down the driveway, and Jeremy grimaced.

"I'm gonna go pet the bunnies," he said, turning abruptly to the barn. The alpacas looked on placidly as he walked past their pen and up to the rabbit hutch. Ben's bunnies were in an adjacent lean-to, and they looked up in anticipation when he entered. Sure enough, he had a pocketful of carrots—pure bunny candy, those, just like in the cartoons. But he reached in to his old friend—the Harvey bunny—who was getting long in the tooth but still seemed to like Jeremy.

Jeremy had learned that the trick with bunnies was to gentle them first, and then hold them firmly. Once they knew they couldn't get away, and that you weren't going to hurt them, they settled into your arms and submitted to all the affection you could heap on them. The trick, though, was to know when the bunny had had quite enough—that was the time to put them back in their cage. Aiden walked in when Harvey had just about had enough, and Jeremy very carefully put him back in his cage.

"Who was that guy?" Aiden asked, and Jeremy looked up at him and tightened his lips.

"Johnny the delivery guy," Jeremy said, but his voice crumpled with irony.

"I'm not shitting around here, Jeremy!"

Jeremy looked at him sadly. "I'm not either, Aiden. If I told you I think he's trying to keep a low profile because he's in danger, would you just believe that his name is Johnny for basic principle?"

Aiden blinked. "Danger?"

Jeremy looked at the bunnies and wondered if it was time he went back to his cage. Then Aiden came up behind him and wrapped his arms firmly around his waist and dug his chin into Jeremy's shoulder. Jeremy leaned back into his arms and melted a little. No. Not time yet.

He liked the safety here in Aiden's arms. If he needed to, there would be plenty of time to hit the road. He didn't want to now.

"Denver WITSEC is nearby," Jeremy said, thinking about how witness protection rumors and truths floated around the con world. His eyes were closed so he could pretend these weren't scary things he was dragging Aiden into. "The last time I saw Gianni was in Vegas."

Aiden let out a breath. "Jeremy, if I went in and used Craw's computer, would you want to give me a name to Google?"

Jeremy closed his eyes. "Carelli. Mario Carelli."

Jeremy fed the alpacas and mucked out their cages, then shoveled out the pile of bunny crap below the bunny cages, and then changed the straw and the bedding underneath the sheep. By the time he was done, Aiden came back in, some printed pages in his hands.

"Do you want to see?" he asked, and Jeremy shook his head.

"Would rather not. What do you have for me?"

"About two years ago, Mario Carelli's goon, one Gianni Caprisi, turned state's evidence against Carelli. Among other things he disclosed the whereabouts of a shallow grave with the bodies of six men that Caprisi said Carelli killed."

Jeremy grimaced. "Any of those names look familiar?"

Aiden nodded, and made sure Jeremy was looking him in the eyes. "One Oscar Norton. That's his real name, by the way."

Jeremy raised his eyebrows. "Norton. Not a bad name. I think I'll stick with Stillson, though. I got all the paperwork for that one."

Aiden looked at him sharply. "Is that all you got for me?"

Jeremy's smile was con man tight. "Yeah, Aiden. I think you maybe should go to your mama's tonight. I think I've got something to do."

"LET ME go with you," Aiden said for the hundredth time on the way back to Jeremy's apartment, and Jeremy said no for the thousandth.

"He wants you!" Aiden snapped, and Jeremy sighed.

"Yeah, I know he does." He looked down at his hands, wondering if he should feel shame for this or not. "Aiden, why do you think he covered for me when my daddy got shot?"

Aiden blinked and his hands flexed on the steering wheel—which was a really good idea, since the roads were icy enough for chains as it was.

"You said—"

"I wasn't lying!" Jeremy shouted, and he heard Aiden take a big breath, which meant you probably shouldn't yell at a man when he was driving in the snow.

"Okay then—"

"It was a blowjob! And a kiss!" Jeremy blurted, which, as much as anything, probably meant his con man days were long gone if he couldn't keep *that* information secret. "And I didn't.... I mean, I thought it might have been more, but he risked his life for me, okay? He risked his life for me, because he knew I was there, and he didn't say anything. That's why I'm pretty sure he's Johnny instead of Gianni, and *that's* why I need to meet him for a beer, you understand?"

He sat there, miserable, leaning his head against the frigid glass of the passenger's side window, until he felt something warm on his knee. He looked down, saw Aiden's hand, and took it.

"So he was a good guy," Aiden said softly.

"He was good," Jeremy confirmed. "He left me money in my bible, so I could catch the bus out of town. That's why I thought WITSEC, you understand?"

"Because he's a good guy."

"Yeah. And I owe him."

"Then why can't I—"

"What if he's not?" Jeremy said bluntly. "What if someone sees us?"

"What if you go running because you get it into your head it's what's best for me, and you won't have to do something scary like commit?"

Jeremy sighed and clenched his hand tighter. "Then you're better off with someone brave," he said quietly.

"Jeremy, I'm better off with you."

Jeremy closed his eyes. "Let me prove it, okay? This is my old mess, baby. Let me clean it up."

Aiden made his "I'm out of options" grunt, and then pulled his hand back to steer the car. When he swung into Jeremy's apartment parking lot, Jeremy went to get out, but he paused.

"C'mere," he said briefly, and Aiden looked at him in surprise and put the car into park and set the brake.

Jeremy knotted his fingers really tight in that curly light brown hair and looked into Aiden's brown-green eyes. "I'm still planning on honest," he said, and Aiden smiled a little.

"That's the best promise you could give," he said, and Jeremy pulled him in for a kiss. In spite of discussions of darkness, and knowing that Aiden liked to be bossy and Jeremy needed that like bunnies needed to be held tight in order to stay, there was nothing in that boy's kiss that didn't taste like fresh air, sunshine, snow, earth, and sky. It was as honest a thing as Jeremy had ever touched, and he thought he very possibly might die without the taste of it in his soul.

"See you Wednesday," he said, and Aiden nodded and let him go.

JEREMY WASN'T even sure the place had a name. If it did, it didn't register—Jeremy just knew it was a bar and grill, and he'd grown up around bars so he knew the type. Families ate there sometimes, and there was a pool table and a jukebox, and after ten, the people who were lonely congregated and played who-am-I-sleeping-with-now. When he walked in, the scarf Ariadne had knitted him last Christmas wrapped firmly around his neck and the jacket Craw had bought him that long-ago January buttoned up against the cold, he scanned the dark interior quickly.

It didn't take him long to see Gianni, back tucked into the corner of the room behind the bar. He was the only one there, and although he spotted Jeremy when Jeremy walked in, he didn't wave. He did smile, though, tentatively, when Jeremy walked up, and Jeremy gave him the same smile back.

Jeremy sat down across from him—even if they were having a rendezvous, he would have done that. This wasn't the type of town where you just macked on another guy without drawing attention to yourself. The waitress was on him in a hot second, and she smiled sweetly, remembering times when Jeremy and Aiden and sometimes Craw would come in.

"Soda?" she said, because Aiden wasn't quite old enough to drink yet, and that's all Jeremy had ever ordered in his presence.

"That'd be fine," he said, and winked at her. She was in her late thirties and had two kids, and although she didn't knit, her mother did and sometimes she brought the kids into the shop.

"Anything to eat, Jer?" she asked, and then looked at Gianni. "Or for your friend?"

"Hamburger would be great, Wendy—mushroom, Swiss, no mayo, lots of ketchup, and some garlic fries. I know it's late—can you come up with that?"

"For you? No problem." She looked pointedly at Gianni and Jeremy smiled at him encouragingly.

"The burgers are first rate," he said. "You can't get beef like this in Albuquerque."

Gianni nodded like Albuquerque was where they'd met and ordered one for himself. And a scotch.

Jeremy laughed softly as the waitress walked away. "That's a mite slick for these parts," he said softly. "Didn't them WITSEC people teach you how to blend in?"

Gianni grimaced. "You always were clever, Jeremy. And no. Nothing they've given me has helped me blend in. I still miss my fucking suit, and I miss my fucking wingtips, and I miss the fucking rentboys who would give it up for a slick hundred bucks. This delivery boy shit? That's no way to live."

Jeremy thought about it. "I could do that," he said thoughtfully. "Before we hired your company, the boy and I were driving out once a week. It wasn't no hardship, really. Talk to people, see different parts of the country. Craw and I went to New York City once to talk to a yarn rep from upstate New York. Actually saw Manhattan from across the river—I'd like to visit someday."

Gianni took a breath and looked at him. Tentatively he reached out with a finger and stroked the back of the half-glove that Jeremy was wearing, and Jeremy caught his breath.

He'd thought about getting something warmer out, and then thought about putting them all in a bag with the cash in case Gianni wasn't in WITSEC and had the mob on his tail. He'd thought about running to get Aiden to run with him and then had figured Aiden would be better off without him and thought about leaving a note. He thought about calling Craw and telling him everything and then thought about how Craw might freak the hell out on Ben and Ariadne and... and... oh God. What if he'd fucked up the lives of everyone he cared for, just by being him?

And he'd almost done it. Almost just grabbed the safe and rabbited out of there. But he looked at the safe and thought of all of the other knitted things he had—not just the gloves, which Aiden had turned into their own code, but the scarf he was wearing and the hat in his pocket, and the blanket on his bed.

He couldn't pack them all. They wouldn't fit into his car. But he *had* to have them. He had to. They were necessary for his existence. He couldn't be Jeremy—this Jeremy, the one who was honest—without them.

He'd looked mournfully at the safe, thinking that unless he had Aiden in there to keep knitting him things and holding him and keeping him from bounding away, he just didn't have enough to travel.

He'd left the safe on the bed, in the end, and had washed off his face and then put on his gloves and his scarf. He wasn't going to dress up for this. He wasn't going to do anything special. He was just going to go meet a friend for a drink and a meal.

Gianni was still petting the glove, but now with a couple of fingers and not just one. "Those are nice," he said, his voice rough. Jeremy looked up and saw those wide brown eyes, that tint of shyness, that light of desire, and he swallowed.

"My boyfriend made them for me," he said quietly, and Gianni's hand stilled. He sighed heavily and pulled his hand away.

"A boyfriend? Like, the whole world knows about you?"

Jeremy grimaced. Oh God—*now* he figured out why that would have been a good idea. "Not yet, but that's 'cause I'm... I'm scared a lot. You know. Two years in jail, and Vegas. I'm not brave—and this, it's going to hurt if it don't work out." He took a deep breath and tried to steady his quivering little rabbit heart. "Is it going to work out?" he asked. "Please tell me you're in WITSEC and not on the run. Please tell me you got people I can go to if the mob shows up looking for you."

Gianni nodded and pulled out a card. "Look, here. Anyone shows, you call these people. But…." He sighed. "Look. Man, I just got here. This is my third relocation in the last two years, and I think we *finally* got everyone under wraps. I told my handler that I saw you. Not who you were, just that you recognized me, and she asked if you were a danger. I said no. Please—that's all. Just… just let me be Johnny here, and I'll let you be Jeremy, and we can just… I don't know. Wave to each other on delivery days." Gianni looked down. "I would really love to see someone I knew who didn't want me dead."

Jeremy sighed. "What made you do it? I mean, that's pretty brave. I didn't do it. My daddy got his brains blown out, and I just stood there and waited 'til it was over."

Gianni shook his head. "You were smart, Jeremy. You did what you had to. See, that's why I liked you. You were smart. Not hard, but smart."

Wendy arrived with their hamburgers then, and they waited until she was gone before they tucked in. They were halfway through their burgers before Gianni spoke again, and the way he looked at his hamburger, Jeremy didn't think he'd be picking it up again.

"There was this rentboy," he said, his voice so low Jeremy almost couldn't hear him. "Sweet kid. Making his way through school. I started being his regular, then started letting him bunk at my place, made sure he was eatin' right, took care of him. He was a good kid. Corn fed, you know, like that kid where you work." Gianni blinked. "Boy, am I a schmuck. Boyfriend?" he asked, and Jeremy grimaced.

"Yeah." He hadn't wanted to bring Aiden's name into it.

"Well, isn't he precious."

"That's what you think. Boy's got a will of fucking iron. Anyway."

Gianni made a noise then. A hurt one. "Yeah, well, he was sleeping in my bedroom when Mario came over and started talking shop. The boy was so scared, and I don't even know how Mario heard him, but he dragged the kid out and asked what he was doing there." Gianni shook his head. "He said he was robbing the place. Can you believe that? Kid lied his ass off, gun to his head. So Mario don't know I'm a queer. I didn't tell him, you know? Didn't tell him that Mario'd fuckin' shoot me if I was queer, but he woulda. And the kid lied to

Mario and Mario… just fuckin' shot him. There in my apartment. Left the mess for me to clean up."

Gianni's voice was coming from a tight, grief-filled place, and Jeremy reached under the table and grabbed his hand, because he was a friend.

"So you decided to go straight," Jeremy said, and Gianni lost a few tears then.

"Yeah. Yeah. What did it for you?"

"Some mob goon told a lie that saved my life, and suddenly I couldn't kite a check to feed myself." Jeremy laughed a little, but it wasn't a nice sound. "Didn't stop me from getting busted. Just stopped me from getting out and doing it all over again."

Gianni took a deep breath and let it out shaky. "Is it worth it? I mean, I don't got a lot of hope for a long life. Is it worth a short one, just living honest?"

Jeremy didn't have to think about it. "It's the best thing you ever do, because it's not the last best thing you ever do," he said, meaning it. "Because everything you do after that is better, and better, and it gets easier."

Gianni squeezed his hand and let go, and smiled gratefully. "Good. Don't worry 'bout me and my problems none, Jeremy. They won't show up on your doorstep. I promise."

Jeremy nodded. "Your promise means a lot to me, Johnny. I'm going to take you at your word."

They finished their hamburgers, and then Jeremy left first. He checked his mirror halfheartedly, to see if Gianni would try and pick things up from where they'd left off, but he was pretty sure they were done.

Gianni had sounded so lonely, though. Jeremy thought maybe all it would take would be a friendly wave and a friendly word, and he could pay back the debt that had saved his life. Maybe have Aiden and Craw do the same. Yeah. You could pay a man back by just letting him know he wasn't alone in the world.

He was happy with that thought, and happy with telling Aiden that, as he pulled into his apartment complex.

Aiden was waiting out front, sitting on a stadium seat and wrapped in a blanket from the back of his car. The pure glowing smile of relief he gave as Jeremy stopped the car and got out was about the most boyish expression Jeremy had ever seen on his small square-jawed face, and he wanted to bottle that look and keep it for when he was feeling low.

Jeremy walked up to him, and instead of going inside, sat down beside him. Aiden opened up the right side of the blanket, and Jeremy cuddled in, letting Aiden wrap his arm and the blanket around his shoulders securely.

"How'd it go?" Aiden said quietly into the hollow of his neck.

"He's in WITSEC, and would be ever so grateful not to be relocated, thank you very much. He'd like it if we gave him a wave, were civil to him."

"How civil?" Aiden growled, burying his nose against Jeremy's skin, and Jeremy yelped.

"A wave and a cup of coffee—holy Jesus, boy, you're freezing. How long you been out here?"

There was a stillness, and Aiden rested his head on Jeremy's shoulder. Jeremy wrapped his arm around Aiden's waist under the blankets. "Long enough to see the safe on the bed through the window," Aiden said quietly. "Long enough to know you were thinking about running."

Jeremy shuddered. "I was afraid," he said. "Not for me, but for you. The last time I saw this guy, my daddy died."

Aiden grunted and held him tighter. "What made you stay?"

"What do you think? Jesus, Aiden—you don't take no for an answer. You know everything about me—shit I didn't even know five years ago. Why wouldn't I run?"

"Because you love me," Aiden said smugly, and Jeremy grunted.

"Arrogant much?"

"And you love it here, and you love what we do."

"Still being an obnoxious fucker, you know that, right?"

Aiden's breath in his ear made Jeremy shiver with the first thing besides fear in what felt like ages. "And because this whole life you love came from being honest, and that's who you want to be now. You're honest, and an honest man doesn't run."

"Not even an honest rabbit, I guess," Jeremy said, and some of his starch leached down his spine to add to the icy mess on the porch.

"No."

"You know how you hold a rabbit, don't you, Aiden?"

"You hold them tight while they struggle, until they know they're safe, and then you pet them until they don't want to leave."

"You *do* know how to hold me," Jeremy whispered. "I don't ever want to leave. Is that awful? I think if I was a better man, I would have left here, and you would have started over and your mama could be asking someone like Ben over to her house for dinner and—"

"I wouldn't have been eating at my mama's table with anyone else," Aiden said softly, "because you would have left me gutted like a sheep. I may have loved someone again, but there'd be a big chunk of my heart missing in that, because a thing like that just doesn't grow back, you hear?"

Jeremy turned and looked at him, earnest in the darkness, and thought of Gianni and the poor rentboy. He took his hand and pushed Aiden's hair back from his face. "My friend," he said gruffly, "he had to make a horrible choice. Speak up and die, or let the boy he loved die alone. I need you to know…." He swallowed. "I'd make a different choice. I'll tell anyone you want. I'll tell your mama at her table, I'll tell Craw, I'll tell Ariadne. I ain't never loved anyone in my life, Aiden. No one but you. I'm sorry it took me so long—"

Aiden's mouth was open, warm, and wet on his own, and Jeremy devoured him, unapologetically, without shame. Aiden broke off too soon and stood up, giving Jeremy a hand up and grabbing the stadium cushions afterward.

"Jeremy," he said, a wicked arch to his eyebrows, "I've got lube in my pocket, and I figure we don't need condoms. You got any idea what I've been imagining while I was waiting for your scrawny ass to pull up?"

Jeremy chuckled, in spite of the heat in his face. "I got some."

"Not yet, but you're gonna."

They burst into the apartment laughing, hands everywhere, clothes coming off in clumps as they kissed and groped, touched, fondled, and suckled their way to the bedroom. When they got to the bed they were naked, but Aiden had the lube in his hand. Jeremy put the safe on the ground next to the bed and pulled back the covers. While he was bent over the bed, Aiden came up behind him, rough, work-hard hands touching Jeremy's stomach, his chest (he'd gotten hairier in the last five years), and his shoulders, while Aiden tracked kisses down his spine. Jeremy arched against him, spreading his knees a little and letting Aiden have his way. The boy ground up against him, his cock hard against Jeremy's backside, and groaned.

"Turn around," he said, "So I can see your face."

Jeremy did, sitting down hard on the bed because Aiden didn't give him much room, and scooting back up against the pillows with his knees wide.

"This is just sex," he cautioned, stroking his own cock in unconscious excitement. "It's... it's not everything."

One corner of Aiden's mouth turned up, and it made him look devilish and very adult. "I know it's just sex, baby. It would just be awesome if it was very *good* sex."

Jeremy laughed and then gasped as Aiden covered his naked body. Oh, all that sweet, supple skin all over his. It was home and haven and coming in from the cold. Aiden did a thing then, a full-body caress that made Jeremy mad for him, made him wrap arms and legs around Aiden's shoulders and hips and beg like a child. Aiden took his mouth, full and wet, and took it again and again. He came up for air and whispered, "You ready?"

"Yeah, sure, why not, it's just—"

"You finish that sentence and I'm outta here."

"God, Aiden... please?"

And Aiden was sitting up on his knees, his fingers sure and confident as he slicked them up and then reached between Jeremy's cheeks and—

"Oooooh!"

Aiden cracked up. "Oh my God! It's a good thing I know I'm gay or that sound might have confused me a little!"

"Where've you been keeping that shit, the fucking... *free*... oh shit... zer?"

Because Aiden had stopped laughing and warmed up his fingers a little, blowing on them, so when they walked their slick path to

Jeremy's tender little orifice, this time they were warm, and soft, and wet, and slippery and… "Oooohhh…."

Jeremy knew his eyes were wide with surprise, and he arched his ass off the bed and thrust his hips to take Aiden's fingers in deeper.

"Good?" Aiden asked, his smile just a little shy as he thrust two fingers in and out.

"Damn."

Aiden thrust and Jeremy gasped, and Aiden asked, "Damn good or damn bad?"

"Damn, boy, is that all you got?" But Jeremy's eyes were still wide and curious, because the sensation was different, good, but different, and he twitched against Aiden until Aiden put his hand on Jeremy's stomach.

"No, it's not. Now hold still."

Aiden positioned himself and moved, slowly moved, thrusting forward, while Jeremy's eyes went big, bigger, and then… *pop*, he had to close them, because Aiden was inside him, and he had to breathe, to get used to things there for a moment.

"Jeremy," Aiden whispered. "Open your eyes."

Jeremy did, and Aiden was right there, leaning on his elbows, brown-green eyes intent on Jeremy's face. "You all good?"

Jeremy grunted, scooted forward a little, took some more. "Mmm…."

Aiden made a little whining sound. "Jeremy?"

"Yeah… yeah… go a—*head*…." Oh God. It felt even better when he moved.

"Yeah?"

"Keep going."

And he did, seated fully in Jeremy's, uhm, seat, he thrust forward and then back and Jeremy watched his face, intent, thoughtful, and then strained as he grew more and more aroused.

And then he…. "Omigod… that was good. Again. Do that again…."

Aiden pulled back and thrust forward.

"*Yes!* Hit that a*gain!*"

Aiden laughed throatily and then started to move faster and harder. He pushed himself up on his knees and grabbed Jeremy's thighs. "Grab yourself, Jer. C'mon… wanna see this…."

"Would you just *keep hitting* that spot?"

And Aiden did… oh God… he was thrusting faster and faster and Jeremy's whole body was going to explode and please, please please please—

"*Whooooaa….*"

Aiden's face was contorted with wonder, and he fell forward, just as Jeremy was… "Omigod!" And then he was spurting and Aiden was spasming and his entire body was white light, and stars.

He had trouble catching his breath—mostly because Aiden was lying on him, so he didn't mind. "God, young'un," he panted, "you're going to wear this old man out."

Aiden pushed himself up on his elbows. "No more of that," he said seriously, but Jeremy saw his brow was slick and shiny with sweat, and he smiled stupidly up into Aiden's eyes.

"You're so easy." He laughed, and Aiden stopped his laugh with a kiss. When the kiss was over, Aiden fell to the side and pulled Jeremy—sweat, come and all—onto his shoulder.

"Jeremy?" he said softly, when their breathing had stilled and the dark had closed around them like sanctuary.

"Yeah?"

"So you're coming to my mom's house for dinner, before Christmas sometime."

"Yeah."

"And I'm telling Craw everything."

"Fine, tomorrow. Ariadne already knows."

"What?" Aiden sat up halfway in bed, dumping Jeremy on the pillows, and Jeremy swore.

"Well, it was Thanksgiving. We had other things to worry about with Ariadne and I forgot until just now."

Aiden flopped back into the bed. "God, Jeremy—you kill me sometimes. All that time I was worried about you taking off, and you already told Ariadne?"

Jeremy glared at him. "Well, the reason I ain't been telling people isn't that I'm ashamed!" he muttered. "It's that I didn't want you to be ashamed of *me*!"

Aiden lay back down in bed and grunted. "Okay, you know something?"

"Obviously not."

"I love you so much I'm stupid with it. How's that? So, dinner at my parents' house sometime soon. But you know what's happening tomorrow?"

"You're going to school."

"Shit. You know what's happening tomorrow night?"

Jeremy smiled a little. He looked so serious in the darkness. "You're staying the night."

"Damned straight. I'm staying all the nights. I'm moving my clothes and my toothbrush and a frickin' picture for the wall. God, Jeremy, two years and you just left that space up there. It's been making me crazy."

Jeremy reached out and touched his cheek. "Make sure you bring your knitting," he said.

"Of course. Why?"

"Because it's cold, and I'm gonna start wearing my gloves. They might get holes."

Aiden smiled. "I'll make you new ones."

Jeremy grinned in the darkness, thinking it was time for all good bunnies to go to bed. "I'm counting on it," he said.

Aiden would get up and wash him off in a few, because Aiden liked to tend to him, and Jeremy liked to let him. They would put on sweats and fall asleep in each other's arms. And Jeremy would dream of quiet pastures, and Aiden's arms around his shoulders, and looking out over the little valley they both loved. He would dream of sunshine on his face, and warmth at his back, and the soft, springy feel of yarn in his hands. He would dream of the two things he'd never thought to dream of, not in thirty years.

He would dream of his lover, and his home, content in his frantically beating heart that both would be there in the morning.

Aiden's Fingerless Mitts
for Jeremy

Okay—this is my go-to pattern for fingerless mittens. Why fingerless, you ask? Because my computer keyboard is under a vent, and in the winter, it is, alas, not my ass I'm freezing off. This pattern is easily adjusted for both heavier and lighter yarn and smaller and larger gloves. Of the two pairs shown, the pair on the right is made of DK-weight yarn and the pair on the left is two strands of sport-weight held together to make a heavy worsted-weight yarn. The only difference in the two patterns is:

A. The number of stitches cast on, and

B. the number of stitches saved for the thumb in the gusset. I'll include both patterns—and the pattern for basic worsted-weight yarn, but just remember: Every cast on number needs to be divisible by four, and every number for the thumb gusset should be odd. Other than that, you can play with yarn weights and sizes to your heart's content.

Instructions:

DK Weight (The Green & Pink Mittens)
Sizes: Small, Medium, Large
Needles: Size 3 DPN, with a stitch holder
Yarn: Madeleine Tosh, DK Sock Yarn
Gauge: 5 ½ stitches per inch

1. Cast on 44 (48, 52) stitches onto DPNs.
2. Start working in 2x2 ribbing for 2 inches, or until you feel like stopping.
3. Work one round plain.
4. At the beginning of next round, M1 stitch before beginning round.
5. Work one round plain.
6. At the beginning of next round, M1, k1, M1
7. Work one round plain.
8. At the beginning of next round, M1, k3, M1

9. Continue to increase the gusset in this manner until there are 13 (13, 13) extra stitches, including the last two increases.
10. Finish the round, put increased stitches on a stitch holder, and skip them, continuing around the mitten.
11. Work 10 rounds even, (more if you want them longer)
12. Work 8 rounds 2x2 rib.
13. Thumb: Pick up three stitches on the side of thumb gusset, work across live stitches from stitch holder, pick up three stitches on the side, join for next round
14. Knit two rounds
15. Purl one round
16. Knit one round
17. Purl one round
18. Bind off, and finish off as usual.

Worsted Weight (The Purple Mittens)
Sizes: Small, Medium, Large
Yarn: Plymouth
Needles: 5
Gauge in Stockinet: 4 1/2 Stitches per inch.

1. Cast on 36 (40, 44) stitches onto DPN's.
2. Start working in 2x2 ribbing for 2 inches, or until you feel like stopping.
3. Work one round plain.
4. At the beginning of next round, M1 stitch before beginning round.
5. Work one round plain.
6. At the beginning of next round, M1, k1, M1
7. Work one round plain.
8. At the beginning of next round, M1, k3, M1
9. Continue to increase the gusset in this manner until there are 11 (13, 13) extra stitches, including the last two increases.

10. Finish the round, put increased stitches on a stitch holder, and skip them, continuing around the mitten.
11. Work 10 rounds even, (more if you want them longer)
12. Work 8 rounds 2x2 rib.
13. Thumb: Pick up three stitches on the side of thumb gusset, work across live stitches from stitch holder, pick up three stitches on the side, join for next round
14. Knit two rounds
15. Purl one round
16. Knit one round
17. Purl one round
18. Bind off, and finish off as usual.

Heavy Worsted (the mixed yarn mittens)
Sizes: Small, Medium, Large
Needles: 6
Yarn: Big Trend Sock Yarn by Kattan and Marsh
Gauge: 4 stitches per inch
*Note—To make these mitts for my friend Andrew, I used one big skein of yarn with long color changes, and I picked a strand of yarn from one and, and a strand of yarn from the other. I combined the strands and knitted them as one, and the result was this heavy worsted-weight yarn with these oddly matching color changes. I was very pleased.

1. Cast on 32 (36, 40) stitches onto DPNs.
2. Start working in 2x2 ribbing for 2 inches, or until you feel like stopping.
3. Work one round plain.
4. At the beginning of next round, M1 stitch before beginning round.
5. Work one round plain.
6. At the beginning of next round, M1, k1, M1
7. Work one round plain.
8. At the beginning of next round, M1, k3, M1

9. Continue to increase the gusset in this manner until there are 9 (11, 11) extra stitches, including the last two increases.

10. Finish the round, put increased stitches on a stitch holder, and skip them, continuing around the mitten.

11. Work 10 rounds even, (more if you want them longer)

12. Work 8 rounds 2x2 rib.

13. Thumb: Pick up three stitches on the side of thumb gusset, work across live stitches from stitch holder, pick up three stitches on the side, join for next round

14. Knit two rounds

15. Purl one round

16. Knit one round

17. Purl one round

18. Bind off, and finish off as usual.

A Knitter in His Natural Habitat

Chapter 1

Watch, as the Innocent Crafter Chooses His Path

STANLEY MISSED Craw ever so.

It wasn't like he'd been in love with the big goober—no. But he'd *liked* Craw's visits, as terse as the guy had usually been. They broke up Stanley's job somewhat, and that's always nice, even if you love your job. And better yet, those visits meant Stanley got *laid*, and, as Stanley sat at the counter and peered moodily into the mid-November slush, it turned out Stanley hadn't been doing a lot of that without Craw.

He couldn't really put a finger on when it had happened, either.

Stanley Shulze had arrived in Boulder a little more than ten years before with a fresh-off-the-turnip-truck business degree, an art minor, and a job as a yarn buyer. God, hadn't *he* been a deprived child in the bowels of fucking Nebransas, because *Boulder* had seemed like a bustling metropolis of gay. He'd gone to the clubs, gotten fucked by anything that cared, gone down on a few more that hadn't, and had enjoyed the hell out of himself.

When had the novelty worn off?

He couldn't put a finger on it. He certainly hadn't started off exclusive when he'd bent over for Craw. He'd seen the guy—a big giant of a bear, covered in curly auburn hair—walking through the doorway of the yarn store and thought "Hel*lo* big daddy bear man! Now wouldn't it be lovely if you were—" And then he'd seen Craw checking out his best ass. The tight, bouncy little bubble one, right on top of his thighs, and Stanley had been in….

Well, not love. But certainly in enough of a dither to grab a lubed condom out of his messenger bag, lock the door between rushes, and follow Craw to the bathroom to proposition him.

Craw had shrugged, said, "Well, if you're fucking serious," and a tradition had begun.

And five years later, Craw had met a nice boy and settled down, and it had ended. And Stanley was left wondering—when had bending over for Craw become the be-all and end-all of his love life?

He wasn't sure. Sometime in there, it had gotten too bothersome to go out to clubs and find a hook-up that he'd maybe had before and then had to forget. Sometime in there, the music got too loud, the kids got too young, and the scorn for an aging fag got too hard to bear. All he knew was that the Friday night after Craw had called it quits, Stanley had gone to Wilde's, his favorite meat market, and had met… well, twenty-one year old children, mostly.

They'd been pretty—omigod, was it possible they were getting *prettier*?—but their conversation?

Well, lacking.

"Dude!"

Stanley looked encouragingly at the young man and crinkled his eyes, which were blue with dark lashes and he'd spent hours looking in the mirror trying to make them alluring. "Yes, sweetie?" he asked, batting those dark lashes.

The young man—tall, with a heavy chest and heavy thighs, who looked like he could probably break Stanley in two if he felt like it— had smiled sweetly and said, "Dude," while nodding his head up and down and taking in Stanley's trim little (five feet seven) body. He seemed to have earned an expression of approval, and Stanley tried to make his smile *extra* special.

"So, would you like to buy me a drink?" he articulated.

The kid nodded, his jaw slack and loose. "Oh yeah. *Dude*."

Stanley had taken a deep breath and realized that blowjobs were never free and a good primal pound in the ass was gonna cost him a fortune in self-respect. Oh well, he'd been living on credit that way for years.

"Awesome. I'll have an Amaretto sour, if that's okay."

The kid blinked and wrinkled his nose. "Dude?"

"Don't worry, sweetie. If you order one, Victor will make it." Stanley looked over at the bartender, who was everything you wanted in a gay-bar-bartender: tattoos, bandana over his bald head, no shirt over his solid body, leather chaps, chains around the groin, and all!

Victor rolled his eyes at Jethro and slid Stanley his sour, and Stanley simpered up at his pretty, dumb friend and tried to seal the deal.

"So," he said, trying for conversation. "Do you go to school around here?"

Jethro looked down a little and blushed. "Construction," he mumbled, and Stanley saw it, and kicked himself for seeing it.

"Don't be embarrassed," he said sweetly, touching the back of the kid's hand with his own. "We do what we're good at, right sweetie?"

The kid looked at Stanley mournfully. "And what are you good at?" he asked, and Stanley almost gave him the easy answer only. But instead he said, "Selling yarn to little old ladies," *before* he said, "and giving blowjobs."

And of *all* things, that lit the kid's face. "Do you *knit*?" he asked, enthralled. "Because my mom knits and *that's* cool!"

Stanley blinked. "You're not impressed by the blowjob even a little?"

The kid shrugged and looked around. "All these guys give blowjobs," he said matter-of-factly. "And I'm hung like a donkey, so I get lots of ass. But you didn't even answer the question. Do you *knit*?"

Stanley shrugged. "A little. You have to, if you're going to help sell the yarn, right?"

The kid's eyes got really big and moony. "Would you knit me a sweater?" he asked, and Stanley's mouth fell open. He knit garter stitch. Plain garter stitch. Back and forth, repeat ad infinitum. And here he was, his first visit to a meat market in a *year*, and this kid wanted to know if he would *knit*?

"Oh, Buttercup! *No* one is that good a fuck, okay?"

The kid considered and then jerked his chin in the general vicinity of the back privacy rooms, where what you did in there might not be seen overtly, but it was really not anything near private. "Well, I *might* be. Want to give a try?"

Stanley pursed his lips. "Yeah, sure. But don't pull my hair—my hair plugs are just starting to look natural, okay?"

The kid patted the top of Stanley's blond head—which he could do easily since he was well over six feet tall. "Yeah, okay."

Stanley looked despairingly at the little darkened cubicles and realized the bathroom in the yarn store where he'd been doing Craw had at least been cleaned once a day and had air freshener and disinfectant and... young Jethro put his hand on Stanley's shoulder.

"Kid," Stanley shouted, because the music gave an extra loud throb at that moment, "what's your name?"

The kid traced a line down the side of Stanley's neck and nibbled his ear. "I've got a condom," he said, close enough for Stanley to hear him. "It's lubed. Do you care?"

"Well, if I'm gonna knit you a sweater, you'd better *make* me care," Stanley grumbled.

A rather sweaty fifteen minutes later, Stanley leaned against the wall of the privacy cubicle and pulled out some wet wipes from a box provided for guest convenience. He wiped off his stomach and his hands, which were wet from come, and turned around to see the kid tying off the condom. Together they threw away their trash and Stanley looked at the kid and shrugged.

"You're right, Junior; I don't think names are necessary. But on the downside, I ain't knitting you shit if I don't know your name."

THAT HAD been about three months before Thanksgiving. The Tuesday before Thanksgiving, Craw had brought his "nice boy" to visit while he made his delivery, which depressed the hell out of Stanley.

Ben really *was* a nice boy. He was funny, he was acerbic, he was *fully* aware that his catch and Stanley's former steady lay was a walking communication dysfunction, and he looked at Craw with such yearning that even *Stanley* had to admit he would have felt bad if he'd gotten between them. Oh for *fuck's* sake, didn't his *jealousy* even function anymore?

The two of them took turns baiting Craw (apparently Ben had been in the dark about Stanley until Craw pulled the truck up to the curb—that was always good for a few chuckles) and then he'd turned that sunshine-poet's face with its hipster's stubble toward Stanley and said, "So, do you knit?"

Stanley had gaped. Seriously? He was getting this from Jethro *and* from the ex's new squeeze? What in the fuck?

"Stanley doesn't knit," Craw grunted, walking by with a box neither Ben *nor* Stanley was bothering to help him with. Big dummy. Bringing the new squeeze to meet the old lay. How desperately tacky. Oh yeah, sure, the guy *called* it being up front, but Stanley knew unintentional emotional punishment when it was flogging him on the tush. Stanley was so put out he didn't even bother to contradict Craw about his knitting, although, by Craw's standards, a little bit of garter stitch didn't count.

"You don't knit?" Ben said, surprised. "Even *I'm* starting to knit. I mean…." Ben gestured around the store, and Stanley rolled his eyes. It was a *huge* chunk of floor space, and he'd done it up right, with smooth black lacquered cabinets artfully overflowing with yarn sorted by brand, type, and color, plush couches set at feng shui angles, cream colored (stain resistant) carpeting, and mirrors on the available walls next to the windows to make the place seem even bigger than it already was.

Stanley looked again and saw the yarn this time and not the floor space. "Yeah," he said, pulling up one corner of his upper lip. "I guess there *is* yarn."

Ben shook his head. "Okay—I've known the guy for three months—I'm telling ya—the yarn is the *only* thing he sees. And I'm starting to get tunnel vision that way too."

Stanley looked at Craw, coming back with another box, and then at Ben, who was just so sunshiny sugary sweet that Stanley wanted to eat him up with whipped cream and chocolate, and then saw the way Craw looked at Ben when Ben didn't know he was looking.

"Yarn," he said, looking around his place of business again. "Go figure."

See, the thing is, Stanley had a business major with an art minor—he'd been going to buy and sell *art*. He'd just taken the job in Boulder as sort of a stop-gap bill-paying measure. Sort of an interim thing to put on his resume. Because those sorts of jobs are a dime a dozen when you're sending your resume to everyone between Boulder and New York, right?

Yeah. That had been ten years ago. He was still here. He had his regulars, he had his club scene, he had his neighbors—and fuck him if he didn't have two cats and a wild attack ficus.

Oh hells. Stanley had a *life* here, one it would sort of piss him off to leave. He hadn't sent his resume anywhere in *years*, and quite frankly? He had no desire to. He liked Alice, his boss. Although he mostly worked in Ewe'll Love This!, the fact was, she owned four different craft boutiques around Boulder and Fort Collins. He got to buy for and design the floor space for *all* of them, and it was fun. It wasn't acquiring art for a Vegas casino ('cause those people had *cash*) and it wasn't designing for Cosmo, but it played into his strengths and, well….

He was damned good at *picking* yarn, yarn that would be fashionable or yarn that would be trendy, yarn that would be practical and yarn that would wear well. If he was going to make his life like this, maybe he should get his hands dirty. (Of course, the allure of yarn in the first place was that you could get your hands dirty while keeping them reasonably clean.) And why not? He'd spent the last eleven years pushing fiber on little old ladies (and a surprising number of trendy young ones). Wasn't it about time he became a user too? God, it beat the hell out of amyl nitrate—he'd had at least three regrettable encounters in college due to that little chemical nightmare. It's not like yarn could be any worse!

And besides. Craw had left him for a man who wanted to learn to knit. The sweet boy at the club had thought his one interesting feature was that he *sort of* knew how to knit. Knitting was a sign of commitment; Stanley knew enough about the craft to know a project took some devotion and had some permanence.

Maybe, if Stanley learned how to knit, he'd figure out how to have some of that in his own life.

So, the day before Thanksgiving, he cashed out two skeins of yarn and some nice square-shank knitting needles to make himself a scarf.

Now, Stanley knew his own limitations. He assumed he'd be interested in knitting like he'd been (thus far) interested in men. He'd see something shiny, try it out, and then think he could probably do better in the next privacy booth. So he started out with big, thick yarn and big, thick, phallic needles (he liked the squareness in the shank—although that did make him do some online research to see if that was a trend in sex toys, because, hey, something he didn't have would be nice! He did find a few plugs in that shape, which he ordered. Why not?)

And he made the yarn something... rich. Yummy. Decadent. A deep, flashy lipstick red. Now Stanley himself usually looked good in cool colors: crisp navies, charcoal grays, ice greens. But that's not what he *wanted* to wear. So he picked this dark, flashy, candy-apple, hot-car, full-lipped I'm-a-superstar red, because he figured, if he was going to get his granny on, he was going to do it like the look-at-me attention whore he was.

He remembered his basics, and the night before Thanksgiving, while the curried lamb dish he was making for his boss's pot luck the next day simmered, he sat down with the some previously DVR'd episodes of *Top Chef* and *Project Runway*, and cast on.

For the first episode, he cursed his own stupidity, struggled with the yarn, struggled with the needles, and felt like an idiot douchebag. He got up, tended to his food for a moment, poured himself a glass of wine (to go with his whine, he supposed), and picked the red in case he got really wasted and spilled the wine on the hand-wash-only merino/cashmere blend.

After the first glass of wine, the repetitive movement became soothing.

After his second glass of wine (and after he, thankfully, took the food off the stove and prepped it to take to the early dinner the next day), the Zen of the color started to seep into his hands.

He never made it to his third glass of wine. He became totally enthralled, sitting there, knitting, watching the skank ho designing the dress try to possibly squeeze one last millimeter of nonboob out of the spider-monkey of a model. Van Gogh, his manic-depressive black cat, curled up in a little ball by his shoulder and Matisse, his big, surly orange tom, was spread out unapologetically on his lap, and their combined weight pretty much arc-welded his ass to the couch. But that was okay; in fact, it was perfect. It was like the permanence he'd been seeking had found him, just by gluing him to the couch and making his activity so soothing he didn't *want* to go anywhere.

He finished the first skein of yarn that night, and when he woke up, he realized he hadn't done half bad. He liked it so much he put it in his messenger bag, so he'd have something to do while Alice's redneck son was monopolizing the television. It was so unfair. Everyone else there—Alice, her daughter Candace, her daughter-in-law Amanda— they *all* wanted to watch the *Thin Man* marathon, every year. But no— not Jed. Jed was going to by golly watch the fucking football games, and even trying to imagine those boys naked didn't make that game any more fun for Stanley, who was not a fan of BDSM even when it was the *fun* stuff, with the leather. But Mandy was sort of a doormat, and Alice was trying to have peace with her children one day a year since their father got them for Christmas, yes, even into adulthood, and waging that sort of war in someone else's house was just déclassé.

The curried lamb was a success—even more so because the curry had a chance to settle in and work up some kick. As a traditional Thanksgiving side dish, well, maybe it didn't blend, but Alice and Candace both kissed him on the cheek and told him thank you, and everyone but Jed (who hated him), including Mandy, used it as an alternative to gravy on the mashed potatoes when they ran out of rice.

Jed, for his part, just sat at the end of the table and glared and muttered things under his breath about pansy food, and Stanley ignored him. The fact was, he hadn't been welcome in his parents' home for years—not even to attend their funerals. The story was so old by now— and Stanley was a big fan of the "It Gets Better" movement, because he was certainly glad to be free of *that* mausoleum—that he couldn't bear repeating it, even for the sympathy. But sometimes, sometimes, he did miss the sound of his mother's voice, with his sister in counterpoint, singing the doxology over their meal, which, as far as he knew was a tradition that was just the Shulzes' with their good old Lutheran upbringing.

But Alice? She more than made up for it. Alice was one of those hard-nosed broads—with a core of solid chocolate. She cut her graying hair short and didn't wear make-up and didn't do battle with time so much as just turn her back on the bitch and go about her business. She wore jeans and a nice sweatshirt to prepare dinner and told Candace, her ultra-feminine daughter, that she looked lovely in a winter white cashmere dress with red trimming. Candace did, too. She'd piled her fiery red (dyed) hair up on the top of her head and left tendrils down and painted her lips almost the exact pop-my-cherry color of Stanley's scarf.

Stanley adored them both. When Stanley had first started working for Ewe'll Love This!, Alice would bring her children into the store while they consulted. Jed had been sixteen, surly, scornful, and obviously a carbon copy of his father, whom Stanley had met once and it had been more than enough. Candace, on the other hand, had been fourteen and shy. Beautiful—God, even through the pimples and the gangliness and the braces and the bad hair, you could still see the snub little nose and the bee-sting mouth and the heart shape to her freckled little face—but shy. Terribly, terribly shy.

Stanley had adored her. He'd ramped up his camp and called her honey and mooned over the boys in the fashion magazines to make her giggle. She reminded him of his own sisters, before he'd come out and they'd hated him like the rest of the family, except *her* mother had told her kids straight out that Stanley was gay and they could like it or they could keep their mouths shut about it. Candace had chosen to like it, and Stanley had chosen to love her with all his gay little heart.

Eleven years later, she was this amazing, fabulous woman who was studying art as an *artist* and not a buyer, way out in New York, which Stanley had wasted his youth thinking of as a metropolis just waiting to discover him. He very possibly could have been bitter that Boulder had been here all along, just waiting for Stanley to discover *it*, except Candace was his darling, and when she had gone off to college and begun to make a name for herself, he'd had a very hazy, wine-soaked conversation with God about giving her all the success he'd never achieved. He wanted her to have it. He wanted her to shine. He was content to sit at her mother's table during the holidays and spice up her time with curried lamb.

But he wasn't sure when she'd grown older than him. That hadn't been part of the deal.

They'd lingered over wine after the dinner clean-up, and she'd smiled at him over her wineglass.

"Stanley," she said, only a little buzzed, because she was a lady like her mother. "How is it you never bring anyone by for Thanksgiving?

Or over Easter? Or for the summer barbecues? I am starting to worry about you!"

Stanley looked back at her, touched to his core and trying not to tear up because Jed would only call him a big flaming mo. "Darling, don't worry about me. I'm learning to knit," he said proudly, and Alice was suddenly at his elbow, with some leftover turkey and gravy (good, he needed some carbs and protein to sop this buzz!) and complete attention.

"Oh, Stanley," she said, sounding sober, "that's wonderful!"

Candace grimaced. "Mom—it's knitting. It's no big…."

Stanley knew he had sort of a sappy smile on his face. "It's all the secrets of the universe wrapped up in one Zen little ball of string," he said happily. "Everything I thought was missing in my life is twisted up in fiber and the magic stitch."

He was aware Candace and her mother were exchanging rather alarmed glances.

"Stanley," Alice said, her voice getting as gentle as it possibly ever did, "I love the craft. I mean, it's why I started the store, but do you really think you should be pinning the secrets of the universe on—"

"Stanley, you need a man."

"Candace!" Alice was scandalized, but Stanley, he understood.

"No," he said sadly. "Don't you see? I don't *get* a man. I've squandered my golden years being a one-night mantrap. I need to own up, Candy darling." He patted her hand serenely. "You get to go out and be fabulous. I've got the cats, the ficus, and now I've got the knitting. These things will fill my time until I shuffle into the sunset. I am content."

"*You're thirty-six!*" Candace squawked, and Stanley held his hand to his chest, mortally wounded.

"Thirty-*five!*" he corrected. "But that's not the point!"

"Oh, that's *exactly* the point," Alice muttered, taking a gulp of her daughter's wine. "Stanley, honey, I'm glad you've embraced knitting, I really am. It'll make you even better at your job, and, quite frankly, I was starting to think you had the morals of a con man. It's good to know you don't. But maybe don't embrace celibacy just yet. Maybe, you know, just embrace a new you."

Stanley looked dispiritedly at his wine. "It's better than the old me, I guess."

Alice was a chunky woman, but that's what made the arm around his shoulder feel solid and real. She kissed his temple. "The only thing wrong with the old you is that you treated dating like finding a vibrator on legs. There's more to finding a life mate than that, honey. I mean, Candace's father fucked like a god—"

"*Mom!*"

"But he fucked *everything* liked that, and who wants that kind of competition? Certainly not someone worthwhile, Stanley. Maybe the knitting is a good thing. You can practice project monogamy and then move on to the human kind."

"Oh Jesus." Candace's eyes were wide, and she stood up and started searching the counter for the other bottle of wine. Stanley didn't have the heart to tell her he was pretty sure he'd killed it while he'd been helping her mother with dinner. "Mom.... God, maybe monogamy just isn't Stanley's way—"

"It could be," Stanley said pathetically. His messenger bag was hanging over the back of his chair, and he found himself suddenly needing the comfort of his yarn very much. "It could be," he repeated, getting out his scarf. He started working the row with dogged determination. The wine was starting to recede, and he was with his people now, his darling, beautiful Candace and her mother, who had been trying to fill in for *his* mother since he'd applied for the job. "I just... I just need to find the right project," he said, thinking this scarf was too short and he was going to need another skein of yarn. That was good. The scarf could go on and on and on and on, and it could be the harlot-red banner of shame that wrapped him up and kept him warm when the nights grew lonely and cold.

Candace managed to find another bottle of wine—Chablis this time; it had been hiding in the fridge—and Alice continued to lean her head on his shoulder soothingly.

"Stanley, you know, I was pretty sure when I divorced their father that I was going to be alone my entire life and I'd never find another man. You know what I discovered?"

Stanley kissed the top of her silver-gray head. "That you're a lesbian?" Jean hadn't been able to make it for Thanksgiving—she had her own kids. The good news was that her kids were there for Christmas, so Stanley got to have family at both the major holidays. Who needed to bring home a boyfriend? It also helped that Jed didn't have to see proof that his mother was everything he professed to hate; he got to pretend she was still his mommy and needed to wait on him, hand and foot, along with his wife. Stanley had never been puzzled by the idea that parents as straight and narrow as his had gone and thrown themselves a Stanley. Nice people like Alice were squirting out assholes like Jed every day.

"Well, yeah, that," Alice conceded. "But you know how I discovered that?"

Candace choked on her Chablis. "If you say 'masturbation,' I am never coming home again, ever."

Stanley grinned at her, thrilled at how quick she'd gone from sophisticated glamour girl to horrified teenager. "Oh baby, you know she lives to make you spit-take. Let mummy finish her story and we can have a lovely game of hand-n-foot over pie."

Candace rolled her eyes and glared at him indulgently. "You know, Stanley, you're still the best father I've ever had." Jed gave a cheer from the living room and pumped his fist. The three of them looked over to where Amanda was sitting next to him, looking longingly at the table. Amanda was tiny and mousy, with dark hair and sloe eyes, and Stanley thought if Jed ever actually laid a hand on her, he would possibly throw a punch for the first time in his life. "And older brother," Candace added with a sympathetic glance at Amanda, "rolled into one. But that doesn't mean you can tell me not to be freaked out by my mother's sex life."

Stanley started to giggle. "You're just lucky your mother *has* a sex life. My parents spawned us in the mud puddle behind the house. I was the egg that got stepped on and that's why I'm gay." He turned to Alice again. "Finish your story, darling. You were trying to give me hope about my love life, and I need some."

"You weren't the egg that got stepped on," Alice muttered. "You were the egg that had the good sense to move out from under the fucking horse." She finished grouching and sat up, suddenly looking as sober as Stanley would have to be before he drove home in the snow. "Anyway, no. There was masturbation because I was alone, but that's not what I discovered. What I discovered was that I *liked* myself. I was alone, and it sucked, but I wasn't a bad person to be with. You're not a bad person to be with, Stanley. You can keep sex in your toy drawer for a while, until you find someone you wouldn't mind meeting us for Thanksgiving."

There was another cheer from the living room, and Alice grimaced. "Or lunch. Tell you what. You name a nonholiday time, and I'll fly Candace out and we can meet Mr. Hasn't Walked Through The Door, okay? That way, we won't let Jed scare him off."

Well, why not? Stanley laughed a little and made his next stitch. Some of the wine was wearing off, and he was starting to crave pie. "Why not," he said grandly, thinking the odds of that happening were as thin as the odds of him actually becoming a knitter for life. "Darling, if that happens, *I'll* fly Candace out."

"As if," Alice grunted. "I know what you make, Stanley, and it ain't that impressive."

Stanley shrugged. "After you give me a raise."

And then there was pie!

Chapter 2

When Tranquilized by Their Craft, Wild Knitters Are Oblivious to Their Mates

BLACK FRIDAY was as insane in the yarn store as it was any other place on the face of the frickin' planet. Stanley had been ready for it—a giant coffee, some Advil, and he was ready to wheel and deal and walk those little old ladies to where they needed to go. What he was *not* ready for was to see Craw and Ben walk in right before closing time, looking tired and worried, and ready to wait until the last customer left before they talked to Stanley.

Alice had worked Ewe'll Love This! with Stanley this year, and Candace had worked the quilting store in the trendy strip mall about four blocks over. During pie, Alice and Stanley had even pressured Jed to let Amanda (let!) work the quilting store as well, so they could maximize their sales presence (i.e., have as many of Alice's employees working each store as possible.) Besides, Alice paid Amanda on the sly, in the vain hope that someday she would leave Jed and Alice could stop inviting him to family meals unless he was going to be an actual human being.

When Stanley looked up and saw Craw, he actually lost his train of thought. He thought that whole "let's be friends" thing was just a crock of crap Craw had fed him to keep him from shrieking like a wounded harpy. It had sort of worked. Stanley was actually humbly grateful. It's not like a newly reformed club baby was long on friends who weren't still in the scene.

Craw scowled his welcoming scowl and nodded his head. It was Ben at his elbow who smiled. He looked resigned, like maybe this hadn't been his idea, but friendly, like maybe he understood Craw wasn't going to go bang Stanley in the bathroom with him there. Something strange—one of those weird tendrils that had bound Stanley to his knitting project (and had him hiding the last two balls of that yarn from a little old lady with blood in her eye so he could finish his scarf)—gave a little yank where Stanley's chest hairs would be if he didn't wax.

He was happy to see these people.

"Go talk to them," Alice said, nodding. "I've got these last folks here."

Stanley excused himself with a smile, almost sad, because those women were buying the same stuff he'd been using for his scarf, and he wanted to dish. First time *that* had ever happened. He was sort of enjoying the novelty. But Craw looked worried, and Stanley was right there.

"Hello, boys," he said with a smile. "Long time no see!"

Craw looked uncomfortable. "You have a good Thanksgiving, Stanley?"

"Yeah," Stanley said, completely sincere for once. "It was really wonderful. What can I do for you?"

"It's about Ariadne."

Stanley tweezed his eyebrows once a week, to make sure they arched just so, and now he arched them just so, in order to look quizzical. "Is she okay?"

Stanley had never actually met Ariadne in person, but he dealt with her on the phone for orders, and they chatted frequently online. He liked her. She was like Candace, except a little less cosmopolitan—and a little less easily scandalized. (When she'd first gotten pregnant, he'd asked her how she was. She'd said, "My boobs hurt, Stanley. Would you like a list of what else is pissing me off about my body today, or would that short circuit your little brain?")

Craw and Ben exchanged glances again. "She's fine so far," Craw said before he could panic (much). "And the baby too. But she's stuck here in Boulder for the next few months until the baby's ready to come. Anyway, we can come visit once, maybe twice a week until the roads close, but her husband's got art shows in the next two months and…."

It was probably more than Craw had said in five years of acquaintanceship, and he looked both highly uncomfortable and sad. Stanley understood. Craw's mother had passed away when Craw was still a young man; Ariadne was the closest thing Craw had to family.

Except for Ben, who put his hand on Craw's arm and stopped him from talking before he broke something.

"She's going to be lonely," Ben said, smiling a little. "When Craw said once or twice a week, that's us once and Jeremy and Aiden once—and maybe Rory once—and that's it. That's a long time to be stuck in a hospital bed without kin, even with a computer and a phone—"

"And knitting!" Stanley said, suddenly wanting to hug the scarf in his messenger bad very, very badly. He *liked* Ariadne. It was as though now that he'd given up on men, the universe was conspiring to show him he had friends and family for the taking. And sometimes, the universe did the fucking taking!

Craw nodded in complete understanding. "That's why we thought of you. We figured if you could stop by once a week and knit with her—"

"I can bring Alice," Stanley said, thinking it sounded like exactly the sort of thing Alice would like, especially when Candace went back to New York on Monday. She was big on power of the sisterhood, right? They could sit around and talk about tits and plumbing, and Stanley could knit and scorn them. "She and Ariadne will get along like a house on fire... it'll be great!" He smiled at them winningly, for some reason wanting these two men to be happy, even if there was no sex at all in it for him.

The relief that broke across Craw's face made Stanley a little warm inside, and Ben actually hugged him. He returned the hug and realized that it was sexless and comforting, just like a hug from Alice or Candace, and he wanted to cry. Alice had told him to be by himself. He'd spent less than twenty-four hours by himself (well, three months if you counted the encounter with Jethro) and as it turned out, being by yourself meant you weren't by yourself after all.

"One more thing," Ben said after some more discussion of where the hospital was and Ariadne's phone number and the best place to park. "While she's laid up, Craw was going to hire a delivery guy. I know Aiden and Jeremy were going to bring an extra shipment on Monday, but the service said the delivery guy will be here on Tuesday instead."

Stanley blinked. "No Jeremy and Aiden?" Well. That was a disappointment. He wasn't sure if either of them were gay. Aiden was like a Craw Junior in the body of a young, green-eyed god, and Jeremy was pathologically charming to pretty much everybody in a ten-mile radius except Aiden. They antagonized each other unmercifully, and Stanley had often speculated they would either end up banging each other or killing each other, and not even *his* practiced eye could tell which. But they were both pretty to look at, and Stanley was never averse to eye candy, especially when it came with Jeremy's slick patter, which, sincere or not, was tailor-made to make people like Stanley feel better about themselves.

Ben cast a rather covert glance at Craw and shook his head and answered the question. "Nope. I'm afraid they're going to be at the shop when they're not running the mill. I can help a little, but I've got my own business to run, and Ariadne left a pretty big hole to fill."

Stanley looked at Craw, who seemed oblivious to the look, and he realized he wanted to be in on that look too. He was in on the little group thing to visit Ariadne, right? Apparently he knew everyone Craw cared about? He wanted to know this!

Stanley looked at Craw and batted his big blue eyes. "Craw, babysweetiehoneydoll, could you go ask Alice for a piece of paper and a pen and then write down all that information you just gave me for her?"

Craw blinked and then looked disgusted. "Oh Jesus—you're not going to figure it out right now, do I have to?"

"Shoo." Stanley even made the motion, and as Craw stomped off, he invited Ben to spill with a wicked arch of his eyebrows. "So?"

"So what?" Ben returned mildly.

"So tell me what you think Craw doesn't know, and then I can dish about it with Ariadne."

Ben tried to look clueless for a moment—and he was really good at it, which made Stanley think more of him when he dropped the façade and moved in to dish. "I think they're screwing around," he said softly, glancing at Craw.

"Who?"

"Jeremy and Aiden. I saw them the other night holding hands, for one thing."

"Aw, isn't that cute? It's like those darling little pictures of babies in flowers!" Even Stanley wasn't sure if that was derision or sincerity dripping off his tongue. "What else?"

Ben looked quickly at Craw again and then grinned conspiratorially. Stanley could tell he'd been *dying* to talk to somebody about this, and Craw did *not* gossip, particularly about Aiden, whom Craw looked upon like some sort of saintly little brother.

"And Aiden's been staying the night at Jeremy's apartment. I've been driving by to go get coffee in the morning—"

"Ellerby's coffee?" Stanley had been to Craw's shop in Granby once or twice, when he'd been feeling like a drive, and that was a place on his list to visit.

"Yeah, only decent place in town. Anyway, his car's been there. I started paying attention, and the thing is, I know Aiden used to pick Jeremy up from work, but now they're driving Jeremy's car sometimes too. Like, you know—"

"Whoever's got the gas!" Stanley interjected, as tickled as if he'd help to solve a major crime. "Oh my God." He looked at Ben, suddenly both happy and sad for these two men he barely knew.

"What?" They both looked furtively at Craw, who was awkwardly engaging Alice in small talk.

"If they're staying the night and trading cars and holding hands, they're not just banging each other. You *know* that, don't you?" Because as sweet and sunshiny as Ben was, he also had the look of a city hipster. Ben probably knew the same rules Stanley did, and when his eyes widened and he nodded, Stanley knew they were on the same wavelength.

"It's really fucking serious," Ben said softly. "That's why they haven't told Craw."

"Would he object?"

Ben grimaced. "He seems to think Aiden walks on water. The kid's as snarly as Craw himself, but Craw doesn't see it."

"Jeremy does," Stanley said, rolling his eyes. He liked Jeremy. There was something in that boy's eyes that reminded Stanley of his favorite person: Stanley. But at that point their conversation was interrupted by a grim-faced Craw, who came back and said he and Ben needed to get a move on before the roads got too icy. Stanley was sorry to see them go.

But it was okay; he had a *job*. A *social job*. Friends who weren't club friends and weren't really work friends either. On Saturday he called Ariadne up before work. She sounded exhausted but told him her husband was going home on Monday; she'd love to have a visitor Tuesday, if he could make it. Stanley usually left work in the early afternoon on Tuesday; he said he'd be happy to.

And he was. Stupidly happy. So stupidly happy he nearly brushed off the love of his goddamned life, because he wanted to go knitting with a laid up pregnant woman he'd never actually seen before.

STANLEY HAD almost forgotten the delivery guy. He was getting ready to leave, going over the receipts and the restocking with Alice and making sure the spring reorganization he'd planned for the stores over the New Year's Day holiday was going to take place. (Nobody liked coming in to work New Year's Day—but the next four weeks were practically dead, so everybody liked the overtime.) He looked up, and there was a guy in a khaki uniform covered with a brand new fleece-lined leather jacket, with the dorky little hat on top of thick, unruly black hair, coming through the doorway with a box of yarn awkwardly held at his hip.

He was so not going to make it.

Stanley hurried over to open the door for him, bitching in his impatience. "Jesus, it's yarn, not a baby—on the hip, really? Your shoulders are wide enough, do you think maybe you could hoist that up a little? Good—very good, Jethro, we may not kill you yet."

The guy made it through the door and set the box of yarn down delicately at Stanley's feet. "Jethro?"

Stanley sniffed with impatience. "I don't know—we'll have to see if you're a super genius later. I've got a friend to visit. Here, grab that and follow me."

"But there's like, two more!" the guy protested—but he had a smile in his voice, and Stanley decided he'd try not to act like too much of a bitch. "Oh, bless Craw anyway, he really decided to stock up. Here, sweetpea, I'll hold the door, but you gotta get a move on! I'm trying to get outta here!"

Stanley stood at the door and opened it to the frigid Colorado cold to let the guy in with the next box and then closed his mouth as he watched him move.

Oh he*llo* eye-candy! Not quite as tall as Craw, the guy had short-cut black hair, swarthy olive skin, and a carefully maintained body and complexion. He set one of the boxes down at Stanley's feet with a smile, and Stanley noticed the even white teeth and the holygodshootmenow... *meltable* chocolate eyes.

Eye candy indeed.

Mr. Eye Candy stood up after the second box, quirked his smile back on one side to show a dimple, and winked, then went back out into the cold for the last trip. Stanley closed the door behind him and noticed the tight... oh Jesus, *tight*, taut ass, and narrow hips and broad chest and....

And he'd been over thirty at least.

Stanley's heart started to pound in his ears as he tried to tell himself that Mr. Melty Eyes Hard Body Eye Candy was not necessarily gay just because he'd winked.

But something in Stanley must have been moved, because Melty Eyes brought back the third box and Stanley did the unthinkable and actually picked up the smallest box (the second one) to help.

"Follow me," he said perkily around the brown cardboard. "We'll just put these in the back to put away tomorrow."

Stanley looked around the box and saw Alice staring at him. Boxes were not something Stanley *did*, unless he was unloading stock from one. He'd warned her ahead of time that he was *not* the sort of man who moved boxes around for women. Most women he knew were taller than him, for one, and there was really only one place he liked to sweat, for another. So when Stanley caught Alice's stare, he jerked his chin toward Mr. Melty Eyes Hard Body and watched her own eyes widen appreciatively. She nodded, and then pointed to her watch and he grimaced.

Well, dammit! He had a resolution about being by himself with friends to keep!

He showed Mr. Melty Eyes into the back storeroom, which was, coincidentally, right by the bathroom where he and Craw had spent their finest moments, and showed him where to set the boxes down.

"I'll let you get the next one, dollbaby; I've got to motor." There was a serious amount of regret in that last statement—even he knew that.

But Mr. Melty Eyes stood up and winked. "Well, it's too bad you gotta leave," he said, his voice every bit as Italian-tough as the man looked. "I would have liked to chat."

Stanley dropped the box on his foot and didn't even give thanks that it was yarn and light. "You would have?" Seriously? Because Stanley's conversation was not usually his strong point in these encounters.

"Well yeah!" the guy said, his smile sweet and sort of indulgent-like. "I'm new to the area. Anyone who wants to chat with me—that's sort of a good thing, right?"

Stanley was nonplussed. "Really? Because usually when guys want to 'chat,' they're talking about a quickie in the bathroom. You know that, right?"

Those melty brown eyes grew hooded, and that full, way-sensual mouth curved up in what could have been the dirtiest smile Stanley had ever seen.

"It wouldn't have been that quick," the guy said, looking Stanley over from head to toe. "You got the sweetest little bubble-ass. I woulda wanted to linger."

Stanley's jaw dropped and his head tilted back, and if he'd been a girl, his panties would have gotten wet. But he wasn't a girl. He was a man, and his balls gave a gleeful throb and his cock woke up, yawned, stretched, and started to sprawl a bit, making Stanley's pants tight.

"I'm Stanley," he said weakly. "And I gotta go."

"I'm, uhm, Johnny," the guy said, grimacing for no reason Stanley could think of. "And I got another delivery to make tomorrow."

Stanley perked up. "Here?"

Johnny winked, the dark fringe of his lashes practically stirring up a draft they were so long. "You betcha, cupcake."

Stanley pursed his lips consideringly. "I *am* too old to be a twinkie," he conceded. His own grin turned evil. "So, you, uhm, like to eat cupcakes?"

"Only if they're cream-filled," Johnny said back, his voice so smooth it felt like a lubed flesh-jack on Stanley's cock. His vision went black and his head got all swoony and he sighed like a starstruck teenager.

"Oh my," he said, shivering. "I'm a big fan of cannoli myself." He had no idea what kind of head this guy would give—but his conversation and eye-humping alone might make Stanley come. If Stanley didn't have to fucking leave!

Stanley shook his head, and only some of the wet heat of the room seemed to dissipate. "Uhm, Johnny, I'll be here tomorrow with bells on."

Johnny blinked. "Please tell me that's a euphemism," he said. "Man, I ain't gotten some in *months*."

Stanley practically cackled. "Okay, I'll be here with a butt-plug and lubed condoms—is it a date?"

"I'll be happy to deliver to you any time you want, cupcake. Any time good for you?"

Stanley's smile turned sultry. "10:30. The aqua aerobics class doesn't get out until 11:00. It'll give us a chance to get acquainted."

"I'd love to get acquainted," Johnny said, and he bent down then and kissed Stanley's cheek. Stanley held his hand up to his cheek in something like awe. Five years Craw had fucked him blind in the bathroom, and he hadn't gotten a kiss until Craw had said good-bye.

His moment of dreaminess was superseded, though, by Alice's impatient voice. "Stanley, unless you're naked and coming, you need to leave *now* if you're going to get to the hospital before traffic fucks you up!"

Stanley snapped out of it and beamed up at his new best friend. "Tomorrow?" he said breathlessly. "You promise?"

"Yeah—if you tell me who you're visiting in the hospital."

"A friend on bed rest," Stanley said, starting his hurry out of the back room. "She's there until she has the baby." And then he was out to the front, grabbing his jacket, gloves, newly knitted fuck-me red scarf, and the messenger bag with his next project in it as he sprinted out of the store.

BLAH BLAH blah traffic, blah blah blah hospital, blah blah blah nasty smell, white corridors, and all. But then hello, Ariadne, who turned out to be everything Stanley expected from her phone conversation and e-chat, except she had one of the warmest smiles Stanley had ever seen.

He decided they were on a hugging basis as soon as he saw her sitting on the bed in her sweats, her dyed fuchsia hair a splash of hallelujah against the standard hospital white and pastel.

"Oh baby, I must!" he exclaimed, and to her credit, she opened her arms and took him in. She was tiny, thin, and almost too delicate-looking for words, but there was wiry strength in her arms, and Stanley felt immediately protected, which was funny, considering she was the one laid up.

"Heya, Stanley," she said when he'd backed away and pulled up a chair. "It's good to see you; you look just like Jeremy described."

Stanley nodded, thinking of Craw's slickly handsome, dapper little employee. "He does seem like he's got an eye for people," he said judiciously. "I'm glad he didn't scare you off."

"Oh no." Ariadne waved her thin hand and then reached to her side and pulled up—what else?—knitting. She was working on a shawl in a deep dramatic red much like Stanley's scarf. "He actually said you were bitchy and sweet." She looked at her work judiciously, like she was trying to remember where she'd been on it. "Considering how much nonbitchy gay I work with, I thought you'd be a refreshing change!"

Stanley laughed. "Nonbitchy gay?"

Ariadne shrugged. "Well, there's Craw, who's just frickin' mean, and Ben, who's as sweet as sunshine, and…." She shook her head and jerked her glance at Stanley, as though realizing she was on the verge of confiding something that wasn't really her business.

Stanley arched his eyebrows with smug innuendo. "There's Aiden and Jeremy," he said slyly, and she narrowed her eyes.

"What makes you think so?"

He grinned at her, so damned tickled to have something to dish he couldn't spill it fast enough. She listened, nodding her head as though it made sense. "Yup—Ben's not stupid. But Aiden isn't either."

Stanley pursed his lips. "I thought it would be Jeremy who'd be keeping the secret."

"Oh, it is," Ariadne said matter-of-factly. "No doubt—that man's doing everything he can to recognize this is *not* a fight or flight situation. But Aiden's the one who's letting him. He's a little like Craw—just sort of gentles a person, then lets her be herself while he's keeping her safe."

Stanley cocked his head. "Her?"

Ariadne smiled a little. "Rory and I were just out of college when we moved to Granby because his mother moved to Florida and Rory got her house. And it almost ended our marriage, because...." She shook her head. "Stanley, I grew up in Seattle, which is a fucking metropolis compared to Granby, Colorado, you know that, right?"

Stanley nodded. "I grew up in Shelter, Nebraska. Which was exactly like Granby, without any mountains and less charm. Boulder is a metropolis compared to Shelter, Nebraska."

"Yeah, well, I was not impressed with Granby. There I was with... I dunno, green hair and six zillion piercings, and I'm thinking this flea shit in the bottom of the mountain bowl isn't going to impress me none. So I go out to find a job, and there's Craw. And he just doesn't give a fuck. And he's so sublimely indifferent to how much of one I don't give either, that... well, we just clicked. And suddenly Granby was a bucolic little frickin' haven, and I was happy."

Stanley laughed a little. Yeah. "Were there dance clubs in Seattle?" he asked wistfully, and Ariadne nodded.

"Yeah. Not so much drive beat, you know, but metal—birthplace of grunge and still rock in its soul—and alternative. I loved those clubs."

Stanley nodded and looked at the hat he was knitting. Cast on in a circle, keep going around, right? This color was a dark, masculine brown in a cleanly spun alpaca/wool mix. He thought it would go well with his deliveryman's uniform, and the thought made him anxious. What if Johnny the deliveryman didn't show up? What if it had all been an empty promise and a kiss on the cheek?

Well, he thought determinedly, at least it was a kiss on the cheek and not a meaningless fuck up the ass.

"I love dance clubs," Stanley said, some of that sadness seeping into his voice. "But I don't think I can go back to them anytime soon."

"Yeah? Well, you sort of grow out of them. I grew out of needing them when I started to love Craw, and Granby. I think that's what Aiden's been doing with Jeremy; that's why all the secrecy. Just getting him to recognize it, is all."

Stanley sniffed and kept knitting. Making a hat was *awesome*. Around and around and around... it was like the forces of physics, making life simple in action. "Well, if I had a guy I was seeing all the freaking time, I'd sing it to the heavens," Stanley huffed. Seriously, if Johnny McMelty-Eyes was banging him in the bathroom once a week—

"You were pretty discreet about Craw," Ariadne said, and Stanley tried not to choke on his tongue.

"He *told* you about me?" For a moment his heart beat a little wildly in hope.

Ariadne shrugged. "No—he's barely spoken about Ben, either. We just showed up for Thanksgiving and Ben was there like he'd spent the night. But he used to shave and put on aftershave before he made deliveries to Boulder. He must have thought something special was going on; the shaving part only happens like once a week at the most, and the aftershave surprised me so much I thought someone had dropped a bottle of Windex."

Oh. Okay. So Stanley was a little special. For a second, he contemplated being terribly hurt and disappointed, and then he realized Craw had been a little special too—but not heartbreaker material. Not like Johnny McMelty-Eyes.

"Stanley?" Ariadne said into the silence, and Stanley made a deliberate stitch and said, "Hm?" back.

"Stanley, I'm laid up in bed here. I got nothing to do but talk to people and knit, and I know you can keep up your end of this, so spill!"

Stanley grinned at her, suddenly realizing he'd been captivated from the moment he'd first heard her voice on the phone. She was his friend; she had been for years, whether they'd met in person before now or not. So he told her everything, from Craw and his curious sadness, to Jethro, and even about Johnny McMelty-Eyes and *not* getting banged in the bathroom, and a kiss on the cheek.

"A kiss on the cheek?" she said, making a careful cable on the back of the shawl she was knitting. The cable itself was pretty complicated—Stanley was impressed with the way this woman knitted. "And not a quickie in the bathroom." She nodded approvingly. "So, you're starting to want something more from your life. I'm impressed, Stanley. Most guys, it would take a near-death experience or something. All it took for you was a little bit of heartbreak."

Stanley sniffed. "My heart *so* wasn't broken," he said.

"Have you ever had your heart broken?"

He shook his head. "No. Because I'm a coward and I can't abide pain. Mine or anybody else's."

She closed her eyes and her mouth tightened a little, and then she put her hand on the swelling at her middle, where, he realized belatedly, a whole lot of pain and a whole lot of heartbreak had the capacity to dwell. "That's too bad," she said, her voice strained. "Sometimes you've got to risk the pain and maybe get your heart broken."

Just that suddenly, her eyes were shadowed and she looked exhausted. Stanley called the nurse, who brought her some dinner, and Stanley left then so she could rest, but she made him hug her again.

"Come back real soon, okay?" she begged, and for all her toughness, he realized she *was* terribly vulnerable, and sometimes, people just needed to be protected.

"You name the time and I'll be here," he promised. "I'll even bring Alice—she can come on her own too."

Ariadne's smile lit up her plain features, and Stanley gave her a firm kiss on the cheek. "I'm crazy about you," he said. "Head over heels. You take care of yourself and that kid, all right?"

She promised she would, and he left then. On the way home, in his little Kia SUV, he found himself being careful of the snow on the roads—and wondering a lot. His older sister had been pregnant before he'd left home; the whole family had fussed over her. He'd outed himself and gone off to college before the baby had been born, but for a few months, he had been part of the excitement, that strange, collective hive mind that took over a family to protect its gestating members.

Now that he was older, he felt some of that excitement again; it was the same excitement he'd had when watching Candace graduate, or helping her choose her prom dress, or even helping her with her math homework.

Stanley wondered about this, because he would have freely told the world he'd spent the last eleven years being as self-centered and narcissistic as possible, when the truth—the whole truth—was that he'd just been looking for someone to love him back.

He thought about that kiss on the cheek and hoped.

Chapter 3
Sometimes a Perfectly Placid Knitter Will Startle

STANLEY TRIED not to look at the clock too assiduously. It helped that the weeks before Christmas were heinously busy, which he always thought was funny, since a knitting project took *time*. Was it really possible to buy more yarn than you'd ever bought all year during the month before Christmas and then knit something for your entire extended family?

Stanley doubted it. He would settle for his practical little brown hat for the nice UPS delivery guy, who'd kissed him on the cheek and flirted with him intelligently and made him feel special. Stanley decided he didn't even want to suppose there would be more to it than that. Maybe he'd been kidding about the promised romp in the bathroom. It didn't matter. The night before, he found he was simply obsessing over the yarn. It was brown and sturdy, with a long staple, and it seemed very practical at the same time it seemed really decadent.

Stanley was having a hard time figuring out how that could possibly be.

But still, he'd worked on it after he'd eaten his little Lean Cuisine meal at his small breakfast table. He'd curled up on the couch with his cats and turned on the television, and… voila! Worked on the hat. He'd finished it while he'd been watching *Love Actually* on cable, and was absolutely stymied with nothing else to do.

He had leftovers from his scarf and from the hat, and he found himself practicing his mitered squares, ending up with five of them before he went to bed. He realized he was going to have to buy more yarn the next day. Not just enough for a project, but enough for a couple of them. The twitchy feeling he'd gotten when he'd finished the hat and hadn't known what to do with his hands had been distracting. He *didn't* want to do *that* again.

So, during his break the next day, while he tried to pretend he wasn't waiting for Mr. Johnny McMelty-Eyes deliveryman, he grabbed a basket and started picking out a couple of projects' worth of yarn. He bought craft products for a living; he knew the projects, and he even knew how to read a pattern, although he'd never done one more difficult than a couple of lines. He started to fantasize who he would make things for—something for Ariadne, something for the baby, something for Alice and Candace, and even for Craw and for Ben.

He refused to look at that decadent, practical brown and think any more about a basic sweater, because that was just way too big a commitment for a kiss on the cheek. So he picked out his yarn and his needles and cashed himself out at the register, and then his break was over and the store was swarming and, oh shit.

There was Johnny.

Stanley looked at him in agony. He'd thought the store would be empty; he'd been so flustered the day before, he'd forgotten about the Christmas rush and the women who skipped their aqua aerobics class in order to knit instead.

Johnny took one look at the crowd and grimaced, and Stanley made his way through the (mostly) women to take the smaller box he had, the one on top, and then guide him through the crush.

They made it back to the relative peace of the stockroom, and Stanley turned to set his box on a shelf. He was surprised when two strong arms reached around him and a cheek already scratchy with stubble rubbed up against his own.

"Bad timing," Johnny muttered against his cheek, and Stanley melted into him, so relieved the whole thing hadn't been his imagination that his knees *literally* went weak.

"I'm sorry," he said breathlessly, folding his arms over Johnny's hands. "I was really looking forward to showing you the bathroom."

Johnny's low rumble started a little electric zing path from the back of his neck to his nipples right down to his groin. "Yeah, you know, I been thinking about you all night, if you know what I mean. I'm thinking this is going to have to be one hell of a bathroom!"

Stanley couldn't remember smiling this wide since his first boy—who was now a fundamentalist preacher in his home town—had offered to go down on him in the locker room.

"It's had its good points," he admitted. He turned his head and saw Johnny's face in close profile. He had a couple of wrinkle lines near the eyes, and the toughened, swarthy skin that showed he knew how to drink. But his eyes were closed like one of Stanley's hedonistic cats when they were basking in the sun, and Stanley had a revelation.

This was a treat for Johnny too.

On impulse, Stanley kissed Johnny's cheek tenderly. "I'm so glad you came in today," he confessed softly. "I'd sort of thought I was hallucinating you in the first place."

Johnny turned his head and caught Stanley's mouth softly. They couldn't get too deep, too passionate, but it was a kiss, a real kiss, a first kiss, and Stanley turned in his arms just as Johnny stepped back reluctantly.

"If you've got a delivery tomorrow...," Stanley said hopefully, and his heart about shattered when Johnny shook his head.

"Nah. You're gonna be busy. But, you know, on Thursday, I'm going to be back in Boulder around seven. Isn't that your closing time?"

Stanley blinked. "But why would you want to get here at closing time?"

Johnny dropped his head and pinched the bridge of his nose. "I don't know, Stanley. Maybe because I'll be hungry."

"But it'll be dinner time—you'd be eating!"

Johnny cocked his head and looked at him. "Not to put too fine a point on this, cupcake, but I've been out with rentboys who expected more from a first date. I'm gonna get here at closing time and take you to dinner, and then, maybe, we can end up having more than a quickie in the bathroom. That okay with you?"

Stanley's jaw dropped, and Alice called him from the front, and he realized he was just standing there, staring at Johnny McMelty Eyes with the expression of a boy with his first Justin Bieber doll.

"Dinner?" he asked in a small voice.

"I'd ask you to see a show, but this ain't Vegas," Johnny said matter-of-factly. "How about a movie?"

Stanley's inner eight-year-old suddenly blossomed. "There's an animated Christmas movie I'm *dying* to see!" he practically squealed, and then, right when he was going to kick himself for being the world's most obnoxious, *celibate* gay man, Johnny's face split into a wide, warm, indulgent grin.

"Yeah! Let's do that! Look up times, and if you got any ideas for where to eat, I *love* a good steak!"

Stanley tried not to let his expression fall. Steak? Well, if they were going to have steak, they'd probably have salad too. Stanley could eat salad. If he could find a steakhouse. Suddenly he perked up for real. He actually *knew* a man who would eat steak—he'd ask Craw.

"*Stan—ley!*" Alice's voice was both shrill and desperate, and Stanley grimaced.

"I'm sorry, Johnny—I gotta go. But come up with me to the counter for a minute, okay? I've got something to give you." He grabbed Johnny's hand, in case he was going to try to escape, and hauled him up to the counter, where Alice was swarmed with little old ladies who all needed their yarn wound from hanks to balls. (Stanley had been trying to make a dirty joke about Hank's balls for *years*, but just when he was going to say something brilliant, his inner twelve-year-old popped up and said, "Balls, heh heh heh heh…" and there went the opportunity.) Anyway, Stanley needed to get in there and help Alice, so his presentation wasn't awesome as he reached into his messenger bag and grabbed his sturdy, decadent brown hat.

"Here," he said, pushing it into Johnny's hands. He was suddenly absurdly embarrassed. It was a hat. He'd met the guy twice and knitted him a hat. What sort of idiot *does* that?

Johnny took the hat and looked at it, and Stanley couldn't stand to see what sort of expression he'd have, in case it was the sort of expression that canceled dinner plans because the bubble-butt you followed down to the storeroom suddenly did something way too serious for what was going to be, initially, a quickie in the bathroom. So Stanley bustled over to the swift to stretch the first hank of yarn across it and was just snipping the little threads that held the hank together when he heard his name called in a dusky, rumbly baritone with Mafioso overtones.

"Yo, Stanley!"

Stanley turned around—and so did every little old lady in the place, but Stanley didn't care. Johnny had pulled the hat on down past his ears, and was grinning at Stanley like he'd won the lottery.

"Thanks, Stanley, it's real nice. I'll see you Thursday."

And then he turned around and made his way through the stunned crowd of women, who all stopped chatting for a moment just to watch his heavily muscled body walk confidently through the door.

The door swung closed behind him and Stanley (and the store) watched Johnny get into his delivery truck, and one of the regulars said, "Way to go, *Stanley*!"

And the store erupted into applause.

Stanley was a pale little man of German descent. Any flush at all could be seen on his face, which is why he was so glad he didn't blush anymore.

Until now, when he grinned foolishly and bowed, his face heated and burning, even as he turned to start winding yarn. The women hooted and hollered and then found something else to talk about, and Stanley concentrated on his work (which could get tricky if you didn't understand how yarn behaved on a swift) while Alice rang up purchases.

Stanley was on his sixth hank of yarn (lace weight, which went for*ever* because it was like, a billion yards!) when Alice had a moment to turn to him quietly and say, "My God, he was handsome. Well chosen, sweetheart! Me likey!"

Stanley managed a little look over his shoulder and found that not only could he still blush, but that he could also be attacked by a shyness he thought he'd killed during his second gang fuck in college. "Me likey too," he said, biting his lip, and he was surprised when Alice leaned in and kissed his cheek before going back to work.

It couldn't be this easy, could it?

STANLEY ASKED Ariadne that the next evening when he went to visit. He was working on another scarf, this one with a basket-weave pattern of knits and purls that he'd sort of saved to start when he was sitting down with her. She knew so much more than he did, and it was embarrassing to ask Alice, because she'd been trying to get him to learn how to knit for years!

"Mm, that's pretty." Ariadne was still working on her red cloak, and as Stanley watched her continue the complicated cable on the back, he realized she was probably making that for herself. He sort of respected that. Babies got all sorts of attention—most of which they didn't appreciate. But moms? Overworked, underslept... who needed some pampering more than a new mom? Good for Ariadne!

"The yarn?" he asked, looking at it critically. Alice tended to stock hand-painted yarns, with color*ways* instead of colors. It was the kind of yarn Craw dyed, and Stanley could appreciate it—but it wasn't what he was buying. No, Stanley was buying one-color yarns, with a clean, predictable twist pattern when it was spun. "It's plain," he said, trying not to sigh. "It's basic cobalt blue."

"Yeah," Ariadne conceded, "but it's also beautiful. I mean, I'm as much a fan of the rainbow wooly madness yarns as anyone—"

"Rainbow wooly madness?"

"It's a Jeremy term. It's what he says when Aiden is designing."

Stanley knit five stitches and very carefully changed to purling. "How are they doing?" he asked, genuinely curious, and Ariadne sighed.

"Let me finish this thought, and then we'll dish, okay?"

Stanley looked at her, surprised. "O-kay?"

"'Kay, Stanley, remember—I've been talking to you for about six years. And six years ago, you were all about the next hot guy at the club. I used to wonder if I shouldn't send you boxes of condoms, because I was worried you'd forget—and remember, we hadn't even *met* yet. Well, that's sort of the novelty yarn phase of your life, you know? Lots of glitter, lots of bells and whistles—sparkly, but it won't keep you warm, you know what I mean?"

Stanley nodded, because he hadn't thought of it like that. "Yeah, I hear you. Novelty—it was all about the 'Oh shiny,' okay. Good. Go on."

"Well, that's not where you're at anymore. I don't know, maybe it was when Craw broke it off—but suddenly, you're about the 'I don't want sparkly. I want real.' Well, that's what you got in your hands. It's pretty—and it's even complicated pretty. Would you look at the color!"

Stanley did, puzzled. "Uhm...."

"No, Stanley—you sell this shit. Tell me about that yarn!"

Stanley did. "Well, it's got sort of a complicated process," he said slowly. "This one's got three dyeing rounds. It's dyed in the wool first off, and then it's vat dyed a slightly lighter color, and then it's veil dyed a slightly different color—so, it's cobalt with a navy base and a sky blue overtone and a little hint of dark gold." He knew what the label said, even though he didn't know what "veil dyeing" really entailed.

Ariadne blinked. "You *are* good at your job," she said, a smile in your voice. "Even if it's one you hadn't thought you'd love."

Oh God, had Stanley told her that? It seemed wrong that a woman who would know all that about him would be sentenced to bed for three months. There was something seriously flawed in the universe because of that.

"Yeah," Stanley said, making another pattern change. "So, this yarn looks simple—"

"But it's really very deep," Ariadne said, and then she winked, like she knew it sounded corny, and Stanley's face heated.

"Oh God," he said, stunned. "You take that back!"

"Not on your life." She was so serene. A plain woman with fuchsia-colored hair and a nose ring, knitting a blood-crimson cape. How could you argue with her?

"So," he said, "We're going on a date."

"The deliveryman?"

"Yeah. He... he kissed me in the stockroom and told me rent boys asked more from a first date, and told me we were going out to dinner and a movie."

Ariadne put down her knitting and looked at him with admiration. "Oh, Stanley! Dinner and a movie with no sex in sight? That sounds serious!"

Stanley knitted when he should have purled and swore, tinking the knitting back to fix the flaw. "It sounds very unlike me," he pronounced when he was going forward instead of backward again. "Can it really be that easy?"

Ariadne said, "Give me the scarf for a second, love—you messed up that entire quadrant, I'll show you how to fix it." She took the knitting from his hands and started dropping stitches. For a moment, Stanley was terrified. That was his *work* she was screwing with, and he almost yanked it back. Then he realized it was only knitting. Ariadne was a friend, and she was helping him. He watched her as she went back stitch by stitch, dropped it, and then went back and worked it the right way.

"That's very clever," he murmured.

"Yeah. That's how you know you're fixing something right," she said with satisfaction. "You look at each small thing and make sure it's on the right path."

Stanley blinked. "Like, say, dinner and a movie instead of sex?"

Ariadne laughed. "My God, you people are easy. I tell you knitting is Zen, and suddenly you're all fiber Buddhists. But yes, like dinner and a movie instead of sex." She handed Stanley back his knitting.

Stanley looked at it and figured it would be much easier to continue from where she left off. "You're good at this," he said thoughtfully, and she grinned, the expression making her thin, plain face seem fuller and softer somehow.

"I'm awesome. So, do you want to hear about Jeremy and Aiden now?"

Stanley found himself ravenous for news, and they stopped talking about his new love life and knitting as Zen and started talking about how Craw's two workmen were dancing around telling Craw that they'd been, in Ariadne's words, "screwing like rabbits" for what, Ariadne guessed, had been a couple of months now.

Stanley's mood when he left the hospital was what he'd term "cautious optimism." On the one hand, sex wasn't guaranteed the next night. On the other, he could count on one hand the number of guys he'd gotten to pay for dinner.

SO THE next day was a misery of waiting. It was a good thing it was a madhouse, because otherwise Stanley would have either gnawed off all his nails or knit himself into a coma. At ten to seven, Stanley was waiting on the last customers, and Johnny wasn't there.

At seven o'clock, Stanley was shooing them all out, and Johnny wasn't there.

At ten after seven, he was wandering the store and putting yarn back in the slots and cleaning up the disaster in the bargain bin when he heard a tap on the glass, and he took his first deep breath all day.

Johnny was here. It wasn't all sunshine and bullshit. Stanley was going to get dinner and a movie, and suddenly, that actually sounded better than sex.

He was wearing slacks and a sport coat—no tie, but still, awfully dressed up for all of that. Stanley couldn't help thinking about his work clothes—black slacks, black loafers, and a burgundy colored turtleneck. He liked to dress nattily—but still, he wasn't sure he was a match for Johnny Mc—oh hells. Stanley was going to have to ask for a last name, wasn't he?

But first he needed to let him in.

"Hi. I'm glad you made it," he said as he swung the door open. "Here, I've got just a few more things to do and then I can count the safe and we can—"

Johnny stepped in, wiped the snow off his shoulders, and grabbed Stanley's arm before the door had even closed behind him. Stanley was suddenly being mauled in a warm, friendly, *happy* open-mouthed kiss that left him panting and wide-eyed as Johnny pulled away.

"Hiya, cupcake," he said with a smirk. "Glad to see you." For a moment, his expression wavered, and Stanley wondered what had happened to make him seem so lost. "You have no idea how happy I am to see you," he repeated softly, and Stanley inched forward and stood on his tiptoes to plant a very brief, reassuring kiss on him.

"I was afraid you'd bailed," he admitted breathlessly, before backing away and trotting around the aisles of the store to make sure everything was where it should be before he dealt with the cash. He wanted to kiss some more, but, *oh God*, he was already hard and his balls felt swollen and he'd built up this sort of mystique over the day about getting laid in an actual *bed*, and not a club privacy room and not even the much nicer yarn store bathroom. A *bed*, where Stanley could explore Johnny's body and see if he waxed his chest and if his ass was as tight bare as it was through his uniform and see if that banter, that intelligence and fun Stanley had seen from him so far was there completely or if it had just shown itself to get the job done.

"Naw," Johnny said, his voice carrying across the empty store to be oddly muffled in the baskets themselves. "I had some business that ran a little late. Didn't mean to scare you."

Stanley almost groaned as he saw an entire cubby of yarn that had been dumped out in an effort to get to that last matching skein in the back. (Or so he assumed—the cubby was short two different colorways; someone had cleaned it out.) "It's just that," Stanley panted, squatting down, "I don't know if I've gone this long *ever* without getting laid. I think you're sort of special."

To his surprise (and relief, actually, since he'd just admitted something so personal,) Johnny laughed. "You're a slutty little bottom," he said, the words clear through his chuckles. "That's awesome. That's my favorite kind of lay." For a moment, Stanley felt a little bit hurt and a little disappointed. "Once he's mine alone," Johnny clarified, and Stanley actually stood on tiptoes to glare at him across the store.

"If that's a line, I'll die of disappointment and come back to haunt you," he said, feeling peevish. God, it's like the guy had been reading his diary, as well as watching all his favorite movies. But he saw a white smile stretch across Johnny's wide, full mouth, and while still standing at the door, Johnny winked at him.

"Stanley, I am, at this moment, a lot hungry, and getting close to damned horny, and really looking forward to spending time with you. Can I help it if I've got a type?"

Stanley flushed for the zillionth time since Johnny first walked through the door. "Can I help it if I didn't?" he asked, maybe feeling shame for the first time since he'd decided to come out to his parents in a big way. (Announcing he was late for curfew because he'd been blowing half the soccer team had been a big way, right?) And on that note, he figured he should probably be honest. He dropped down again, talking more to the yarn probably than to Johnny, but trying to be honest nonetheless.

"I mean, I could help it," he said, gathering up all the skeins into his lap. (It was a pretty sage green. He made a mental note to buy some.) "It wasn't like I was being controlled by aliens. I just, you know—"

"Liked to get laid." And Johnny was suddenly right there by his shelf, bending to pick up another couple of skeins that Stanley hadn't gotten to yet and placing them respectfully with their buddies.

"Yeah," Stanley said, standing up and smiling at him gratefully. He finished with his last armload and looked around again, refusing to admit how very handy it was that doing so meant he didn't have to look Johnny in the eye.

"Me too," Johnny said gently, and now that there wasn't any yarn in the way, he could get up close and personal again, and Stanley had a chance to think, *He smells like leather and soap and car and a little bit like Calvin Klein's Obsession for Men*, before Johnny leaned over and whispered, "That's why I like my bottoms slutty."

He pulled back and winked, and Stanley hid his burning face in the shoulder of Johnny's sport coat. Oooh… fine wool. Nice.

"Yeah?" Pathetic, Stanley, real pathetic.

"Yeah," Johnny reassured. "Once I know he's not giving it out all over town, I'm reasonably sure he's going to be putting out for me and me alone. A lot. Is that so wrong?"

Stanley smiled shyly at him. "I haven't…. I mean, I've never cheated, but, well, I've never been monogamous, either. No chance to cheat."

Johnny chuckled, and the sound rumbled in his chest. "Well, do you think you got it in you?"

Stanley reached up and tugged on Johnny's brown hat. It was a little bit small—probably could have used another couple of stitches around and some more inches on the bottom. Stanley wanted to make him a new one. "I seem to be able to knit one thing at a time," he said, taking the question seriously. He managed to look Johnny in the eye then. "And I haven't seen anybody I've wanted to be with seriously in a long, long time."

Johnny smiled then, and Stanley thought he could probably skip his morning aerobics workout, because that smile right there made his pulse race in alarming ways.

"Yeah, cupcake. Me neither." His face fell then, into quiet, saturnine lines, and Stanley was overwhelmed with the urge to cup his cheek.

"You look so sad," he said, surprised—not just at the sadness, but at his own sensitivity to it. Stanley wasn't the most empathetic guy— even *he* knew that.

"You think you're the only one with a past?" Johnny asked, but his voice was tired and kind and not bitter.

Stanley shook his head. "No," he said softly. "I just always hope it's a happy one. Here. I'm starving. Give me ten minutes in the back, and we can go eat."

Chapter 4
Knitters Prefer Strong Fibers

THEY ACTUALLY made it to the movie, which surprised Stanley. He took Johnny to a steakhouse nearby (yes, he'd asked Ariadne and she'd asked Craw and the report was that even if the waitresses were always trying to flash their racks, that didn't mean the steak wasn't damned good). Like he'd planned, he ordered salad, but Johnny kept feeding him bites of steak and potato, so Stanley decided that calories taken off your friend's (lover's?) fork didn't really count. He'd take an absolutely swoony bite of forbidden food, make appreciative food-gasm sounds, and the sweetness that lit up Johnny's face made it totally worth an extra twenty minutes on the treadmill the next morning to keep his trim little bubble butt from becoming big and squishy.

They talked over dinner about pretty much everything. Stanley didn't know a whole lot about sports, so Johnny told him about the Yankees, and how everyone in his father's family was a Yankees fan, and even though Johnny had lived the last ten years in the southwest, he still listened to Yankees games in his car as he drove.

Stanley told him about Candace, his darling, and how he'd cried like a baby when she'd graduated and how she still got horrified when her mother talked about sex, and how she'd once snuck frogs into her brother's bed when she realized what the word "faggot" meant and that Jed was using it to talk about Stanley. She'd told Jed it was so he wouldn't confuse frogs with anything else, and she'd told Stanley… nothing. It had been Alice who had spilled the beans, because, as Alice told Stanley, "Her father's a redneck asshole, Stanley. If that girl's going to grow up with a lick of sense, it's going to have to be you and me." He left out the part about passing up a chance to go into New York to buy for some high-end department stores after that—but he didn't have to.

"So you stuck around here to watch the girl grow?" Johnny asked around one of his last bites of steak. Stanley shrugged.

"You know, I grew up with sisters and a brother. I guess it was worth it, to see her grow up."

Johnny closed his eyes for a second. "Whoever told you about this place deserves something nice for Christmas," he said with heartfelt satisfaction. "And I hear what you're not telling me. What you're not telling me is that even if it would have been better for your career to go somewhere else, you really wanted to stay here for her."

Stanley took a sip of his Chablis, trying not to feel defensive. "I helped her with her homework," he muttered.

"Your family told you not to come back, didn't they?" Johnny said, and Stanley scowled at him.

"We weren't talking about that!"

"We didn't have to. You came here and made your own family. But you didn't want to find a man because you were worried that someone you cared for—like you cared for your mom and dad and your sisters and your brother—you worried that they'd kick you in the gut too. See, Candace and her mom—they can be your family, and you're happy that way. But someone permanent? That's why I'm your first date in forever."

Stanley bristled. "You're being awfully fucking presumptuous," he snapped.

Johnny shook his head and wiped his mouth politely with his napkin. "Naw, you don't get it. You're a good guy, Stanley. You're all afraid that you can't have a relationship 'cause you like to play around—you been having them, just not the romantic kind. You and me, we're not gonna be no different. Once I get you all settled and comfortable, you ain't gonna want to leave."

Stanley stared at him. "Seriously? Just that? Dinner and a movie and a romp back at my pl—"

Johnny shook his head and covered Stanley's hand with one massive paw while taking another bite of loaded baked potato with the other. "There ain't gonna be no sex. Not tonight. Not now that I know all this about you."

"All what? I just told you about a friend's daughter—"

"And you love her. And she's special. And you go knit with another friend while she's laid up in the hospital. And you keep working for your boss when you could be making more money and getting all your props and shit because *she's* your friend too. I know what I need to know about you, Stanley. You're loyal. If you fall for me, it'll be like falling off a building. You'll punch a hole through the soul of the earth before you break. I can put off some sex for that. That sort of love—that's fucking worth it, you know?"

"I don't know," Stanley said miserably, that kiss on the cheek from Craw growing further and further away. "I've never had it."

Johnny's smile—God. It was so gentle. It was wide, and handsome, and it set off the grooves in his cheeks, but mostly it promised to treat Stanley with kid gloves and softness, and Stanley was not sure he'd ever been smiled at in quite that way.

"Don't you think it'll be worth it if you could have it?" Johnny said, and Stanley swallowed.

"That," he said with a sniff, "is a supremely stupid question."

Johnny's smile amped up a little, became a wicked grin. "You're scared to death, aren't you?"

Stanley rolled his eyes. "Oh puhleeze. The only thing I'm afraid of is that my equipment will malfunction with lack of use."

Johnny's laugh echoed through their little corner of the steakhouse, and Johnny leaned forward, putting two fingers under Stanley's chin so he had better access to whisper in Stanley's ear. "You prime the pump a little tonight while you think of me, and I guarantee it'll be up and running when you need it."

And his lips were touching Stanley's ear and his breath was dusting in and out and Stanley's stomach went liquid and his cock went solid and he did everything but just faint, face down in his chicken soup and salad.

Johnny pulled back and resumed eating his steak. "Okay?" he asked, and Stanley just nodded, completely beyond words.

"Ungungh."

Johnny chuckled through the rest of his steak.

STANLEY HAD known Craw for six years, and mostly, he'd known that the guy was thrilled to be getting off when they were together. He'd known Johnny for a week, and by the time the Disney movie started, Stanley knew that he'd grown up back east, that he'd lived in the southwest for a while, and that he was new to driving a delivery van, but he liked it okay.

"Visiting people who are happy to see you—that's something new," he said contemplatively over popcorn. Stanley had asked him what he meant by that and Johnny had shrugged and smiled—but there was trouble in his smile and Stanley didn't know what to say. There had been a couple of times that night when Stanley had seen trouble in Johnny's smile—the worst one had been when Stanley had asked him about his last "slutty little bottom." That warm, smiling face turned to stone, and Johnny's voice said, "He, uhm... uhm, can we not talk about that?" And Stanley nodded, thinking that here, right here, that expression on Johnny's face, was the reason why he'd never gotten that involved, never fallen in love. God, Stanley didn't think he could take that kind of pain.

For a moment, he contemplated ending the date after dinner. He could get cold and snotty, and basically make Johnny not want to come back. The idea was appealing, but Stanley had already put his hand in motion to pat Johnny's, and Johnny seized his hand there, mid pat, and squeezed it so tightly, Stanley had no choice but to look into his face and see the naked gratitude there.

Oh my heavens—Stanley was already *important* to Johnny. Important—like, he'd just given him something no one else could.

Stanley had scooted his chair around the table then, and leaned his head against Johnny's shoulder and watched as Johnny finished his cheesecake, which Stanley couldn't have any part of because his stomach got delicate around dairy. When he thought about that moment, he realized that neither of them had talked for a while, but still—there seemed to be something significant about it anyway.

And the movie... it was a charming kid's movie, and Stanley was a sucker for them just like he was a sucker for movies like *Love Actually* and *While You Were Sleeping*. This wasn't one of the great animated films—it wasn't *Up* or *Wall-E*. But it was sweet, and it made them both laugh, and Johnny's laugh... God. Stanley stopped his own, mid cackle, and turned to watch Johnny throw his head back and laugh out loud from his diaphragm, like he meant it. Who laughed like that? It was marvelous. Brilliant and marvelous. Stanley wanted to capture it in a bottle, but it was too big for that. It would break the bottle. He swallowed then, and smiled back to Johnny's smile when the guy looked at him to check—the way people do—to see if Stanley thought that part in the movie was as good as Johnny did. Stanley nodded and leaned his head on Johnny's shoulder again and Johnny grabbed his hand. His body was big and warm and Stanley's libido took a breathless second, because oh God....

What would it be like to be surrounded by that body? Not just have it moving behind him, but to have those shoulders covering his, or soft kisses along the back of his neck or all that warmth pressing him into the mattress from (it made him giddy to think about) the front, while Johnny kissed him?

Oh God. The thought of it made Stanley shiver and ache, and the feeling was just so delicious! He couldn't remember the last time he'd shivered and ached, and he realized, with a shock, that he wouldn't trade this moment of breathless desire, of *yearning*, in a laughter-filled movie theater for all the quickie-fucks in a club he'd ever had.

The movie ended and they filed out with the other patrons. Stanley was in mid burble about how wonderful the flying reindeer were when he felt Johnny's hand, sans glove, cover his, the fingers lacing together.

Stanley stopped burbling and tightened his grip on Johnny's hand. They got into the car—a plain black Cadillac—and Johnny drove them back to the yarn store, where Stanley's car was parked. It was quiet for part of the way, and then Johnny started speaking.

"I haven't always lived an honest life," he said quietly. "And I haven't always been the nicest guy. But you make me smile when nothing about nothing has made me smile in a couple of years. Do you think we could do this again?"

"Dinner and a movie?" Stanley asked, and to his embarrassment, he sounded... enchanted. Excited. Enthralled. A teenage virgin, excited about his first prom.

"With the possibility for more, when it's right," Johnny told him. He drove that Caddy like the car had no choice but to do what he said. Stanley didn't worry at all about this man making his way through the slush on the streets of Boulder this cold December night, not even a little. Stanley thought carefully about what he was offering as Johnny swung the car into the yarn store parking lot, and as Johnny set the car in park and then let it idle, he finally figured out what to say.

"That's a really grown-up relationship for someone who doesn't do those," he cautioned. "If I decide to throw a big fuck-me tantrum, are you going to leave because I was a bitch for ten minutes?"

Johnny's smile lit up the darkness inside the car, and he turned to Stanley and caught his chin between two blunt, callused fingers. "If you want it so bad you got to throw a tantrum, Stanley, I just might have to fuck you," he said. He sounded amused, but his voice was so deep, even being amused sounded sexy. Stanley looked at him in the darkness and spent a moment loving the yearn. They were inches apart, and he could feel Johnny's breath against his forehead, and Stanley let the wanting build until he couldn't stand it anymore and tilted back his head, and even as Stanley closed his eyes, Johnny's mouth descended and the kiss began.

This one started face to face, and Stanley was so ready. His lips were sensitized and the first whisper across them made him groan, reach back, and tangle his fingers in Johnny's thick hair, and pull Johnny in close.

Oh... oh wow. His mouth was warm and his lips were soft and his hands... one cupped Stanley's face and the other reached down and cupped his ass, and Stanley was pulled close enough to put his hands up under Johnny's coat and feel that magnificent heat from his broad, heavily muscled chest. And in the meantime, Johnny's tongue was sweeping inside Stanley's mouth and Stanley practically wiggled in excitement. Johnny groaned when Stanley's fingers found his nipples through his undershirt, and another thrill raced Stanley's spine.

Oh God, he wants me!

Johnny pulled away just long enough to kiss down Stanley's throat, and he nuzzled the turtleneck sweater down enough to suckle on Stanley's neck until Stanley gasped and pulled away.

"Don't like that?" Johnny murmured in his ear, and Stanley leaned his head against Johnny's shoulder and panted.

"Loved it," he muttered, "but if I came from getting a hickey, I'd never be able to forgive myself."

Johnny's rumbling laughter was growing familiar by now, but Stanley didn't mind. Johnny pulled back and planted a quick one on Stanley's mouth.

"Now go," Johnny said, unlocking the door from his side. "I'll watch you start your car."

Stanley felt a whimper start. "But…."

Johnny gave another brief, hard kiss. "Saturday night, cupcake. I'll bring a change of clothes; it'll be a sleepover. That okay?"

Stanley beamed. "I thought you said a couple of dates," he purred, not really caring, and Johnny knew it too.

"And I thought I could resist you for more than tonight. I got somewhere to be in Denver early," he said regretfully. "And trust me, Stanley, it's real fucking important. If you think I don't want to get to a bed and show you what we just started should look like naked, you're wrong. But I'll be back. Are we good?"

Stanley nodded, and pressed his lips up against Johnny's again until Johnny opened his mouth and groaned. Stanley's groin was swollen and his nipples were on defcon-1 and his entire body was strung so tightly he thought if Johnny tried the hickey thing again he really *would* come. But if he felt this good now, in a car… oh God. Imagine what a second date would be like! Imagine what doing this in bed would be like!

Stanley pulled back and bit his lip in a little bit of uncertainty. "Can I give you my number? You can call if you can't make it."

Johnny nodded and pulled out his cell for Stanley to dial it in— which he did with shaking fingers. God… it was like being starving and having a… a… a *steak dinner* right there for the taking, but putting it off until you could get out the good silverware. But then, Stanley had eaten plenty of steak dinners on the fly; maybe the good silverware and some clean sheets were worth the price of going home and dreaming into his fist. When Stanley was done with the number, Johnny pressed call, so Stanley would have his number too, and Stanley blushed in the confines of the car.

"I had a very nice time," he said primly. "I do hope we can do it again sometime."

Johnny chuckled, grabbed him by the back of the neck, and hauled him in for another open-mouthed kiss, and this one didn't stop until Stanley was grinding his crotch up against Johnny's massive thigh. This time, when Johnny pulled away, *he* groaned with arousal, and he reached around Stanley's shoulder and shoved the door of the Caddy open into the frigid night.

"You're making me crazy, Stanley. I want you. Just… just trust me, okay? I swear, I won't let you down."

Stanley smiled at him, thinking that just hearing someone promise that was worth nursing the hard-on until he got home.

"You're a real good egg, Johnny," he said. But it wasn't until he got outside and had shut the door that he realized he still didn't know Johnny's last name. Had his cell phone number, but didn't know his last name.

It didn't matter. Johnny was idling and gesturing, and Stanley hopped into his Kia Sportage and started the engine. They both pulled out of the parking lot and drove, Stanley to his apartment and Johnny to the mysterious life he hadn't spoken much about during the date. And for a minute, Stanley thought about being overly curious about someone else's business, but then he got home and plugged in his phone and saw that he had a message.

He checked it, and heard Johnny's voice. *Hey, cupcake. I just wanted to tell you that I had a real good time. I appreciate the hell out of your giving me a chance to be a stand-up guy and come back and keep my promises. I'll do you right, Stanley. I promise.*

Stanley wasn't sure at the end how long he'd been standing there, cuddling the phone to his chest, but when he finally went to bed, his feet were cold, his hard-on was gone, and his eyes burned like he'd been crying, just a little bit, from happiness.

ARIADNE THOUGHT it was promising, but Alice was skeptical. The two of them sat in Ariadne's hospital room and dissected Stanley's date, all of them working on projects as they talked. Ariadne had finished the scarlet cloak and hood, and it hugged her shoulders as she worked on what looked like a pair of tiny baby socks for a friend back in Granby. (Or that's what Stanley thought, until he saw her make three of them. She told Stanley most mothers had assured her that three socks really did make a perfect pair. Apparently even the ones colored like clown puke tended to disappear.)

Stanley told them about dinner, about conversation, about the movie—but he found himself curiously reluctant to part with the most personal bits. For instance, he didn't want to tell them about the sadness on Johnny's face when he mentioned his last lover, or his admiration when he talked about "slutty little bottoms." He didn't want to tell them about his own embarrassment at being a "slutty little bottom," and he didn't want to tell them that Johnny had said nice things about his friendship or his loyalty. He didn't want to tell them about the sultry promise of that last phone message, because that right there was tempting fate.

But they were smart women, canny women, who listened and discussed like a chorus of fates. "He fed you bites of steak? That's almost kinky, you think?" Ariadne made some thoughtful stitches as she spoke, and Alice (who knitted overhand, throwing her yarn like a world class pitcher) threw a beauty of a fiber pitch and nodded.

"That's intimate right there," she said seriously. "And it shows a little class. If he'd just plowed through the plate, he'd be just a guy, but this one—no, no, that's sort of classy."

So when Stanley was done, they all fell silent for a moment, knitting in contemplation, before Ariadne spoke up. "You're keeping something back, aren't you? Don't you think so, Alice? He's keeping something back?"

Alice looked at her in admiration. The two women (who had also known each other by phone, and who had squealed like teenagers upon meeting and settled right into their rightful role as Stanley's clique) were completely in agreement. "Oh yes," she agreed. "I think so." But then she stopped thoughtfully. "No, Stanley—don't deny it. But don't tell us either."

Stanley gaped at her in surprise, and Ariadne nodded her head in agreement. "Oh, definitely."

"You don't want to know?" He wasn't sure to be hurt or outraged—or reassured.

"No," they both said, and then Ariadne (who was probably used to filling in the blanks for Craw) added, "It's yours, Stanley. It's private. It's not a quickie or a club hook-up. It's real. It can be yours if you want." She smiled her own secretive smile and patted her tummy. "There's some stuff between lovers that should be theirs alone."

Alice impulsively leaned over and kissed her cheek. "You're totally scrumptious," she pronounced. "I'm adopting you. Candace isn't going to gestate for another ten years or so; I want the right to hold your offspring."

Ariadne sniffled. "My mom still lives in Seattle, sweetie. You can hold the little spawn whenever we can hook up."

They hugged, and Stanley smiled at them distractedly. Inside, he was thinking that he'd grown up in a busy house. About the only thing he'd ever had that had been his and his alone was his sexuality, and he'd damned near hired a skywriter to give that away. Maybe it was about time he had something just for Stanley.

Then Ariadne must have decided the silence had gone on too long, because she said, "So, does anyone want to hear about Aiden and Jeremy?" And the dishing was on!

"Have they told Craw yet?" Stanley asked, genuinely interested.

Ariadne shook her head "no." "Okay, so Jeremy was minding the store today, right, and I called in right before it opened. The thing about Jeremy is that when he's nervous, he can't shut up. He doesn't talk about anything *important*, right, but he just talks. So he was going *off*, about the alpacas and how they weren't behaving and how the new delivery guy was someone he knew from back in the day, and I knew the store was about to open, so I said, 'Cut the crap, Jeremy—what's the story with you and Aiden?'"

"And?" Stanley and Alice said in tandem. You just didn't leave somebody hanging like that, did you?

Ariadne shook her head. "See, the thing is, you guys both know Aiden, right? He's done deliveries and shit for you, right? So anyway, he's turning twenty-one this January, and Craw still thinks of him as a little kid. And he went in to talk to Craw—I guess they were out in the barn—and Jeremy didn't hear what happened. All he knew was that Craw stalked out of the barn yelling, 'It's not happening because I say it's not!' and that was that."

Stanley looked at her a little horrified—and she looked concerned too. "But... what about Jeremy? He's not going to lose his job or anything, is he?"

Ariadne looked at him then, sharply, and almost like she'd said too much. She took her time answering. "No," she said softly. "No.

Craw wouldn't cut Jeremy loose." She sighed, and smiled at him, like she was gauging how much to say. "Jeremy needs the farm. He's... he's sort of helpless on his own."

Stanley frowned, thinking about the slick, fast-talking little man. "Seriously? I always got the impression he could take care of himself wherever."

Ariadne nodded, thinking hard. "Physically, yes. But...." She shook her head. "Let's just say that neither of them are going anywhere, because Craw doesn't want to lose them, but they're not talking a whole lot right now either."

Stanley cocked his head. "What aren't you telling us?"

Ariadne grimaced. "You know how I said some stuff is yours, right?"

"Yeah."

"Well, this stuff is sort of Jeremy's. I hope that's okay."

Stanley nodded. Of course it was. But.... "If Jeremy knew the delivery guy, that'd be Johnny. I wonder how they knew each other," he mused. He'd have to ask Johnny if... *when* Johnny showed up for their second date.

YEAH, HE showed.

He was there about half an hour before the store closed, and he sat down on one of the couches next to Gretchen, a regular, and heard all about how she was knitting all six of her grandchildren sweaters, and her ungrateful children had damned well better send her a picture of the kids in their sweaters or she wasn't making them *shit*, ever fucking again. (Gretchen had been a fry cook in a diner for over thirty years. She was being mild today.)

Of course, Lily-Anne, their little church-going junior college student, was (as always) appalled by Gretchen—she had the big eyes and the shocked face to prove it. But that didn't stop her from sitting next to the tall, rawboned Gretchen and getting an earful *whenever* they attended Saturday knit night at the same time. Stanley finished up with his customers and exchanged glances with Alice. Johnny was nodding at both of them, treating them like ladies and generally showing himself to be a gentleman of the first water, and Stanley?

Was trying not to die inside a little at how wonderful it was to see Johnny just sitting there, melding perfectly into his little world.

Alice gave his arm a playful shove and whispered, "Go!" and Stanley grabbed his messenger bag and his current project (still the basket-weave scarf, with enough yarn for a hat tucked in there, in case he finished that), and walked over to where Johnny was sitting. He tapped his shoulder. "You ready to go?"

Johnny turned his head and winked. "Yeah." He stood up and said, "Regretfully, ladies, I must depart, but I look forward to seeing you on many knit-nights to come!"

A chorus of "Bye, Johnny!" came from the women on the surrounding couches, and Johnny grinned at them and bowed. Then he turned and put his hand in the small of Stanley's back and escorted him out to the Cadillac.

Stanley grinned the whole way. "So where to?" he asked, and Johnny smiled with excitement.

"Did you know that there's a ballet company in Boulder?" he asked, and Stanley was actually pretty damned surprised.

"I had no idea."

"Well they're doing *The Nutcracker Suite*. It's on the junior college stage. You want to go and then get a late dinner?"

And Stanley was tickled pink. "You know," he said in wonder, "I don't remember the last time I thought about the ballet or the opera," and Johnny turned to him quickly, his grin flashing wickedly in the dark.

"Oh, cupcake—you'll know it's serious when I take you to the opera."

Stanley swallowed. "I'd love to see the opera with you," he said softly, and Johnny waggled his eyebrows.

"I'll see if I can arrange that," he said softly.

The ballet? It was little kids running around in tights; life didn't get much cuter than that. Johnny held his hand all the way through it, and Stanley felt a sort of deliciousness suffusing his body at the contact of their hands. It was thick and hot, like blood, and strong, like yarn, and soft, like roving before it was spun, and it settled into his chest and seeped throughout his limbs, making his movements languorous and his skin just sing with the blood thundering underneath.

Holding this man's hand was a sensual experience. What would making love be like?

Oh God. Stanley had actually thought "making love" and not "having sex." Somebody alert the media, that was probably a first!

Some of his swoony-ness had receded by the time the ballet was over, and he was ready to eat and to talk, and that's what they did. While eating his chicken Caesar salad and chicken noodle soup at the same steakhouse, Stanley actually remembered his conversation with Ariadne.

"So," he said, taking a bite, "you used to know Jeremy? The kid who works at Craw's mill?"

Johnny couldn't have looked more startled if Stanley had pulled out a gun and started shooting. "Jeremy?" he said, after a moment when Stanley wasn't sure if his big, liquid brown eyes weren't going to just pop right out of his head.

"Yeah—you know. One of the two guys Craw hired. The place you keep delivering from."

Johnny nodded and swallowed what he'd been eating (a grilled salmon this time) and said, "Yeah, yeah. Jeremy and I go way back. His old man and me, we worked for the same guy once upon a time."

Stanley nodded. "What did you do?"

Johnny grimaced like he couldn't answer that question. "Let's just say," he started, and then shook his head. "Let's say we both worked for a not-very-nice man. And Jeremy—he didn't belong there. Not even a little. So, when his father was… uhm, terminated, I made sure Jeremy got some… uhm, benefits from the transaction."

Stanley nodded like he could even pretend he knew what Johnny was talking about, but pursued it doggedly, because he'd been about to start bragging about his cats before that particular topic had come to mind, and he wanted to talk about something else because nothing scared off a big, alpha male like talking about your cats!

"So, Jeremy—what was he like back then?" he asked. "I mean, he's pretty funny now, and I've *never* heard him talking about what his life was like before he came to Craw's."

Johnny took a careful bite of salmon. "Stanley?" he asked, thinking hard, just like Ariadne had been when Stanley had asked about Jeremy.

"Yeah?"

"You've got a pretty good life here, you know?"

Stanley nodded. "I know that," he said softly.

"I mean, you've been lonely, and I'd like to fix that, but you've always had enough to eat, and a cushion of... I don't know, education and resources, right?"

Stanley thought about it and nodded some more. "Yes. That's true."

"The world isn't like that for everybody. It wasn't like that for Jeremy. It wasn't like that for me. Sometimes, the person you become without those things, that's not the sort of person you want to remember. Do you understand?"

Stanley thought about it, remembered Johnny saying he hadn't always been a good person, and tried really, really hard to be what Johnny needed him to be. And failed.

"No," he said apologetically, and then, even as Johnny's face fell, "but I'd like to. I think I need some more information first."

Johnny nodded and took another bite of salmon. "Can you go on faith for tonight?" he asked. "I...." He looked down. "It's not fair of me to ask, I know it."

Stanley felt that warmth, shivering through his body again, and shuddered. "It's more than fair," he said, thinking that he could have banged serial killers he hadn't known about, and that Johnny was at least trying to be honest. "I need to remember, it's as hard for you to jump in the deep end of the pool as it is for me."

Johnny smiled at him, but it was a veiled smile, one with more mystery behind it than light. "I'd love to jump into the deep end of the pool with you," he said softly. "I would just rather not drag you down to the bottom if I don't have to."

And then he started talking about opera, and that was the end of that.

Chapter 5
Mating Habits May Vary

THE RIDE to Stanley's apartment was breathless, and Stanley felt himself besieged by an unusual idea.

Nerves. He was *nervous* about having sex. He tried to deny it— told himself it was silliness of the most bizarre sort—but that didn't change that his hands were clammy in his gloves and his stomach kept giving little twitches and he talked for five minutes straight about Vincent Van Gogh's hairballs and his laughter was shrill enough to shatter glass.

It wasn't until his voice cracked two octaves when telling Johnny to turn left that Johnny started to laugh.

"Nervous, are we?" He took his hand from the steering wheel and patted Stanley's hands as they wrung together in his lap.

"I have no idea what you're talking about," Stanley lied. He couldn't seem to control his breathing.

"I love this part," Johnny confessed like he hadn't heard the lie. "I love the nerves. The more nervous you are, the more important it is. The more important it is, the *better* it is."

"It's only the first time, right?" Oh God. Didn't that sound pathetic? And then Johnny shook his head "no" and Stanley almost cried.

"No—don't you see? That's the best part. It gets *better* and then you're *still* nervous, and then it's all like new again!"

Stanley caught his breath then. He liked new. He liked shiny and exciting. "With the same person?" He had to ask, because he could actually imagine it. He could imagine Johnny being next to him in the car, and he could imagine them coming back from a movie or a play or even, oh God, the *opera*, and being aware of Johnny's every move. He could imagine knowing that Johnny wanted to kiss him, except, by then, he'd *know* what Johnny's touch felt like all over his body, and...

and oh my God, it would be *exquisite*. For the first time ever, Stanley looked forward to the time after the first time.

But that didn't mean the first time wasn't going to be special, either, did it?

Suddenly the sweating palms and the tingling skin and the nervous stomach weren't horrifying at all. Suddenly, they were *electrifying*, and he was so much more excited about this moment, this night with Johnny, than he had been about anything since his first lay. (Which really hadn't been anything to write home about. Not that he hadn't, there at the end.)

Suddenly he remembered whining to Candace about being old. He couldn't possibly be old, could he? He felt so extraordinarily new!

He felt new for the rest of the night.

Johnny had an overnight bag—not a duffel bag, or a gym bag, an honest-to-god piece of gray luggage—and he hefted it easily in one hand and grabbed Stanley's hand with the other after he parked the car in front of Stanley's little row of condos and set the car alarm. Stanley tugged gently and brought him along the cleared sidewalks and up the granite stairs, opening his door and decoding his alarm, then gesturing Johnny in.

"Condo sweet condo," he said whimsically, and Johnny looked around appreciatively. Stanley had taken full advantage of his contract and painted the walls in rich colors—cobalt blue, spring green, bright crimson—with complementary trim and stencils in some rooms and those lovely little wallpaper trims in others. Johnny looked around, taking in the tapestry couches, the white carpets, and even the treadmill and yoga mat in the corner, clearly delighted.

"It looks just like your yarn," he said in wonder. "It's all these deep, complicated colors—and they're gorgeous. You're like a frickin' rainbow!"

Stanley giggled. "That doesn't automatically come with the gay, you know."

Johnny smiled. "Yeah, I hear you. You can't get me out of black, gray, and brown."

Stanley closed the door behind him and locked it, then turned around and looked critically at Johnny, who was wearing a brown sweater and black slacks. In Stanley's living room, he offered a somber counterpoint, but like Ariadne had said about simple colors, sometimes a deep and simple color was a lot more complicated than it was on the surface.

"It suits you," he said sincerely. "It's... it's got depth."

Johnny laughed softly, still looking around. Van Gogh opened one eye lazily and then went back to his twentieth hour of REM cycle. Henry Matisse hissed and darted away, presumably under Stanley's bed where he usually hung out. Johnny laughed again.

"You got a really nice place here," he said softly. "It's happy."

Stanley looked at his feet, absurdly pleased. "I *am* happy," he said, feeling stupid for being honest. "I had no idea how happy until you came by last week."

Johnny frowned. "So I made you—"

"No!" Stanley grimaced. "No—you *do* made me happy. I just... I sort of had this epiphany, you know? About how good I had it, and how maybe I should stop looking for the wrong things in the wrong places and be happy about the things I'd done right... does that make sense?"

Johnny looked startled, like maybe he'd been thinking the same thing. "Yeah—that makes complete sense."

"Yeah? Good. Because I was just starting to realize that my life was really pretty damned good, and then you walked in, and it got better."

Johnny's smile was the kind that made the grooves wreathe around his cheeks. "You too," he said, nodding. "And that's good. That's real good."

Stanley suddenly felt the awkwardness of standing there at the doorway and staring at Johnny in the middle of his floor. "Uhm, the bedroom is right down the hall," he said. "If you, uhm, go put your stuff in there, I can pour you a glass of wine for a nightcap."

Johnny's smile grew soft. "Stanley?"

"Yeah?"

"I want to kiss you real bad. How 'bout you turn off most of the lights, take me back to the bedroom, and let me do that. We had our wine with dinner."

Stanley's face stayed turned toward his bright, shiny short leather boots, but his eyes cut sideways to Johnny, who was still looking at him kindly. Stanley reached behind him and turned off the track lighting in the living room, leaving just the stove light in the adjoining kitchen on, and then took Johnny's hand to walk with him down the hallway.

Stanley's bedroom was a study in burgundy and brown, with white walls and burgundy trim. It wasn't bright so much as a bold color choice, and his bed had brown sheets and a burgundy comforter. He couldn't explain it to anyone else and not feel foolish, but the colors made him feel… protected, somehow. Wrapped in the muscles-and-sweat masculinity he'd never had himself, but had always desired in other men.

Of course, with all of that, it was meticulously organized, and the first thing he did was divest himself of his long coat, his hat, his scarf (the pop-my-cherry red one), and his gloves (a present from Alice), putting each thing in its appropriate cubby along the wall and his shoes in the shoe rack in the bottom of the closet. It was his evening routine, and it soothed him, and when he turned around, he saw that of all things, Johnny had done the same. His coat was hung up on the peg on the door—his scarf too—and his hat (the one Stanley had made him) was tucked in the pocket with his gloves. He'd pulled his garment bag out of his suitcase and hung that under the coat, and Stanley felt a quirky little smile bloom on his face.

"That's amazing," he said, and Johnny looked over his shoulder from where he was brushing his coat.

"What?"

"You're… I don't know… civilized…."

Johnny's grin came out, the one that made his teeth glint and the grooves in his cheeks pop, and he said, "I'm not *that* civilized," before he took two steps toward Stanley, that was all, just two, and grabbed his arm and hauled him in for savage, brutal kiss.

Stanley blossomed like a pinecone in the heat of a fire. All his sarcastic prickles and his nervous little layers opened and it was just him, just the way he'd always wanted to be during sex—sweet and pliable and heated to the core. All he'd ever wanted was to open to Johnny's mouth and his hands and the relentless way his body strove to dominate Stanley's own.

Stanley groaned—the better to give Johnny access to his tonsils—and grabbed Johnny around the waist, reaching down to cup his ass and haul him close. Oh *yes*—Stanley had wondered, who wouldn't? But the bulge, hard and thick, pressing above the belt buckle of Stanley's jeans, was plenty big enough, plenty powerful enough, and Stanley shivered again to realize that Johnny really *was* everything he'd ever wanted.

Johnny ground against him, and Stanley started fumbling with his belt buckle immediately. Oh *yes*, yes yes yes yes yes… he knew where this was going, it was his favorite destination, and he was going to get there *right now*!

And then Johnny put his hands on Stanley's and whispered, "Slower."

Stanley's heart went triple-time in his ears.

"Slower?"

Johnny pulled away and placed a series of small, languid, nipping kisses down Stanley's cheek. When he spoke, his voice was a gravel whisper. "Slower."

Stanley had to hold on to something besides Johnny's ass for slower. He reached up and put one hand on Johnny's neck and the other on his shoulder and held on. The warm skin under his palm grew heated and damp as Johnny moved his kisses down Stanley's neck. Johnny didn't fumble with Stanley's clothes—he backed up and pulled off Stanley's thin, ribbed turtleneck (to hide his *last* hickey!) and then the undershirt beneath it and moved forward, his body all heat and hard muscle, to resume those tender, languid kisses down Stanley's collarbone, down his chest, to his nipples.

Oh dear God, his nipples.

Johnny suckled and laved for a moment and Stanley buried his hands in that thick hair and moaned. Johnny's hands were rooted firmly on his hips, and Stanley needed them there, because he was about two seconds away from flopping on the bed, spreading himself out like a starfish, and just letting Johnny do whatever he wanted. Oh God… if it was as good as that tight, pinpoint arousal from his nipples to his groin, it couldn't possibly be a bad thing to do!

Johnny worked his belt buckle and Stanley managed some self-assertion. "*I* wanted to give the blowjob," he panted, and Johnny laughed against the soft skin of his stomach. (Stanley did crunchies every morning; his abs were hard, but his skin was like buttermilk, pale and smooth.)

"I like it when we both give the blowjob," Johnny said, and then suckled in some of Stanley's pale skin with enough bite to leave another hickey.

Stanley's knees went weak from the hickey alone. He was going to ask if he could sit down, or lie down, or maybe suck Johnny's cock first so he didn't have to humiliate himself, when Johnny dragged his pants down, boxers and all, and Stanley was naked, pale and aroused, in the middle of his own bedroom.

Had he ever had another man in his bedroom?

As soon as the thought hit, Johnny pushed him backward until he was sitting on the bed, and Johnny pushed him one more time so he was lying down, and then? Oh yeah… Johnny's hands were big, and he wrapped his big, hard hand around Stanley's pale, hard cock and squeezed, and stroked, and then his mouth, hot and wet, surrounded the head and Stanley's fingers scrabbled on his comforter as he tried to get a handle on what to do when his entire nervous system was exploding.

"I'm going to come…," he hissed and swallowed and closed his eyes and thought of tax returns. "Way too soon. I'm going to come way too soon if you don't give me something to do."

Johnny's response was to take him down into the back of his throat, tighten his lips around the base, and gently tug on Stanley's balls.

Stanley arched his hips off the bed and cried out, coming fast and hot and hard enough to make his eyes roll back in his head, and Johnny just kept swallowing, while Stanley clenched his fingers in his hair tight enough to hurt. He came back down to earth (and his ass came back down to the bed) and he fought hard against the urge to cry.

"Too soon," he muttered sadly, and in response, Johnny pulled himself on the bed next to him and kissed him. Oh geez… had Stanley ever tasted his own come in someone's mouth? It was… intimate. Electrifying, and his kiss back was starving and rapacious and like he hadn't just come at all. Johnny pulled back from the kiss and smiled, his eyes half-closed, looking supremely satisfied and leonine.

"Not too soon, cupcake," he purred. "Just getting started."

Stanley's response was to jump his bones. He pushed off the bed and kissed him back, flipping them both around until Johnny was on his back and Stanley was on top. Johnny was mostly dressed, and Stanley burrowed like a gopher, slipping open the buttons of his shirt and working his belt and the fastener of his slacks, moving quickly and nimbly so he could get under Johnny's clothes and touch his skin. He wiggled off the bed to shuck Johnny's pants and socks, and he left them with the rest of his own clothes, on a puddle at the foot of the bed. He came back up and caught his breath.

Johnny—*Johnny*—was spread out on his queen-sized bed, his cock thick and erect against his stomach, his swarthy skin golden and his muscles heavy and defined. He was beautiful, massive from long, thick cock to tree-trunk thighs to hairy chest, and Stanley wanted to just fall on him and devour him like a wolf.

He went for the soft skin of his stomach first and licked it, to see if Johnny was ticklish. He was sensitive, that was for sure, because his cock flexed and smacked against his tummy until Stanley had to wrap his hand around it and stroke to make it behave. Johnny groaned and started massaging Stanley's bare back as he stroked. Stanley moved up to nibble on Johnny's nipples while he was stroking. Johnny groaned again and said, "Suck it, just for a minute, 'cause I've got plans for you."

Oh heavens—was there anything sexier than that? *Pleasure me so I can blow your mind?*

And Johnny's cock tasted *so good*. A little salty, and Stanley had to stretch his mouth around the shaft and relax his throat to get halfway down, but he used his fist for the other half and was rewarded when Johnny shuddered and spread his legs a little wider, inviting exploration.

Every part of him was like virgin territory—even if he was anything but virginal.

"Oh God... yeah, like that. C'mon, cupcake... oh yeah... deeper... deeper...." Stanley lunged forward, gratified by the groan that he'd actually felt emanating from Johnny's stomach as his diaphragm flexed under Stanley's hand. He switched hands and palmed Johnny's thighs and then snuck under and cupped his flexing, hairy ass. (The hair was sublime. The hair meant this was a man, not a preening club boy.)

Stanley let a little bit of spit dribble down so he could use it to slicken his finger and skate it down in Johnny's crease.

"Whoa!" Johnny gasped, and Stanley pulled back.

"You don't like that?"

"Love it," Johnny muttered. "I'm crazy about it. But I got a job to do tonight." With that, Johnny's fingers were firm on Stanley's shoulders, and suddenly Johnny was scooting, and without much effort, he'd put his hands on Stanley's hips and positioned Stanley on top of him, his (erect again!) cock dangling over Johnny's mouth in a basic 69.

Stanley was a little stunned at the turnaround, and then, oh he*llo!* Would he ever get used to that slick heat? Johnny liked to blow with a little bit of tongue and just the tiniest edge of teeth, and when Stanley felt that combo on his crown he whimpered and thrashed, and only Johnny's firm hands on his hips kept him from wriggling off and just quivering in a hyper-sensitized lump of orgasm on top of the cover. In retaliation, he found Johnny's crease again and tickled the little puckered divot he found there, and Johnny grunted around his cock in approval. Suddenly Stanley was being manhandled again, and when things were settled, he found himself on his back, with Johnny's big, firm hands on his lower thighs while Johnny nuzzled his backside, burrowing with his tongue.

Stanley grabbed his upper thighs and held them wide and spread so Johnny could use his hands for other things, and then realized what he was doing.

"Uhm…," he said, suddenly a little amazed at the intimacy. It wasn't that he didn't *want* to do this, or that he wasn't sure it wouldn't feel *wonderful*, but, again, it wasn't something you *did* on a one or two time hook-up.

But Johnny took his cue and spread Stanley's bubble-butt cheeks. Then he looked up between Stanley's legs, over his cock, and winked.

"Don't worry," he said, his teeth glinting in a smile. "I learned how to do this from a pro."

In a moment Stanley was wide open to the world and Johnny's mouth was right *there*, and his tongue was wriggling around right *omigodandholyhell* right *there*! And it wasn't a sharp kind of pleasure, not a "Holy God fuck me *now*!" kind of pleasure; it was more a delirious, dreamy, drugging sort of pleasure, and Stanley probably could have let Johnny do that all night, but Johnny looked up and started giving orders.

"C'mon, Stanley, grab your cock. I want to hear you—"

Stanley moaned, and Johnny buried his tongue against Stanley's clenching entrance again.

"Mmm…." Johnny sighed, and Stanley let loose with the noises, because oh hell, anything he could do to reward Johnny for a job well done, Stanley was all for.

Suddenly he was close again, oh God, all it would take would be a tug on the balls, a finger where Johnny's tongue was, and he must have gibbered something like that because Johnny disappeared for a moment, and Stanley heard the (familiar) tearing of a condom wrapper and there was the feeling of a lubed rubber, right up where Johnny's tongue had been.

Stanley looked up then, realized that Johnny was big enough to loom, and that his own eyes were big and luminous. Oh wow. After all of that, he was going to get fucked too? Fan*tast*ic!

Johnny was pushing slowly inside, and he was so wide, and Stanley was *so* ready, and the stretch and the fullness and the pleasure/pain… oh God, it was *exquisite*, and omigod, Johnny was inside of him, thrusting forward, until he was all the way in and they were both gasping.

"Hey," Johnny rasped. "Open your eyes."

Stanley did, and Johnny stayed buried inside Stanley's ass, but he fell forward and cupped Stanley's face, holding him there for a long, wet, pleasurable, drugging kiss. And again, and again, he kept kissing Stanley until Stanley's body was quivering, begging, and he couldn't take the amping and the arousal and the….

"Oh God, Johnny, please!"

Johnny chuckled and pushed up again, holding Stanley's thighs back with his big hands.

"Please what?"

"Please please?"

Johnny pulled his hips back so the head of his cock stretched Stanley's entrance.

"Please what?"

Stanley moved his hand to his cock, desperate to jerk himself to some relief, but Johnny captured his hand and wove their fingers together.

"Say it, Stanley," he said, still smiling, and Stanley looked at him, helplessly, needing, and begged.

"God, Johnny, fuck me hard... fuck me so hard... fuck me until I can taste you in my mouth... *oh God, yes!*"

Johnny was thrusting, pounding, stretching, and Stanley wanted it, wanted it so bad that when Johnny moved his hand back to the back of Stanley's thigh, Stanley didn't even need to put his hand on his cock, because he was erect, and sensitive, and Johnny was slamming into him and it just... oh it just... oh God....

"Jerk it now," Johnny ordered, and Stanley managed to focus just long enough to grab himself and stroke, hard and fast and....

"*Yesss!*" He came all over his abdomen and a little on his chest, and Johnny grunted, "*Yess!*" and shuddered and shuddered, groaning like he was pushing a fence post through a needle (which it felt like he was) and finally falling forward and clutching Stanley close to his sweating chest while the two of them quivered in climax.

THE DARK was silent, soft, and kind. It covered Stanley's shoulders when they were shaking, shaded spots dancing in front of his eyes, and masked the terrible vulnerability that was left behind when he'd just poured his soul out in orgasm with a man he'd known for a week.

How could he ever think a week was enough time to know a person before doing this?

Suddenly all those meaningless club hook-ups assumed a pitiful color—is *this* what he'd been trying to do when he'd been blowing strangers in back rooms? Is *this* what he'd wanted when he'd bent over, spread his ass cheeks, and allowed his body to be invaded on a whim? God, how arrogant could he have been, thinking fifteen minutes of chat in a loud room, or over a drink, or, hell, in the bathroom of the yarn store with Craw, gave someone he didn't know the license to his body?

How could he have assumed sex was for anything less than the total annihilation of his individual person, and the merging of himself and another human being into one?

Johnny was placing little, gentle kisses on his cheeks, his forehead, over his closed eyes, and along his jaw, and Stanley was in no shape to do anything but let him.

Finally his breathing stilled, and Johnny's erection shrank a little and fell out of his body. After some thrashing and flailing with the covers and getting rid of the used condom, Johnny rolled off him and situated them both under the sheets and the comforter, naked and sticky and warming after the chill of the room.

Johnny tucked Stanley against his chest and kissed his temple. "You okay?" he murmured, and they were probably the first words either of them had said since that extraordinary climax.

"I'm sort of stunned," Stanley said. "In fact, I'm reassembling the world as I knew it."

Johnny's laugh was low and intimate in his ear, and Stanley turned his head and kissed him, surprising them both. The kiss lingered, and Stanley pulled away, then rolled over and propped his chin on Johnny's chest.

"Do you know I don't even know your last name?" he said, and that quality around them, that air of peaceful melancholy, changed.

"Russo," Johnny said with reluctance. "Very Italian."

Stanley smiled at him winningly, hoping to release some of the tension from Johnny's body. "I never would have guessed," he said and managed to maintain a straight face.

Johnny laughed and as he released his breath, he relaxed just a little. "You're very perceptive," he said dryly, and Stanley grinned like he'd won something.

"Okay," he murmured. "Okay, Johnny Russo. That was amazing. And you know, I'm usually a pretty self-obsessed sort of guy, but right now? Right now, I want to know everything about you. Isn't that strange?"

Johnny's hand came up and smoothed Stanley's hair back from his forehead. "No, no, that's natural. Lovers do that, when they want to stay together."

Stanley beamed and dropped his head to kiss Johnny's chest, and his skin tasted so good he did it again.

"So who was the pro?" he asked, smiling, and he was a little dismayed when Johnny scowled back.

"What?"

"The rim-job—you told me you'd learned from a pro. Who was the pro?"

Johnny's expression did a very careful dance then, between neutrality, dismay, and yearning. "Stanley," he said, and he sounded too desperate for a man who'd just rocked Stanley's world, "is there any way…." Johnny's voice dropped. "I want you to think the world of me," he said after a moment, and Stanley grimaced at him.

"Honey, I'm a manwhore," he said frankly. "And I'm a manwhore because I'm a coward. Until *literally* five minutes ago, I was too damned afraid of what would happen if we did what we just did. And now we did it, and…." He sighed and realized his way had never been anything but honest. "I'm feeling very naked here, Johnny. I just did something with you I haven't done with anyone else: I had sex and meant it. Can you give me anything that makes me feel safer than the dark?"

Johnny's massive hand came up and splayed on his back, and Stanley shivered, feeling protected.

"He was really a pro," Johnny said softly, his eyes focused anywhere but on Stanley's face. "I… I picked him up one night because I was too busy to date and…."

"The loneliness," Stanley finished with a swallow, thinking of Jethro and Craw and the fact that he would have fucked anyone, anytime, just for that momentary spark of *maybe* connecting with another human being.

"Yeah," Johnny whispered. "Anyway, he was a sweet kid." Johnny's smile was so crooked it drew blood. "Way too young for me. And he was really trying to get through college. And… you know. He'd learned all these tricks, and…." Johnny's voice thinned, leaving only a brief sound trail in the darkness. "He was a real sweet kid."

Stanley's heart gave a big thump. *Was* a sweet kid? Oh. *Oh.* Before, when he'd bargained with his self-respect, he'd thought that was the only currency he had in sex. He never realized that *this*, this painful moment right here, was the highest rate of trade a lover had.

And for a moment he didn't want to pay it. For a moment, he didn't want to ask the hard question. He thought about kissing Johnny on the forehead and curling up into a ball and hoping they could stay together in spite of what he hadn't been willing to give.

But Johnny had given him…. God. It was like getting a color television after living with a black and white TV your whole life. The least Stanley owed him was the hard question.

"What happened to him?"

Johnny swallowed and closed his eyes. "Well, you know, he was in the wrong bedroom at the wrong time. He heard some mob guy's secrets and got caught. And… and the lowlife he'd hooked up with, well, he knew the only reason he was breathing air was that his boss didn't know he was gay. And the kid didn't give him up, either. Told some cock-and-bull story about breaking in there to steal, but it didn't matter. The boss guy blew him away. And… and the fucking coward he was with… he just cleaned up the fucking body like he always cleaned up the fucking body, and that… that sweet kid, who used to watch cartoons on my couch, eating cereal in his underwear, he… he got dumped in a shallow fucking grave."

Johnny's voice was tight and squeaky, and Stanley had a horrible moment of his own cowardice, thinking *I can't do this. I don't know pain. I've never had pain. I've spent my entire life running the hell away from it.* But Johnny was here in his arms, and Stanley didn't want him anywhere but right here.

He kissed Johnny's chest again. "There was nothing you could do," he said, and even before Johnny opened his mouth, Stanley knew the truth.

"I could have stood up for him," Johnny said thickly.

For a moment, Stanley thought about playing dumb and saying "How?" but he didn't. He could pretend he didn't know Johnny was talking about himself as the "fucking coward," could pretend Johnny didn't have a past that maybe Stanley shouldn't know about, but then, would he ever have another moment like this one? Would he ever have another chance to have all of Johnny in his arms? If he played dumb, he could go on in innocence, and pretend the man who'd just rocked his world wasn't hooked up with a mob boss and guns and violent death—but he'd maybe lose the chance to ever be more to Johnny than a body in the dark. Maybe bravery was just a matter of knowing which loss would hurt worse.

"If you'd stood up for him, you'd be dead too," Stanley told him, and Johnny's eyes squeezed shut tight, but even in the moonlight coming through the window behind the bed, Stanley could see the shiny glint beneath his black lashes.

"At least I wouldn't be a coward," Johnny whispered.

"Did you know? Did you know he was going to get...." God, Stanley couldn't even say "shot" or "blown away." People in Stanley's world didn't *get* shot or blown away. That was for television people, or the newspapers, that wasn't for real life.

Johnny shook his head. "I ask myself every day," he said. "Every day, I ask myself how I couldn't have seen it coming. But the kid... there was no reason, you know? No reason, except he said he was a hooker-thief, and... and Mario, he didn't like hookers, 'cause he knew what they were doing. And suddenly...." Johnny shook his head and passed his hand over his eyes. Stanley rolled to his side and grabbed a couple of Kleenex from the end table and handed them over.

Johnny smiled through his tears and took the tissue and wiped his eyes and blew his nose and rolled over and dropped the tissue in the garbage can, then rolled back over.

Stanley was there, propping himself up on one elbow, gathering Johnny in, holding his face against his chest and letting him cry. He knew there was more to the story, knew there were things he should probably know, but right now, what mattered was that he was still here, and Johnny was in his bed, and that's where he was going to stay.

Chapter 6
Predators Should Be Wary of a Knitter's Surprise Weapons

STANLEY ACTUALLY had to work Sunday, but he put it off until the last minute. He and Johnny fell asleep after making love (that was a real word now—Stanley had always assumed it was just a nice way of saying "came") and then awakened sometime in the night to do it again, slowly, gently, without penetration, which Stanley would have claimed to be impossible at one point in his life.

But it happened, Johnny gliding slowly and sensually between Stanley's thighs, his big arm wrapped around Stanley's waist to stroke Stanley while Stanley lost his mind. The next morning Stanley woke up and Johnny was wrapped around his shoulders, so warmly, so securely, Stanley wondered how he could have slept without a Johnny-blanket for most of his entire life.

He tried to wriggle out of the embrace after a moment—he was sticky and his flaccid cock was damned near glued to his thighs with come—but Johnny tightened his arms.

"Not yet," he murmured, and started kissing languidly down from the nape of Stanley's neck down to between his collarbone, and Stanley melted.

"I"—gasp—"never really thought of that as"—oh God—"an errogen... erro... errogen... oh crap..." because Johnny was down to the small of his back now. Johnny chuckled against him then and stuck out his tongue and licked a pointed path all the way back up before placing a careful bite on Stanley's shoulder.

Stanley lay there, panting, in the early morning sunlight. Sometime in the night, Johnny had gotten up and come back with a limp and sleepy Vincent Van Gogh, who was stretched out in front of Stanley now, looking bored. Stanley reached out and scratched his stomach, and the cat started up a purring from his belly that shook the bed. Johnny was still pressed up against Stanley's back, growing hard, and Stanley laughed helplessly.

"Again?" he asked in disbelief.

Johnny kissed his neck again. "The way I figure it, you got a choice. Now in bed or later in the shower?"

Stanley shoved Vincent Van Gogh off the bed, rolled over in Johnny's arms, and kissed him, morning breath and all. "Both," he whispered, thinking he'd take it all.

"Both?" Johnny rocked his body hard against Stanley's stomach, and Stanley purred just like his cat.

"Both."

So they did both.

When they got out of the shower, Stanley didn't have much time. He hustled, making them egg-white omelets with spinach, mushrooms, and lo-fat Swiss cheese, and was pleased when Johnny—who seemed to take his food seriously—enjoyed the whole thing, without ketchup.

They got to the store—where Stanley had left his car—and Johnny put the car into park and leaned over, seizing his chin and pulling him in for a kiss.

"I've got a delivery here tomorrow morning," he said softly, and Stanley heated, both from the whispered, coy little kiss and from the implication.

"I can have my break with you," he said, looking at the big, dark-skinned man with the liquid eyes and the gentle touch from under his lashes.

"I'd like that. I can come back after, we could, I don't know—"

"Order takeout and watch TV?" Stanley said hopefully, and Johnny's grin brightened the pissiness of the gray sleet that was falling around them.

"That sounds a little tame, cupcake; you really up for that?"

"I want… I want to cuddle," Stanley said, sniffing and looking out his window, like it was casual and he said those words to every guy he laid.

"Yeah?"

Stanley cut his eyes sideways and saw that terribly, terribly gentle smile on Johnny's face, like he knew cuddling on the couch with someone besides the cats or his girlfriends was a luxury Stanley had dreamed not of.

"Yeah," Stanley said, returning his gaze back to the front of the store. He frowned a little. Some asshole had stood about five feet to the left of the store and smoked what looked like half a pack. The butts were all ground out in the slush on the sidewalk and Stanley wrinkled his nose. He'd have to go out there with the little broom and dustpan-on-a-stick to sweep that up. That was just… just *tacky*.

But Johnny's body was warm next to his, and Johnny's hand on his shoulder was insistent that Stanley's complete concentration be right on Johnny, where it belonged.

"You sure you're ready to try snuggling?" he asked. "You know, that could lead to all sorts of horrible things—whole weekends together, more dates—"

Stanley grinned impishly. "Opera?"

Johnny actually giggled. "Stanley, I'd *so* take you to the opera."

"Yeah?"

"Yeah."

"Well, maybe later. Maybe tomorrow night, we can start with a snuggle."

Johnny's kiss was so warm and kind, Stanley didn't want to leave.

THE NEXT evening, they did end up snuggling—but Stanley had to go Christmas shopping first. He dragged Johnny along, looking for a present for Alice, for Candace, for Craw and Ariadne—even for Aiden and Jeremy, who had given him matching gloves and a scarf the year before.

"Why don't you knit for them?" Johnny asked, and Stanley shrugged, almost as embarrassed to confess this as he had been to confess to being a manwhore.

"'Cause I just really started to knit," he mumbled, as they were walking from The Body Shop to a specialized beauty boutique.

"But I thought you worked there for, what?"

"Eleven years," Stanley told him, looking in the window. "Oh my heavens! Would you just look at that gemstone mosaic piece? It was *exactly* what Candace would wear right now!" Stanley mentally consigned the entire shower set he'd just bought for Candace at l'Occitane to Amanda's gift and decided he *must* buy that for his darling, price be damned.

"So you worked in a yarn store for eleven years and just learned to knit?"

Stanley shot him a look of annoyance. "She also owns a paper craft store, a quilting boutique, and an entire store devoted to cake decorating. You don't see me taking up any of *those* hobbies, do you?"

Johnny thought about it as they walked into the store, the little bell tinkling to announce their arrival. "I know, I know—but I just never see you without it. You wear the hobby like you wear your scarf. It's adorable."

Stanley wrinkled his forehead, not in irritation as much as thought. "I like it," he said simply. "It's… it's *real*. I guess I just hit a phase where I wanted something real. I didn't know how to make it a man, so I made it something else I'd been looking at for years and hadn't figured out how to work."

Johnny loomed over him and kissed his cheek. "And then the man came."

Oh, Candace's gift was just sitting there, in the glass case, looking gorgeous and perfect. Stanley caught the sales clerk's eye and saw the man coming to free Candace's most perfect gift. While they were waiting, he turned to Johnny, who was wearing the hat Stanley had knit, and winked flirtily. "Yup. The man came, and I knit for him!"

Johnny's chuckle warmed him as he serenely paid a crapload of money for the only present he could give his darling with a whole heart.

That night, he curled up on Johnny and knit while they watched *Santa Claus is Coming to Town*.

"I can't believe this is how we're spending our date night," Johnny muttered when Stanley teared up at the wedding scene between Jessica and Chris Cringle.

"I can't believe you've never seen this," Stanley sniffled. He went to wipe his eyes with his shirt, but Johnny handed him the box of tissues he kept on the end table just for movies like this one, the kind that snuck up and bit you on the ass with unrepentant sentimentality.

"My mother let us watch two kinds of movies," Johnny said bluntly. "*The Godfather I-IV*, and anything by Martin Scorsese."

Stanley stopped sniffling over the Christmas movie long enough to stare. "Mobster movies? Really?"

Johnny watched the TV with immense concentration, even though it was now advertising some sort of whirling pink and silver thing for four-year-old girls.

"It was a family thing," he said after a few heartbeats. He looked at Stanley with a sigh. "You know... *family*. Like, it was my *family* that killed Neil for being a rent boy in my house?"

Stanley's breath stopped, and he watched Johnny's careful study of nonchalance. "Oh," he said, raising his eyebrows. "Johnny, how long ago did that happen?"

Johnny sighed. "A little over three years."

Okay. That was some distance. For a moment, Stanley had panicked, wondering if he'd be fighting the ghost of Johnny's rent boy for as long as they... well, made dates to cuddle on the couch. And then he focused on the word "family," because Johnny kept saying it like he was trying to tell Stanley something.

"Is there something I'm missing about that word?" Stanley asked after a moment.

"Which word?"

"Family?"

Johnny squeezed his eyes shut in helpless laughter. "It means different things to east coast Italians than it does to Colorado cupcakes, I guess," he said after a moment, and Stanley blinked.

"Really?" he asked, suddenly remembering that he'd watched *The Sopranos* religiously for all eight seasons. But... but... that wasn't *real*, was it? And now that he'd made the connection (feeling stupid, because he should have made it when Johnny had told him about his poor, doomed lover two nights ago), Stanley had to ask.

"Johnny, were you... are you...?"

"I wasn't made," Johnny said quickly. He pulled Stanley back into his chest, gently running his fingers through Stanley's white-blond hair (which looked completely natural now, and Stanley was absurdly proud of that, if only for this moment).

"Good," Stanley said, feeling cowardly and relieved at the same time. The thought of his gentle Johnny, doing that final, violent thing.... He shuddered, and then realized the truth. "Good. I might have been able to live with it anyway, but... good."

The commercial ended and the program came back on, and Stanley was suddenly wrapped up in the here and now—Johnny's heat against his back, the goofy sentimentality in front of him, and the knowledge that sometimes truth was a gift.

And, of course, more questions. "You know," Stanley said after a moment, "I can dish about people I hardly know for hours, but asking you questions right now is sort of scary. Can I make a suggestion?"

"I'm game."

"Yeah. Uhm, anything you want to tell me, you just assume I want to know."

"So like for instance?"

Stanley thought about it. "Did you love your rent boy?"

Johnny was quiet. "Would it be awful if I said yes?"

Stanley thought about it some more. "No," he said after a moment. "I've never been in love. It would be good if one of us knew what it felt like, right?"

Johnny's arms tightened around Stanley's shoulders. "I did love him," he whispered. "And I miss him at the strangest fuckin' times."

Santa Claus Is Coming To Town was running credits, and Stanley's other favorite—*Rudolph the Red-Nosed Reindeer*—was about to come on. Stanley loved that little mangy puppet thing. He knew what it was like to be run out of town for having a light that shined in all the wrong places.

"Like when?" he asked, wanting to turn up the volume of the kid's show so nothing would hurt him again. But this was Johnny, and he'd given Stanley some precious moments as it was.

"Like when I first saw you, cupcake, in the yarn store."

Stanley thought of the moment. "Yeah?"

"Yeah. See, I'd just seen an old friend, right? And I'd sort of been hoping—you know... *that* kind of friend."

"To reconnect," Stanley said delicately, trying not to be bitchy.

"Yeah, like that. To reconnect. Except," Johnny's voice dropped, and Stanley heard the regret there—not like he could hear when he was talking about "his rent boy," but regret just the same. "He was seeing somebody—it looked serious, and you know? I was glad. This guy—I mean, at first glance he could take care of himself, right? But after I saw he was with someone, I realized how worried I'd been, the whole five years I hadn't seen him. Some people—they just need a safe place, and that's something this guy ain't never had. So I was a little sad, 'cause I didn't know anyone here, and it woulda been nice to see someone I knew, but I was happy for him too. Anyway, so there I was, sad and happy, and then I saw you. And you were flirty and bitchy and... just everything Neil was, except you were old enough to make it really fly, you know?"

Stanley, who worked out, tanned, ate, and moisturized in a frantic attempt to capture his fading youth, suddenly realized he'd put up with an entire phalanx of the ghosts of old lovers past, just to know this man didn't pity him as an aging queer. Johnny *liked* his age, *liked* his bubble butt, *liked* his past. God, if these men helped make Johnny the sort of guy who'd like *Stanley*, they were welcome to stay in this conversation as long as Johnny needed them to.

"I'm glad you thought so," Stanley said, putting his nose in the air. "I'm certainly glad it took an ex-boyfriend to make you grateful for the piece of ass you saw when you walked into the store." Okay. So maybe he wasn't *that* well-adjusted about it, but he was reassured by Johnny's chuckle.

"You're adorable when you're jealous, cupcake. Don't worry. You don't need to be jealous. You weren't easy, or convenient—"

Stanley cleared his throat, and Johnny laughed again.

"Okay. Easy. Definitely easy. But I wanted to grab that ass the minute you turned it to me, and your eyes.... God. Such an amazing blue. I wanted you, and you were just so much fun. You *are* so much fun." There was quiet, and Johnny nuzzled his temple. "And you're really humane to listen to my bullshit about the past when we got maybe a week under our belt, you know?"

Stanley turned around in his arms, leaving Rudolph to struggle alone.

"Would you believe this is the longest relationship I've ever had?"

Johnny laughed a little, sadly. "Then buckle up, cupcake. I got dreams about kissing you under the Christmas mistletoe and getting a tree and ringing in the New Year, okay? You got a problem with that?"

Stanley placed his pouty little lips over Johnny's full, sensual ones and pushed until Johnny opened his mouth, just a little.

The kiss was gentle, and slow, and Stanley pulled back and smiled. "I got no problem at all with that, Johnny. Just keep talking about my pretty blue eyes, my darling, and you've got me!"

THE NEXT day when Stanley went into the store, someone had broken in. They hadn't taken anything, but the lock was jimmied and the security system had been set off, and there were a couple of policemen there as Johnny pulled up to let him off.

"Oh hells," Stanley muttered as he opened the car door.

"Do you want me to stay?" Johnny asked, but the reluctance in his voice was clear. Well, yeah, right? What sort of mob muscle really wanted to hang out and face the police?

Stanley shook his head. "No, but I'll give you odds it's the same asshole who keeps smoking outside in the middle of the night."

Johnny—who had just put the car in park—grew really, really still.

"How many nights now?" he asked carefully.

Stanley shrugged and slid out, turning around and talking to Johnny with the door held in one hand. "Three—no, four. Since our date on Saturday—and look there? Same fucking cigarettes, and I could swear—Zappos boots. Seriously. What kind of thief wears Zappos and smokes Pall Malls?"

Johnny's eyes got big, but Stanley was already out of the car. "I'll see you…?" he asked hopefully—so hopefully, in fact, he didn't realize that he'd taken Johnny both for granted, and at his word, until Johnny shook his head and eyeballed the police with a hard, calculating look. "Cupcake, I know I said I was in it for a while, but right now, I'm not so sure that's a good idea."

Stanley blinked. "I'm sorry?"

"I think maybe it's time to cool it for a while, just until—"

Stanley's outrage could not be adequately expressed on the ground next to the car, and he scrambled back up into the Cadillac because the last *he'd* heard, he was going to have a boyfriend for Christmas, *damn it!*

"What in the hell?" he demanded furiously. "You're not sure *what's* a good idea?"

Johnny actually had the balls to look startled, and he backed up against the door of the SUV, eyeing Stanley like he might eye a poisonous snake. "It's just...," he started, and then one of the policemen, who had been standing outside, stomping his feet in the cold and talking to his fellow officers about something serious, came and banged on the window.

"Sir, do you have any business here?" he asked Stanley, and Stanley glowered at him.

"I'm the manager. Have you called the owner, Alice Sinclair?"

"No sir, we're still tracking her down."

Stanley nodded and glowered, feeling a full-on homo-cidal snit blowing in. "Look, officer, I'll be right there to call Alice and tell you what was stolen—I just need a word with my boyfriend first, okay?"

The guy widened his eyes, like hearing a gay man talk about his boyfriend wasn't such a usual thing, but he held up two hands and backed away from the SUV.

"So when am I going to see you again, mob-boy?" he snapped, glaring at Johnny and pushing out his lower lip. Johnny, who was still looking at surprise at the police officer, shook his head and grimaced.

"Cupcake, I am real fucking worried about the fact that someone who wears Italian boots and smokes Pall Malls is hanging out outside your store. I did not exactly leave my family under the best of circumstances, and if my cover here is blown, you are in one hell of a lot of danger, do you understand?"

Stanley sucked in a breath, and *finally* remembered that he watched television like it was an Olympic sport. "Are you in Witness Protection?" he asked, feeling dim, and Johnny rolled his eyes.

"You know, considering how easy people keep jumping to that conclusion, I do not know how safe this shit is. But yeah. So I'm thinking—"

"That you're going to talk to whomever you need to talk to and show back up at my doorstep sometime this week," Stanley snapped. "We're baking cookies, remember? I told you. I even looked up the recipe for biscotti, just for you!" Oh hells—he had to go talk to the police, and he had to call Alice, and for all he knew, his yarn (oh geez, not the spring green cashmere that looked like the Colorado hills on an April morning!) was trashed and destroyed and strewn over the fucking floor.

Johnny looked at him like he'd suddenly turned into an ocelot. "Jesus, you just got fierce. I had no idea you could be so possessive."

Stanley sniffed and pulled his attitude around him like a cloak. "Well, I had no idea I could ever have anything I didn't want to lose this bad. I'm going to go be a grown-up now, and I'll see you—?"

Johnny laughed a little. "Saturday. I'll have to spend my day off at the office, talking to… whomever I need to talk to."

Stanley nodded. "Good," he said. "Let me know if you want to see a show or something. Otherwise—" And suddenly he smiled, thinking this would be a wonderful thing to do. "—otherwise, after cookies, I'll cook for real."

"You any good at that?"

Stanley's grin popped out and his shoulders scrunched up and he practically danced away into the chaos that awaited him. "I can make cupcakes," he said smugly, and then he hopped out of the SUV and shut the door.

SO THAT ended on a good note, but the break-in still sucked large. Huge. Unmercifully. The yarn was mostly undamaged, but the door had been open for what police estimated was about four hours, and there was snow and moisture damage at the entryway, including an entire shelf of hanks that had gotten wet and needed to be untwisted and then set out on a rack over the floor vent to dry. The automatic heating system had kicked in, and the store was about a thousand zillion hundred degrees and would stay that way unless Stanley could get a repairman in to fix the door so it stayed shut instead of sneaking open an inch every time they left it alone.

The policeman Stanley had snitted at while he was in the car with Johnny followed him around as he bemoaned his beautiful hand-painted hanks of yarn, carrying them over to the heating vent in a box he'd gathered from the back room and giving his information as he went.

"So Stanley… uhm… how do you spell your last name?"

"S-C-H-U-L-Z-E. Could you not stand on the heating vent? I need to keep it clean when I set these down."

"Can't you just order more from the factory?" the guy asked, looking at the mass of color in Stanley's arms like he couldn't see the appeal.

Stanley glared at him. This particular yarn was from Craw's farm—he actually *knew the names* of the animals that belonged to it.

"This alpaca has won *awards*," he snapped, outraged. "Burlingame is a premiere stud animal—his fleece is measured at barely fourteen microns. That animal gets shaved once a year, and this, right here in my arms, is what happens when he does. The 'alpaca factory,' as you so eloquently put it, is currently growing his goddamned fur back over the winter, so we can have some more of this lovely fucking yarn! And the colors? Were individually designed according to the owner's frickin' whim, and quite frankly? I haven't seen Craw or Aiden in this good a mood since they got a new drum carder for his mill, and that was around three years ago. *This* particular yarn in my arms may *never* be back again, and I'm *not* going to just throw it all away and go send for more at the 'factory.' Now do you have any idea who did this?"

The cop shrugged. "We can take some prints and look at the security camera—"

"Oh fuck Tim Gunn with a chainsaw!" Stanley snapped, and then looked at the wide-eyed police officer in almost-apology. "Look over there, Junior. The damned camera has been vandalized."

Junior—who was pretty much your average police officer, in a blue uniform with a cap over his sandy-brown hair and a lean, fresh face with still-healing acne scars—blinked at the digital security camera that looked over the door. It basically looked like someone had taken a sledgehammer to it, and it was, in fact, pitched drunkenly over sideways, just waiting to plummet from its little ledge and fall on someone's head.

Stanley sighed and hurried up with the yarn arrangement and added unbolting the damned camera and buying a replacement for it to his list of things to do.

In the end, he was a little disappointed. He watched enough television to expect the police to have access to a vast crime lab, and that the break-in at the yarn store would be top priority. (Why he expected this wasn't really clear. It just seemed like the yarn was precious enough to gather that much attention, that was all.) All that really happened was that Officer Junior followed him around, asked him a lot of questions, wrote shit down in his little notebook, took some fingerprints off the door, hit on Stanley, and then left.

The thing he did before the leaving took Stanley by surprise.

"So," Officer Junior said, making sure he had Stanley's home phone number and his cell too, in case anything should arise, "so, that guy in the SUV with you, your boyfriend?"

"Yes?" Stanley tried to maintain a front of polite indifference, afraid they would ask him for Johnny's last name and occupation and family history. Stanley was *really* bad at fabricating a story, but he was pretty good at not saying important things that he knew and someone else didn't. Like when there was a sale at Nordstrom's, or that someone's designer pashmina was passé.

"So, are you two, like, exclusive?"

Stanley blinked, and the running list in his head of things he had to do to fix the damned store before he could open it stopped scrolling, and he found he was standing there with his mouth open.

"Are you?" Officer Junior asked insistently, and Stanley closed his mouth abruptly and answered.

"Yes. Why?"

The boy was crestfallen. "Oh. That's too bad. You have got *the* sweetest little ass."

And for a moment Stanley was completely himself. "Well, before you grab my ass, Junior, you'd better notice my eyes."

And then Officer Junior left just as Alice drove up, and Stanley was left having to explain the whole thing to her while dealing with a shitload of work.

THE DETRITUS of the break-in occupied them for the next two days, and it wasn't until they went to knit with Ariadne that he got a chance to dish a little about Johnny. Ariadne had been forced by the doctors to lie on her left side—a position that made it difficult for her to knit at all—so Stanley and Alice were both doubly glad that they'd cleared time to come visit.

"So," Ariadne said, her face tight with discomfort, "you have no idea who broke into the store, and why?"

Stanley looked at Alice, who shrugged. He'd talked to Alice about it. He'd *had* to, given Johnny's suspicions and the fact it was Alice's store. Alice had been a little worried for Stanley—and a little fearless for herself.

"Don't worry about my shop, Stanley; worry about your little gay ass. Why would these guys be sniffing around us?

Stanley shrugged. "Because, well, I think Johnny pissed off the mob, and they're probably trying to figure out who he's hanging out with."

Alice had gaped at him. "Your new boyfriend pissed off the mob? How in the hell did he do that?"

Stanley shrugged. Johnny hadn't said a lot, he realized. A lot of this had been artfully dropped hints and Stanley's own extrapolations, but he was pretty sure he was right. "I think he probably...." For a moment, he stumbled, and then all his Sopranos expertise came flooding back. "Ratted them out, dropped a dime, rolled over... you know...."

"Got a bunch of them thrown in jail?" Alice supplied bluntly, and Stanley nodded. "Why did he do it, did he say?"

Stanley looked down, not wanting to share something so personal, and then looked around Alice's store with its wonderful cream carpet and plush couches, and at the yarn drying on the heating vent and at the workmen remounting a new camera and fixing the door. Johnny loved... liked... hung out with him because he was loyal. He'd said that, and Stanley wouldn't be loyal if he wasn't loyal to this woman who had given him family.

"They killed his boyfriend," Stanley said quietly. "They didn't know... didn't know about him, and the kid covered for him, said he was a thief, and... Johnny didn't see it coming. It...." God, it sounded so melodramatic, even for Stanley to say, but he somehow couldn't be snarky about this, or light, or flip, or anything. "It really hurt him. He hasn't given me details; I don't think he wants me involved. But I'm pretty sure that's when he left."

Alice sighed. "Okay. We keep this from the police—for the moment, okay? But when you see him again, I want a contact number, something. I want a way for us to get help, okay?"

Stanley nodded. He'd already thought of that—and, from what Johnny had said before he'd left that morning, so had Johnny.

"WE DO a little," Stanley said now. And then he told her about Johnny's problems. He was to the point where he talked about Johnny trying to reconnect with an old boyfriend when Ariadne swore.

"Oh Jesus. Stanley?"

"Yeah?"

"You actually know the old boyfriend. You've met him. We've been gossiping about him for weeks."

Stanley looked at her blankly. "Honey, I have no idea *who* you are talking about. The only people we've ever gossiped about are—"

"Jeremy and Aiden," she supplied helpfully, and Stanley blinked.

"Aiden is *way* too young for him!"

Ariadne glared at him from her position on the hospital bed. From her waist down she was covered in a sumptuous, multi-colored alpaca and wool afghan Stanley was pretty sure Craw had dyed and knitted just for her.

"Alice," she complained, "could you do me a favor and smack him on the back of the head for me?"

"Sure," Alice said cheerfully, but as she went to stand and walk over to where Stanley was sitting, he put his hand on the back of his head and protested.

"Don't do that! My hair plugs are finally stable, dammit!" Alice retreated in the face of his besieged glare, and he turned back to Ariadne. "So why are we smacking me upside the hair-plugs?"

Ariadne shook her head. "Because Aiden isn't Johnny's old boyfriend, *Jeremy* is Johnny's old boyfriend. Why would you not make that connection?"

Stanley wrinkled his nose. "I don't know—Jeremy doesn't seem his type. He's sort of... you know, slick and self-assured." Stanley blushed when he said it, but still, he had to say it. "Johnny sort of likes his guys sweet and slutty."

Ariadne grimaced. "Well, I think maybe, for Jeremy, he liked 'em sweet and not-so-slutty. Jeremy—I mean, I've told you this before, but you've got to listen to me now, and I'm going to be more direct, because I think Jeremy would agree this isn't a time for secrets. Jeremy lived a *very* odd life before he came to Craw's. He was born and raised on the grift, and after two years at Fort Lyon—"

"The *prison*?" Stanley asked, aghast, and Ariadne grunted.

"Why does that spaz you out so badly? You're sleeping with ex-mob, when everybody knows the only way you get to be ex-mob is by rolling over on someone and going into WITSEC, or, you know, by showing up dead. Yes, you're sleeping with ex-mob, and Craw hired an ex-con. But Jeremy isn't like any ex-con you've ever met. He...." She shook her head. "Jeremy is fragile, Stanley. Think like a bunny. Sweet, and delicate, and sometimes, if you startle it too bad, it'll drop dead just from fear. He puts on a good, brave front, but if Aiden hadn't made him a pet project, the guy would have been in the wind by now, and he would have been lost and...."

Ariadne stunned them both by wiping her eyes with her hand, and Stanley was so shocked he dropped his project—a very basic sweater, he was working on the sleeves—and ran to her side to get her a tissue.

"Oh, honey, what's wrong?" Stanley was dancing in anxiety.

Ariadne sniffled. "They're just both so defenseless, Stanley. He told us about your friend Johnny—and he's a stand-up guy. A real good guy. You're right—he's ex-mob, but he saved Jeremy's life, and... and if he's seeing you, that's a big deal for him. But you need to tell him. You need to tell Johnny you know Jeremy and tell Jeremy Johnny's okay—don't you see? They both need to know if there's mob involved, and they both need to know they've got family here, okay?"

Stanley nodded, although at the moment, he didn't see what the big fuss was about. He was more thinking, "It's a small world! Isn't that weird?" He wasn't thinking, "Oh my God! I know my boyfriend's old hook-up!" but, he discovered, that was because, in spite of the fact he'd met him a couple of times, enough to know him by sight and exchange pleasantries, the fact was, he really didn't know Jeremy.

Funny, how some of the most important people of your life can be dismissed as inconsequential, just because you believe the bullshit they've spent their entire lives selling.

Chapter 7
Knitters Can Be Known To Defend Their Packs Fiercely

CHRISTMAS WAS coming at its usual breakneck, shop-i-cidal pace, and Stanley was suddenly caught up in a quandary. He was used to baking up a storm—that was what he did. He produced hundreds upon hundreds of cookies; he gave them to customers, he gave them to Alice and shipped them to Candace, and even (under the guise of giving them to Jed) produced a whopping big bunch for Amanda, because he figured if anyone had earned the right to self-medicate with sugar, it was Jed's long-suffering wife who could probably fit into the eye of a needle—or a size zero Dior.

So, baking was his *thing*, just like exotic, inappropriate dishes for holiday dinners were his *thing*, but he was suddenly caught up in the desire not to bake, but to *knit*. And not just to knit, to knit for *Johnny*, because even if the break-in at the store had no mob implications whatsoever, and even if the entire thing was a product of Johnny's speckled past and Stanley's (and Ariadne's and Alice's) overactive imaginations, Stanley wanted Johnny to have some sort of armor against his secret, scary past life that was somehow looming like a knife-ridden shadow over their sweet little nascent beginning.

Stanley wanted to insulate Johnny from the harsh realities of the world using wool.

The project he'd been working on when he'd gone to visit Ariadne was a very (*very*) basic sweater. Knit almost entirely in garter stitch, using thick yarn, it was really a study in rectangles. A rectangle for each arm, two rectangles for the body—the sweater wasn't going to flatter anyone, or give them illusions of a body they didn't have, or show off any knitting talent Stanley had not yet earned by right of practice and assiduous application.

It was simply going to shelter Johnny from the cold.

Stanley liked to think he was under no illusions about much in the world. He was aware that Johnny likely did bad things in his past, and he didn't like to think about his lover hurting people—so he didn't. Instead, he concentrated on the things he knew from movies like *Casino* and *Goodfellas* and *Donnie Brasco*—which is that some guys in the mob are just doing their jobs. They make a living, and they concentrate on the people they love and being loyal to *them*. Stanley himself was aware *he* was very shallow. His world was very narrow, and although it had expanded of late to accommodate *everyone* at Craw's farm (whether they knew of his new interest or not) the fact was, if he was not somehow involved in another person's life, he couldn't possibly conceptualize of another person's pain.

So he didn't.

Johnny needed protection, from his demons, from his past, and from the elements at large. Stanley could really only protect him in one way—from the elements. So Stanley focused on the knitting.

Which meant that—although he still baked like a fiend—he planned it a little differently; that is to say, he planned it at all. He usually spent three days in a frantic, unplanned baking orgy, looking around at the end at his demolished kitchen and stacks upon stacks of cookies in festive little decorated tins with a sublime amount of amazement and triumph.

This time, he actually started early. Usually, he spent his two days off cooking, and then called in sick for the third, to the point where Alice had finally just caved and gave it to him anyway—mostly because she sort of lived for his Russian tea cakes. That usually happened the week before Christmas.

Now, three weeks before Christmas, Stanley actually planned, and all because of an ex-mob boyfriend he didn't know he'd have when he'd bemoaned his single-hood in a wine-sodden pity party.

And whom he planned to keep for a good long time.

So really, it seemed Stanley had either completely gone around the bend, or he had wholly and completely embraced emotional maturity. He supposed he'd go for emotional maturity, even though it was so much more fun to say he'd gone around the bend.

Anyway, he started by picking out recipes for freezer cookies—the kind that could be kept cold for a week or so before baking—and then, as soon as he got home from work, he would make one double batch and put it in the refrigerator. His goal? To spend one day baking—and only baking—so he could knit while the cookies were in the oven, and decorate them all in one go.

He felt like it was a good goal; he was proud of it.

He was even prouder when Johnny came over and blew it all to hell, but in a good way, by helping him knock out not just one or two batches of dough, but five, and when they were done, Stanley looked in awe into his freezer before shutting the door.

"You're amazing!" he said in wonder. "That would have taken me forever! How did you do that?"

Johnny—who seemed to have the rhythm of baking and cleaning up and baking again locked into his bones—had spooned a little bit of leftover batter into his mouth with gusto and smiled. "I helped my mom in the kitchen from the time I was a baby. I loved it, you know? I love that you do it. Of course…." Johnny wrinkled his nose. "Who are you doing that for again?"

"Oh, everybody!" Stanley said excitedly. "Alice and Candace, of course, and Alice's daughter-in-law—"

"The one married to the 'useless redneck phobic bastard,'" Johnny supplied, like a child who had studied well.

"Yes, exactly. Anyway, so some for Amanda, and some for Craw—"

"The guy who used to bang you in the bathroom?" Johnny sounded outraged, but Stanley waved him off.

"Well, yes, but it wasn't personal. Not really on my part, either. I just got distracted because he was a good guy, and I didn't know many of those. Anyway, him and Ben, and Ariadne and her husband—"

"Whom you've never met!" Johnny was pretty amazed, but Stanley shrugged him off.

"Well, I've met her, and she's tremendous. Her husband gets some just for visiting her three times a week when it's a huge pain in the ass, and he has to travel over ice. Anyway, if anyone deserves cookies, it's a pregnant woman stuck in the hospital over Christmas, right?"

"Yes. Anyway, so there's them, and…."

Stanley took a breath and turned away from the freezer, then took the cookie dough from Johnny and reveled in a fortifying spoonful. Johnny had called him and said he'd be able to come over and stay the night, and then they'd baked cookies. They'd had a lot of fun—and eaten an astounding amount of sugar, butter, and spices—but they had not yet talked. Stanley swallowed the cookie dough and his pride. "And there's Jeremy and Aiden, and you told me you knew Jeremy back in the day, and I think maybe Jeremy should be aware of things like the break-in at Alice's store."

Johnny closed his eyes. "Yeah. Damn, cupcake, I was hoping we could put that off for a little while longer."

"So you didn't just know Jeremy, you knew him as a criminal? And he knows who you are now?"

Johnny shrugged. "Yeah. And he offered to be my friend. *Just* my friend. I may be muscle, but I'm not stupid. I took him up on it."

Stanley pursed his lips. "You see Jeremy a lot, do you?" and Johnny shook his head with what looked to be a relieved smile on his face.

"Not like that—not like we were back in the day. Look—he's happy. He's better off with that kid anyway, because I gotta tell you something: that kid is stronger and braver and more of a person than I ever was, right up until I broke away from the mob."

Stanley scowled, feeling disgruntled and off-balance. "Well, I'm not going to go track down some toppy-the-twinkie to take your place, so I'm pretty sure I'll be happy with you."

Johnny grinned. "God, you're cute when you're jealous. But you owe Jeremy—you really do."

"Yeah? Why's that?"

"Because I was thinking about losing WITSEC, going underground, maybe moving someplace far away. I'd just started the delivery route and I hated it, and I thought Jeremy was my last best hope, because he'd known me when I was a bad guy, and he'd seemed to think I was something anyway."

Oh wonderful. Unconditional acceptance from con man the ex-con. Stanley was unimpressed. "I'm missing the part where I owe him something," Stanley snapped, and Johnny—God, he was *so* tall, and his hands were so big! And when he ran his hands through his thick, curly hair, he looked larger than life, like some big Sicilian god.

"Because Jeremy was straight up with me—which blew my mind, by the way, because back in the day, he would have told you the sky was green and had you believing it in about five minutes. But he told me that going straight was worth it. He said it was the best thing I'd ever do, because it wasn't the last best thing I'd ever do. And then I delivered a box from the place he worked to the place you worked, and suddenly I knew what I wanted the last best thing I'd ever do to be."

Stanley took a deep breath and abruptly forgave Jeremy, who had always been nice to him anyway, for being a part of Johnny's past. Oh look! More emotional maturity. Even more so when he found he had the courage to ask the hard question.

"Are my friends in danger, Johnny? Am I?"

Johnny shook his head. "I don't know. But I talked to my contact at WITSEC, told her about the break in, the stalker. She's already started poking her nose into the local police stuff, so she's going to try to find out." Johnny sighed and leaned back against the table and held out his arms. Stanley didn't even hesitate. He insinuated himself between Johnny's thighs and leaned against his chest. Two weeks. They'd been doing this for two weeks, and he already felt at home, right here. He didn't want to give this up, not for anything as pesky as fear.

"I have a theory," Johnny said softly. "I told Margie, and she thinks I could be right."

"Let's hear it," Stanley said, feeling serious.

"See, I made a list of people I knew would be gunning for me, and we could account for every one of them. They were either dead or in prison, and there was no wiggle room. And then I made a list of secondary people—people I wouldn't have accounted for when I was working in the family, but who may have crawled out of the woodwork anyway, because the head guy got put away."

Stanley wrinkled his nose. "Like… cousins who couldn't cut it in the day, so they think they're going to be the big guy now?"

Johnny nodded. "Yeah. Exactly. Anyway, I finished my list, and we had a pretty good bead on everyone…." He trailed off significantly.

"Except…?" Stanley asked, in the haven of his arms.

"Except the boss's idiot son, who was away at boarding school when he was put away. Now his mother's one of those people who didn't know what her husband was doing. I made sure, when I was doing the dance with the WITSEC people, that she'd be provided for. She had enough money to finish the boy's education, get started on her own life, still keep the house—that sort of thing, 'cause she's a real nice lady and I didn't want to screw her over. But her kid...." Johnny shook his head. "Bad news. 'Course, his old man's a piece of work, and his mom's had to be a dishrag to survive. Mikey, he never had a fuckin' chance. But he's not bright, and he's been using since he was a kid; he's crazier than a shithouse rat. If he thinks he's got a line on me, he's not gonna do anything sane about it. He was smart, he woulda taken me out and then just gone and picked up the organization. But Mikey— he's gonna make it into a game or something, and that's...."

"Well, it's good, on one hand," Stanley said, trying not to shake. "Because I'm really fucking glad he didn't just take you out, because no matter how casually you just said that, you almost ended my world, you asshole, so we're not going to talk about that."

Johnny's big hand cupped the back of Stanley's with absurd gentleness, and Stanley didn't want to think about the fact that it had only been two weeks and this guy could seriously fuck up his life.

"So, that's the good," Johnny said, and Stanley could tell he really didn't want to add this part, but that he had to. Well, good for him. Stanley's emotional maturity was capped out at planning cookies. "The bad is, if he finds out about you, he's gonna wanna fuck with you, and that's unacceptable to me."

Stanley sighed. "Will he hurt my friends, Johnny? I'm serious. I can be afraid for me, and I can deal with that, but these people in my life, they're my family—"

"See, Mikey won't see it like that. I think, if it's him, your friends are safe."

"And if it's not?" Oh geez. Stanley wanted some reassurance, he really did. But even he knew that reassurance was for children.

"Do you want out, cupcake?" Johnny said softly. "I wouldn't blame you if you did. I could go my own way, maybe come back when this was over and we had a bead on where Mikey was. I don't want you hurt. I don't want your friends hurt. You got a real nice life here, and I don't wanna fuck it up for you."

Stanley sighed. "I don't want to be the last best thing you ever do, Johnny. I'll stick around. I think you've got some more best things coming down the line."

Johnny bent over and dropped a kiss in Stanley's for-real-now growing hair. "You want me to make a batch of them cookies now? I'll bake, you sit and watch a show and knit some. You still feel that way when the cookies are done, maybe we, you know, can fool around some more."

Stanley nodded. They would do that, in a moment. Stanley would sit and knit and watch Project Runway and make catty comments about the contestants, and Johnny would look at them critically and agree or disagree. And then, when three trays of cookies sat cooling on the counter, Johnny would come up behind Stanley and started kissing his neck.

"You still want me, cupcake?" he asked, right in Stanley's ear.

"More than all those damned cookies combined," Stanley confessed—and it was the truth and it was definitely saying something because the cookies smelled heavenly and they were *so* tempting him off the good and righteous path of diet that he'd thought he could walk while cooking them on his own.

But Johnny didn't give him a chance to eat the cookies; he was too busy kissing a line down Stanley's spine and stripping off his shirt. Stanley put the knitting to the side and pulled out the condom and the lube he'd stashed in the corner of the couch for just this reason, and committed with his body when he couldn't seem to find the right words to use to commit any other way.

TWO DAYS later, Jeremy and Aiden were actually visiting Ariadne when Stanley arrived. Jeremy saw him hovering outside of the curtained room and moved to the side.

"C'mon in and sit a bit, Stanley. Don't mind us. I can sit on the edge of the bed here, and Aiden, he don't mind standing none," he said, his cheeks wreathing in smiles and his dark eyes crinkling in the corners. His hair hung straight and shaggy from a part in the middle, which was funny because he'd almost always had it slicked back when Stanley had seen him before.

Jeremy's voice was a mish-mash of places, classes, and education levels—but Stanley always had the feeling that he'd grown up country poor. He certainly had the manners of someone who was used to giving up their own comfort for someone else. Of course, after talking to Ariadne, maybe that was because he was used to putting people at ease, and Stanley waited to distrust Craw's hired man, based on the new information about his past.

Whatever else the motor-mouthed millworker might have been, at the moment, Stanley was willing to believe he was 100 percent genuine.

Ariadne grabbed Jeremy's hand. "Stanley's been my savior," she said, from her sideways position on the bed. "He keeps coming in and gossiping about women at the shop and I pay him back by gossiping about you guys—"

"Us?" Aiden asked, and Stanley turned to look at him just because the boy was particularly easy on the eyes. Aiden was tall and broad shouldered, with curly brown hair and brownish eyes. His smile was startling in his tanned face, and he looked like he smiled a lot, judging by the divots in his cheeks. When he looked at Jeremy, though—that's what was interesting. Suddenly he went from smiling young man to a rather fierce predator, and through the course of their conversation, Stanley realized that Johnny and Ariadne had been right—everything they'd said about Jeremy and Aiden had been right. Jeremy wasn't the strong one, or even the older one, regardless of his age. Jeremy was the fragile one, and Aiden was his pet wolf, ready to protect him.

"What's so interesting about us?" Aiden was asking now, and Ariadne laughed.

"You two? Between you two and Stanley, your love life has pretty much filled up our days. Whether or not you've told Craw, how serious you are, which one of you wears the pants—"

"Aiden," Jeremy said promptly, smiling like it was a joke. "He's more stubborn than I'll ever be."

Ariadne took his hand to her lips and kissed it. "I could argue that," she said gently, "but I won't. Now, about being serious—"

"I moved in," Aiden said shortly. "With my parents blessing, and my little brother's profound thanks because now he gets my room."

Ariadne looked at him and gasped. "Now *that* we did not know."

Jeremy looked at her and shook his head like it was no big deal. "It happened right after Thanksgiving, Ari—and he pretty much just told me he was bringing his toothbrush and his clothes and shit for the walls."

Ariadne's look was... gentle and fierce at once. "Don't think I don't know what a big deal that is for you," she said gruffly, and Jeremy shrugged and looked away.

"It's a picture of a goddamned sunset, sweetheart. Aiden, tell her—"

"He's mine," Aiden said implacably. "Ain't changing. Craw seems to think it will, but then, Craw seems to think I'm still fifteen. My mom said old people do that, and that when the baby comes, I'll see."

Ariadne snorted, and so did Stanley, and the two of them met eyes. Aiden may have been young, but there was something of Colorado's weathered stone in him. Yes—whatever he felt for Jeremy, that was there to stay. But Jeremy was fidgeting, probably because he was being talked about and not doing the talking, and he looked at Stanley with hope in his eyes.

"So, Stanley—you got yourself a love life? That's promising. Let's hear about you, since you're here."

Stanley and Ariadne met eyes again, and this time they grimaced. Well, time to let the cat out of the bag and see how much damage he'd done.

"Actually," Stanley said, looking Jeremy straight in the eyes, "it's a case of a small world and big men. You sort of know him. In fact, you sort of sent him my way."

Jeremy wasn't stupid. "Oh hell...." He closed his eyes then, and for a moment he looked... well, Stanley looked from Aiden's face, taut, protective, and fierce, and then back to Jeremy. He looked young. And vulnerable. And sad.

"Gi... Johnny?" Jeremy asked, and then grimaced.

Stanley wasn't stupid either—he heard. Johnny had another name—and Stanley should have been ready for that, but for some reason he wasn't. But, well, he'd been the master of denial for more than ten years now; he had that to fall back on.

"Yes—I understand you know him?"

Jeremy nodded, his eyes darting everywhere but Stanley. Finally they rested on Aiden, and Jeremy's whole body posture relaxed, including what must have been a death grip on Ariadne's hand. "Yeah. He's a good guy. The best. But he comes with a whole lot of trouble on his back. You ready for that sort of trouble?"

Stanley thought about it. Well, hadn't he answered that question two nights before, when Johnny had come over to make cookies and stayed over because Stanley had told him it was all right?

"I hope so," he said brightly, "because a little bit of it seems to have come my way."

And with that, he pulled out his knitting and told them about the store break in and some mobster's idiot son.

They listened, fascinated, and when Stanley got to the part about the idiot son, Aiden actually stood up, walked over, grabbed Jeremy by the hand, and dragged him back to where Aiden was sitting, perching the smaller man on his lap.

"I ain't a kid," Jeremy muttered resentfully, and Aiden started a slow, soothing rub on his back.

"You're not a rabbit, either," he said with some meaning, and Jeremy visibly relaxed.

"So," Ariadne asked when he was done, "are you in danger?"

Stanley shrugged, wanting to say he highly doubted it but not sure if that wasn't just the height of denial right there. "I don't know. I don't." He looked up at Jeremy then. "But I think you're right," he said seriously. "I think he's a really good guy. I think…." Stanley didn't want to go on. It sounded so maudlin. He shook his head and sniffed.

"What do you think?" Ariadne asked from the bed, and Stanley looked at the very, very basic sweater he was working on.

"I think if I'm going to knit for him, the least I should do is see if it fits," he said, trying to be snarky, but no one in the little hospital room laughed.

"I think," Aiden said with some deliberation, "it's time to tell Craw about this part too."

Stanley looked at him. "What do you mean, 'too'?"

"We told him about Johnny," Jeremy said, and he seemed to have shrunk a little. His shoulders sloped, and if Stanley didn't know better, he'd say the man was about a second away from bolting out of the room. "He's worried, but says it's good he knows. Granby's pretty small—someone new, especially someone slick like Johnny, he'll stick out. So we'll tell him there might be someone around, looking for Johnny, and for you. I... I think Johnny's right. I think really, you're the only one this guy will worry about. These mob guys... they... they sort of rely on setting an example. If someone fucks with them, they'll take them out, and witnesses—everyone else sort of stays in line, because, hello, they're the fucking mob."

There was a tense silence then, and Aiden suddenly spoke. "Jeremy has to go to the bathroom."

Jeremy turned his head and glared. "I do not."

Aiden just looked at him levelly. "Yes. Yes you do. And I have to go with you. Like girls at a party, or so I've been told."

"I'm not a child," Jeremy said, his voice dropping to an intimate enough level that Stanley felt uncomfortable.

"Yes, but you keep telling me I am, so maybe we're going for me."

It wouldn't have worked for Stanley, he realized. He would have snarked, he would have demanded, he would have refused.

But it worked for Jeremy. He stood up and walked out of the room, and Aiden followed him somberly, neither of them saying another word.

Ariadne watched them go with a sad little smile on her face. "You're not even going to ask?"

Stanley shrugged and looked at his knitting. "It doesn't feel right," he said, feeling subdued.

"That mobster Johnny turned on? He killed Jeremy's father. Jeremy was hiding nearby; he heard the whole thing. Johnny kept quiet, smuggled Jeremy some money—basically saved his life. Jeremy—he knows what he's talking about when he says Johnny's a good guy. He also knows what he's talking about when he says he's worried for you. Have you considered taking a time out? A break? Something?"

Stanley's hand were suddenly shaking so hard his left needle couldn't hold still enough for his right needle to go under the stitch. "Please," he said, keeping his eyes on his knitting and his voice nonchalant. "Do you have any idea what sort of effort it took for me to *find* this relationship? I had to go without sex—for three months! I had to take up knitting. I had to resign myself to a life alone—"

"For three months," Ariadne said gently.

"It was a fucking lifetime," Stanley snapped, his mock-irritation enough to stop his hands from trembling. "I have no idea how I survived."

"You depended on your friends," she said, and Stanley looked up and went for a snarky grin.

"Well, hopefully they won't desert me now," he said, and Ariadne nodded, as grave as she could be from lying on her side in a hospital bed.

"Count on it."

Jeremy and Aiden came back in at that point and she looked up at them and smiled.

"It's no use, guys. I tried to talk him into running the fuck away but he's not going for it."

Jeremy's smile was tight to his cheeks, but it looked sincere. "Well, that makes him a good guy in my book," he said. "Hey, Ari— you wouldn't want some dinner, would you? Me and Aiden will treat."

"Where you going?" she asked, and his smile relaxed a little.

"McDonalds."

Ariadne closed her eyes like she should have expected it. "Chicken sandwich, no mayo, make them add mushrooms and Swiss cheese."

"Oh geez," Aiden protested. "Ari, you know that makes the people crazy when you do that—"

"I thought you were down here to make me feel better!" she said, laughing, and Aiden shook his head and turned to Stanley.

"Anything for you?"

Stanley sniffed. "As *if*! I've got leftover curry at home I'd much rather have. God, you people. Just because you live in Granby doesn't mean you have to live like savages!"

"Well, you let me know when they open a Thai food drive-thru, and we'll think about stopping by," Aiden said, so matter-of-factly Stanley had to look twice to make sure he wasn't really Craw. "In the meantime, if you're gone before we get back, Stanley, you make sure to take care now. Jeremy told me to make sure you felt like you could come by any time you need to, okay? You get scared, you think you see a shadow—anything. Anything at all, you show up at the mill, we'll find a place to keep you, okay?"

Stanley looked at them, so naked with gratitude he might as well have been grinding against a pole. "That's swell," he said, managing not to cry and drool. "And I'll let you know when that Thai-food drive-thru opens up, 'kay, sugar?"

Aiden grimaced and Jeremy cackled behind him like a little kid. "We'll do that," he grunted, and the two of them turned around to leave.

Stanley stayed for another half-an-hour, ready to leave when they returned, and he and Ariadne spent the time talking about how cute Aiden was, and how surprisingly sad Jeremy was, and what an adorable couple they made when you weren't expecting it. Stanley went home a little later, hoping for a phone call from Johnny on his cell, and was happy when he saw a missed one.

He walked through the mild slush on the sidewalk outside his apartment building in a rush, because it was cold and because he wanted to talk to Johnny and get some reassurance. As he turned left to get to his door, he saw a lone cigarette butt in the slush at the crossroads for the little complex, and shivered.

A talk with Johnny, he figured. A talk with Johnny, and he might not think every smoker in Colorado was a complete psychopath, out for his queer little ass and blood.

Chapter 8
When a Knitter Migrates, He Does His Best to Find His Own Kind

JOHNNY LIVED in Denver, which was forty-five minutes from Boulder in average traffic. That night, Johnny made it to Stanley's in an hour, and Stanley assumed that came with packing an overnight bag and calling in sick to his delivery job and placing another call to his handler at WITSEC.

What boggled Stanley was that one minute he was on the phone, tired, saying he didn't want to be paranoid about litter, and the next minute, Johnny was making plans to be at his little apartment.

And an hour later, he was *there*.

And it wasn't until Stanley threw open the door that he realized how much that meant. It meant that Johnny worried about him, that Johnny cared. It meant that the first real relationship Stanley had *ever* had was a man who may have called him "cupcake" but who actually took him very seriously, and who would literally move heaven and earth to make sure he was okay.

Stanley's last lay barely moved the curtain of the privacy cubicle.

And Craw would probably put himself out for Stanley—but he'd do it out of duty and friendship, not because he was worried.

And there Johnny was, big, tired, worried, capable, and Stanley just buried himself in his man's arms and stayed there for a long time.

THERE WAS no sex that night, which Stanley would later think about regretting, but he couldn't. Johnny lay there next to him in the darkness, petting Vincent Van Gogh and talking to him.

It was innocuous at first.

He talked about baking cookies, and how much he'd liked it, and how he'd loved cooking with his mother. He talked about his mother, and how he missed her, but he didn't miss "the family" or the expectations or the fear. He didn't miss hurting people, and he didn't miss having to use the word "faggot" when he was one.

He did, however, miss the clothes, and the nice wing-tip shoes, and being able to wear a fedora and not feel like an asshole.

It wasn't until he told Stanley about the clothes and the shoes that Stanley could admit it, at least to himself.

It had to be love.

"Yes," he said, lying in front of Johnny in the darkness, Henri Matisse giving him little peeks over the bed, "in a fire, I'd rescue the cats first. But it would be close."

"So," Johnny said, humor lacing his voice with the idea of a game, "the cats first, the clothes second—when would the knitting come in?"

"In the same bag with the cats," Stanley replied pertly, and the sound of Johnny's laughter in the dark would fortify Stanley for a lot of long, lonely weeks.

THE NEXT morning, Johnny drove Stanley to work and then sat quietly on one of the couches, reading a book of gay humor (of all things!) and looking quiet and unassuming for a big Italian guy in a yarn store, while Stanley did his thing. About the time Alice came in to spell Stanley for lunch, a nice, middle-aged woman wearing a power suit under her trench coat and worn, comfortable leather shoes came walking in. She nodded to Johnny, who stood up and said, "Stanley, this is my, uh, cousin. Margie. She uhm, wants to meet you."

The woman's wide-set hazel eyes widened and her lip came up in sort of a disbelieving scowl. Stanley heard her mutter, "Cousin? That was the best you could do?"

Johnny shrugged, looking at Stanley with sheepish brown eyes. "I coulda said you were my sister?"

"Yeah. Cousin is probably much better, Johnny." The woman's hair was streaked blonde—but her complexion said it was probably her natural color before the grays had started to set in. "Why don't you introduce us?"

Johnny was a big guy—the kind of guy who probably didn't get ordered around a lot, but "Margie"? She had the sort of build and carriage that suggested that underneath her jacket and trench coat, there was a lot of muscles and attitude.

Stanley thought he might like her—if she didn't scare the crap out of him.

"Uhm, Margie, this is Stanley. Stanley, this is my, uhm, cousin. Do we wanna go somewhere and maybe talk?"

Stanley looked up at Alice, who had come in with some of his favorite Thai takeout, and asked if they could use the stock room. She gave Margie a stare and then a grimace at Stanley that said they'd talk later, and then told him to knock himself out.

Stanley tried to put extra swish in his step as he led the way back to the site of his and Johnny's first date.

Once they got there, Margie looked around appreciatively.

"Nice," she said softly. "My sister knits—I might come back here and shop. But right now, we've got more to worry about. Stanley, Johnny said you felt stupid about raising a ruckus about a little trash on the ground. Don't. Don't feel bad about raising a ruckus, don't feel bad about calling us—we're not thrilled Johnny told you his life story, but he's right about one thing: you deserve to be protected, do you understand?"

Stanley tried very hard not to cry. God, *finally* he was starting to understand that exact thing, and it had taken Johnny to show him. He deserved to be protected.

"It was litter," he said nonchalantly. "But, you know, I have people here. I want them safe."

Margie nodded and pulled out a card. "I hear you. Here—you see anything, you call me. You get a creepy feeling over your shoulder, you call me. You imagine an Italian accent, you call me, do you understand?"

Stanley nodded and took the card, then pulled his cell phone out of his pocket and entered the number for all he was worth. "Smile!" he said, and took the picture quickly while Margie was blinking in surprise, because he liked having the pictures of people in his phone, dammit—Johnny's was right there too, a self-conscious smile, his brown eyes looking up into the corner like he could avoid it. The pictures made them really his people—he was the first to admit it.

"There," he said, showing her the picture in the phone. "Got you. Is there anything else?"

She laughed a little and then nodded. "A place. We're going to be doing drive-bys on your place, Stanley; we've got local law enforcement wandering by a little more than usual. Do you have a place you can go? Someplace people might not know?"

Stanley blinked, thought about it, thought about the people who made him feel safe. Somehow it all came back to a kiss on the cheek and a request to enter a circle of friends. He turned around and started rooting around in one of the first boxes Johnny had ever delivered; it wasn't quite empty, and he came up with a really gorgeous skein of sock yarn, done in layered shades of brown, purple, and red. Aiden's work, Stanley thought critically; Craw was usually more restrained.

"Give this to your sister," he said abruptly. "It's made locally. See? Granby. It even has the address on the label."

Margie looked at him in confusion and then looked at the label closely—and then lived up to Stanley's best expectation and smiled in appreciation.

"It does!" she said, nodding. "And it's as good a place as any. Johnny—isn't this the address of the guy who used to know you?"

Johnny nodded. "Yeah. Jeremy will keep him safe."

Stanley had his doubts there, but that didn't change the fact that not only had Jeremy offered, but Craw's little farm and mill seemed like the best choice of sanctuary he could think of.

Margie seemed satisfied too. "If you see something that frightens you, I want you to call me, then call Johnny, and don't stop, don't get your stuff—"

"Not even my cats?"

"They're not after your cats, Stanley. If it is Mikey, he's going to be after you, and he's not going to be merciful, you understand?"

Stanley looked at Johnny unhappily, and Johnny reached out—disregarding Margie, the Federal Marshal—and cupped his cheek.

"I really want you safe, cupcake. It'll hurt if your kitties get hurt, but…." Johnny swallowed. "I can't… I can't do that again, okay? I…

not someone else, okay? I… I'm so stupid." He closed his eyes miserably. "You were just so fun to flirt with, and I… I just wanted to be a part of you so bad."

Stanley twitched his shoulders with his best vamp. "Of course I'm fun to flirt with. I've been practicing my whole damned life."

Johnny opened his eyes and gave a watery grin. "It's gonna be a long one, me and Margie have anything to say about it, okay?"

Stanley nodded and thought about his kitties and how it would suck to desert them. "Matisse would probably jump on their heads before they got anywhere near the middle of the apartment anyway. I promise, if I see anything, I'll let you know."

"And you'll set the alarm?" Johnny cautioned, and Stanley rolled his eyes.

"Oh please. Why would I even *pay* for the damned thing if I wasn't going to set it?"

Johnny surprised him then with a mauling, engulfing hug, and Stanley let down his attitude and his self-protection long enough to snuggle in. "Be careful, cupcake. For me, okay?"

"I didn't need you to be careful, Johnny-angel. But yeah. Yeah. Am I gonna see you tonight?"

Johnny shook his head. "I gotta work late; I traded shifts so I could be here and introduce you to Margie, okay?"

Stanley nodded. "Okay." Without thinking, he raised his face and closed his eyes, but Johnny didn't leave him hanging. The kiss was brief and needy, and then Margie cleared her throat and Johnny stepped back.

"It was good to meet you, Stanley. You take care, okay? And remember—nothing's stupid with this. Until we get Mikey under wraps, everything's important."

She stuck out her hand and Stanley shook it, and Alice called a little frantically from the front. Was it weird that it didn't even seem out of place? That Alice, who had been a part of his life for eleven years, was as much a part of his life as this Federal Marshal and this big man who was looking at him with a pathetic combination of worry and guilt?

"I'll see you tomorrow, cupcake," Johnny said, and Stanley pulled up his best grin.

"You'd better, big boy! We've got cookies to bake."

"Oh hell," Margie muttered as they turned around and walked out of the back room. She was placing the skein of yarn carefully in her coat pocket as they went. "That had better not be a euphemism."

"No, really!" Johnny protested. "He's got a freezer full. We'll even give you a tin!"

Margie let out a little laugh and patted Johnny's shoulder as they moved through the store and toward the door. "You're okay, Johnny, you know that?"

Johnny's laugh was a little subdued but still sound. When he got to the door, though, he turned around and caught Stanley's eyes, his own eyes dark with worry. Stanley gave him a little wave and Johnny nodded and walked through the door.

As good-byes went, Stanley had been through worse. He was pretty sure Johnny had mouthed "I love you," there at the end.

ALICE HAD him over for dinner that night. Jean was working late, which was too bad, because Jean was the softer, sweeter counterpoint to Alice, and Stanley could have used someone on his side.

"Stanley, what the hell are you doing here?" she asked, over a chopping board full of broiled chicken.

"I thought I was being a grown-up," Stanley said with poise. No wine tonight—he was sticking to vitamin water, oh yes he was.

"You're dating a mobster—"

"*Ex*-mobster," Stanley said with dignity. Johnny didn't do that anymore. That counted for something. "For a guy who watched *The Godfather* on his mother's knee, that's saying a lot."

Alice looked like she was going to say something bitchy—and she wasn't above that or she wouldn't have been Stanley's best friend—and then she swallowed the bitchiness and tried again.

"Okay, look. You're in danger. You're afraid for us and I don't blame you, even if you try to mask it. Christmas is barreling down on us like a shotgun shell, and seriously, who needs the fucking aggravation, right? Just tell me why. Why this guy is special. Stanley, in eleven years, you haven't brought home one guy—not one. We've been waiting. Not one of them has been worth knowing the guy's name in the time it takes for the condom to hit the trash. Why this guy?"

Stanley stopped and thought about it, really thought, because she was right. The store had been broken into, and that was scary. He'd met an honest-to-God US Marshal, and he was worrying his friends—*his family*—because he'd finally met a guy worth laying twice.

"He liked my ass," Stanley said, and before she could interrupt, he added, "but that's not *all* he liked."

Alice nodded, also being considerate. "Stanley, there's no rule book that says he's the only guy that'll ever do that."

"Maybe not," Stanley said with a shrug. He closed his eyes and could see, in minute detail, the delighted look on Johnny's face when he'd put on the hat, and the sound of his laughter at the silly children's Christmas show. He saw the way his eyes had crinkled in the corners, and the way his full lips had tilted up as he'd pondered whether or not he'd liked the sugar cookies more than the Russian teacakes or less than the biscotti.

He saw the serious look in Johnny's eyes as Johnny had taken him, face to face, and showed Stanley that sex was awesome, but making love was *incredible*.

He swallowed and opened his eyes. "Maybe you're right," he said to Alice, trying hard to hold onto his insouciance. "But Johnny's the only one I *want* to do that. Is that bad?"

Alice sighed. She threw the chicken in with the stir-fry and washed her hands, and Stanley waited for her, because he craved her good opinion in a way he'd never been aware of until this moment. He was afraid, and he was fully aware he was not a hero, and he'd never been a faithful lover and his decision to be one now was frightening. He needed Alice, and he needed her to allow him into her family, and he needed to know he would have them if this all went terribly, terribly south.

When she was done drying her hands on the towel (with the hand-crocheted little triangle that anchored it to the handle of the kitchen drawer), she turned to Stanley and threw her arms over his shoulders, pulling his head to her shoulder and kissing his temple.

"Stanley," she said softly, "I'm scared shitless for you. I'm glad you seem to have found someone, but I'm not gonna lie. I'd rather have you break up with him and nurse a broken heart than have something else get broken, okay?"

Stanley whimpered and tried to move away, but Alice wrapped her arms around his shoulders a little tighter.

"But it's not my decision to make," she said, and Stanley relaxed.

"God, I wish you were my mom," he said, and even though his own mother had passed away five years earlier, he felt nothing but truth in the words. He'd known; he'd put off coming out until he was going away to college, because he'd been under no delusions about his parents. After they'd told him to go away and not to come back until he'd "come back to Jesus," he'd spent the next fifteen years telling himself that cynicism was a good thing and that he had no delusions about anything anymore.

Oh God. Please, let his sudden belief in love not be a delusion. Please? Didn't all reformed boy-sluts need a belief in happy-ever-after? Wasn't it in the rulebook?

"Who says I'm not your mom," Alice said, and Stanley pulled back and rubbed his hands through his short—and blessedly growing—blond hair, and then over her gray-blonde buzz cut.

"We even look alike," he said with a smirk, and she smirked back, just for him.

"You even like knitting," she said, and he nodded and wiped his eyes.

"If you don't stir the wok, we're going to be eating take-out," he warned, and she wiped her eyes too and did just that. They talked about Christmas—knitting, cooking, and planning—for the rest of the evening, and not another word was spoken about breaking up with Johnny or about worrying for their lives.

Chapter 9

Knitters Have Proven to Be Surprisingly Brave

STANLEY TRIED to put that disturbing thought about lives in danger out of his mind. Johnny was coming over the next night, and they were going to make cookies, and Stanley would be eating some and cooking some more, and his little tins for his family members were threatening to fill up way before he finished cooking all the dough in his freezer. He'd had to buy his produce fresh instead of relying on the frozen stuff that *should* have been still in his freezer, but that he'd had to thaw out and cook every night for a week.

With that in mind, he stopped by the market the night Johnny was coming over to buy some fresh vegetables for a salad, and even some nice marinated chicken breasts so he could grill them quick. He had some soup (made with the frozen vegetables and some thawed stew meat) for a main course and he'd chop up the salad and—

His happy musings on the comfort of cooking were stopped short as he turned the corner in front of his condo building. There was a stranger outside his apartment, smoking purposefully in the frigid air.

For a moment, Stanley froze, and then he remembered not to make eye contact, and then he stepped on the accelerator a little hard and had to focus on driving because he started skidding on the icy road. He couldn't be sure—but he thought maybe the guy had looked up and seen him as he rounded the corner for the next block.

Stanley wasn't going to look back and see. He was going to need gas for the next leg of the trip, so he circled the block and went the long way to the freeway, stopping at a station near the freeway entrance, and made his phone calls then.

He got Jeremy when he called Craw's; apparently Ben and Craw were at the little Granby movie theater, and Jeremy was tending to an alpaca who had miscarried her winter cria while Aiden did homework in their apartment.

"Say what?" Jeremy said, sounding stunned after Stanley spilled out the story.

"There was a big Italian guy smoking cigarettes outside my apartment," Stanley snapped, more out of panic than out of true irritation. "I told the Marshal I'd drive to Granby if anything bad happened, because they wouldn't know to look for me there." He looked around the gas station and didn't see anybody, for which he was thankful. He had put his Bluetooth in his ear as he finished pumping his gas, so he was still talking to Jeremy as he hopped in his little Kia and started out. He drove with purposeful slowness; the roads were icy, and he was very aware that he was more likely to spin the damned car out than actually get captured by the mob.

Jeremy grunted into the earpiece, and Stanley thought belatedly this might not be the safest move for *Jeremy*. Oh fuck, how could he take this ba—

"I'll be here," Jeremy said evenly. "How soon will you be here?"

Oh God—once Stanley hit the mountains, he'd be going ten miles an hour through about a thousand hairpin turns. "An hour and a half?" he guessed, and Jeremy made a measuring sound.

"Good. Aiden expects me to stay here all night, and Craw and Ben aren't due for a couple of hours. We can get you hid, maybe even hand you off to the Marshal before any of this affects them. We're good. Drive safe, Stanley, okay?"

Stanley was surprised when Jeremy signed off, and it wasn't until he did that he realized Jeremy had just set himself up to be the only person at the mill when Stanley got there. Oh God. What if they found him? What if Jeremy was there and got hurt? Why would he do that? Stanley looked in his rearview mirror as he got on the freeway and tried not to freak out at the sight of a pair of lights back there. What, he was the only idiot who could get on the freeway at seven o'clock at night? Oh fuck. That reminded him. He had Johnny's number on voice activation, and in a minute, Johnny's warm voice resonated in his ear.

"Hey, cupcake, I'm about half an hour out—"

"There was someone outside my apartment," Stanley broke in brusquely. "I'm on the way to Granby."

"Fuck."

"Yeah. Johnny, is there any way you could call your Marshal friend? I'm… I'm sort of dragging this thing into Craw's backyard without asking permission and—"

"It's done," Johnny cut in, his voice thick. "God, Stanley, in a thousand years I never expected—"

Stanley swallowed and tried really hard to concentrate on his driving. "I know, Johnny. You… I mean, I'm worth it, right?"

"Stanley, you are worth everything. You're worth going straight for. You're worth staying there. If you want to keep having anything to do with me, I'd be stupid to say no."

Stanley nodded and felt a stupid smile crossing his face. "You're not stupid," he said gruffly. "And I'm not either. Do me a favor and call Margie, would you?"

"Yeah. Love you, cupcake."

Stanley made a little noise of surprise. "Love you too, Johnny. Bye."

He disconnected before he remembered that it wasn't even Johnny's real name. Oh God. He was in very real danger of dying for a guy whose name he didn't really know. Well, hells. Maybe it didn't matter; he was already in love with the guy. Why in the fuck not?

The Kia threatened to skid on the nonskid asphalt and Stanley got a real grip on the wheel and paid some fucking attention. He had a moral obligation to get to Granby without wiping out on the damned freeway.

AN HOUR and a half later, he wondered if the muscles in his neck and back could actually tighten down so much that his head really *would* pop off.

Holy fuck, he *never* wanted to do that again.

The road had been plowed, but there were fences on the looming cliff face to hold back the snow and the boulders that kept threatening to slide down the hill. The hairpin curves all had signs in front of them that insisted fifteen miles an hour was the maximum, but Stanley was pretty sure he would have died in a fiery explosion if he'd gone faster than ten. And to make matters worse, he was also pretty sure someone was following him. As the road had flattened out near the bottom of the hill, he could see the glow of headlights still executing hairpin turns through the trees.

Well, shit. He came to the giant straightaway that was Granby and gunned it, barely slowing down enough to take the turn into town and then the hairpin turn to the "residential" area. He was might have torn something vital in the Kia's suspension on the ice-crusted gravel road to Craw's, but he was rewarded by Jeremy, standing in the driveway/parking lot of the mill/shop/farm. Craw's hired man was swathed from head to foot in a motley assortment of hand-knitted things. Bright green and purple thrummed mittens (which Stanley envied because they were warm!), a brown cabled scarf, and a very, very red hat all helped insulate him from the cold. When Stanley rolled down the window, he thought it might not be enough. My *God*, he'd thought it had been cold in *Boulder*!

Jeremy looked at him seriously from that colorful tornado of knitted alpaca as Stanley blurted, "I think I was followed."

Jeremy nodded. "Best park behind the barn, then. There's a garage there; Craw usually uses it, but no one really knows it's there because it's tucked back near the critters. Take the driveway around, you'll see it. I'll meet you there."

Stanley followed his directions and saw the little carport. Jeremy was a genius, he thought, because the Kia really *was* hidden, and by the time he'd killed the motor and gotten out, Jeremy had emerged from a door that connected the carport to the barn.

To Stanley's immense surprise, after Jeremy led him through the door to the carport and across the warm, dim animal closeness of the barn, he took him through another door into what looked to be a little apartment.

It had an all-weather sleeping bag, a space heater, and an adjoining bathroom. It also had shelves that probably held food, indoor/outdoor carpeting, a kitchenette, a tiny table with a chair, and a cot. Jeremy got on his hands and knees and started rooting under the bed, pulling out books and throwing them at Stanley.

"Put them on the shelves," he muttered. "Make them neat as you can, like they belong there."

"Oh my God!" Stanley took the books on automatic, but he was still impressed by the tiny little room. "Who in the hell does Craw keep in here? Oompa Loompas?"

Jeremy grimaced at him over his shoulder. "I'm sorry," he apologized. "I haven't read that book. But since I moved out, mostly we use it when we're out here late tending stock."

Jeremy stood up and started helping Stanley with the book stacking, and Stanley stopped in the middle and looked at him in shock.

"You *lived* here?"

Jeremy nodded. "Yeah, after Craw took me in. It was a regular luxury suite after living in shelters." He shuddered. "That first month after prison was *not* friendly at all. I almost went back."

Stanley sobered, remembering Johnny's words about going straight.

"How hard was it?" he asked, his voice rasping. "Going straight?"

Jeremy stopped his fussing with the books and looked at Stanley shyly, slantways from under his brows. "It's hard," he said gruffly. "I was lucky. Craw gave me a break, Ariadne gave me some mothering, and Aiden...." He looked down at his hands, which were still covered in the thick, warm mittens. "Aiden gave me strength."

He looked back up and smiled at Stanley, and then looked beyond him. "Fuck," he muttered, and shoved Stanley back against the bed. "Look, Stanley—they're coming up the road." Sure enough, in the ice-clear dark, the car could be seen about half a mile away, making the turn to the road that led to Craw's gravel-covered street. "Here, wrap up in the sleeping bag and get under the bed—"

Stanley blanched and looked under the bed. "Oh my God, no, seriously—"

"You said people are coming out here, right? Well, I'll buy you some time. Now scoot. I'm going to close the door and turn out the light, okay? But once you get wrapped up, stay wrapped up; keep your head in the bag and roll it tight around your body. You're pretending to be a bedroll, and don't ever stop!"

"But what about you?" Stanley asked, and Jeremy's face— narrow, pretty, with its slick smile and pretty dimples—hardened abruptly.

"Don't worry 'bout me. I owe Johnny, okay? And," Jeremy swallowed. "Look, Stanley? If this goes south, you need to tell Johnny that it's okay. I owed him, it's fine." He closed his eyes and opened them, then blinked again. "And tell Aiden I'm sorry. I didn't mean to gut him like a sheep. Now *move!*"

And with that, Jeremy turned off the light and slammed the door shut, leaving Stanley to wrap himself firmly in the musty bedroll in the dark and then roll himself under the cot, huddling in the pitch black and trying not to shiver so hard he gave himself away.

AT FIRST, all he heard was Jeremy, going around to the animals. He was talking to them, soothingly, and sometimes Stanley caught murmurs of "It's all right now," and "Don't fret none, okay?" He remembered Johnny telling him that Jeremy was more fragile than people knew, and he wondered how many people knew how strong he was capable of being. Stanley was huddling under the damned cot on the force of Jeremy's nerves alone. Stanley dug deeper into the sleeping bag and rolled tighter, tucking his head in and making sure a flap of the bag covered his bright hair. It was occurring to him that Jeremy was putting his life on the line for him; Stanley didn't want to pay him back by getting found. He was pretty sure that would be the death of both of them.

All too soon, he heard the crunch of snow tires on gravel, and he literally cringed as a voice—young, brassy, harsh—screamed out into the cold country quiet.

"Yo! Yo! Is anyone fuckin' there? Get your ass out here, I need ya to answer my questions!"

Oh Jesus. Stanley had wondered—he'd wondered if these people were as bad as Johnny had said. He'd thought maybe Johnny had exaggerated, and, well, Jeremy had the look of someone who could panic easy. But apparently not. Anyone who could scream like that, someplace where there were animals and quiet and....

This person respected nothing. That's all Stanley could think about: he respected nothing.

"Hey there!" Jeremy's voice was pleasant and unruffled. "Can I help you fellas? You all seem to be a mite lost!" Nothing to see here, just a country boy, out about his chores, oh yessirree! Nothing to worry about, and don't even think for a second this country boy would be lyin' to ya, cause he just ain't that smart!

"We're lookin' for someone!" that brassy voice said. "Angie! Yo—Angelo! Get your sorry ass out of the car and go lookin'!"

"But Mikey! Boss…." Angelo sounded big and dumb. Stanley sort of wished he'd sounded small and cowardly, because he thought maybe small and cowardly could be scared out of Craw's barn, but big and dumb—that was harder.

"But boss what?" Oh God. Mikey sounded mean and crazy. In twenty words, Stanley was in a bedroll, hiding from his worst nightmares, while Johnny and Margie the Marshal were half an hour away, at the least. God. So much could happen in half an hour.

"Get your ass out of the car and go looking!" Mikey sneered, and Angelo made a reluctant sound.

"It's one of them barn things. I don't know what's in there."

"Nothin' that'll hurt ya!" Jeremy said winningly. "Some alpacas, some horses, a whole mess of sheep and some rabbits—"

"What is this, some sort of farm or somethin'?" Mikey asked, and even tucked in the bedroll, Stanley rolled his eyes. Oh yeah. Proof that you didn't need a degree in squat to be in the mob.

"It's a yarn mill," Jeremy said. "If you come back tomorrow, when we're open, we can give you a tour." Stanley had to hand it to him. Craw's man wasn't stupid and he must have been scared, but he kept his voice even and friendly and very, very willing to work with the two goombahs who had pulled up to what must have been his safe place. Stanley was living his worst nightmare; Jeremy was reliving his worst *life*. Stanley had the thought, as awful as it was, that Jeremy was getting the raw end of the deal.

"If this is a mill, what the hell are you doin' here this time of night?" Mikey wanted to know. Stanley was distracted by his voice for a minute, and then became aware that Angelo must have gotten out of the car. There was a heavy tread on the fine gravel that led into the barn's big entrance, and it was heading Stanley's way.

"Oh, I'm tending stock. There was a poor alpaca mama, had herself a miscarriage. I needed to clean her up, get rid of the fetus— nasty shit, shit that can't be waited on in the morning. Sad shit, too.

That mama's gonna need herself some attention and maybe some more mating, or she'll mourn her cria—they do that, you know."

"I have no fuckin' idea," Mikey said distastefully, and now his voice was getting closer along with his footsteps. "I get my clothes from a store like fuckin' human bein'. No buying it in yarn and making do, ya fuckin' retard."

Jeremy's voice did a passable "wounded" and Stanley allowed himself a shallow breath in, because that was good. A real person would know he was being insulted.

"Now hey, this here's a good place. Making this stuff's a skill. And like I said, we could show you the mill itself when—hey now, whatya doin' there—ouch!"

Stanley stopped in the middle of his breath. The door to the little room was being thrown open and the light came on. There was some rooting around, and Stanley heard the books hitting the floor, and then those heavy footsteps yanked on the door to the bathroom so hard the frame probably splintered.

Stanley tried very hard to be a bedroll.

"Naw, boss," Angelo said, and he must have flipped off the light because the space around Stanley went dark. "Nothin' in there worth seein'." The door slammed then, and Stanley dared to peek out of the bedroll, discovering he'd been given a gift.

The door had rebounded open a few inches, and he could actually *see* out of the little apartment. Granted, his field of vision was small— mostly it was limited to legs and shoes, but still. It wasn't hard to guess whose legs and shoes were whose.

Jeremy's were easy. He had on worn, steel-toed work boots and faded jeans. Well, that was a no-brainer. The other two sets of legs were a little more difficult; they both wore expensive wool suits, only one was a burnt umber and the other—the one belonging to the slimmer set of legs—was charcoal gray. The burnt umber pants had the brown wing-tips, and the charcoal gray had the gray and white saddle shoes, and as those gray and white saddle shoes started to pace while their owner spoke, Stanley figured those shoes belonged to Mikey.

"So, uhm, what's yer name again?"

"Jeremy," Jeremy said. "Jeremy Corker."

Inside the bedroll, Stanley's jaw dropped. He knew Jeremy's last name was Stillson, but that lie rolled off his tongue so smoothly, if Stanley hadn't been an adrenalized nervous wreck, he would have believed Jeremy right off the bat.

"Jeremy Corker? You any relation to that Jeremy my dad was looking for a few years back?"

Jeremy's voice, when he spoke, was dry as the fucking Sahara, and twice as droll. "Contrary to popular belief, sir, not all of us Jeremys are related. I have no idea who your daddy is, but I don't recall being looked for by anyone recently."

"You being smart with me?" Mikey asked, and suddenly, the burnt umber set of trousers was right behind Jeremy's jeans, the shiny brown shoes wedged on the insides of Jeremy's work boots.

Jeremy grunted like he was in pain and said, "No sir, no sirree, I just don't have any idea as to what you fellas is lookin' for, that's all! I'll help ya, I will, but first off I gotta know—"

"We're lookin' for a fairy," Mikey growled, and Stanley wasn't sure whether to roll his eyes or smack Jeremy when he said, "Then don't you need a set of bells and a jar?" just as quick as his smart mouth would let him.

There was some scuffling, and Jeremy's grunt sounded like it came with a lot of pain this time.

"Not that kind of fairy, asshole," Mikey snarled, and then there was the sudden, sickening thud of flesh against flesh.

Stanley heard someone hawk spit, and what landed in the dust of the barn floor near Angelo's shoes was dark with blood.

"Once again," Jeremy said patiently, although his voice sounded strained and garbled, "I am really sort of confused as to what you two boys want from—" and *smack!* Mikey hit him again.

"I'm lookin' for a faggot!" Mikey growled, and Jeremy spat again, giving Stanley just enough time to pray, *Oh please don't take that opening, oh please don't take that opening!* But apparently Jeremy's quick tongue was the quickest part of him, because sure enough, when he spoke again, he made it worse.

"Well now, Granby's not really that sort of place, but I understand that there's some artist colonies up near Michigan that go for that sort of—*fuck!*"

This time the blows were quick and savage, and not confined to Jeremy's face. They also hit his midriff and his chest and there were a couple of well-aimed kicks at his shins. One of those came with a blow to the back of his knee from Angelo, and Jeremy collapsed to his knees in the dust. Stanley saw his face and bit through the skin on his wrist in an effort not to gasp.

Oh God. His nose was broken, there was no two ways about it, and pouring blood, and both his eyes were swollen, and so were his lips, which had split over his teeth. One of his ears had split at the side and was rapidly filling with blood. Oh God. Oh, Jeremy. Jesus. Silence. Yeah, you swore silence, but did you know what it would cost you?

Apparently he must have. Stanley could swear the man smiled in his direction, and then looked up into Mikey's face.

"I'b sobby," he said, struggling hard to enunciate through the nose and the lips and the blood, "I stibb dob bo who you'b wookieb fob!"

Angelo still had a hold of his wrist and now he twisted his arm *hard* behind his back.

Jeremy screamed, and Stanley actually heard the breaking of bones and the tearing of cartilage as something snapped and gave in Jeremy's slight body. He had to close his eyes then as Jeremy fell face first into the dirty, slushy straw. Mikey went into a frenzy then, screaming, kicking, and Stanley wept into his hand, wishing… praying… God, anything.

"Boss!" Angelo shouted, and Mikey came to himself. "Boss— he's done for. Couldn't tell us even if he wanted to! You never even asked him the fuckin' question!"

"*Fuck!*" Mikey said succinctly, and then pulled out his gun. He wiped his face, and his hand came away bloody from what was dripping out his own nose, and Stanley wanted to cry. Oh no—oh, Johnny, you were so right. Mikey was insane. Jeremy was still breathing on the ground, every breath sputtering, but not for long, and Stanley, oh Christ. Stanley, who wouldn't have given Jeremy the time of day six months ago, was suddenly huddling in a bedroll, thinking that he owed it to Jeremy to live, and not to just burst out crying and end it all right then.

"Jesus," Mikey muttered. "We'd better make sure he doesn't fucking live to tell the tale."

"But boss—he didn't do anything!"

"Yeah, well, I don't give a shit. He shoulda fuckin' told us what we needed to know!"

And with that, Mikey aimed his gun at Jeremy's head. A shot rang out, and Stanley screamed against his own hand, and then Mikey's body seemed to blow sideways, in a shower of blood and bone.

Angelo turned toward the shout with his hands up, dropping the gun he'd been clutching in his own hand to the ground. Stanley still lay there in the dust, looking at Jeremy's still-breathing body and sobbing.

FIRST, THERE was a flash of footsteps and Stanley saw Aiden hauling ass into the barn with a shotgun, which he aimed stock-first to crash into Angelo's face. Angelo went down and then Craw was looming over him with his own shotgun while Aiden went to Jeremy and gingerly rolled him over.

Stanley couldn't see his face, but it was enough to make Aiden burst into tears right there.

"Sobby," Jeremy muttered. "Coubn pwetty ub fob boo," and Aiden sank to the slushy gravel on the floor of the barn and cradled his head in his lap.

"You vain bastard," he snapped through his tears. "You need to focus on your real fuck-up, and that was failing to call us. Craw, call the fucking ambulance right the fuck now!"

But Craw was already fumbling for his phone with one hand and Stanley closed his eyes in relief. Good. Good. Jeremy would get help. He lost track of how long he laid there, wrapped in the stuffy comfort of the sleeping bag, staring out at the wake of two beatings and an unlamented death. Aiden kept talking to Jeremy, and Jeremy seemed conscious enough to answer, so Stanley could keep hoping there. Yes, hoping he could do, but crawling out from under the bed seemed to be beyond him.

Craw finished his phone call and then prodded Angelo's prone body with his toe. When the big man didn't move, he grabbed what looked like an alpaca halter off of the post and tied a quick figure eight around the guy's wrists and then, without compunction, around his feet, leaving him trussed up bending backward and looking both ludicrous and pathetic. Stanley didn't give a fuck, and apparently neither did Craw. Neither Craw nor Aiden—nor Stanley, for that matter—wasted a glance at the carcass on the ground in the gray charcoal suit. Suddenly there was more crunching of gravel and more cars rolled up, and still, Stanley couldn't move from his place.

Jeremy had told him to stay put. Jeremy, who was bleeding in his boyfriend's arms, had told him to stay put. Stanley was by fucking God going to stay the hell put.

"*Stanley!*" Johnny's voice was unmistakable, and Stanley thought he might be able to answer. "*Stanley*—oh *fuck*!" Stanley could see more now, because there were lights, and because people were far enough away for him to see more than their feet. He saw Johnny skid to a halt in front of Jeremy and crouch down next to Aiden.

"Oh God. Jeremy?" And yeah. He had to ask, because Jeremy's face was so swollen by now, Stanley was surprised Aiden had known him.

"Don't touch him!" Aiden snarled. "Get the fuck away!"

"Aibn," Jeremy said. Stanley supposed the word was supposed to calm him down, but it didn't work.

"Look what he did to you!" Aiden said, his voice sodden and breaking. "Look! You were honest. You were *happy*. Does he have any idea how hard you worked for that? *Does he?*"

"I obed hib," Jeremy said, struggling for every syllable.

"You didn't owe him *shit*!" Aiden screamed, a sob in every word.

"I bib," Jeremy insisted, and even Johnny shook his head.

"You didn't owe me this, Jeremy," he said softly. "I never would have asked you to do this." He looked up then, and from his position squatting next to Aiden, he must have been able to see Stanley's pale face in the dark of the small apartment. "Oh Jesus," he said, his voice breaking. "I'm so sorry, Jeremy. I never would have asked you to do this, but God… God, I'm so glad you did." Johnny stood up then, conscious, Stanley was sure, of the glare from Aiden and from Craw, as he walked to the little apartment and switched on the light.

Suddenly he was crouching down by the cot and looking underneath it, his brown eyes bloodshot and the lines in his face particularly deep, even in the soft overhead light from the bigger part of the barn.

"You can come out now, cupcake," he said softly, and Stanley nodded, but by now, he was sobbing so hard he could hardly move, much less disentangle himself from the fucking bedroll.

Johnny and Craw dragged the bedroll out, and Stanley finally managed to scramble up and into Johnny's wide, safe chest and long, long arms, where he tried to get hold of himself.

"Jeremy," he hiccupped. "Jeremy…." There were more people: Margie was stalking up toward them, and the ambulance was there and police cars and sirens and Ben and even Ariadne's husband, Rory, whom Stanley had only seen in pictures, but Stanley didn't give a flying fuck about any of them. He needed to see Jeremy, because the man had saved his life.

He managed to make it to Jeremy's side before the EMTs, but barely.

"Thank you… thank you…." He choked, unsure of how to thank a guy who would do that. God, he could barely look at him; Rocky had looked better after his second fight. Jeremy smiled through missing and broken teeth, though, and Stanley looked for Aiden's permission before reaching for his good hand—the one not hanging limply and twisted from a shoulder that was just not where it should be.

"Teb Bonny," Jeremy said, his smile growing almost saintly, "wab eabier on dis sibe."

"Fuck," Aiden groaned. "For you, maybe, asshole. It was easier for *you*." And then the EMTs were in the way, and Stanley had to move back into Johnny's waiting arms. They were trying to get Aiden to step aside, but he wouldn't because he was too busy snarling at everyone who came near, even though the two EMTs seemed to know him. He would have been there forever, but Craw bent down and wrapped an arm around his shoulders and whispered something in his ear. Aiden looked up to a spot in the barn—the rabbit hutch, if Stanley remembered right from his quick look around—and nodded before bending down and kissing Jeremy's forehead. He came up with a mouth smeared with blood, and then the EMTs helped lower Jeremy's head and shoulders down to the ground as Aiden stood.

Aiden moved restlessly to the rabbit hutch and stood there, Craw on one side of him and Ben—who had come in with the rest of the world—on the other, and together they watched as Jeremy was assessed and then strapped to the board and hefted onto the gurney. Stanley was still crying on Johnny's chest, and that's where they were when Margie—who had stopped to admire the carcass and the trussed-up bad guy—came to stand in front of them.

She shook her head as they wheeled Jeremy out—Aiden in his wake, so he could ride in the ambulance—and then looked at Johnny and Stanley.

"You were supposed to be my quiet one, do you know that, Johnny? And then we found out about Stanley, and it got better. We were gonna get cookies in Denver this year. But I gotta tell you, it's gonna take a lotta fuckin' cookies to make up for this disaster here." She looked over at Mikey's corpse again. "But then, you also saved the Justice Department a whole lot of money too. So, who was responsible for the dead guy?"

Stanley sighed and looked at the ambulance as it disappeared down the road. "The guy freaking out on his boyfriend in that ambulance over there."

Margie's eyes widened. "Oh dear," she muttered. "This is really gonna be a fuckin' mess."

IT WAS. It was a real fucking mess. It took nearly six hours for the interviews and the reports and the paperwork to be over. They drove to the hospital and Stanley got to hear Aiden, Craw, and Ben answer questions and put together some of the things he'd missed from the teeny-tiny reality window that was all he'd been able to see.

Aiden had apparently tried to call Jeremy on his cell phone and hadn't gotten an answer. Margie asked, "So that sent you over to the barn? Just that? Isn't that overreacting?"

Aiden's face—pretty in youth, and younger tonight in absolute vulnerability—suddenly grew hard and adult.

"Jeremy is fragile," he said seriously. "He said he's fine, but he was going to be in the barn all alone after finding out the mob was in town. If he wasn't answering his phone, something was wrong."

Margie pursed her lips and nodded. "Okay. Your 'fragile' boyfriend just survived a beating that might have killed half my department, but okay. And then what?"

"Then what" turned out to be Aiden seeing the strange car as he was driving up and calling Craw, and both of them parking at the house down the block (it was technically Ben's, but he was mostly living at Craw's now). Craw had snuck into his own house to get the shotguns, and they'd gotten there about in time to watch Mikey holding a gun to Jeremy's head.

"So you fired to save Jeremy," Margie said gently. Aiden looked like he needed some gentleness by this time, but at her words, he bristled and glared.

"Did you see him?" he demanded, and Margie grimaced. "Did you? Did you see what that psycho did to him? I would have—"

And at that point Craw literally clapped his hand over Aiden's mouth before Aiden could say anything incriminating, and judging by the relief on Margie's face, this was a good thing.

And still the questions went on.

Stanley put his head in his arms at one point, and when he woke up, Johnny's arm was around his shoulder, Johnny's head next to his. For a moment in the madness, Stanley kissed his temple and smiled. Johnny was safe. Later he'd decide whether to feel angry or violated or frightened. But this moment right here, with Johnny doing his best to protect him and Stanley feeling protected for the first time in his life— that was what sustained him. That was what would make him strong.

Because in the end, the Marshal's service took Johnny away. Margie told Stanley that when the investigation was over, they would probably let him go—and that he would probably even be able to leave WITSEC at this point, because after Mikey, no one who was a threat to Johnny's safety was left alive. But that was the future, and maybe, and probably. What happened in the brutal chill of the Colorado morning, right in front of the tiny, ill-equipped hospital from which Jeremy had been helicoptered out to be taken to Boulder for surgery, was that Johnny hugged Stanley one last time and kissed him long and deep in front of several highly amused federal marshals.

Stanley was too numb and too heartbroken by then to snap at them and ask them why it was funny that Johnny would want to say good-bye to Stanley with as much tenderness as any man to a woman or a wife. It wasn't funny, dammit. Nothing about it was funny.

"You're leaving me?" he asked plaintively, feeling stupid and weak. A man he barely knew had just almost died for him, and he couldn't sac up any better than this?

"I'll be back, cupcake. I promise. As soon as they pull me out of hiding, I'll be right here, I swear. Margie'll check up on you. Remember—you promised that woman cookies. She holds a grudge!"

Stanley barely refrained from shouting *"Fuck cookies!"* and stamping his little foot. But Margie had pretty much blown through any legal hassle for Aiden, and she'd jumped in a car and brought the frickin' cavalry out to bumfuck Granby to save his weenie ass. The fact that the real hero had been an ex-con-man and ex-con, who seemed more inclined to go bounding out into a meadow searching for clover than standing up to a crazed mob goon, didn't really figure; Johnny had brought the cavalry. Even Jeremy's heroism had been spawned by a debt to Johnny, which had been paid in full to keep Stanley alive.

And now he was leaving.

If Stanley hadn't blown his un-manly-tear wad in the panicky sobs after they'd found him huddling like child under the bed, he might have gone for some sort of record now.

But he didn't. Johnny just held him and kissed the top of his head. Stanley shivered, and Johnny whispered, "You need a hat, cupcake. Your skin is all pink under your hair."

"Should I make one to match yours?" Stanley asked, his voice soft against the skin of Johnny's neck, and Johnny shook his head—but didn't dislodge the basic brown hat Stanley had made him before they'd even dated.

"No. You don't match anyone. You make yourself something stylish and flamboyant and in-your-face. When I see you again, I want you to be all Stanley, you hear me? I want your ass to wiggle, I want your voice to hit that high place girls can't reach. I want you to knit every fucking day. I want to think of you in your condo, knitting with the cats on your feet, cooking bizarre shit, and eating dinner with your friends. When I walk back in your life, I want you to be just as free and just as fucking happy as you were that first day, when you didn't barely have time for me, you hear me?"

"It was a lie," Stanley confessed. "All that happened was I'd given up on Mr. Right and realized Mr. Right-now was a sham."

"Yeah?"

Stanley looked up into his eyes, and saw that he was tired and sad. "Yeah."

"You feel different now?"

"Yeah," Stanley said certainly. "Mr. Right is here. I've had him."

"He's going to be back. Can you trust in that?"

Stanley sniffed and pulled his shoulders back and tried a smile. "Baby, I have not sucked you off *nearly* enough for you to get tired of me. We have a whole lot of shit to do together before I let you go."

Johnny nodded and stepped back. "You just keep planning, cupcake. Don't worry 'bout me. I'm in it as long as you are."

Margie was waiting patiently by a big, scary-looking black SUV with tinted windows, and Johnny walked up to her so she could let him in the back. He waved once, and then Margie gestured to one of the uniformed police officers who came forward to escort Stanley down into the hospital again. Wearily, Stanley wondered if Craw would let him crash on his couch before they took the emergency plane to Boulder to see if Jeremy was going to be all right.

CRAW DID, and he even let Stanley use the shower and borrow some of Ben's clothes (sweats—*ugh!*). Ben was nice enough to volunteer to drive the Kia, so Stanley could see Jeremy first and then go home, and that, too, was nice.

Stanley felt stupid, helpless, and useless, to be the recipient of this much generosity when it was Jeremy who had done the hero thing.

Aiden must have figured that out. He sat next to Stanley in the tiny Piper Cub, and for the first five minutes of the twenty-minute flight he was silent. When he started talking, his voice was so quiet, Stanley missed the first part of what he was saying—but he tuned in for the important part.

"He was such a rabbit, you know? He was afraid... of the dumbest things. We couldn't get him to stop buying ramen noodles; I guess it's like manna from con man heaven or something, but he hated it. God...." Aiden's laugh was strained. "Craw had the worst time getting rid of the mice. I think he adopted half the local cat shelter, just to keep the fuckers from running the bigger animals out of the barn."

Stanley listened, suddenly, desperate for more information on the "rabbit" who had stood up to the mob for him. "Did he ever stop? Buying the ramen, I mean."

Aiden looked at him, his eyes red and puffy, and nodded. "Yeah. Yeah. When he committed to renting an apartment, he left the ramen thing alone. Still bought peanut butter like mad, but at least peanut butter doesn't bring in the mice." Aiden swallowed. "He had nightmares about when his father was killed, about hiding in the curtains and knowing Johnny was the only thing standing between him and death. But Johnny, he didn't say anything—even managed to get Jeremy some money so Jeremy could get out of town. And I guess the whole thing scared him—made him want to go straight, so he felt like he owed the guy. But God...." Aiden looked past Craw, who was listening with that broad, Scots warrior face as impassive as the stone of the mountains they were crossing, and apparently tried to find some landmarks out the small plane window. Apparently, all he saw were the Colorado Rockies, slicing and dicing the view below.

"God, Stanley. Even when he was a con man, it was all small shit. I know he hurt people, and he feels it, you know? That he was a bad guy? But that whole time, inside, there was the heart of someone who didn't want to hurt a fly. I hope he feels like it's all put paid now. I hope he feels like he's all evened up, because I don't think I can ever look at him and see that again. I don't. If you only knew... oh God... if you only knew what sort of guy he was, for real...." Aiden started taking deep, shuddering breaths, and Stanley put his arms around the boy's shoulders because he seemed to need it. On the other side of him, Craw shocked the hell out of them both by doing the same.

"I know," he said, making sure his voice could carry over the plane's engine. "I know. He shoved me under the bed and told me to tell Craw thank you for taking him in, and to tell you he was sorry."

Aiden and Craw both looked at him sharply. "Sorry for what?" they asked, almost in tandem.

Stanley swallowed, feeling acutely uncomfortable, because the image was so painful. "For gutting you like a sheep?"

Aiden started laughing helplessly, a sort of pained, thin sound, and Craw's arm tightened around his shoulders.

"He didn't, did he?" Craw demanded sharply, and Aiden shook his head and wiped his hand across his eyes.

"No," he said gruffly. "I may be pissed at him at the moment, but you've got to admit, that's the one thing he didn't do."

The plane got ready to land then, and Stanley got to chew on that mystery for a while, because it was easier than his own, but when they were all ranged outside the waiting room, hoping to hear from the surgeon about Jeremy's status, Stanley managed to ask Craw.

"What did he mean?"

"What did what mean?" Craw was scanning the exit door, maybe hoping Ben would arrive as they waited.

"What did Jeremy mean about gutting Aiden like a sheep?"

Craw looked at him then, and the harsh, inscrutable lines of his face eased for a moment. "You said good-bye to Johnny?"

Stanley swallowed. "Yeah. He's... he's got to go do his legal duty or some such crap. I don't know. He'll be back."

Craw nodded. "Stanley, I felt real fuckin' bad, when I broke it off. I'd been thinking we were casual, and you were thinking something else. I probably hurt your feelings because I'm a bastard and a clod and I don't know better—but how bad did I hurt you, really?"

Stanley thought about it for a moment, actually comforted by Craw's bald admission that he felt badly about it. "I was hurt," he said after a moment. "But I got over it."

"How do you feel without Johnny?" Craw asked mercilessly, and Stanley smacked him in the stomach.

"Ouch!" Craw squawked, obviously startled.

"Yeah, well, thanks for the reminder, you clueless bastard."

"Hurts?" Craw asked, and Stanley shifted uncomfortably, because he'd been trying not to think about it.

"Like I was gutted," he said tonelessly, and Craw draped a comforting arm around his shoulders.

Ben walked in right before the doctor came out, and instead of kicking Stanley off his man, he simply cuddled into Craw's other side.

Stanley had to admit to a certain amount of wonder that the same guy, with a lover on each side, could put so much difference into each touch.

But then, Stanley's touch was different too.

The doctor came in at that moment and told them all that Jeremy would be fine—for the night—but there were a couple more operations in his future, and some cosmetic surgery and dentistry, if they had the right insurance.

Aiden, apparently, wasn't going to be able to be stoic through all of that, because when the doctor said his family could sit with him through the night, he sank down on the hard plastic chair and started to cry in earnest. "Me," he sobbed. "Me. I need to sit with him. Me."

Craw disengaged himself from Stanley and Ben and went to pat the boy on the shoulder, and Stanley had to wonder at Jeremy after all, because it looked like Aiden was gutted like a sheep, and Jeremy was still alive.

Chapter 10

A True Knitter Doesn't Need a Mate to Survive

ALMOST TWO weeks later, Stanley was knitting his fingers to the bone. Christmas was in two days, and he'd already finished Johnny's sweater, which Stanley had dutifully turned over to Margie, along with enough cookies to give an Olympic rowing team diabetes, and he was hard pressed to finish Jeremy's socks.

So sue him. He'd never made socks before. But Jeremy had complained bitterly about how cold his feet were in the hospital, and since that was the *only* thing he complained about, Stanley needed to make sure he could do this one thing to help Jeremy out.

Because Jeremy's life was by no means going back to normal any time soon.

Jeremy had to have three more surgeries in that first week, and as Stanley hustled into the hospital, he saw Craw up at the front desk, arguing for a fourth one, mainly cosmetic, to help minimize the scarring in his face.

"It's not a necessary procedure," the doctor was saying patiently, "and according to the nurse, your health insurance doesn't cover it."

Craw closed his eyes for a minute, and when he opened them, Stanley saw true desperation. "You don't understand," he said gruffly. "This boy—for most of his life, the only thing he thought he had going for him was his face and his fast-talking mouth. You take away his face, that prettiness, and he's gonna.... He pulled himself up out of nothing, you understand? He made himself a good person with just his will and... and sort of a hope, you know? That it would be worth it? And we can't let him... let him go through life feeling like this face is his reward!"

Stanley gasped. Jeremy's bandages had come off and what lay under them.... Mikey had worn a big ring, with a big fucking diamond, and Jeremy's pretty face was never going to be the same. And Craw—Ariadne had told him that Craw was paying her hospital expenses, and he was now officially down two people in his little operation. He was a small business owner; he didn't have the money. Stanley took a deep breath and thought about the padding of savings he had in his bank account. He took three steps forward, Alice at his heels (because he was going to visit Ariadne today too) and said, "I can help pay."

Craw looked at him, and to his credit, Stanley didn't see any pride there, just gratitude. "Ben said the same thing," he said quietly. "Unless you're a lot richer than you look, we're still…."

"I can help," Alice said behind Stanley. She had her hand on Stanley's shoulder and he looked at her in surprise. "The boy saved your life," she said, as though it were a given to just fork over big honking sums of money for Stanley Shulze. Stanley was thinking about getting all *verklempt* over that, but then Margie strolled in, her matte black suit a stark contrast to the beige and white hospital.

"Heya, Stanley," she said with a genuine smile. "The cookies were amazing—thanks a lot!"

Stanley gaped at her and then closed his mouth. "I hope *Johnny* got some of those!" he said indignantly, and she grinned.

"Yeah, yeah he did. We gave him the present, too, and to be honest? I don't think he waited until Christmas to open it."

Stanley swallowed. It was the sweater he'd been working on, plainly made but with a rich yarn, and he hoped it comforted Johnny as much to wear as it had comforted Stanley to finish it for him. It had been the one thing that got him through that first week; he was making a worsted wool suit of armor for Johnny, who was alone.

"What are you doing here?" he asked baldly. He didn't have a lot in him for bitchiness or cleverness these days. In fact, if he had to describe the last two weeks in one word, it would be *subdued*. "I didn't realize you people made house calls!"

Margie rolled her eyes. "Careful, Stanley—your bitch is showing." Okay. Maybe he didn't have a lot left for *cleverness*. "I'm here," she said pleasantly, swinging around to the doctor, "to front Jeremy's hospital bills. All of them. Let him order room service from a five star restaurant, boys, it's all on the government's tab."

They all gaped at her as the doctor handed her three clipboards full of paperwork to start filling out and directed her to the nurse's desk down the hall.

"Really?" Stanley asked quietly as she balanced the clipboards on the counter and went to work with the pen chained to the first one.

"Really," Margie said mildly, raising an eyebrow dearly in need of sculpting. "All compliments of your pal, Johnny."

Stanley swallowed hard. "Really?"

Margie nodded and pulled something out of her pocket so she could fill in a part of the paperwork. "He's still turning state's evidence, Stanley, so we can sew this all up pretty. He gets to set conditions. His one condition was that you and Jeremy be taken care of. Craw too—let's just say we've got some cheap labor ready to show up to help after Christmas. He was real firm about taking care of you all, Stanley. In case you, you know, were wondering."

Stanley closed his eyes and tried not to get too emotional. He was *Stanley*, after all. "Well, it's damned human of him," he sniffed. "Tell him we're all pretty fucking grateful."

Margie grimaced. "Just keep knitting for him, okay? I think that's all he really wants."

Stanley nodded and then managed to pull his shoulders back into a snitty little shrug. "Well, after Jeremy's socks, of course."

Margie smiled before scowling at the paperwork again. "Of course. Go visit your friends, Stanley. I'll give Johnny your regards."

"You'd better not, bitch!" Stanley protested, and he was rewarded with Margie's full-out grin.

"Maybe not *those* regards," she said, genuinely pleased. "But I'll tell him you said hi."

Stanley turned around and looked to Craw and Alice, who were standing by looking bemused, and started walking. "What, are we cattle? Jeremy needs to know he's going under the knife again! I'm sure he'll be thrilled. I'm sure the high of the anesthesia is the most fun he's had all year."

HE HAD Christmas Eve with Alice and Jean, and Christmas Day in the hospital with all of Craw's people. Candace blew her father off for

Christmas Eve to fawn over Stanley and make him feel special, and he appreciated that. He snuggled with her on the couch and watched *It's A Wonderful Life* and made sure Jean (who was plump and sweet and soft as warm cookie dough) got enough of her favorite Christmas cookies. He allowed himself to be petted like the family cat and catered to and made much of—"Oh, what a horrible ordeal!" "You were so very brave!" "Oh, Stanley! You'll be dishing about this for a year!"—and all of it sounded perfectly natural and very true when he was with his people, warm and full of wine and with his darling laying her head on his shoulder and telling him he had to be careful because she had plans for him to be Uncle Stanley to her children, whenever they should arrive.

But the next day he helped bring Christmas breakfast to the hospital, where—with much roaring and cursing from Craw and Aiden—Jeremy and Ariadne had been given permission to share a room.

Everyone was there—Craw, Ben, Aiden, Rory—and Stanley and Candace walked in with bags upon bags filled with containers of homemade curry, pad thai, turkey, mashed potatoes, chicken stir fry, prime rib, three-layer cake, and Christmas cookies, which they unloaded to coos of wonder and accolades.

"I don't know what the big deal is," Stanley sniffed as they settled (sort of) in with the chow. "I *told* you I'd bring Christmas."

"Yeah, Stanley," Ariadne said, looking at her plate, which had been heaped high with *everything* by her attentive (and very quiet) husband. "You told us you'd bring Christmas dinner; you didn't tell us you were feeding a small country afterward!"

"Don't mind Stanley," Candace said cheekily, commandeering an empty rolling cart from the hallway and dragging it in so she could set up dessert. "He loves with food."

Ariadne laughed and took a forkful of pad Thai. "Well, he must absolutely adore us!" she said when she'd swallowed. "This is delicious!"

"Oh, he loves you all to death," Candace said blithely. She'd been introduced to them all as "Stanley's darling" and no one had questioned the blood or family relationship after that. Stanley thought he could love these people for that alone. "Ever since Thanksgiving, he's talked about nothing but you guys. I know more about Aiden and Jeremy's sex life than I know about my own!"

Stanley blanched. "You don't have one, darling. You're a virgin forever; we made that deal."

Candace's full lips puffed out into a little smirk. "Of course we did, Stanley. I haven't forgotten." There was general laughter, but Stanley didn't miss Jeremy and Aiden's pained look (through Jeremy's new bandages, which showed very little besides fine brown eyes and a mop of straight brown hair) as they realized once again they'd been the subject of gossip. Candace didn't miss it either.

"Don't be embarrassed, guys," she said seriously. "You were his gold standard. All of you: Craw and his 'nice boy,' the two of you, Ariadne and Rory." Rory was a strapping blond man with a layer of stubble, faint freckles on his cheeks, and a tongue-tied smile, even around Craw, whom he must have known for ten years. Candace smiled at him extra sweet before she continued. "Every time he got on the phone to talk about Johnny, he'd talk about you." She had a plate full of curry and pad thai, and she put her free arm around Stanley's shoulders. "It's like he'd never seen real couples like him; he needed to see how they worked."

Stanley suddenly felt like a bug pinned to a board. The other six people in the room were looking at him curiously, while Candace blithely forked pad Thai into her mouth and chewed.

"What?" he asked, taking a bite of his own curry. "You all *know* the only role models I have over here were one-off-wonders. How *else* was I going to figure out how to be boyfriend material? Craw ditched me for a nice boy. I figured if I wanted my own man, I needed to be a nice boy too."

The silence was acute and exquisitely painful. Craw spoke up into it, so Stanley gave him points for bravery because *Stanley* sure as hell wasn't going to say anything else.

"So, uhm, Stanley," he said, looking at Ben's wide-eyed bemusement and soldiering on, "how exactly did you *become* a nice boy?"

Stanley swallowed but kept his eyes on his food. "It was pretty easy, actually," he said thinking. "I mean, the raw materials were all around me. I learned to knit."

He figured this could be the one room full of people in all of Colorado—perhaps in all of the whole known world—who would not laugh when he said that.

"It worked for me," Jeremy said carefully through the gaps in his teeth. He was getting new teeth, too, care of the US government, and Stanley knew it took all the bravery he possessed, *every time* he looked at the healing ruins of the timid, pretty man who had shoved him under a cot and told him to stay.

"It worked for you because your heart was good," Aiden said gruffly. He looked up at Stanley and smiled a little. "Both your hearts. I don't think it was the knitting."

Jeremy made a raw sound, and his next words were hard to make out. "That's only because you didn't have an Aiden to knit for you."

Aiden closed his eyes and leaned over, kissing Jeremy very gently on top of his bandages. "You will *always* have an Aiden to knit for you," he said gruffly. "Always. Always and forever. Just like Gianni will *always* have a Stanley. That's why knitters knit for other people. Because their hearts are good."

Stanley tried not to get sniffly and failed. He distracted himself with trivia. "So," he said into the sweet and sad silence, "his name's Gianni?"

"Gianni Caprisi," Jeremy said carefully. "But not to you. He can be Johnny for you."

Stanley liked that. He smiled gratefully, and in spite of the worry in the room—for Ariadne, for the baby, for Jeremy, and even for Johnny—they told stories then, and laughed. Jeremy took his socks (brightly hard, masculine purple and blue) and had Aiden put them on for him, and Candace regaled them all with quirky, funny stories of people from New York, and how sometimes she was proud she didn't fit in.

"Jesus," she muttered through a mouthful of sparkling cider, "whatever happened to dating with*out* sex? I know it's passé, but really? Why does every guy want past the front door on the first date?"

"Because they have dicks?" Aiden asked, like it was obvious.

Stanley spit out his sparkling cider. "Like you would know?" he asked, because no matter how bad the scarring was when Jeremy came out of surgery, Stanley was pretty sure Aiden wouldn't trade him for a Rockette line of prom queens on their knees.

Aiden smiled a little and laced his fingers tighter with Jeremy's good ones.

"Hey—I may be a hick from Granby, but even *I* know class when I see it." And then he earned Stanley's approval and love forever (like he hadn't already with the shotgun that nobody talked about either) by winking at Candace until she shook her head and grinned.

"He may be a catch, Jeremy," she said throatily, "but I don't think you have anything to worry about; he looks pretty firmly caught."

Aiden smiled, and Stanley looked at him for the first time and didn't think "kid." It was the first time Stanley got it—*really* got it, about what it was that bound the two of them together. And, like all the other small moments of peace following the events at Craw's farm in Granby, it was one of those moments that gave Stanley hope.

Hope was something Stanley sorely needed.

That lovely moment of Christmas notwithstanding, the next few months stretched out interminably.

He was not alone; he was *never* alone, and that was something he never lost his gratitude for. New Year's Eve he spent with Alice and Jean, and New Year's Day, he was back in the hospital room.

In fact, hope seemed to live there. Ariadne wasn't due until March, and she admitted—and not quietly either—that as much as she hated to see Jeremy hurt (and he was—hurt and in pain, every fucking day), she was beyond grateful for his company.

"God, he can talk," she said one day after the nurse had come by and given him a sedative. He was going into yet another surgery, and the recovery for each one got harder and harder. Some men would have complained—but not Jeremy. He spent his time before surgeries talking a mile a minute about what he was going to do when he and Aiden got to move into Ben's house, and how they were going to decorate it, and maybe, even, get their own rabbits. (Rabbits seemed to be something Jeremy loved a lot, and Stanley had been looking up the expensive ones with the long, silky fur, just for him.)

But now the nurse had come by and Jeremy was asleep, and it was just Stanley and Ariadne in the silence of the hospital room with their knitting.

Ariadne was finally, for the first time since Stanley had started visiting nearly two months before, knitting something for her own baby. It was a wee little hat, one in plain white, with complex cables and seed stitch, and Stanley thought it might have been the most precious thing he'd ever seen. He, himself, was knitting a very simple baby jacket for the baby—but not where Ariadne could see.

"He *can* talk," Stanley agreed, then looked at the silent figure on the other side of the room. Jeremy's bandages were off by this time in mid-January, and he looked like a tired young man who had been in a fight. There would be scarring, but most of the disfigurement would be mild, and that was something Aiden had actually wept tears of joy over when the cosmetic surgery bandages had first come off. "It's reassuring, actually. Jeremy talks and the world spins on, and everything is as it should be."

Ariadne was unusually pensive now that Jeremy was asleep. Aiden had left for a few to go have a soda and get hold of himself. He hated the surgeries; he was there until Jeremy fell asleep for each one, but he hated them.

"Is everything as it should be in your world?" she asked quietly, and although it had been nearly a month, she was the first person to ask. Alice didn't want to know, and Candace told him quite frankly that she would do everything to distract him because she knew the truth.

But not Ariadne. Ariadne would ask.

"I miss him," Stanley admitted baldly, and Ariadne smiled like this alone gave him comfort.

"Then he'll come back," she said simply.

Stanley rolled his eyes. "He'd better. Do you realize I've been making that man a fucking blanket? Can you *imagine*?"

"Really? What kind?"

"Mitered squares. I had to do *something* with my leftover yarn!"

Ariadne laughed. "Of course you did," she said softly, and Stanley had hope some more.

THE NEXT week, as the snow continued to blanket Colorado, Stanley continued to work on his little jacket for Ariadne's baby, and the blanket for Johnny with the mitered squares, and hope.

The blanket was good for it. The squares could be worked independently or joined on as they went, and Stanley did the second thing, so the blanket just kept growing every time he finished another project, and since he tended to work with bright, bold, worsted weight, the blanket was turning out a lot like Johnny. Bright, bold, warm, soft, and strong.

It wasn't as good as having Johnny in his apartment, cooking or talking or sitting on the couch and watching movies, but it was a promise that he would be.

But January was slow at work: a time to stock the shelves and rearrange things, to put up the newest posters from the yarn companies, and organize the patterns. Stanley worked on his knitting, too, when he manned the registers, and spent hours (especially now that he was a member of the club) looking through samples of yarn (and fabric and paper and tools) to figure out what to order when things picked up a bit.

One day near the end of January, Stanley was actually knitting another pair of socks in worsted weight for Jeremy (who would be getting out of the hospital in a week) when the bell rang. Stanley looked up and saw Gretchen, the regular with the six grandchildren, walk into the store on the arm of a young man in his late twenties. Stanley greeted her by name, and she looked up at him with a vaguely predatory, mostly triumphant look.

"Hi, Stanley! This is my oldest grandson, Joshua—he's twenty-six."

Stanley opened his eyes wide. Joshua was wearing a very bright green, red, and blue sweater that Stanley definitely recognized because he'd helped Gretchen pick out the yarn and the pattern for six grandchildren. When Gretchen had been picking out sweaters, Stanley had assumed the oldest would be in his teens and torture-able like that.

"Hi, Joshua," Stanley said, trying hard to leach the snark out of his voice. "I would have known you were Gretchen's grandkid anywhere!"

Josh was plainly pretty, with brown hair that parted in the middle and feathered at the sides and a wide-at-the-cheekbone face. His grimace, though, was anything but provincial.

"You recognized the sweater, didn't you?" he said, and all the snark Stanley had tried to lose was right there, riding the undercurrent of Joshua's voice.

"Blindfolded in the dark!" Stanley said cheerfully. He turned to Gretchen with sincere affection, though, and said, "I hope he wrote a thank-you note, sweetheart. That turned out wonderfully!"

"Oh, he did more than that!" Gretchen crowed. "He bought me a membership in the sock-of-the-month club!" She patted Joshua's arm. "I'm going to go look for an instruction book for magic-loop, dear. You and Stanley get to know each other, okay?"

She toddled away looking very pleased with herself, and Josh came over to lean on the counter.

"You're the only other gay man she knows," Joshua said apologetically. "I came out to my parents this Christmas."

Stanley put his hand over his mouth and tried to stifle the giggles. He failed.

"Are we a set-up?" he burbled. "Is this a date?"

Joshua looked sheepish and shrugged. "Well, you are, in her words, damned cute. You wanna?"

Stanley's giggles faded. "Oh, you're cute, sweetie—absolutely scrumptious, and you'd probably even top."

"But...?" Joshua finished for him, looking sincerely disappointed, and that was flattering.

"But the love of my life is going to get out of witness protection soon enough. He's worth waiting for."

Joshua grimaced. "Worst. Rejection line. Ever."

Stanley found his giggles again. "I swear to God, it's the truth." He sobered. "You're sweet," he said sincerely, "and you could be hot with a little bit of product and a sweater your grandma didn't make, but my dance card is all danced out. I really am waiting for someone. He's worth it. You'll find someone worth it too."

Joshua shrugged, seeming to be okay with that, and then asked, "So, what would *you* do with my hair?" he asked. "Because I am getting *no* love at all at the present, and I'd really like to change that."

They had a nice conversation after that, and Stanley gave him tips on fashion and hair, on the clubs and how to work them, and what not to do if you didn't want to be the biggest manwhore in Boulder since Stanley himself. As Stanley rang up Gretchen's purchases—a how-to book and some really long size 1 circular needles—Joshua said he'd be back with Gretchen again just to talk, and Stanley said that was fine. They left the store, and Alice, who had been there doing inventory during the entire conversation, walked up behind him and smacked him on the head.

"Why'd you do that?" he asked, outraged and patting his hair back into place.

"I could ask you the same question! He was a perfectly nice man!"

Stanley sighed and grimaced. "He was. But he wasn't *the* perfectly nice man."

Alice shook her head. "*Now* you get picky. Jesus fucking Christ." She stalked off, but Stanley was reassured. Apparently he really was a faithful lover—and it was no skin off his nose, when all was said and done.

JEREMY WENT home at the end of January, and Stanley was there at the hospital when he was released. Ben was there too and told Stanley that he and Craw (with the help of the laborer Margie had sent over) had moved all of Jeremy and Aiden's stuff into his old house. Jeremy was moving into an honest-to-God home, with his lover, and with the rabbits Stanley had bought for him, and with apparently a floor safe full of Aiden's knitting that was his most prized possession. (Stanley had spent a lot of time at the hospital, and Jeremy and Aiden communicated by bickering. The floor safe came up a lot. Aiden wanted it gone and Jeremy liked it. Claimed it was mothproof. Craw told Ben and Stanley that he'd spend the summer making a cedar cabinet if that's what it took for Jeremy to lose this one last reminder of what it had been like for Jeremy to not have a home. Apparently the fact that he kept money in an actual bank now and not a floor safe was a big step as it was.)

Jeremy had looked... well, tired. Tired and thin, and there were scars on his once-pretty face that no amount of plastic surgery would take away. But Aiden looked at him like he was as mighty and as gorgeous as the dawn, and Jeremy apparently fed on that look alone. Stanley had hugged him before he'd gotten into Rory's SUV and thanked him quietly for his life.

Jeremy had shrugged. "I'm just glad you're such a good guy, Stanley. It would have sucked if I'd done all that and you were screwing around on Johnny already. You're worth it!"

He also said the only thing Stanley had to do to pay him back was to be there for Ariadne until the baby was born. Stanley told him that would have happened anyway, and he'd spent the rest of that day in her hospital room, trying to take up the slack of Jeremy now that her roommate was gone.

February was just as long and just as cold as January; the only good thing that could be said about it was that it was shorter than March by three whole days. Ariadne continued to get larger and larger—and more and more dispirited. Stanley started bringing in not just Alice, but Amanda, now that Candace had gone back to New York. Alice's daughter-in-law was not as bubbly or as charming as Stanley's darling, but she did seem to have a sort of quiet strength. Stanley figured she must have needed it, coping with Alice's snarling, bigoted son, but that was not his place. His place was to see that the two women got along, and knitted together, and Ariadne could rely on him to keep her happy in Boulder.

March—now, March had some possibilities. March had at least a warmer *smell*, and the snow in Boulder was more slush than powder, and that too sort of teased the back of Stanley's taint about spring being in the air. (Lots of things were teasing the back of Stanley's taint these days, all of them man-made and none of them men. Just because he was faithful didn't mean he wasn't getting off; that would have been *inhuman!*) Ariadne was due in the second week of March; they'd taken her off of the drugs that would stall her labor. The baby would be born with a cleft palate, but otherwise was pronounced healthy, and every day of March was a moment of breathless anticipation.

Something would happen this month, Stanley firmly believed it. *Something.*

In the middle of March, in the evening about fifteen minutes before closing time, Stanley was supervising (and actually teaching) a class in how to knit cables (Ariadne had taught him; he hoped he was as patient as she was!) when the bell over the door to the shop rang. Stanley looked up automatically, his professional smile firmly on his face, and then he froze.

He was wearing a black trench coat, and his hair was cut close to the back of his neck under the brown wool hat, and he must have lost at least twenty pounds since that dreadful morning in front of the small hospital in Granby.

But it was him, and he was gorgeous, and his eyes were still kind and his smile still wreathed around his cheeks, and Stanley dropped his knitting without another word and ran across the room.

"*Johnny!*"

He wasn't even aware that he'd squealed like a girl, and he wouldn't have cared anyway. Johnny opened his arms and caught him as he wrapped his arms around that man's neck and jumped up to wrap his short little legs around Johnny's trim waist. Johnny's mouth was suddenly on his, hard and hot and warm and wonderful while Johnny's big hands came up under his ass and held Stanley close, so close, Stanley could hardly believe they'd ever been separated at all.

He wasn't sure what happened to the knitting class after that. He looked up after more (Ten minutes? Twenty?) of that wonderful kiss and realized the store had cleared out and he and Johnny were still necking in the middle of it. He managed to put his feet on the ground and recover enough to see that someone had turned the sign on the door to "Closed," and he found he was laughing semihysterically with his head on Johnny's shoulder.

"We cleared the room," he said hoarsely, reveling in Johnny's arms wrapped around his shoulders and surrounded by Johnny's shoulders and his chest and the fact that he'd kept his promise and returned.

"You didn't hear the applause when we started?" Johnny asked gruffly. Stanley was standing up on his own now, and Johnny ground up against his middle with a little bit of frustration. "It was epic."

"I missed the applause." Stanley looked up into his dear, dear face and cupped his cheek with a trembling hand. "All I could see was you."

THERE WERE grown-up things to do. Stanley was *not* going to have reunion sex in the goddamned bathroom. He just wasn't. He cleaned up the store—with Johnny's help—and closed it fifteen minutes early, but he figured just this once, Alice would forgive him. He got out to the front and realized Johnny's Cadillac was nowhere to be seen.

"It's still in storage, cupcake," Johnny said apologetically. "Along with all my stuff from my apartment. I finished testifying, WITSEC said I could go, and… well, they vouchered a cab for me. Here I am." He grimaced. "No apartment, no clothes, no job… just me."

Stanley beamed up at him as they got in the car. "You'll get them," he said, not caring if Johnny lived in his apartment and fed his cats and did nothing else for the rest of his life. "You're here. That's *really* the only thing that matters."

Johnny smiled at him, his eyes crinkling, his white teeth flashing against his dark skin, and suddenly March felt like spring. "It's all I'm caring about too, cupcake. Although my clothes would be nice. And a job." God, he was warm and big and *there*, making the front seat of the Kia seem small.

Stanley nodded. "But you'll stay with me, right?" He suddenly felt nervous. They'd been apart longer than they'd been together, but *God*, did he want Johnny there in his bed every night.

Johnny looked at him shyly and nodded. "If that's okay with you, cupcake. I'd love to set up house."

Stanley grinned and kissed him, quickly and chastely, thinking about the many things, some of them legal, that he planned to do with Johnny's hard, strong body when they got together, alone, in Stanley's apartment.

They had just pulled up to the front of the condos when Stanley's phone buzzed with a text.

It was Ariadne. She'd had a girl.

"Oh God," he said, gazing at the text blindly. He clapped his hand over his mouth and looked at Johnny in an agony. He wanted the reunion sex. He'd *earned* the reunion sex. Oh my God, didn't Stanley get reunion sex?

Johnny smiled gently and reached out and took the phone from him. His smile deepened, and he leaned over the shift console and took Stanley's mouth in a deep, dark, chocolate promise of a kiss.

"Do you think I'm here for a minute, Stanley? Do you think I'm here for a week? You just told me I could live with you. I'm planning on doing that forever. *Forever*. Do you understand that? You're my reason for going straight. I'll worry about you when you're out of my sight and celebrate *every time* you walk through that door. I'll be family for your family here, or in Granby, or on the fuckin' moon. Your family just had a baby. Let's go celebrate like family, okay?"

Stanley put his hand over his mouth and tried very hard not to sniffle and then nodded.

"I have to go inside and get her present," he apologized. "Can you stay here?"

Johnny looked surprised. "You don't have to clean up for me, cupcake."

"No, it's not that." Stanley shook his head and gave it up and let some tears trickle down, because damn, he really was this happy and who in the fuck was going to tell him not to cry?

"Then what?" God, Johnny's hand was so big and safe on his cheek. Stanley leaned into it and answered from his heart.

"I don't want your first moments in our home to be on the fly," he said, feeling stupid and sentimental and giving into it, just like the tears. "If they're going to be forever, they're going to be forever, and we're going to have the rest of the night. Is that okay?"

Johnny pulled him in for another kiss, another promise, and when he let Stanley go, Stanley closed the car door behind him with an almost chipper walk down the slushy sidewalk.

Just like spring in Boulder, his life held so much promise of beauty and life, he thought his heart might burst wide open to embrace it all. When Johnny walked through his door that night, he'd be coming home.

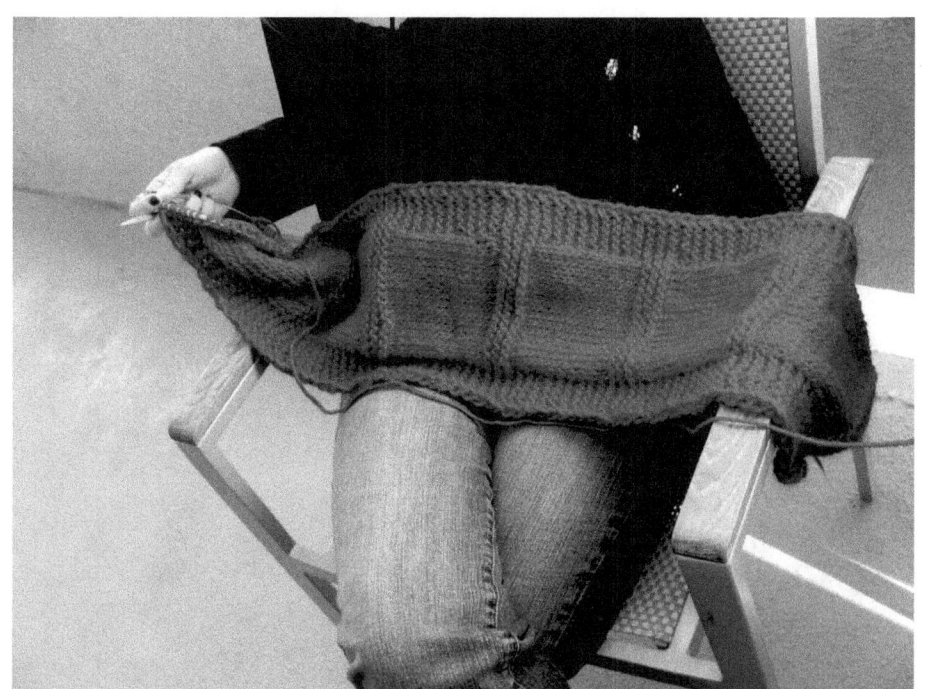

The Stanley Scarf

Stanley's first scarf was probably a garter stitch scarf—knit first row, repeat until your eyeballs bleed. This scarf has a very easy pattern for interest, and it uses a fluffy, lofty yarn—Pastaza by Cascade—and a slightly large needle for a lofty, bright, bold scarf that very definitely makes a Stanley statement.

Yarn: Pastaza by Cascade, 2-3 skeins, color 309—let's call it "Pop-Your-Cherry-Red." Two skeins will make a very handsome scarf that will wrap around the neck once. If you like your scarves longer and more Who-vian, you will need more yarn to repeat the pattern until you are happy with the length.

Needles: 10 ½

Gauge: 3 ¾ stitches to the inch (4 is fine, so is 3—it's a scarf! It fits everybody!)

Needs scissors and yarn needle!

Cast on 30 stitches.

Row 1 and all odd numbered rows: Knit
Row 2, 4, & 6: Knit
Row 8-26—all even rows: Knit 7, purl 16, knit 7
All odd rows: Knit

Repeat rows 1-26 for pattern 9 more times, for a total of 10 pattern repeats.

Repeat rows 1-6
Bind off, weave in ends and block.

And here is the lovely Ariel Tachna, working on the Stanley Scarf

AMY LANE is a mother of four and a compulsive knitter who writes because she can't silence the voices in her head. She adores cats, Chi-who-whats, knitting socks, and hawt menz, and she dislikes moths, cat boxes, and knuckle-headed macspazzmatrons. She is rarely found cooking, cleaning, or doing domestic chores, but she has been known to knit up an emergency hat/blanket/pair of socks for any occasion whatsoever, or sometimes for no reason at all. She writes in the shower, while at the gym, while taxiing children to soccer/dance/gymnastics/band oh my! and has learned from necessity to type like the wind. She lives in a spider-infested, crumbling house in a shoddy suburb and counts on her beloved Mate to keep her tethered to reality—which he does, while keeping her cell phone charged as a bonus. She's been married for twenty-plus years and still believes in Twu Wuv, with a capital Twu and a capital Wuv, and she doesn't see any reason at all for that to change.

Website: www.greenshill.com
Blog: www.writerslane.blogspot.com
E-mail: amylane@greenshill.com
Facebook: www.facebook.com/amy.lane.167
Twitter: @amymaclane

The Johnnies Series from AMY LANE

http://www.dreamspinnerpress.com

Keeping Promise Rock Series from AMY LANE

http://www.dreamspinnerpress.com

More novels from AMY LANE

http://www.dreamspinnerpress.com

More novels from AMY LANE

http://www.dreamspinnerpress.com

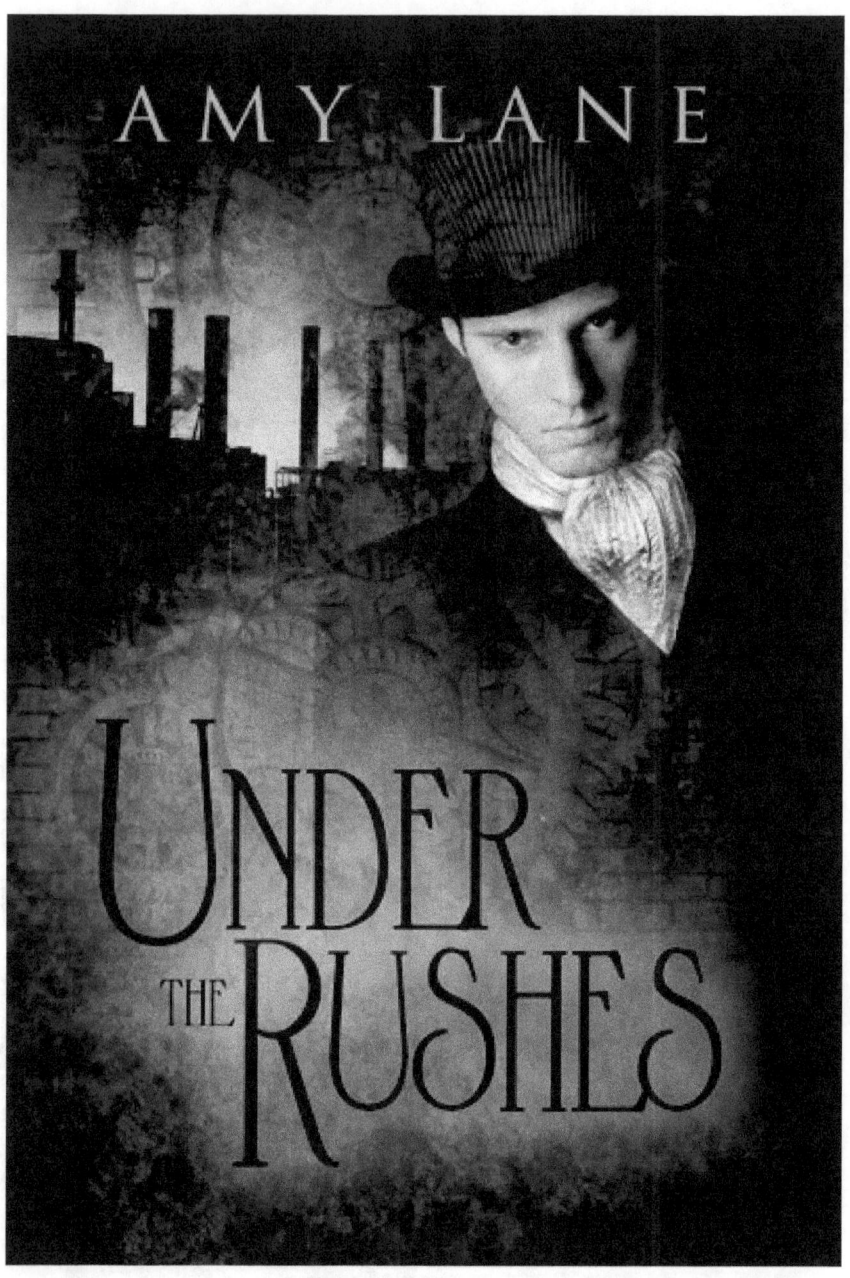

AMY LANE

UNDER THE RUSHES

The Talker Series from AMY LANE

http://www.dreamspinnerpress.com

Green's Hill Stories from AMY LANE

http://www.dreamspinnerpress.com

More novellas from AMY LANE

http://www.dreamspinnerpress.com

More novellas from AMY LANE

Also from AMY LANE

Turkey in the Snow

Amy Lane

http://www.dreamspinnerpress.com